Ilsa

Ancient Celtic Leader

Paul Williamson

Copyright © 2014 Paul Williamson.

All rights reserved. No part of this book may be used or reproduced by any means, graphic, electronic, or mechanical, including photocopying, recording, taping or by any information storage retrieval system without the written permission of the publisher except in the case of brief quotations embodied in critical articles and reviews.

Balboa Press books may be ordered through booksellers or by contacting:

Balboa Press
A Division of Hay House
1663 Liberty Drive
Bloomington, IN 47403
www.balboapress.com
1 (877) 407-4847

Because of the dynamic nature of the Internet, any web addresses or links contained in this book may have changed since publication and may no longer be valid. The views expressed in this work are solely those of the author and do not necessarily reflect the views of the publisher, and the publisher hereby disclaims any responsibility for them.

The author of this book does not dispense medical advice or prescribe the use of any technique as a form of treatment for physical, emotional, or medical problems without the advice of a physician, either directly or indirectly. The intent of the author is only to offer information of a general nature to help you in your quest for emotional and spiritual well-being. In the event you use any of the information in this book for yourself, which is your constitutional right, the author and the publisher assume no responsibility for your actions.

Any people depicted in stock imagery provided by Thinkstock are models, and such images are being used for illustrative purposes only.
Certain stock imagery © Thinkstock.

Printed in the United States of America.

ISBN: 978-1-4525-1477-2 (sc)
ISBN: 978-1-4525-1479-6 (hc)
ISBN: 978-1-4525-1478-9 (e)

Library of Congress Control Number: 2014908812

Balboa Press rev. date: 05/29/2014

Dedication

To Catherine, whose love and support has been inspirational during the writing of this book. Thank you.

Contents

Prologue ix
Chapter 1: Early life at home 1
Chapter 2: Eurydice and the Circle of stones 13
Chapter 3: Parting from family 23
Chapter 4: Arrival 37
Chapter 5: Beginning my training 43
Chapter 6: Experiences from my youth 51
Chapter 7: Trials and training 73
Chapter 8: Transition 101
Chapter 9: Initiation and responsibility 109
Chapter 10: Karka's fate 133
Chapter 11: A dark shadow over the Land 157
Chapter 12: A Great Loss 187
Chapter 13: The time of trial for the land 211
Chapter 14: Family Tragedy 247
Chapter 15: Children 263
Chapter 16: Later Stages 273
Chapter 17: My transition to Spirit 289
Chapter 18: Reflections 295

Prologue

I could feel the lightness dimming and narrowing my vision. My friends were there; they were still there. Some of them were coming with me. We were going to that earthly place, a hard place, but a world with great promise, where we could accomplish such a lot. I wanted to move forward; I wanted to do this, and accomplish all my goals. I felt eager and full of purpose, and yet, I also felt the pain and the restriction, and as I approached closer, there was also that cold energy of fear. It had been such a long while since I had felt it, and I still did not like it. I shivered inside. These feelings made me want to contract and withdraw, but I couldn't do that, not now. The emotional whirlpools around me swirled as I sank deeper and deeper into that darkened compacted world. It felt so dark, and yet, inside my chest, there was still that faint slither of light, and I could discern the thread of it extending upwards, going way up to that beautiful homeland from where I had come. This world where I was placing myself was so much more dark, but it was the lightness in that thread that I needed to bring with me, and pull it down into this dark world, pull it as much as I could, until this new world glowed with more happiness and home feelings. Then I could feel satisfied that I had done my job.

I felt a strange whoosh, and I was further trapped, less able to move, and I could feel the strange whirring of emotions of the being enclosing me. Yes, I was loved, and I was wanted – I could feel that. But so many other concerns were flowing by me, and I knew that many of these thoughts and feelings were not part of me, and were distractive from what I was coming to do. With effort, I prayed, and I asked to be still. If I was going to succeed, I would have to be very strong, I would need to listen within very closely, and I would need to be exceedingly brave, to follow my instinct at all times, and I would need to state my truth with passion, so that others would listen to me.

Very soon, it would be time for me to enter this world. I was ready, as ready as I would ever be. It was not a moment to hesitate. I knew that in this body, I would be the first; I would go in front of the others. Action would be easy for me; it was wisdom that I would need, and gentleness, so I would not overwhelm the others with my strength. My time to do this was now. I could feel the pulling was beginning. This did hurt, but I would push my way forward. I would not take long. Just a while longer to the opening and I would be there.

Chapter 1

Early life at home

Family

I wished that my family could be happy together. We were good people. My mother and father were both kind and attentive. They both tried to live their lives as well as they could. My parents were sincere people, and devoted to their faith. I could not understand why I could feel the simmering resentment, the underlying sorrow, and the unease in how they related to each other. It was evident every time we had food together, in the awkward silences, the way that my mother and father never looked at one another. It was disquieting and confusing.

As a young child, I could not understand this; I could only vaguely wish for ways that would be different and more harmonious. I loved everyone in our family very much, and wanted everyone to be happy. But then, this was not quite true, for I did struggle very much with my older brother.

We were a family with four children, and we lived in the outskirts of the village in our thatched wooden dwelling place. In the mornings, I would wake up and watch with fascination the billowing smoke from the fire as it drifted upwards, and I would see my mother tending to cooking and cleaning and looking after the needs of my younger brother and sister.

In our culture, we were supposed to care for each other, and were expected to enjoy our lives, and participate in rituals and dancing and singing in the festivals we shared. But our village was a sad place. People did not talk about it. I could feel it though, for I was sensitive to energies, and I had learnt that I could see and perceive a lot of things that others did not recognize. I had to decide to withhold many of my thoughts, for I did not know how safe it was for me to share.

My mother was very dedicated to her children, and she loved all of us as fully as she could. She held a special position within our community, for she had trained with the Order of the Wise, and she was a qualified priestess that could lead our ceremonies and festivals by the stones. I felt proud of her, and I loved to watch her when she preformed her duties. But most of the time, she was with us, and I enjoyed to be close to her warm body, and for her to show me how I could learn the basic practical skills I needed to function in our home. She was very patient most of the time, and when she was on her own, I felt a quietness about her that was comforting.

I felt very close to my young brother and sister, but not to my elder brother, Skife, even though I tried to be kind to him. He could be very hostile towards me, as if he was jealous. And he looked different from the rest of us, for his body was much more thick set and stocky, and his speech was not easy for me to understand. Inside, I felt that he was dissimilar too, for he did not think like us, and I questioned at times how he could be part of our family.

Most of the time, I did not think about him though, for I had lots of other activities to enjoy. As well as helping me manage practical tasks, my mother also spent time with me to teach me meditation and how to use my mind to perceive energies. She also gave lessons on these subjects to my younger siblings, for they had gifts like me, but Skife did not seem either interested or capable, and at times, I could see him looking on at us with envy and hatred in his eyes.

I knew that when I became older, I was going to travel far away and train with the Order of the Wise like my mother, for I had been chosen, and I accepted that. Sometimes, I asked myself how I would feel to leave my family and go to be in a place where I did not know anybody, but it felt right inside me, and the little bit of fear that I discerned within my chest was not large enough to persuade me not to go. If I stayed too long with my family, it would affect me, and I wanted to explore what else there was in the world.

Disturbance of the peace

Where I felt most at home was not with the people but in the nature, and by the trees and the Earth, and there were special places where I liked to be. Here I would feel like dancing and singing, and this was where I was free.

There was a clearing in the wood that stretched over the slope overlooking the community, and I used to go there often. On the edges of this clearing there were a group of oak trees that felt very familiar to me, and I used to talk to them and tell them my problems, and I sensed that they talked back to me, and I would listen to what they said. Beneath my feet, I could perceive the living energy of the Earth Spirit and this helped me to feel more alive and purposeful. Also, there were a lot of animals in the wood, and especially birds. I regarded animals as my friends, and I spoke to them as well. There were some fiercer animals where I was wary and I stayed away from them. However, nothing in the woods prompted me to feel afraid, and the strongest impression I gained in this place was a feeling of being connected with all life, and it was a feeling that grew with warmth in my heart the more that I opened to it.

One day, these ample feelings of well-being were disturbed, and it came as a great shock to me when this happened.

It was morning and I was sitting underneath one of the oak trees, and I was just enjoying the peace and vibration beneath me and around me. I was trying to listen to the Earth Spirit, and had my eyes closed in meditation. I was hardly aware of anything that was going on around me. Then suddenly, I felt a piercing pain in my shoulder. I gasped and was thrust out of my meditative state with a jolt. My arm was hurting and then my other shoulder was suffering too. Somebody was hitting me, and pushing me. It was very violent, and fear shot up through me like a cold arrow. There were blows following on from one another in rapid succession, and I had to adjust my sense of reality very quickly. It was like a blur, and I instinctively put up my arm to try and protect myself.

But then when I opened my eyes and looked, it was my brother, Skife hitting me. Why was he doing that? In his hand, he had a big stick and he was assaulting me with it, and trying to push me over. His eyes looked vicious, and I knew that I was in danger. I felt that he wanted to hurt me badly. There was no sign that he would stop. Already, I was bleeding, and I felt weak inside.

Roughly he pushed me over, and began to inflict further blows. He was aiming for my head, and I couldn't let him do that. What could I do? He was stronger and bigger than me, and I had no experience in fighting. I desperately needed help. Frantically, I slithered my body from side to side so he wouldn't be able to hit me so much. I was nimble and agile, but my body hurt so much.

I did the only thing I felt I could do, and called on the energy of the trees and the Spirit of the Earth to help me. I did not know what they could do, but I trusted the Earth Spirit, and I had to have help from somewhere.

Immediately I asked for this help, I felt compelled to tune in to the vibration of the Earth Spirit, and the vibration of it surged up through my back and into my limbs, giving me strength and resolution. Skife was attempting to get his knees on top of me and hold me down, while continuing to hack at me with the stick. There was a strong power arising in me, urging me to push against him, so I did this, and I cried out at the top of my voice with huge determination and resistance. For some moments we struggled, but I felt strength in me that I had never experienced before. With all my might, I forced myself against Skife's body, and he fell backwards. While he was off balance, I grabbed his stick and hurled it away with all my force, through the trees, and away from him.

I glared at him, and stood up to him, defying his violence, and communicated that I wasn't going to tolerate it. I yelled at him again. He appeared to be shocked and mystified, not comprehending how I was not submitting to his aggression. I stepped forward as if I was ready to strike him, and for a moment he stood there with fear in his eyes, but then he turned and ran.

For a while, as I continued to stand there, I just felt the calming power of the energy of the Earth Spirit, and it was an amazing feeling, but then this energy rapidly diminished, and the pain of my injuries became apparent. Soon weakness and tiredness overcame me, and I felt that my body was trembling. No longer could I could stand up. I leant back against the tree and felt warmth enter my body, sliding slowly down, and then my agitation began to subside.

I listened as the trees spoke to me, and they tried to reassure me that they would protect me, and their presence was so calming and peaceful that I must have drifted off to sleep.

When I awoke I got up and looked for healing herbs that I needed to ease the pain of the beating I had suffered. My mother had shown me these and I knew how to apply them. I needed time on my own to think, and recover from this attack.

Why did Skife hate me so much? Why were people in the village so sad?

Later that evening, when we had our meal, I chose to sit next to my father. There was an uncomfortable, awkward atmosphere around our eating circle, even more than normal. Everyone could feel it, and the tension between Skife and me. My father was the first to react to it, and he put his arm around me in a gesture of warm affection. When he touched me, I winced with pain, but I tried not to let anyone else see. My father and Skife were almost like strangers to each other. They hardly ever spoke. Skife was with us physically, but I felt that energetically, he was on his own. The only one that seemed concerned about him was my mother, who fidgeted with her hands nervously.

Skife glanced at me from time to time, but mostly his face turned down towards the fire and his expression was dark.

I knew he would attack me again; I just knew it. But at least I had some support to defend myself and some confidence that I could stand up for myself with the help of the nature elements. But how could I ever relax in the woods again, if I knew that he could be around?

It was easy to take refuge with my father; I felt safe with him, and I snuggled closer against him. But as I looked around our table, it was my mother that worried me. She was unhappy, and her energy was torn. I had to speak with her and ask her, for I had to know and understand why our family was like this.

Origins

It was a few days later, when I was with my mother in the woods and collecting herbs. I decided to be brave and tell her about the incident with Skife. My mother was very sensitive about energies. She could tell there had been a disturbance from the atmosphere at the dinner table, and she became more and more agitated as I told her the details. To my astonishment, her first comments were about her concern for Skife, not me, and whether he was OK, and she showed me very little sympathy. I was shocked by her attitude and had to contain my anger, and I did not know what to say.

I had to take a deep breath and remind myself of my intention. So I changed the subject to the one that was important to me, and asked her my questions about Skife and the tension in our family. My mother paused for some moments, and then must have decided to tell me.

We sat down together on a fallen branch. It was late afternoon and the air was moist and a little damp. My mother was crying, and I tried to wait patiently. I asked if she wanted me to go, but she grabbed me by the arm and told me to stay.

She started by telling me about the relationship she had with my father. There had not always been tension between them, and when they first got together, they had loved each other very much. When they had celebrated their joining ceremony, they had hopes of building a happy family life and growing old together. They were both leading members of the village and loved and cherished the home where they lived. While she worked as a priestess conducting ceremonies, he hunted and was the main protector of the village. People looked up to him for their security and safety, and he was an excellent provider of food, for everyone. His approach to hunting followed sacred traditions and he was very much respected for this.

Our village was situated quite close to the sea, and although we lived a peaceful life as a community, there was always the concern that invaders would come from across the seas, as they had done before. No-one wanted this, but it was always at the back of our minds, from stories that had been passed down from our ancestors.

Then, one terrible day, while my father was out hunting, the invaders did come. My father was not there. And the wild barbaric intruders poured into our village with their spears and knives and set fire to our houses. They were so rough and cruel, killing people and destroying all we had.

My mother began to relive this trauma, and she could hardly speak through her tears. Her body was convulsing, and all she could say was how much they hurt her, and the screams she heard were terrible. My mother's body was curling up, and I did not know what to do. I put my hands on her and asked the Earth Spirit to support her. I had to stay doing this for a long time, until finally she appeared to grow a bit calmer and so she could continue.

After the raid, she was lying by the roadside for ages, and the fires died down, and there were just faint sounds of whimpering from those survivors that were left. My mother hardly knew if she would live or die, and her body ached from head to toe. She felt completely revolted by what happened, and could hardly inform me of the details.

The hunting party finally returned and my father found her. He was enraged, and barely stayed with my mother long enough to ensure that she was comfortable before he was chasing after these murderous barbarians that had done this. The only thought that seemed to occupy him was revenge, and she heard afterwards how he had ruthlessly hunted down every last one of these invaders that had not left on their boats, and he killed them all.

But the trauma was not over there. In the months that followed, as people convalesced, and the village was rebuilt, and people began to resume a semblance of the lives they had lived before, my mother found that she was pregnant.

My father was blamed for not protecting his people. He felt tremendous guilt for his absence and lack of foresight on that day. My father could not understand or forgive himself, and there were people in the village that were angry with him. On top of this my mother was carrying the child of one of these barbarians. My father hoped so much that my mother would decide not to carry the child, and they argued many times about this. For my mother, she felt inwardly that she had a choice.

The voice of Spirit within her suggested that if she let the soul live then this soul would have a very difficult journey through life. Eventually, it may find peace and acceptance within our community, but would struggle because of the linage of its father.

My mother did not feel that she could kill her own child, even with the circumstances of how it was conceived. She valued life too much, and she decided that she would accept this child with as much love as with any other children that she would have.

For my father, the decision she made was much more difficult because he had to struggle with the feelings of hate that he felt towards the men that violated my mother and caused so much destruction to the village. He could never accept this child, and its existence reminded him also of his guilt and how he had failed in his duty of protection. And thus a great wound formed in the relationship between my mother and father, that would be so difficult to heal.

Skife was born, and in the days leading to the birth, my father went away on his own, and only returned afterwards. He did all he could to ignore that my brother existed, even though my mother pleaded with him to accept him and to give my brother a chance, and open up his heart. My father couldn't do it, but he would not leave my mother, because then the sense of failure he felt would be even more complete. So an uneasy tension ensued, and this never went away.

As a baby, Skife was heavier and smaller than our native born babies. He took a long time to learn to speak our language, but physically he was very agile and able to stand at an early age. Even as a toddler, Skife behaved like an outsider; his temperament was more aggressive than other children. While other children played, did craft work, domestic chores, and joined in the life of the community, Skife stood back and apart. My mother tried to encourage him while my father felt awkward and did very little for him. Yet, Skife did watch and absorb the life of the community, even occasionally joining in. He did have the blood of my mother within him.

My mother had noted Skife's jealousy and his difficulties, especially with regards to me, and he resented attention that I received and how easily I adapted to the life of the village. As we sat on the branch together, my mother looked at me in the eyes, and pleaded with me to be understanding and tolerant of Skife, to give him the best chance of finding peace in his life. My mother obviously felt that Skife was more vulnerable than me. With this, I could tell that my mother also felt guilt and wished so much that her family would accept my brother.

It was strange for me to listen to my mother. So much of what she told me put pieces into place in my mind, as if some part of me already knew what she told me. Although my mother sympathized with the plight of Skife, the person with whom I felt most compassion now was my father, and in my heart I wished to seek him out and show him that I loved him. I could only imagine how alone he had felt since this all happened.

Father

I had always felt a kinship with my father and liked being with him very much. Although he had not trained with the Order of the Wise, my father was a warrior and expert hunter, and he used psychic skills to help him with his work. He was quite a tall and slender man, strong in the shoulders, with long legs. My father often remarked how he felt that his body structure had been passed down to me, for, although I was a girl, I also had long legs and a lot of physical stamina.

Sometimes, he would take me with him when he went hunting, and he taught me some of his skills that he used in his craft. The only weapons he carried were a spear and a sharpened knife made of stone. I felt very honored when he made me a spear and stone knife that I could take with me when I went with him.

For a big man, he moved across the undergrowth and terrain with surprising lightness and agility. He was sensitive to the energies of the environment and made sure that he was in harmony with those. My father taught me how to step and balance my body and move like him, and I noticed the difference in feeling, and how much more I could blend into the environment when I did this. When I accompanied him I became very still and felt that our beings became as one.

I did not like to eat animals and preferred to eat the fruits and vegetables of our land, but we did need meat in our community to survive, and my father provided most of this through his hunting. His instinct told him where to find animals we could kill for food, and he showed me how we could do this in a way that caused the least amount of hurt to our animal friends.

On one occasion, we had been hiding in wait behind some trees by a pond, when a herd of deer came by. My father had been expecting them. For a few minutes, we watched and my father pointed to indicate the positioning of the various members of this herd. Then, he lifted his head, and with his breath, he sent out a fierce silent call to this group of deer. I could feel the shrill vibration of this call in my ears and right through my body. I became very alert, and the energy of it shook me.

All at once, the deer looked up startled as if frozen, and then, just as abruptly, they dashed towards the cover of the thicker woodland to our right. One lingered a little longer. My father checked with his inner perception. This was indeed the deer that the herd had chosen to sacrifice. My father had shared with me how with his inner sight, he could perceive a direct line from his spear right forward to the heart of his prey.

Now I could sense my father aligning his inner sight with the rump of the deer. In one movement, he thrust the spear forward, and I watched spellbound as the weapon flew through the air. The deer stood motionless, as if transfixed, but then, when the spear thundered into its body, she slumped to the ground, motionless, and we leapt forward to see.

After each kill, my father prayed and gave thanks to the animal kingdom for what it provided, and he got me to join with him. I knew that my father would never kill more animals that what was necessary for our survival. He hunted with respect and cared for the kingdoms of nature.

I could learn a lot from my father, even though it was not my path to be a hunter. He was quite a solitary man, but in his values, I felt great love for him, and wanted him to know that by my spending time with him. Whatever mistakes he had made did not affect my appreciation for him, and I wished that he could find peace.

CHAPTER 2

Eurydice and the Circle of stones

Perceiving energies

When I was little, I lived in a state of wonder. We were told stories about the Earth Spirit and how we needed to honor her in all our actions, but for me, the Earth Spirit was a living experience. I felt the ground beneath my feet as being alive with energy. Every rock, plant, tree, animal and person had contained within it, its own feeling and light. I could see lights around people and these lights had feelings associated with them. When people's lights were brighter and clear, then that person would be happy and positive, and it would be pleasant to be with that person. When the energy of someone was duller or red, or even dark, it was best for me to stay away from them. The light that people carried was not always apparent to me, but I noticed that after I visited the peaceful trees within the forest, that I could perceive these energies much more strongly. It was as if the trees helped my inner perception to be more open.

With my brother Skife, for instance, his energy was not very bright. He would often be sitting on his own, and in his brooding presence, his energy would be quite closed, with dark red and sometimes a darkness that felt quite menacing. It was only on those rare occasions when he took an interest in our community life, and was watching from the edges of our camp, times when my mother was close by, that the colors of his energy was brighter, with some yellows and greens and brown starting to appear.

Other people had quite different lights. My mother had a much more intense energy field. It was deep blue and green that marked her out. When she was caring for her family, a beautiful pink color was present around her heart. In her natural state, she was truly a being dedicated to serving and helping others. The feeling of colors in her energy was of quiet love and devotion. However, when there was tension around, her energy field contracted considerably and became quite jittery. There were areas of grey in her energy that I wished were not present.

The influence of her energy upon Skife was plain to see. However, even though the benefit for him of being near to her was clear, for reasons of his own, he still preferred most of the time, to be far removed from everyone, and this made me feel uneasy.

When we had community meetings, I noticed how the energy fields of people tended to merge together, and if there was feasting and happy celebration, the energy of the whole group would be dancing in union. But then, in the course of everyday life, there were many whose energy seemed heavy with the historical residues of sadness that was pervasive. There was an ongoing struggle within the community about whether it was possible to lift the energy of the people, and I wished that I could help.

There was something else that I noticed. Other lights were connected to people too. This energy was subtler and less distinct, and seemed to come from some Spiritual source that was beyond us. Although in my early years, I did not understand these energy forms, I never felt afraid of them. There was something about them that was very loving and alive. I came to realize, that as humans, we were not alone, even within our own energy field. When I sensed my own energy field, I could feel that I was accompanied by an additional energy form too.

From as early as I could remember, I felt that I had a lady with me. Most of the time, I felt her standing behind me, sometimes very faint, but at other times, more prominently. Her name was Eurydice; she had told me this once when I asked her. It was a strange name, not a name of our people, but it was how she liked to be called. She was a source of great comfort to me, and I accepted her as a friend and teacher from the less visible world.

I saw her in human-like form, even though she was light. She was very tall and upright, and her energy was very soft and loving, but firm as well. Her hair was long and straight, almost white, and her eyes, I perceived as a deep penetrating blue. She wore long gowns that appeared as fine as silk, and for a lot of the time, if I did not focus on her, I would hardly notice that she was there.

I had felt her energy to be strongly present with me when Skife had attacked me, but I knew that she would not interfere, and she encouraged me in many ways, to learn to fight my own battles, and to grow in my own awareness of how I could cope with people and situations that confronted me. If she intervened, I would never acquire the strength that I needed to live my own life, and so for most of the time, she remained in the background, more as a witness.

However, there were instances when I observed guides trying to help and direct their subjects. The most dramatic of these from when I was young occurred when I viewed a fight concerning my father.

Fight

At the time, I was in our home hut trying to mend some of my clothes while my father was working outside. I felt prompted to look up, and noticed a man that was approaching my father from behind. He was carrying a knife and his intention appeared quite dangerous. I knew this man, and he lived on his own. His wife had been killed in the raid from all those years earlier, but I had never seen him happy, and his energy was very brooding, a bit like Skife. I cried out, and my father reacted and turned around, immediately discerning his assailant. My father did not have a weapon, and the other man, in addition to his knife, also carried a big hard stick. With a gasp that I could scarcely suppress, I realized that this man wanted to kill my father. He was very, very angry, as if his feelings had been simmering for a long time. I felt terrified, and my body started shaking. I did not know what my father would do. This man was a big man, and he appeared to be physically stronger than my father, but my father was more nimble and quick moving.

The man lunged and struck out at my father with his knife, attempting to land a telling blow. My father dodged and evaded, stepping back and maintaining his balance, looking in the eye of his attacker the whole time. I could tell by his energy that my father did not wish to harm this man and he only wanted to preserve his own life. My father's actions were defensive.

Cautiously, I came forward to the edge of the hut and crouched huddled there, shivering and watching anxiously. That is when I felt the calming presence of my guide, Eurydice. For once, she came without being called and I felt very grateful for that. With her being there, I slowly relaxed and I could hear the words in my mind urging me to watch my father very carefully.

As I followed my guide's directions, I was able to perceive that there was a Spirit man shadowing my father very closely. In fact, he was trying to direct my father and prefigure moves that my father could make with his opponent. My father was physically very sensitive to energies, and in this time, I could sense that my father was listening very attentively to this Spirit man, and following what he directed. Because my father wanted to do the right thing, Spirit was supporting him. This Spirit man must have been my father's guide. It was amazing to perceive how much harmony and cooperation was evident between them. This other man was wild with rage and destructive ambition, but no matter how forcefully he wielded his knife and stick, he kept missing my father, and my father kept moving away.

As my attention switched to the angry man, I could perceive that he too, had a Spirit person with him. This presence was much more distant and fainter. I could feel this guide more female, and maybe even the spirit of his wife was there too. They were attempting to project love towards him, but in his hostile mood, he was unaware of any other influence. All he wanted to do was to make my father suffer for what he had felt himself.

It was not long before this man had exhausted himself, and my father was able to release the knife from his hands, but he still refused to strike his attacker. Instead, my father stared at him, and waited as the man slowly retreated and sank away.

My father had a pained expression. It was difficult for him that members of the community still held him responsible for what had happened to them. It gave him no joy to have been able to repel this man's rage. In a moment, my father threw away the knife in disgust, and then he came over to console me. It was one of those times when I admired my father, and learnt from him, not so much because of his defensive fighting ability, but in the way that he had opened himself for Spirit to help him, and his ability to contain his own emotions in a time of threat.

Support from my guide

I enjoyed times that I spent with Eurydice, and we had some wonderful conversations. The old oak trees where I communed with the Earth Spirit were also my favorite place to be with Eurydice. Here I would sit and I would feel her presence very close and loving.

We had many topics of conversation together. She could express various moods with me. Sometimes she would be playful, and at other times, serious. If I was willful in my behavior and disregarding of her promptings, she would withdraw until I was ready to ask for help. She would always be very forgiving and sometimes laugh at my mistakes in a light-hearted way, until I was able to laugh with her.

Eurydice could be consoling too. I did not like to witness suffering, whether it was human, animal, or even my friends, the trees. For others, I would try to remain strong; I felt from an early age that I was needed to be the reliable one, which others could lean on if they needed it.

So I would usually do my crying on my own, and then I would feel Eurydice's gentle love and support close by me.

I was very concerned about the struggles of members of my family, but Eurydice counseled me not to become too caught up in this. She implored me to enjoy what happy times I could with both my parents. It would not be long before I would be leaving all my family and moving on to the next phase of my life. The next phase was to be my training, and Eurydice emphasized many times, how important this would be for me. The love bond with my parents would always be strong, but they would have to rely on their own resources to overcome their problems. I needed to appreciate that and be prepared to release them and all the attachments I felt to my village life. I needed to trust and let Spirit guide me, and allow that Spirit would support the members of my family as well.

At times I resisted this attitude and wanted only to feel the safety and security of home, and to stay with that, but in the winter before I was due to leave for my training, I had an inner experience that both shocked me and also inspired me to look forward to a future beyond what I had known.

Ceremony

People trained as members of the Order of the Wise were the Spiritual guardians of our community. They conducted ceremonies and rituals for us so that we could be in harmony with the Spirit of Mother Earth. Also, they talked to us about our behavior so that we would live correctly, and with awareness for others and all kingdoms of life. The Order of the Wise was responsible for administration and leadership of all significant aspects of our society. Its members were greatly respected by the people, and they lived according to a vow to conduct themselves with the utmost integrity. Sometimes we had visitors when members of the Order would come to our village and meet with members of our community. They were always regarded with great reverence. For my mother to have been trained at the College of the Central Council was a great honor. I felt privileged to be able to follow in her footsteps.

When we had a ceremony, my mother let me watch from the outer ring of stones. She had taught me how to hum to summon the energy, and when we did this, I could feel the vibration like a current of energy through my body. The seasonal celebrations attracted a great gathering of people from all of our local settlements. While we were humming, the Priest and Priestess and other officials would conduct the ceremony. I liked the feeling of these ceremonies very much, and with my inner sight, I could see funnels of light and glorious color dancing about in response to the invocations of the Priestess. When I mentioned the colors to my mother, she nodded her head in recognition. I knew that she saw the colors too.

The location where the ceremonies were conducted was the circles of stones that were like pillars at the heart of our community. I could feel the stones as amplifiers and conductors of energy, so that when ceremonies took place, I would see a light in the centre of our circle, and the stones held the energy of this. We regarded the stones as living beings, and we had two keepers in the village that cared for the stones and were responsible for their welfare.

Sometimes the children of the community were allowed, under supervision, to go and feel the qualities of the various stones. My mother organized this, and on the occasion when she took me, I felt my hands become very hot when I touched the individual stones. They all had their own essence. Our people loved the stones, and felt that they helped to look after us. They had been brought to our community, to the place of power that existed here, by our ancestors, long ago.

During actual ceremonies, the stones appeared to channel abundant energy, and different stones would be more prominent depending upon what ceremony was being conducted. During the ritual, people would be invited to walk past the stone and touch it on the way to the centre of the circle where they would receive a blessing from the Priest and Priestess.

I had been longing for the opportunity to do this myself, and was overjoyed that I would be able to do this once in the winter ceremony before I departed for my training.

The symbolism of the winter Ceremony was orientated around us connecting with our inner light and the seeds in our consciousness that needed to grow and expand as the physical light of our world returned. For this ceremony, my mother would accompany me rather than participating in the ceremony as she usually did.

As I approached the big entrance stone, I felt strangely nervous and excited, as if there was some inner anticipation in me that was unusual and new. My mother urged me to reach out and touch it as the people in front of me had done. For a moment I hesitated, and then I did it. Immediately, I felt a tremor through my body and a rush of energy, and so I closed my eyes. It was as though my inner awareness was thrusting forward, and I felt bewildered by it and wondered if I should resist. But somewhere in the background I could sense the voice of my guide, Eurydice, insisting that I go on. There was a kaleidoscope of images and then it settled and I was in another time.

Suddenly I was there. I was wearing robes and could feel that I had an adult body. It was still me, Ilsa, but I was much older. As I looked around me, I was standing in the centre of an enormous ring of stones, and there were many, many people present. I could feel my power with a strong sense of leadership. All the people were looking to me, and I was their leader. I was the one conducting the ceremony.

For my child mind, this felt almost too much for me to comprehend or to accept, and I recoiled and started to separate from what I had seen. In an instant I was able to step out of the body of my future self and dissociate from her, but before the vision could completely vanish, my adult self turned around from the ceremony she was conducting and smiled at me, and I smiled back. I knew that it was more than a dream.

Abruptly, I returned to my normal consciousness and my hand withdrew from the stone. I wanted my mother there and to hold her, and be comforted. My mother stood back, so I could absorb this myself. She could sense that I had had an intense experience, but this was something that was private for me, and I knew that I would have to keep the knowledge of this vision within myself until a time when I would be able to share it.

I had so many questions in my mind, and the rest of this evening was like a daze, and I hardly slept that night. It was as though I had been given a glimpse of my destiny, and I had to decide whether I wanted it or not, and I knew from deep inside my heart, that I did.

CHAPTER 3

Parting from family

Goodbyes

It was supposed to be a celebration. There were so many people, all gathered in our village. Some were standing talking, while others nestled around fires. My family was with me in the large communal hut, and I sat watching, and was snuggled up next to my mother. The fire in the centre of the hut billowed smoke upwards towards the opening in the thatched roof at the top, and disappeared beyond. There was a chill wind, and dampness in the air. We wrapped our bodies in our animal skins close to the fire, to keep warm.

As I watched my family, I could see that they were unsettled. My father was striding anxiously around the hut, fiddling with his spear, keeping his eyes alert with the masses of people that were present. I was afraid that he would feel lost once I left, for he did not have many allies within the community, and I was one person who accepted him. With my mother, although her body was still, I could feel the stress and strain that she was carrying in her limbs. She was wrestling with her own feelings, and I could tell that there was a big part of her that did not want to let me go. But for my sake, she was desperately trying to relax to be supportive of me. My younger brother and sister were on the other side of mother. They seemed so tiny and vulnerable. Both of them kept gaping at me, as if looking for some reassurance that I was still with them. My older brother, Skife, was nowhere to be seen. Altogether, the energy of our community on that day was very tense, with nervous flashes of inner light erupting between people. I could have believed that it was all to do with me, but I knew that there was more to it than that.

These were the days when I would be leaving to go with my new companions to the Training College of the Order of the Wise. People were there to honor me, but there was also an important visitor coming from the Order, and she was going to be meeting with the community leaders of our district. I rather felt that the people were more occupied with this meeting than about what was happening with me.

Although my family was proud of me that I could go, and had been chosen to attend the training, they all valued my companionship. They each were dependant on me in their own manner and would miss me. I would miss them too.

My own feelings were a mixture of anxiety and excitement. To steady my own nerves, I could feel Eurydice behind me. I had invited her there to help me find peace, and for me to remain within my centre as the occasion progressed. The feeling of her presence certainly calmed me, for it was a day when I very much needed some extra assistance.

I tried to work out how it was that I could have been chosen, for I was not aware of any special tests that I had done. It was my mother that had told me one evening, just as if it was a fact that I needed to absorb. I did not question it, for I felt somewhere inside that it was right, and I felt very peaceful when she told me.

As it grew dark, we feasted on game, and there was shouting and dancing around the outside fire. Our guests would be coming soon. I could sense them approaching.

Soon there were shouts heralding that a travelling party had reached the outlying reaches of the village. It was not the one that our community leaders were anticipating, but it was the ones that were arriving for me.

They came to the entrance of our communal hut. Pushing myself, out of my mother's grasp, I could not stop myself, and I had to stand up. There were six in their group, but only three that mattered to me. I was able to identify them at once.

What I noticed immediately was their energy, and how it contrasted with the energy of the other villagers present. These ones brought tranquility with them, but there was also a subtle sensitivity and individuality within each one of them. They were my people. It was as though, from the core of my being, I recognized them and knew them in my soul. My heart was thumping and I had to go to them. Two of them were children, of similar age to me. The third was a young woman with her arms around the two children. She was acting as a protector for them, and I sensed that she would do that for me as well.

Now we were introduced. The girl's name was Nianda. Although she was quite shy, there was playfulness in her eyes. Her body was slighter than mine, but I felt that she held an inner strength. Instinctively, I wanted to touch her, and so I put my arm around her. That was when we became friends.

The boy was even quieter, and smaller. He was called Gracon. His eyes were intense and passionate, but very private. He was not comfortable with the masses of people around us, and I could discern that he preferred more intimate settings. I couched down and held his hands. He held my hands tightly in reply. We both felt the connection between us. I knew that from that moment, I would be looking after these children, supporting them, and that they would be looking after me, and looking to my lead. That would be my role. There was something very familiar, almost magical, as the three of us were together.

Standing over us was the young woman. Her name was Muela. She was to be our housemother in our new home. I could feel her embracing, nurturing energy, kind and friendly, humorous, but firm. As she saw us hold hands together, she laughed, a deep joyful laugh, and it felt as if a circle was completing itself from a plan that had been drawn up before we were born.

Feeling comforted, I knew that with these two children and Muela as well, that I would be together with them for a long time. All other people, including my family, seemed to disappear just then, and I felt a wonderful union take place.

We sat down together, and I introduced my two young companions to my parents and my brother and sister. They were pleased to be included, and for the first time that day, my father sat down briefly sat down, and although he was polite, I could see sadness in his eyes. He could tell in the way that I was bonding with my new friends, how my energy and my heart was now with them, and reaching forward towards my new home.

Visitor

It was only later, when I was almost sleeping, that I heard the commotion signifying the arrival of the important visitor. I was vaguely aware of my mother rising and departing, but my mind was too full with impressions, thoughts and feelings from the day, for me to give this any more attention.

In the next moment, it was morning. The air was clear, with a wonderful freshness. Many around me were still sleeping, but I got up to look outside the hut. People were milling about quietly, slowly awakening to the new day. There was a woman walking across the middle ground of our village, next to my mother. They were approaching, and coming to our family hut.

The woman I saw was slimly built, slightly smaller stature than my mother. Her clothing was plain, a rough cloth tunic, just as other people would wear. She had long brown hair, tied back behind her, but her eyes, even from a distance, commanded attention. They were eyes that saw, but were not easily intruded upon. However, it was her age that struck me. She was only a young woman.

As I gazed further, I noticed how she walked, and she strode lightly, in the manner of my father when he was out hunting. She had an air of grace about her, and she was very watchful, while appearing to be relaxed as well. Around her, there was a brilliant light, a light that was contained, and I sensed that she kept her energy very much within her control. She gave the appearance of being strong, but her aura held sensitivity and firmness about it that needed protecting.

I had never seen anyone like her, and I observed how people drew back as she passed them. There was something about her that was quite formidable, and people also seemed to avoid looking at her, allowing her to see into their souls. Part of me instinctively felt that I should retreat from her, because I did not know what she would see in me, but I sensed Eurydice behind me, urging me to stand firm, and so I did.

When they reached the entrance to the hut, my mother introduced me, and told me that this lady's name was Berenice. Time seemed to slow down. In that instant, I felt that the attention of Berenice was completely upon me. Her gaze was at first very gentle, but then became more intense. I could not help but look at her. Soon, it was like my whole world was taken up with Berenice's stare. It was as though, I was entirely with her, and nothing else mattered. Something unusual was happening. I could not stop it. It felt like it was going beyond my control, and even though part of me wanted to break free, from the edge of my awareness, I could sense Eurydice urging me not to resist, to go with it, and let Berenice come inside me.

I felt that Berenice was exploring every cavity of my consciousness and my soul. It was the strangest feeling. And yet, it did not feel intrusive, more as a sharing of experience. And then it went deeper, into unknown places within me, and for a moment, I was frightened, not knowing what would be exposed, and I felt interplay of many different emotions. I did not understand where these emotions had originated, but the process continued. At some point, the dynamic changed, and it was no longer just Berenice exploring me, but there was an essence of me that was meeting her too. We were joining together, and there was a feeling that we belonged together. It was a great feeling of love, such as I had never felt before, but at the same time, it felt very familiar. For some reason, Berenice was opening herself to reveal herself to me, and I knew that meeting her was something that had been prepared long ago.

As souls, we danced together, and belonged very close. Now we were meeting in our physical life too, and I started to sense how we would be together and what we would share. With that, I felt this vast energy traveling up my spine.

But then, it suddenly stopped, and my consciousness was being pulled forward. In a jolt, I opened my eyes, and there was Berenice looking at me. I felt so full of love in my heart, that I thought it might burst. Berenice wiped a tear from my eye, but as she did that, I could feel how her hand trembled with emotion.

To my astonishment, I discovered that I was sitting down, and she motioned me to stand up. 'Come child, we have work to do'. Berenice used her formal demeanor, but I knew that this was only the surface. From the others in the hut, our exchange was hidden. I marveled at her trust, and felt so many questions bubbling up inside me. Here was someone with me that would be very precious to me, someone who would remain close for as long as we both lived. I was very happy then to hold her hand.

Soon I noticed how Berenice addressed my new companions, Nianda and Gracon, for she spoke as if she knew them very well even though she was meeting them for the first time. And she included Muela too. It was only Muela that smiled back. My companions looked confused at first, but the kindness and firmness that Berenice displayed helped them feel more comfortable and at ease.

Later that morning, Muela took me to one side, and explained to me about Berenice. Muela told me that Berenice was a leading member of the central Order of the Wise, a Seeress, someone who commanded a huge amount of respect throughout the land. Her work was in visiting communities to offer support and guidance on all matters relating to social and Spiritual law of the land. She had considerable powers, and her reputation was redoubtable. People regarded her as ruthless, and very strict, with a perception that could reach right into the depth of people's souls. What she decreed was not to be contradicted, and was expected to be obeyed with immediacy. No wonder, people from our village had been nervous to meet her.

Berenice was also one of those that selected children that could be trained to develop their inner skills with the Order of the Wise. And she had been the one to choose me when I had been very little.

Then Muela disclosed information that made me gasp. Berenice would be my main teacher in my training to come. I was to be her only pupil, and my companions, Nianda and Gracon, would also be learning very closely by my side.

A shiver of anticipation passed through my body. This was a momentous day. Inside, I felt very happy.

Attack

Goodbyes with my family were brief, and they all offered their blessing. As we walked past the outskirts of the village, I gave my family a last look in gratitude, and then walked on. Tears rolled down my face, but I also felt peace inside me. All that had been in my life, my family, the community, even the beloved woodland where I used to go – all of this was behind me now, and I was venturing forward into something that was completely unknown, yet also exciting.

However, as we walked on, into the neighboring hills that marked the first stage of our passage together, I felt more and more tense. I could not explain it, but in my stomach, I felt what I could only describe as a knot of fear. When I looked at the others, I tried to analyze what was causing this, but I felt comfortable with all of them. I did not have any resistance that I could discern to what I was doing with them all.

My first reaction was to call on Eurydice, but for some reason, although I could still feel her, she felt quite distant, and I did not understand why she would not come closer. Was there something I had to go through on my own?

With every step, my body reactions became more pronounced and I felt increasingly crippled by fear. My legs started to shiver and wobble, and felt so heavy. I began to doubt if they would continue to support me. The thought came into my mind that something was going to happen to me, and I could not prevent it. I could feel my heart beating faster and perspiration on my brow.

There was no one near me in our group. The other children and Muela with our other attendants had gone on ahead, and Berenice was some distance behind. We had come to a narrow track between two small rocky hills. With the anxiety I was feeling, I wondered if I should try to catch up to the others in front of me. I did not want to follow this track, and part of me was screaming to go back. But my feet kept stepping forward.

Suddenly, there was a movement from above me. I did not know what it was. But then, within an instant, I felt a sharp heavy pain between my shoulder blades. There was no time to react. This pain brought with it a massive jolt that pushed me forcefully to the ground. The pain was immense and shocking, and I struggled to move, and stay conscious. But then, all at once, I was out of my body, and I could see it all below me.

My body was there in a crumpled heap on the ground. There was a wound in the middle of my back, and blood was seeping from it through my clothes. My body was lying motionless and awkwardly, as if my back could have been broken. And next to the body was a quite large heavy angular rock. It looked as if this rock had been thrown at me.

By being out of my body, I felt detached and free of pain but my emotions were spinning, and crying out in confusion and anger. How had this happened?

Turning my attention upwards, I saw a ledge, and there, looking down from this ledge, was my brother Skife. I could see the smirk and self-satisfied grin on his face, and his eyes held an expression of pure hatred and menace. He had another sharp rock ready, and I could tell he wanted to throw that at me too. He actually wanted to kill me – I could tell his intentions. How dare he do this? What had I ever done to him to deserve this? From my detached position, I could sense his overwhelming feelings of jealousy and resentment.

I cried out for help, and I inwardly screamed. In only seconds my body would be dead. Someone had to save me.

Berenice was with my body in a moment. Her physical movement had been more rapid than I could have imagined possible. She became aware of my brother, and looked up at him, and saw the second projectile. From my viewpoint, I could perceive how she rapidly filled herself with light energy, and drew it to her from above. It was an incredible sight. I could sense her molding this light like a shield around my body, and then moving it closer and closer towards Skife. It was like a reflector beam, so that all his negative feelings, rather than reaching me, were bouncing back at him. She was not attacking him, but merely redirecting his energy, so he could feel and sense the energy that he was trying to direct at me.

At first, my brother looked confused, and then he became afraid. He did not know what was happening to him, and he appeared startled. In moments, he had dropped the rock and ran. He had to run, and what he didn't realize was that he was being chased by his own negative energy.

Meanwhile, Berenice turned her attention to me. She put her hands on my back, and suddenly, I was forced into my body. With a deep breath, I felt enormous pain and discomfort in my back. I wanted to be out of there again. Running down my back, I could feel the trail of sticky liquid that must have been my blood. I was struggling to cope, and did not know what to do. As Berenice kept her hands over my wound, I could then feel a huge injection of heat, penetrating light into me. It was a stronger energy sensation of healing than I had ever felt, and it did feel overwhelming. Part of me wanted to shriek and stop her, but I could not prevent what she was doing, and amazingly, the pain began to transform into calm. Although part of me continued to wish to escape, there was a stronger need for me to lie still, and accept what was being given to me. As she worked, I could sense the faint assurances from Eurydice, that I would be OK

After what seemed an age of enduring heat, she lifted her hands and called Nianda over. 'You finish this', Berenice said to her. How could Nianda do anything, she was only a child? But, to my astonishment, Nianda's hands were hot, just like those of Berenice. And I felt some strange sensations in my back, as if my bones were being adjusted, and soon after that, I felt very sleepy, and could not keep my eyes open. I just remember my last waking thought was the wish that I hoped that I would never see my brother, Skife, again!

When I opened my eyes, I did not know where I was. I must have been in some deep dream state, but my mind felt strangely relaxed. I tried to stretch a little, and could only do that with effort. Beneath me, I could feel that I was resting comfortably on some moss. Berenice stroked my hair tenderly and told me to be still and rest. She wanted me to sleep. I flexed my back a little, and was no longer in pain. I knew that it was healing. How amazing that Berenice and Nianda could do what they had done. I was amongst remarkable companions. Very soon, I drifted off again, and I do not know for how long I slept, but finally, when I did awake, it was evening, and my new friends were gathered around me.

That evening, we all shared stories of our homelands. The other children seemed much more reticent than me, so I did a lot of the talking, but they joined in a little, especially when I got tired. Muela and Berenice sat with us, quietly enjoying our chatter. Inside my heart, I felt growing warmth. I had a new family with me now.

Journey

I was surprised how quickly my energy returned to normal, and the next day, I was able to walk with the others and keep up with their pace, even though on that first full day of walking, I needed to rest more often than I would have liked. It was a very good bonding experience to walk such a long way together.

On the second evening of our journey, I sat down with Gracon. Somewhere inside, I felt the urge to do this. He looked slightly nervous to have me sitting close, so I moved away slightly, until I felt that I was distant enough for him to be comfortable. Out of the corner of my eye, I noticed from the other side of our campfire, that Berenice was studying me.

Bravely, I ventured to tell Gracon that I wanted to be his friend. He smiled a little, and I could tell that this touched him, but he also started trembling, so I could tell that he was afraid. I asked about how he was enjoying our walking together, but he did not answer. So I just sat silently with him to share my company. We sat together for a long time, without me saying a word, and even though it felt awkward at first, gradually he seemed to relax. I felt as if I was doing the right thing with his sensitivity and shyness by not putting pressure on him. He was not a person that would trust others easily.

After a while, Nianda joined us. We spoke about our guides, and I discovered that they had both had strong spiritual experiences like I had had, and being in contact with their guides and the Earth Spirit was a very important part of their lives, just as it was with me.

On the next day of our travel, suddenly, Berenice indicated that we needed to go away from our chosen path, up a hill, and to our left. We did that. After some distance, there was a small valley in front of us. Berenice was at my side, and the others were trailing behind. What I noticed was that there was deadness in the energy of this valley. There were trees and vegetation, but they were not flourishing in the manner that I would expect. The light of those trees was sad and droopy. It was as if there was some sickness or disturbance in the land there.

When the others caught up, we descended into the valley. Even though the temperature was quite mild, it felt cold, somehow. At the foot of the valley, Berenice stopped and spoke to Gracon. 'This is your work', she told him.

Gracon looked up startled and hesitant, but then he stepped forward. In typical fashion, his head had been rather hunched forward, a gesture of hiding and protecting his thoughts from others. But now he was focusing upon what was in front of him, and I caught a glimpse of his eyes. He was examining the ground, feeling the energy and the environment. There was light supporting him as he did his work. Within the valley, there were some fallen stones and logs that did not appear to belong. Gracon asked for help to remove these from their positions. He looked up at us and spoke softly.

'There has been fighting here, suffering and unhappiness. The land is sad. It needs healing.'

He knelt down in prayer, and then took out a stone from a pouch he carried in his belt. It was a black stone. Placing this carefully in the middle of the clearing at the base of the valley, Gracon worked with his hands to energize this stone. I could sense light growing around it. This light was reaching out, and I could feel that a web of light that had been damaged was now linking up again. Berenice motioned for us to observe carefully. With my inner sight, I began to see numerous broken twigs of light that were now moving to form faint streams of light. As Gracon continued to work, the light became brighter, and I watched amazed, as the energy of the valley seemed to be gaining its strength to rejoin the matrix of earthlight that flowed around us.

We stayed there for a long time, watching and sensing, saying prayers together for those that had suffered, and for the Earth Spirit. Berenice insisted upon us being there until the whole process completed itself.

Later, when we had set up our camp for the night, I reflected about Gracon, and struggled to comprehend how he could have performed the tasks that he did. He was only a child, like me. It went completely beyond the experience of my life. I asked him who had taught him. He replied simply that it was his work to do. Spirit had shown him.

Family longings

In all the time of our travel, I was very grateful to Muela. She would offer us cuddles, help us unknot our hair, attend to our cuts and bruises, sing to us. I felt her like a mother, and she was very vigilant, so if any of us were feeling vulnerable, she would be there. It was good to be able to rely on her.

One evening, we had camped beside a magnificent old beech tree in an undulating stretch of land. Nearby, there was the gushing sound of water passing over rocks from a small stream. The air was cold, and it was a clear night. We had walked long that day, and the others had gone to sleep. In the distance, I could hear the hooting of an owl, and I kept listening for other sounds of nocturnal animal life. This was something that I had done often at home. I would have my bed skins outside, and lie awake for hours just listening and enjoying the environment.

My thoughts turned to home, and my family, my mother and my father, my siblings. How were they getting on? I wondered if they were missing me. Even Skife, I thought of him too. I started to cry, and tears were rolling down my cheeks. In a few moments, I was sobbing, and I just could not help myself.

Suddenly, I felt an arm around me, and it was Muela, gently comforting me. I let myself sink into her arms, gratefully accepting that I was not on my own. My sobs persisted for some time, and she continued to hold me, and I rejoiced in the warmth of her body, until slowly, I let go, and allowed myself to sleep.

But then, in another instant, I was awake, and on my own again. The moon was low in the sky, lighting up the ground around me. But there was another light as well, and I sensed the presence of my beloved guide, Eurydice.

'Come Ilsa' she beckoned. 'Come and travel with me.' She was very insistent, using soft and gentle tomes. I found her voice and presence quite hypnotic, and I wanted to follow her and do what she asked.

Eurydice was close to me, and I felt that she was pulling at me, so I drifted out of my body. It was a strange sensation, and I found myself rising high above the campsite. She led me and coaxed me along. We were travelling over the tree line, moving rapidly, revisiting terrain where we had been on our journey so far. Then we were above the village community of my home, the home of my birth, what would be my former home. Eurydice led me downwards, and we approached the hut of my family. We went inside, and there huddled in separate beds, sleeping under their skins were my mother and father. My brothers and sister had their places too, and they were all sleeping peacefully.

Eurydice spoke to me through her mind. 'I can teach you so you can come and visit them whenever you want. Then you can check on them, and know that they are safe. You can even communicate with them. Your mother will sense you, maybe the others too! Do not despair Ilsa. All this is possible.'

But then she looked at me and her gaze deepened.

'You need to decide, Ilsa, where you truly want to be. Is it here or there? You cannot split between the two. You need to choose.'

I felt the challenge in Eurydice's words, and I had to consider the choices she was offering me. I felt the longing to be with my family, to be there sleeping besides them, just like I always did. But, as I listened further within myself, I could also feel the drive to learn, to grow, and fulfill my destiny, and be what was intended for me. I could perceive the image of Berenice in my mind's eye, and also see my two new young friends. From the moment earlier in the evening, when I felt my tears, I could recall the comfort of Muela's arm around me. It was very clear what my choice needed to be.

'Let's go', I motioned to Eurydice, and she smiled at me knowingly. In the next moment, I was in my physical body again at the campsite, and the experience of where I had been was like a dream. Inside though, I felt content and my heart felt lighter. The next moment, I knew, I was being jolted awake, and the light was bright around me. Muela was gently shaking me, informing me that we were preparing to go, and begin the next stage of our journey. There would be another day's walking ahead of us.

Chapter 4

Arrival

The College

As we crossed the hills on the last day of our journey, there was a different energy in our group. I felt an excitement in my heart, a growing tension of anticipation and unknowingness. With every step, I felt the vibration of the Earth Spirit beneath my feet, as if it was beckoning me forward. When I tuned into my inner feelings, I even felt as if Eurydice was smiling and cajoling me to be happy.

We had changed our direction slightly, and now, we were climbing up a striking hill that had the appearance of being a very large mound. I could hear sounds of human habitation. When we reached the top of this hill, Berenice paused and waited until we all reached her. I had reached this vantage point ahead of her, and was impatient for the others to join us. But while we were waiting, I gazed below in amazement at what was in front of us. Then, when we were finally all gathered, Berenice announced simply that below laid the community of the College of the Order of the Wise.

The expanse of settlement we saw was quite extraordinary to me. It was far bigger than my birth village and of any other place with people where I had been. There were numerous clumps of living huts, and networks of other larger buildings and outdoor fireplaces. Tracks were marked out that interlaced between the various sections of the community, and in terms of energy, the whole area felt to be tremendously alive. As I tuned in, the vibrancy of it made me feel even a little unsteady on my feet.

I could see the small figures of numerous people, in groups and on their own. All were moving around with their own pattern, but with a purpose that seemed to link together. In my mind, I discerned that there must be several hundred people here, maybe even a thousand, or more. I stared in awe, and needed to breathe deeply to take it all in.

The huts were arranged in clumps, and Muela pointed to try and show us the hut where we would be staying. Students were placed together in groups of three, each group with its own house mother. Then, huts were arranged close to each other for students of similar age, so, as an age group, we could progress through our necessary stages of learning together, and live in close proximity to each other for the duration of our study. There were several large clusters of huts that separated students of various ages. In addition, there were also larger wooden buildings that functioned as gathering places for groups within the community, with one enormous wooden building in the Centre with a thick column of smoke that wisped upwards through the open roof top. This was our main community building.

The oldest group of students within the College had just graduated and they were now moving on to their next steps, so this meant that there were a cluster of huts that had been emptied for us and other young students of our age. We were the new ones and the youngest students to be there. Many others would be arriving over these next days in preparation for the beginning of our training.

Muela pointed out where the teachers lived, and they had their own huts on the other side of the community. There was no division though, for we or would live and mingle and share many of our meals together.

As well as being a college of learning, this settlement was also the administration headquarters for our land, the centre of government.

Some of the teachers, such as Berenice had dual roles, both as teachers for the students and also as representatives of the governing body.

As I explored more of the area with my gaze, I was drawn very powerfully, to a large copse of trees to the left of the main settlement, going down towards the river that snaked through the valley. I was impressed by the energy of these trees, for they felt so peaceful.

'Those trees form our Sacred Grove,' Berenice whispered in my ear, and I knew that this was somewhere that I would want to explore as soon as I could.

The mound where we were standing also had its purpose. Many from the community would come here in the mornings to greet the new day in meditation, for it faced east, towards the sun. Berenice pointed out a smaller mound on the other side of the settlement that faced west. This was where many people went in the evening as a private place of prayer and giving thanks what had been.

We were a people that honored the Earth Spirit as the living force that supported and nurtured our existence, and also the sun, that gave us the warmth we needed to live. Both were vital and we were appreciative of all the joy we could experience.

Muela showed us to our hut. It was a small traditional thatched hut, made with wood and mud. The interior of the hut was swept clean, and there were spaces for each of us to have our bed and personal belongings. Muela had her own little cubicle within the hut where she slept and there was a common area with fireplace where we could be together. Our beds were comfortable and we had skins to lie on and keep us warm. Muela's warmth and pride of keeping our home as a clear and functional place encouraged us to care for our hut together. Already, I could feel that I would be happy and content in this place, and that together with Nianda, Gracon and Muela, I could feel a close sense of belonging as is only possible when people share the same living quarters together.

Meditation

At dawn, Berenice came to our hut and woke me up. She took me high above the encampment to the top of the mound where people gathered to meditate. She explained that she had come early so we could be on our own. It was a beautiful scene with purple and pink and orange colors on the horizon that beckoned the approach of the sun. Berenice told me that this was one of the main power points in the area, somewhere to deeply connect with the Earth Spirit.

The mound was quite flat at the top, with leafy grass that was pleasant and soft to lie on. I had been instructed to bring some skins to lie on, and so now, I did that, and they cushioned me from the physical cold of the ground.

When I closed my eyes, my vision felt immediately very dark and deep. I was conscious of Berenice being next to me, and her energy was very quiet and reassuring. Through her presence, I felt myself going further and further down. There was a whoosh and then a sudden rush of energy through my body, and it was as if I was right inside the mound and the Spirit of the Earth surrounded me, and I felt at one with it. I could feel a very slow pulsing, and a stillness that felt incredibly comfortable. In my heart, I wanted to cry, for the experience in its simplicity moved me. In my feelings, I felt as though I was merging with the Earth, and knew that I was the Earth, that the Earth and I were one. I could stay in this stillness and rejoice in this, and a part of me wished to remain in this state forever.

But I could hear faintly, the voice of Berenice, and she was insisting on my return. She spoke many times repeating these instructions until I obeyed, and forced myself to rise again to the surface of the mound and the surface of my consciousness.

When I opened my eyes, I could see the outline of the sun, just peeping over the edge of the horizon. There were others nearby now, but I wanted to cuddle next to Berenice and she let me near.

Ilsa

We stayed there enjoying the first rays of the day for a long time, and then a moment came when Berenice turned me around gently to face her. In her hands she had a ring.

'Do you choose to be my student,' she asked, 'for if you do agree to this, you can have this ring? It has come a long way to reach you.'

The ring was very beautiful. It was simple and small, just right for my slender fingers. I felt a slither of joy through my body, and I instinctively reached out for the ring. Of course I wanted to accept this. I had no doubt. Berenice smiled when I put it on.

'This is your commitment,' she stated to me, 'to follow my teachings and learn with me for all your childhood days, until you are ready to go further. Do you agree?'

'I do,' I responded simply, and looked at her clearly in the eye, to show that I meant it.

Chapter 5

Beginning my training

Daily rhythms

The early years of my training were very busy and full. There was so much to learn. Each morning, there would be teachers coming to our quarter offering skills that we could learn. Included in this were practical skills, such as cooking, making cloth, pottery, hut construction, learning about plants and animals, hunting, and how to protect ourselves from predators. We learned about our history and traditions, the makeup of our communities, about our ceremonies, about the Earth Spirit and meditation practices, dancing and music, healing, and how to develop our inner sight and gifts. Various teachers came that had specialized knowledge in one or more of these subjects, and we were able to choose to join their classes, or other ones that may be of more interest to us. From a young age, that responsibility was left to us. There was some pressure for us to learn as much as we could, because later on, we would be tested, and those that were most capable overall would have the best chance of being offered a high position in our society, and perhaps even the entitlement to become a member of the Order of the Wise. So there was some competitiveness amongst us, but also a lot of support and cooperation.

In addition to the general learning that we all had to do, we also had our own personal teacher to help guide us, and allow us to develop our own specialization of skill training. Some of the teachers had a number of pupils, not just one, and these students were engaged in a more general education that they could later use in their local communities. For those that were their teacher's only pupil, a lot more was expected. These were ones who had more exceptional potential for what they could achieve, and the standards for these students were much higher.

I felt very privileged to be Berenice's only pupil, and was pleased that for both Nianda and Gracon, that they also had personal teachers that worked exclusively with them. We met with our personal teachers at times that suited them. For me, in the beginning, I hardly saw Berenice, for she was away so often. But later, she started to allow me to accompany her on her travels and her work, and that's when the learning with her commenced in earnest.

At the beginning of each day, I went to the mound to meditate and connect with the Earth Spirit, and then I would be enthusiastic for what the day would bring. I was keen and eager to learn, and I also found much that I needed to learn to be very interesting, so often, at the end of the day, I would feel quite exhausted from all the concentration.

I was closest to Nianda and Gracon, but over time I developed many other friendships with my fellow students. Many of the teachers and older children were also friendly.

In the evenings, we would regularly sing and dance and have fun together. We were a people that liked to be happy.

When I wanted to be alone and relax, my favorite place to go was the Sacred Grove. I felt blessed that I was allowed to go there. It was available for us at all times, except when it was being prepared for ceremonies or used for such. Whenever I went there, I felt an intense peace and sense of oneness with the Earth. There was a yew tree in the centre of the Grove, and this was the tree that I loved most. It had a feeling of ancientness about it, and when I sat there, I felt connected with all that had been before in this part of our land.

Usually it was late in the day when I went to the Yew. Rarely would I find anyone else there. It felt as though the Spirits gave me this space to be there on my own. The branches were very gnarled and old. As soon as I touched the branches, I would feel a shiver and rush of energy through my body. Then, as I sat down, it would feel as though I was joining with the tree and could feel its consciousness, and it could feel mine. Then I became very still and could contemplate on my day. I felt the quiet wisdom of the tree, but it did not intrude. It left me with my own thoughts, and I would feel underneath me its calm support and strength in the background, enabling me to draw on greater energies than my own. This tree was my friend, and I would hug it, as I would one of my human friends, just to let it know how much I appreciated it.

Karka

The person in charge of our Order was a man named Karka. He also lived in the community with us, and his hut was very close to the centre of our community. His role was not only as an overseer of the work in the college, but also as a director of the life and structure of our society within our whole land. He had tremendous responsibility, and everyone seemed to respect him, and he was very busy.

Karka was a friendly man, and sadly, I did not see him very often. Within our settlement, when he was around, there were always people talking to him, or there would be meetings that he was attending. He wore a distinctive brown cloak, and had a staff with him, wherever he went. One of the qualities that I liked about him was his humor. He would joke with us and make light of serious situations. Some evenings, he joined us when we were sitting by the fire, and he told us stories and joined our games. Karka had a lot of energy, and in his eyes, I saw much determination and vision. We all felt safe with him.

Learning with Berenice

Berenice also had a very high position within our land. She operated very freely and independently, and in terms of authority, she was second only to Karka. Her concerns were with the management of people and communities, and for the inner well being of our life together as a society. Berenice was acknowledged to have a gift of perceptual ability, where she could see deep into people's souls. It was one of her tasks to teach me to develop my own capacity to undertake similar work.

People who were not being honest would tend to be afraid to look at her or even be in her vicinity, because she could discern their thoughts and inner motivations, often with greater clarity than they could tell for themselves. She could also channel healing for humans and all life forms, including stones. Her psychic sense was very strong, and she could project energy and move energy through her own thought processes and intention. There were occasions where I saw her move objects such as stones, by the force of her will and intention, and her attunement to spirit.

Berenice commanded much respect from everyone whom she met, but she was not one to become involved with other people, preferring to remain aloof as an administrator and authority figure, and keeping her own human side hidden.

My training with her began in simple ways. She gave me instructions for meditation. When I meditated on the Mound or the Yew tree, she would question me in detail about what I experienced. She would encourage me to speak inwardly with the Yew and the Earth Spirit and open myself to impressions of what they wanted to communicate, and further she would intently to what I described. Then she would give me assignments to meditate in different environments in the surrounding area, and report what impressions I gained from these, so I could learn about the distinctiveness of each place. Next she would select people, and in a discreet fashion, she would expect me to tune into those people and their energy, and sense what was occupying them, and use my inner listening skills to enhance what I could determine psychically of these people. After a while, she encouraged me to do this as I was walking and moving around, so I could develop my capacity to attune to others in a form of waking meditation, by tuning into myself and inner listening, rather than needing to sit in meditation.

Berenice made it clear to me that what people presented of themselves, through their physical appearance and what they said, was only a tiny fraction of the totality of who they were. As souls, the resources and energy we each carried in us was immense. As human beings, we would typically try to hide elements of who we were, like our jealousies, resentments, fears irritations, prejudices, and shame. But these energies were visible to our inner eyes if we looked closely enough. With Spirit's help, we could do this. If we were going to help people and communities to find clarity and worthwhile solutions to problems that they had, then we could counsel them more effectively by knowing inwardly about their limitations and distortions.

When I was open and in my own centre, I could sense people's energy fields, as I had been doing since I was a young child. But now I needed to learn to interpret the information that I was receiving, and to do that very precisely. At times, I would turn to Eurydice, but she also encouraged me to listen to myself and my own inner capacity to discern truth and wisdom. As I asked to be able to do this, my abilities to succeed in this improved.

Berenice would go away on long journeys to help with troubled communities in our land. In the early stages of my training, she would give me assignments and leave without me, and it could be days before I saw her again. But when she returned, she always checked very thoroughly what I had been doing in her absence, and what I had learnt. If I was not very attentive to the tasks she had given, she would rebuke me, and she would always remind me that ultimately, my progress would depend entirely upon my own efforts.

Eventually, Berenice began to take me with her on her travels and I would be able to attend meetings she had with leaders from communities when she was doing her work. She told me to observe. And then, when the meeting was over, she would take me to one side, and question me closely about what I perceived was happening.

Sometimes, I would stumble, and she would question me further until I reached a necessary insight that I needed. If my perceptions were accurate and helpful, she would give a small smile. And once she suddenly laughed aloud when she realized that the conclusion I had reached was something quite different from what she had considered, but nonetheless, was valid and useful.

Before we went away, she would ask me to meditate and tune in to the place where we would be going, and the dynamics that were proceeding there. Very often I did not know anything about the conditions of what this community would be. So I had to trust myself, and have faith in my impressions. Again she would question and even guide me so I could learn techniques with my mind for increasing my skills. This was a form of telepathy that I was learning, and we also practiced telepathy between us, so it was possible for us to exchange thoughts with each other without speaking, and recognize the vibration of each other's mind. I felt privileged to be able to do this with Berenice, and she acknowledged that to let people into her inner worlds was not something that she generally allowed others to do with her. She could close her mind to me if she wished, and she taught me, how I too, could close my mind when this was necessary.

I was quite enthralled by what I was learning with my teacher, but I felt quite nervous and even a little fearful when she started to give me assignments, where I would be the one to work with members of a community, and speak with them, and try to find a solution – while she sat next to me to give me support.

Berenice introduced me to this gradually, first giving me minor pieces of work with people and slowly increasing the level of responsibility she gave me as I was able to cope with it. I had a child's mind though and I did not have the experience of the adults in these communities. Berenice put to me that even though I was young, my mind would have to learn to stretch so I could do this.

Ilsa

There was such a lot for me to learn and absorb. I was developing my capacity to have empathy, so by opening myself to people, I would have the thoughts and feelings of these people as if they were my own thoughts and feelings. And I had to be able to distinguish the difference between them and me so that what I channeled would not overwhelm me.

When I tuned into people, there were thoughts and feelings which would come into me, that I sometimes found very confusing, because I did not recognize them. I had to speak with Berenice about these, and she needed to explain to me what they meant. Slowly, I was able to develop an understanding of the psychology of the human mind. I was exposed to fears, jealousy, envy, greed, power struggles, loss, and desires between people, attachments, and many other forms of distorted perceptions. And each time that I did this, it would bring up more questions for me to ask Berenice, and many times, she had to help me to detach so I would not be carrying energies that did not belong to me. These experiences all helped me with my inner development, but with many of them, I did not find it easy.

My teacher was very patient with me, for she knew that it was vitally important for me to be able to protect myself and manage the perceptions and energies around me. She showed me how I could be selective about when I opened myself to others, and with whom I should do this. In the early stages, she insisted that I not do this while she was away travelling, but only when she was present to monitor and support me.

Berenice emphasized to me that my own child thoughts and feelings were important and I must not get lost in the issues and energies of others. I had to learn to distinguish between work and play, and that my playtime and relaxing time by myself and with my friends was very precious and that I had to preserve that and grow through my childhood. I was not to become an adult too early. Although she could be very stern and serious a lot of the time, there were moments when she relaxed and we laughed and I could tell that she had a child consciousness within her as well.

During the years of my training, Berenice was by far, the most important person to me in my life. I needed her and I had to place my trust in her to an enormous degree. She never let me down, and supported me step by step so I could develop myself and learn the work that I would have to do. She got to know me very well, and I felt a sense of harmony and great love for her where I both felt safe and a fierce desire to learn more.

Chapter 6

Experiences from my youth

There were many occasions in my young life, when I faced challenges, not only with my growing body, but also my character. Several of these events occurred when I was not with my teacher, Berenice, but with others from the community. Some of these trials were difficult for me, even painful. Here are three stories of those instances that felt most important to me.

The mountain

It is springtime. The sun is shining, plants are thrusting their life forces outwards, buds on trees bursting with the potential growth that is waiting, and the animals and birdsongs are buzzing in the atmosphere around us. The energy of the ground feels like a current that surges up my legs.

We are out walking. There is a group of us, and I am leading. We are exploring some of the neighboring hills in a nearby valley. I feel so alive, that I am unable to contain myself. It is not a day for walking; I want to run. I want to test my strength, and feel those magnificent forces of nature straining through my body.

As I look upwards, there is a large hill in front of us. The face of it looks quite sheer, and there are jagged rocks obscuring the summit of the hill from our view. This is a worthwhile challenge. The height and steepness of it will be a fine task for us to accomplish. It will do.

When I decide this, feelings of inner resolve and determination arise in me. This will be exciting, and a chance to show my strength.

'Let's race', I cry, and I indicate the hill in front of us where we need to go. There is no question of anyone refusing. I have decided, and therefore, we all must do it together. My friend, Nianda is ready. She smiles, and stretches her legs. I sense that she feels she can beat me – I know that, but I feel very confident that I can win.

The others look less certain. Gracon gives me a pained glance, but he knows he cannot argue with me when I am determined like this.

Out of generosity, I tell the others to go first, to give them a start, and even Nianda; I tell to go ahead of me to begin. They start to run, with Gracon lumbering at the rear. I should let them get well ahead, but I am impatient, and cannot bear to wait long. The will to race from within me is like a pressure of desire that I cannot resist.

Once Nianda steps forward, I am soon after her. Nianda is fast, like a loping animal, lightly traveling almost effortlessly over the terrain. With me, it is more sheer effort that drives me on, and my will propels me forward. Soon, we overtake the others, and the foot of the mountain is upon us.

This is where I have the advantage over Nianda. My strength helps me to maneuver up the slope. She cannot keep up with me, and glances ruefully in my direction. So now, it is a race with my Self. I go like crazy, tearing upwards, just as a vain quest to prove my ability, and push myself to my limit. As I head upwards, the panorama below me increases, but I hardly wish to view it. I must keep going, and show myself how mighty and fast I can be.

I reach the overhanging rocks now, and although the passes up through them look very narrow and fragile in places, I trust my instinct and keep going. Nothing can stop me. I have so much energy surging through me. This feels like a day I will not forget.

The gradient of the slope of the mountain increases, but I just swing confidently from one hold to the next. I am almost there. Just a few more holds and I will be at the summit.

But then as I look up, I do not reach for the next hold properly, and the hold gives way. It does not support me. Desperately, I try to adjust, and find another hold, anywhere. My arms, feet lunge about, but there is nowhere for me to hang on, and I am falling, and the distance below is huge.

All at once, it feels as if everything is in slow motion. This could be the end of my life. I could be dying. What a fool I have been. It suddenly dawns on me, with horrifying regret, that I could have just thrown my life away. What have I done? Within an instant, I sense my rashness, and my arrogance, and my lack of regard for anyone's interests, except my own – just wanting to show that I was better than them, and faster. I was so struck on what I wanted to do, and now I could have forsaken my life.

In the next instant, my body is shaking with fear. I really do not want to die. Inwardly, I cry out and plead for another chance, and as I do that, my guide is there, my beautiful guide, and she is shaking her head.

'Not so fast,' she speaks to me, in a very soothing voice.

My arms are flailing, but then, my left arm is grabbing at an outstretched jutting rock. I had not even realized that it was there. My body thunders against it in a sickening crash, but it holds, and I feel a force propel my feet to the tiniest of ledges just below me, where, even with the violent shaking of my limbs, I manage to cling on, and not fall further.

For many moments, I just remain there in stunned disbelief. My life has been saved from a personal disaster of my own making. I have just realized how truly much I want to live, and there is no question. My life is incredibly important to me, and I do not want to give it up unless I absolutely have to.

In the silence, I thank my guide, and I thank spirit. I know I have been given another chance, and I want to make sure that I earn it.

Then Nianda is there, reaching down to me with her hand. She assures me, she has the other one locked around a tree. After a few moments of hesitation, I reach up my arms, and she pulls me up. How did she know I was there? I am surprised how strong she is.

My body is a mass of blood and bruises. When I look up at her, she smiles, as if she knows. I feel safe with her, and for a while, I just sit there with her, and sob.

Then, I know what I have to do, and we go down the hill to the others below us. I need to make sure that they are OK. We manage to check in with all of them except Gracon.

Finally, when we reach the bottom of the hill, we find him nestled in a small crevice, crouched down and shivering. To climb this steep hill is too much for him. His strength is in other directions. I have to respect and appreciate that. He accepts my support, and I give him a gentle hug.

Later that day, we do go up that hill, but we go up all together, and we support each other every step of the way. Once we reach the top of the hill, we all enjoy it, and I feel happy to have learned my lesson and gained some understanding about respect.

Nianda

From the first time when I met her, I liked Nianda. She was very slight in build, and she rarely spoke. Usually, her footsteps were so quiet that it was hard to notice her. Yet, in her eyes, there was a kindness that shone outwards. Whenever she was around, the whole atmosphere of whatever I was doing would become more peaceful. She brought with her, the presence of healing, and it was this gift that was the reason that she had been summoned to train with the Order of the Wise.

Sharing a house with Nianda felt very natural and easy, as if we already knew each other very well as souls from ancient times. She felt very close to me. Like me, she had a strong faith, and we were both very dedicated to our practices. Even though we had so much contact, I still felt as though she kept parts of herself hidden. In nature, she was considerate; she could laugh and dance and have fun; she would easily

Ilsa

give help to others. But rarely did she talk about anything to do with herself, or take help from others.

I wanted to learn what it was that made Nianda so protective of herself? Why was she so reluctant to open herself to others?

Sometimes, if I saw Nianda sitting alone, I would join her in quietness, like I would with Gracon. She seemed to like this, although she would say very little. I sensed that she had great need to receive love and tenderness, and my inner senses suggested to me that locked away deep inside of her, there was some huge sadness that she did not want anyone to see.

Nianda went away on trips that were unexplained. They were not with her teacher, and she never said anything about these absences. However, when I asked her teacher, Dosha, about this once, he responded that this was a private matter for Nianda, but that the trips she made had his consent.

What I noticed was that upon her return from these trips, her mood would be lighter, and she would be happier for a while.

From my training with Berenice, I was developing my capacity to be able to enter into people's minds, to discern truth and disturbances that were there. I had to be respectful about this, but I was very curious to know what secrets existed within Nianda. However, whenever I approached her mind, I felt that she shielded herself so I could not enter into her. What I did notice was that she had an attentive male guide working with her, and he gave her Spiritual support, and helped to keep her safe from prying eyes like mine!

There came a time though, when Nianda could not hide her inner unhappiness so well, anymore. Her energy became listless, and she was spending very little time with others, and appeared to be losing interest in what was going on around her, and even in our classes, I saw her staring into space rather than concentrating. We were all concerned about her, and yet, she still would not speak. She had been away again for a long period, but on this occasion, whatever she had been doing had not helped her mood. In fact, she became more restless than I had ever known her. At night time, I sometimes woke up, and she would not be sleeping, and when I asked if I could help her, she gave a small smile to acknowledge me and then said that it was nothing.

I began to feel anxious that the elders might ask her to leave, because she was giving so little attention to her studies. The problem was not to do with our College; it was from far away. I asked my guide and the Earth Spirit to support me so I could help Nianda.

A few evenings later, she was sitting under a beech tree on her own. I decided to give her my company, but as I approached, her head went down. For some time, I sat with her in silence. Then I felt a light growing within me, and I reached over to stroke her hair. I did this gently and affectionately, and then at one point, I felt a droplet of water on my arm, and then another. It was teardrops from Nianda's eyes. In response, I drew myself closer to her, and she put her head on my shoulder.

'What is it, Nianda?' I asked her.

For a few minutes, she continued to sit there, and I waited patiently, sending her love, hoping she would be brave enough to tell me. Then she began to tremble, and I could tell that the emotion was rising to the surface. From there, she started sobbing, and her body convulsed with all the emotion.

'Tell me', I implored her, and then she told me that it was her father, and that he was dying. She was his only family, and missed him terribly.

I paused in shock and felt a tightening in my stomach. It was an important time in our studies with assessments and initiation practices being taught to all of us. The Elders would not want anyone to be away, and that was surely why Nianda was here. But this had to be more important.

'We must go to him,' I insisted. And within minutes, I had taken Nianda with me for us to meet with both Berenice and Nianda's teacher, Dosha.

It was Dosha who looked gently down upon her student.

'You must resolve this now,' he declared to her. 'You have to heal yourself, if you are going to be able to meaningfully heal others. Make your decision when you are there, child.'

Nianda nodded to Dosha in acknowledgement and looked across at me. She looked brighter than I had seen her in a long time, for she knew that we would leave in the morning.

Just before dawn, we set off at a run. There was no one we wished to see; we just needed to get there. Much later in the day, when we finally rested, I confronted Nianda, and was adamant that she tell me her story. We leaned against the rocks where we stood and I looked in her eyes. I felt that the previous resistance that had been there was gone.

She described the beauty of her homeland where she had been born, the coast and sea, and the wonderful energy that was there. I felt her passion and her love for this place. With strong endearment, she spoke fondly of her family, her mother and father, and her baby sister, and how precious they were to her.

Then her eyes filled up, and once more her body trembled. Gradually the dreadful story tumbled out about what had happened to her community. It reminded me of the raiders that wreaked havoc in the village where I was born and with my family. But this was much worse.

Nianda was only four at the time. The raiders appeared suddenly and without warning. They destroyed and pillaged all around them, and set fire to the buildings. Her mother was cast down, raped and killed in front of her eyes while Nianda watched in horror. Her sister had her throat slit and died, and then Nianda herself, was sexually molested and beaten, and discarded by the side of the road to die. Her father screamed and fought and tried to prevent the agonies happening around him, but they knifed him repeatedly until he slumped not far from her in a pool of blood.

As the violence of the raid receded, Nianda had crawled across to her father, and sought comfort and solace from being close. The stench of death was about him, but she was desperate not to let him go. She pleaded with all the Spirits around her, and her guide, that she was willing to do anything, if only they would let her father live. As a small child, she could not bear to be without him.

'Then do this,' a voice within her commanded her. And then Nianda felt the energy vibrating in her hands, and she placed her hands on her father's body, and the heat became more and more intense. Listening to Spirit, she obeyed where she needed to place her hands, and she felt masses of energy being injected into him, until he finally responded, and she had felt life returning to him. And although he never was fit enough again to work, he recovered enough to look after her while she was little, and Nianda remained utterly devoted to her father.

So, when she was told to prepare herself to go to the College of the Order of the Wise, she did not want to go. In her heart, she wanted to stay with her father, and she would always want to be with him. But she remembered her promise, and it was Spirit that was directing her to go for her training. So she went, but only on condition that she could visit him regularly. This is what she did. So in all the years while she had been training to learn healing, she had never released her attachment to her father. And the child in her would never let him go. Now he was dying.

After her most recent visit, she had wanted to stay and make him well again, but the elders had refused to give her further leave, and inside her, Nianda had felt like giving up, that part of her was dying too.

Later, when we finally reached the village, Nianda went straight to her father. Nianda was kind enough to allow me into her father's hut with her. A couple of women were with her father, mopping his brow, but I was shocked when I saw him. His body was inert, and painfully thin, and he was hardly breathing at all. I could see the alarm on Nianda's face, and the women moved to one side. Energetically, I could sense that Nianda's father's life force had all but left the body. Nianda could not accept that, and she summoned all the light energy of Spirit that she could muster, and she injected that as powerfully as she could into her father's body. He stirred as she forced his energy back into him. This gave her hope, and she continued to work with him, attempting to strengthen his system, anything, so that he would live.

The color returned a little to his body, and she tried to get him to drink a little water from a pouch. However, every time, Nianda stopped to rest through sheer exhaustion, her father's life energy appeared to slip away again, as if he did not want to be physically alive any more. But Nianda would not give up, and she tried over and over again. She even asked me to work with her, and I joined her, and felt the Spirit of her father very close. He appeared to want Nianda to know that she had done enough for him. She had to let him go, and it was his time. But Nianda did not feel that she had done enough, and she was desperate that her father should stay with her. I felt that Spirit was working even more with Nianda now, to calm her, and help her relax. And for a long while, she would not let Spirit into her, but wanted that energy to flow straight out of her to him, and her attention was wholly with her father, anxiously looking for any sign that his condition could improve. Her efforts were futile, but she still would not permit herself to stop.

Finally, I asked her 'Who are you doing this for?' And for some moments, she could not look at me, but her eyes were filling up, and she buried her face in my arms.

'I can't live without my father', she sobbed, and for a long time, I held her, until my clothes were wet with her tears.

For several days, we stayed there, and I tried to support Nianda and her father as much as I could. The atmosphere grew slowly more peaceful, until one evening, Nianda asked me to go, so she could be alone with her father. I respected her wishes, and all night, I sat outside the hut, under the light of the moon, and from inside, there was not a sound.

When the sun rose, I felt that I needed to go in, and when I did, I saw in front of me, two motionless bodies. Nianda's father was dead. I could tell by the color of his skin, and he was not breathing. But Nianda appeared not to be breathing either, and then I felt waves of panic and grief welling up inside me. Could Nianda have chosen to die so she would not be separated from her father? I felt for Nianda's pulse, and checked to hear if her heart was beating, and there were the faintest of signs that she was still alive.

I knew then that she had gone with her father on his passage to Spirit. She would be able to do that. But would she return?

For a long time, I sat by the two bodies, and I prayed. Over and over, I prayed to Nianda for her to choose to live, and embrace all the experiences of physical life that her soul wished for her. I prayed that she would have the strength to live, and I implored her to come back into her body. Passionately, I asked Spirit to help her. I did not want to lose my friend.

Finally, Nianda gave a big sigh, and her body moved. She moaned, and I could tell that she wanted to go again, and I shouted at her to wait. I had made a hot broth, and I made her drink. She had to be grounded.

When she opened her eyes, she had a far away expression.

'I saw them,' she told me, and afterwards, when she could talk more coherently, she related how she had met her family in Spirit and shared love with them, and how she had watched and waited while her father was reunited with them. But she had been pulled down and couldn't stay however much she wanted to. She had to come into her physical body, but at least she knew that the members of her family were happy and well in Spirit, and that meant a lot to her.

Nianda continued to look pale and fragile, and we waited in the village until her father's cremation was over. The Elder of the village spoke to Nianda and told her that they were proud of her, and they wished for her to complete her training, and not to give up on life.

I felt a growing stirring in me, and one morning, I looked into Nianda's eyes, and I told her that she could stay with me, and I invited her to join my family, so we would be like sisters, and I wanted her to be like my sister for the rest of our lives, so she would have a family, and I would look after her, and we could support each other. I meant this from the depth of my heart.

She cried and hugged me. Little did I know how much help and support I would need and receive from Nianda in the times to come, and that this vow we made to each other would stay with us until the rest of our lives.

When we prepared to leave, I put to Nianda that she needed to bring all of her with her to our training college and not leave any of herself behind in the village of her family. She needed all of her energy with her to live her life fully, so she could accomplish all the important things she needed to do in her life.

Nianda smiled, and told me that she would do that.

This was the day when Nianda became my most loyal friend, and as we stepped away onto our journey to the college, we both felt joy, and for Nianda, it was a most significant beginning of a new chapter in her life.

Greystook

Greystook was a student from our intake. She lived in a dwelling place right next to ours. Like us, she was part of a group of three. Her companions were called Mulaid and Kiend. I noticed that, as a group, they were not as close as us, and they existed more as individuals and I wondered what kept them separate. We knew them well, because they attended many of the same classes as us, and shared a lot.

Mulaid and Kiend both had remarkable talents in their own areas. Mulaid was extremely sensitive around music, and was in training to develop these skills. I had watched Mulaid from an early age when he was taught to play music, plucking sounds from his beautiful stringed instruments, with his teacher, Dulon. Now, he was developing wonderfully as a musician in his own right. When Mulaid played music, people would stop, and it would be like enchantment in the air. Mulaid could play with the energies in our vicinity, and bring forth beautiful light streams by the sounds that he created. There were times when I listened to him, and I could perceive the subtle colors of these streams of light, manifesting through his creativity and his attunement to Spirit. My body tingled when I heard him.

Kiend's training concerned his love of animals. They came to him, feeling both attracted and safe with him. In turn, Kiend protected his friends, the animals, and cared for the creatures that were injured. When he touched a living creature, he did it with such tenderness and love, that the animal would have no fear of him. Wild animals would approach him as a friend. Kiend was learning to communicate with members of the animal kingdom, so that he could become both a protector and representative of these creatures within our Order.

It was quite a privilege to be so closely associated with two such outstanding youths.

With Greystook though, it was difficult to discern any great areas of capability. She could talk, and liked to explain things to others. But this was her intellect and not her heart. When our teachers explained things to us, Greystook would gravitate to the front of our group and appear to take a great interest in proceedings. Greystook understood the concepts being imparted, sure enough, and she would be quick to tell the others what they should know. However, it was often in the silences and the subtle energies that our teachers conveyed the deeper secrets of our Order, and Greystook appeared to miss this altogether.

At our meetings, Greystook would cock her head slightly, and I would sense her straining with her mind, but her psychic centers were not as developed as everyone else. Greystook would pretend to understand, and in talking so much, tried to compensate and impress the others with her knowledge, but most were not interested in her, and she must have felt it. She tried not to let it show though, and generally, whenever there was a group of us together, Greystook would position herself in the centre, talking away. Many of us were put off by this, and preferred not to gather in a big group, so we would not have to listen to Greystook dominating the conversation.

Sometimes, I would study Greystook's energy field, and I felt puzzled by her presence. One day, while I was working with Berenice, I asked her why Greystook was with us. She just did not seem to belong or have anything substantial to offer the community. Berenice gave me a strange smile. It was one of those occasions when she would not give me a full answer. All she told me was that Greystook had a special purpose, and she urged me to accept her as well as I could.

Over the course of time, I tried to befriend Greystook, but I found it very difficult. Although Greystook could talk in concepts, she opened very little in her heart. When I tried to sense about this, I felt acute loneliness and lack of self-worth beneath the surface. Here was someone who was desperate to attract attention through her intellect and gain love and appreciation from others. However, on a feeling level, she

Ilsa

expected rejection and did not actually believe in herself. Beneath the bravado, I felt that Greystook was a very sad person, and very isolated.

When Mulaid picked up his instrument, Greystook would come close, and it was the one time when she would be quiet and still. Although she could hardly play herself, she had a great appreciation for the beautiful sounds and vibrations of the music. Mulaid noticed this, and smiled when he saw Greystook listening. She cocked her head in her characteristic fashion, but I could tell that with music, she was attentive with her heart and soul, and this did make a positive difference to her.

Once, when Mulaid was playing, I glanced over to Greystook, and saw her wiping tears from her eyes. Quickly, she put her hands down to try to hide this, and it was very apparent that she did not wish for others to be aware of her vulnerability. But on this occasion, she knew that I had seen her, and rather than turning away, I felt the urge to acknowledge her feelings, and so I rose up from my seat, and moved over to her, and quietly put my arm around her. I was surprised how open she was, and she let me stay with her. The longer, I sat with her, the more relaxed she became, and eventually, she even rested her head on my shoulder.

When the music finished, she looked up rather embarrassed, but I took her hand, and showed her that I accepted her. We did not say much more, but this interaction marked the beginning of my friendship with her. In general, she relaxed more around me, and I noticed, with Mulaid too. She had revealed some essence of her inner self to us, and neither of us had rejected her.

This opening for her did not alter her behavior at classes though, and she continued to give her speeches, and insist of being at the centre of attention, and none of the other students found her to be very easy to be around.

Once, I saw some of the students mimic Greystook, and make fun of her. Out of the corner of my eye, I saw that Greystook had seen them, and her head went down, and she moved away. I wanted to shout at these students for being so insensitive, but I stopped myself, and instead, asked to speak to them privately. I told them that they were not being respectful and what they did denigrated Greystook's soul. It was not the way we had been trained to treat others. One of them smirked at me, and I confronted him, telling him firmly that his reaction betrayed his own feelings of inadequacy. This made the others thoughtful, and I stared at them forcefully, daring them to acknowledge the truth of what I was saying. They left me without further words. There was something about Greystook that made me want to protect her, and I wished that she could more fully express her true self.

There were some very important initiation tests that were approaching. These were intermediate exams, and would determine for some of us, whether we would be able to continue our education at the college, or not. During the build up to this, I had been preoccupied with the trials that Nianda had been suffering with her father. Upon my return, though, my attention turned to Greystook.

I felt fearful about how Greystook would manage these tests, and was anxious that she may be humiliated in front of the other students. I shared this with Greystook, and she was brave enough to admit that she held similar fears. As she spoke of this, her mouth trembled and tears ran down her face. She so much wanted to cope with her studies and succeed with them as well as everyone else. She did not want to fail. Her studies were what she lived for. But beneath her mask, she had very little confidence in herself.

I did not want Greystook to fail either, and I was relieved that she trusted me enough to confide in me. It disturbed me that none of her teachers had sought to give her extra tuition, but Greystook confessed that she was too proud to ask. The only one that she felt she could trust was me.

Together we made a resolution for me to help her as much as I could, and for her to be open to learn from me as well as she could. With this pact, we then discussed a program of tuition where I would try to help her. I did not have the training to teach, but I felt desperate for Greystook, and determined to help her reach her potential.

So, every afternoon after our lessons, we went together to the Sacred Grove, and sat by the old Yew tree. I tried to coax Greystook to listen

Ilsa

and perceive with her inner senses rather than her intellect, and for her to learn the difference.

At first she did not understand and she tried to bluff me that she understood, when I knew that she did not. She could not pretend with me, because I would tell her and give her honest feedback. I insisted that she admit when she did not know something, as then, she would be more open to learn.

Greystook needed to learn to feel with the wisdom of her heart, and not to be afraid of her feelings. I thought that if she could tune into the trees and listen to what they were communicating, then this would help her in other areas too. For days on end, I insisted that she come with me, so we could practice. I tried to encourage her to meditate, but she found it very difficult to quiet her mind. When I asked her to tell me what the trees were communicating, she would just tell me some thoughts that came into her head. It was very frustrating.

One day, it got too much for me and I shouted at Greystook, and she started to cry. But then in the midst of all her distress, she heard a voice inside her telling her to quiet herself, and that was when her inner listening skills began to open.

Once she made the initial breakthrough, she had a genuine eagerness to go further. And I tried to encourage her and push her to learn more. But I just was not certain if we had sufficient space of time for her to learn what she needed.

Her main subject was history, but although Greystook knew lots of facts, it was the moral truth and Spiritual teachings that could be gained from examining specific epochs in our history that was important. Our history existed through the telling of stories and myths. Knowing the facts was not enough. It puzzled me why her teacher had ignored her so much.

When we had our final history lesson before the tests, Broden, the elder that was teaching us, spoke about troubled periods in our past, when there had been warfare between our people, and our collective Spiritual commitment to serve the land and support each other had broken down. For once, when I looked across at Greystook, I felt that she was really listening. The energy of her concentration was no longer just with her thinking brain. Her energy was more spread and inwardly focused.

Broden led us on inner journeys into those times, so that we could sense the consciousness of the people then, and perceive reasons that these conditions had formed. When I considered this, my instinct told me that there had been an absence of Spiritual clarity and authority then. As I followed this inwardly, I could sense the impact that this had upon the people, and how when the people did not have nourishment for their Spiritual being, other drives and instincts came much more to the fore, including aggression and greed.

In these past times, those who took control, had no Spiritual depth to their beliefs, and applied their wills to use force over others. The seers, Spiritual Initiates and sensitive ones, were relegated to the fringes of society and sometimes even persecuted, so they could not assert themselves.

How important, it felt to me, for us to preserve the present structures of our society, and engender our community life with love and dedication to Spirit, so we could live in peace and harmony.

When I opened my eyes from the meditation, I gazed towards Greystook, and her eyes were still closed. Her eyelids were moving so I could tell that she was in a deeper state. This delighted me. She was one of the last to return to our normal awareness, and I sensed that for her, perhaps as an experience of genuine self-discovery, she had been truly travelling within her inner consciousness. When she opened her eyes, she gently looked at me, and smiled.

At the conclusion of this class, a group of us assembled outside by the fire. There was much thoughtful contemplation. Greystook claimed her place at the forefront of this group, in typical fashion. She raised her forefinger to attract attention, and was just about to commence one of her speeches to paraphrase the discourse we had just been given. Immediately, the others began to turn away, not having the patience to listen to her. But then, something changed. It was like an energy being released in the air, as a deeply held pattern was being broken.

Ilsa

I saw Greystook hesitate, and then she stopped. She did not speak, and she stepped back a little to give space to the others. My heart leapt with joy. I sensed a tremor of energy ripple through Greystook's body. It felt like a very important moment for her, an instant when she recognized, perhaps for the first time in her life, that she could be silent in a group. She did not have to impress anybody.

There was a palpable change in her energy. She turned around and her eyes again met mine briefly, and there was peace in her eyes. Part of me wanted to rush over to her and embrace her, but instead, I stood my ground.

Greystook moved to take a few steps away from the group. She plainly did not need the attention any more. I felt like dancing with joy. I was so happy for her. But then, suddenly, there was a shiver of fear rippling through my body. I felt compelled to turn back to Greystook. She was not walking any more, but had stopped, and then she appeared to stagger. Her right hand went up to her chest, and she clutched at it, as if she was in pain. I saw her half turn as if to reach out towards me. And then she was collapsing, falling down. Something was wrong, very wrong.

I felt a surge of panic rise up inside me. Immediately I was running and shouting at the same time. 'Nianda', I screamed out. I needed my friend.

We had a special dwelling place where healing was given. This was where Nianda trained and spent most of her days. She came rushing. By now, Greystook was motionless on the ground. I crouched beside her and felt her life energy very weak and fading. She must not die. How could this happen now? Greystook was my friend. She had learnt so much.

'Save her,' I implored Nianda. I cleared a space from the gathering crowd so Nianda could get in. She gave Greystook a huge injection of energy. Greystook's head moved slightly, and it seemed to revive her. But her vital energy was not returning. It was starting to fade again. Nianda's teacher, Dosha, appeared, and they both worked frantically to try and help.

Greystook was carefully placed on a stretcher, and transferred to the healing room. I was not going to leave her. As much as Greystook's energy wanted to withdraw and leave, my will demanded that she stay. And I believe that it was my will and the continuing injections of healing energy that kept her alive.

It was her heart that had collapsed. On a physical level, her pulse was very weak. Energetically, she was all but gone. We were only just holding onto her by threads. I was not going to let her go.

At one point, Nianda looked over at me longingly. They were at the limits of what they could do. But there was something else in her eyes as well. I remembered her struggle with her father, and wanting to keep him alive, and eventually she had had to surrender to forces greater than her own. I was not ready for that. It was a desperate struggle.

For some hours, I stayed there. Outside, I could hear the murmurs of concerned onlookers. My will was focused only on keeping Greystook alive. I was determined not to lose her. However, every time that there was a pause, I felt a wave coming over me, and as much as I tried to fight it, it kept coming at me and permeating through me. It actually felt very peaceful and accepting, and was urging me to let go. But that was not what I wanted. I had to keep Greystook alive.

More and more, this energy entered me, and eventually, I had little choice but to surrender to it. My eyes closed, and there, in front of me, there was a brilliant light. I did not want to see it, for I could sense the identity of this being. There were others supporting her. I had to look up. It was Greystook in her Spiritual form. She implored me to release her, because it was her time.

Her voice was so gentle and pure, but I wanted to fight against her, and not accept what she told me. She had an initiation test to pass, and I could help her succeed. There was so much in front of her, and I felt like my ambitions for her were crumbling in front of my eyes.

When I looked at her again, she was smiling. The thoughts she imparted to me, told me that she had passed her initiation as a soul, because she had learnt her lesson and opened her heart to Spirit. Her life purpose was fulfilled, and there was nothing more for her to do in this body.

I felt a strong wave of love from her. My hold loosened. It was not only my will that counted, I realized. She was waiting to die.

My head dropped, and the tears rolled down my cheeks. Greystook's body shook momentarily, and then was silent. Nianda and Dosha checked to be certain of what had just taken place, and then they stared at me, and I felt Nianda's calming hand on my shoulder. Greystook's body was now completely still, and her vital life force had departed.

For a long time, I stayed there, watching her, with many contrasting feelings rising up inside me. Meanwhile, others came and went, paying their respects.

Even though she had told me differently, it felt cruel that she should die so prematurely, before she could show the elders what she had learned. But, as I considered this, it dawned on me, that this was my wish and desire. What Greystook had needed was now accomplished. Then I realized that this was a lesson for me; another lesson for my will, for me to trust in the greater divine forces rather than what I wanted, myself. Through her actions, Greystook had been my teacher, showing me how I could open my heart in times of crisis, and I could only shed tears of joy for all that she had taught me.

We had a special sacred ground in a clearing surrounded by a small birch wood. This was where we conducted cremations for those that had passed on. It was situated near the Sacred Grove. When someone died, Elder Initiates of our community would conduct silent rituals in the Grove, and then the body would be taken and placed on a burial pyre on this sacred ground. There the body would be burnt, and while the burning was taking place, the Elders would join together energetically to accompany the soul of the departed one to ascend into the Spirit realm. This is something that we, as students, could join in as much as we were able.

In honor of the soul, a Eulogy of praise and appreciation for Greystook's life would be given. With the death being one of the students, I fully expected that this eulogy would be performed by Karka, our leader, and head of the community.

However, when I checked with Berenice, she confirmed that Karka would be attending the ceremony, but someone else would utter the Eulogy. Berenice stared at me with a strange smile, and I suddenly felt very nervous. Then she confirmed the source of my anxiety. Berenice and Karka wanted me to do the Eulogy because of the closeness in relationship that I had shared with Greystook. I was in shock. As I thought about it, I could acknowledge that it made logical sense for me to do it, for I knew and appreciated Greystook's qualities better than anyone. I was still surprised, but I accepted that it would be appropriate for me to be the one to honor her and pay tribute to her, in front of the others.

I must have looked very startled, because Berenice moved her arms and reached out for me. So many elders were better placed to speak in front of our community than me. It was unknown, in my experience, for students to be given the opportunity to speak at any of our community rituals. But, as Berenice held me, I felt again the light presence of Greystook's soul, near me, and I sensed that I had her blessing as well. This was something that I had to do.

When the funeral was about to commence, I watched as the clearing by the pyre in the Sacred Birch wood, filled with people. Many had returned from travels to attend. There was Karka, Berenice, and all the other elders that I knew and respected. I felt in awe of their superior knowledge, and wondered what I could say that would be meaningful to them. It was unprecedented to be asked to do this, but it also felt very daunting. My body was trembling with fear, and I hoped for everyone's sake, especially for Greystook, and the memory of her, that I could do it right.

I called on my guide, Eurydice, and felt her loving, firm energy behind me, giving me strength. It would have been tempting for me to lean on her and use her wisdom, but Eurydice was not going to let me do this. 'Trust your Self, Ilsa,' she told me. 'You will know what to say.' My guide was encouraging me, while making it clear that this was a task that I had to do myself.

Ilsa

When the time came, and I stood in front of our community, with hundreds of eyes looking at me, I had to swallow to clear my throat before I could start but I could feel Greystook's presence was close by me. As I breathed in, I filled up with emotion for the love that I felt for my friend. My voice rang out, lucid and loud, for all to hear.

I spoke about how we needed to help the weak as well as the strong; those that struggled, as well as those that appeared gifted. We could all learn and grow, even those that might appear quite limited in ability. And from there, I told the story of Greystook, and the great transformation that had occurred at the end of her life, and the light that had shone from her soul, just before she died. Her crowning achievement had been to overcome a pattern of behavior that had limited her all her life. We could all overcome our weaknesses, and we all had that light of spirit within us, a light, that if we nurtured it with tolerance and understanding, could spread out love, and help our community to be a place of peace and well-being.

Greystook's presence was a brilliant light, with many light beings supporting her. As I finished my speech, a whole host of representatives from the Elders of our community sent their energy bodies spiraling upwards to accompany Greystook's soul as it ascended to the high realms of Spirit, where she would be at home.

Part of me wanted to go with them, but my attention was with Mother Earth, and all of us that remained. As Greystook's body lay burning on the funeral pyre, I wept tears of joy at the beauty of what had befallen.

At the conclusion of the ceremony, two students came over to join me, and Nianda was with them. They were Mulaid and Kiend, the other two members of the group that had included Greystook. Without her, they felt incomplete, and they wanted support. We were already friends with them, and they told us, that if we agreed to it, that we could be given a larger hut where we could all live together, and that we could then become effectively, a group of five.

There was a strong light with their presence, and I knew that their joining us was right. I welcomed them and embraced them, as they did me. It felt as though the circle of those that were closest and most meaningful for me, was enlarging, and this felt another important development.

Afterwards, when I reflected upon the speech that I had given, it came to me how for Greystook, the learning of her lesson about opening her heart had been her initiation test. Now I felt that giving the Eulogy in front of all those people, had been my initiation, and with the joy I felt, I knew that I had passed.

Chapter 7

Trials and training

Healing

As students in the College, we had to gain basic knowledge and experience in a number of disciplines as well as the area that was our specialization.

I was fortunate that my personal teacher, Berenice, was proficient and very knowledgeable in many areas. In fact, I probably could have learnt what I needed from her in nearly every subject, but she insisted that I train in some of my disciplines with the other students and also other teachers. She did not want me to focus only upon her. However, I always felt very privileged to be taught by her.

One field of knowledge that Berenice did help me to learn though was the art of Spiritual healing. For this, I was invited, along with the other students, to attend public ceremonies held at the Standing Stones in the large community to the East of our College. It was traditional that if people were in need of healing, then they could receive this following the main ritual of these festivals. Berenice insisted that I join in with those offering healing... With her backing, I was then invited to help channel healing to people that asked for it. She introduced me to basic techniques and ensured that I was sufficiently proficient to be able to support the people in need that attended, but then she let me work on my own, and we would both consult with people independently and hold a feedback session afterwards.

On one occasion, I was working with a woman who had just given birth. Berenice was in attendance, but had stepped back to give me the opportunity to do the actual healing.

This woman was still experiencing a lot of pain in her lower abdomen, and as I opened my senses, I could see the energetic colors around her. By her womb, there was a lot of darkness, and the energy felt thick and sludgy. I had become aware that when I did healing that there were Spiritual beings to help me, a group of them, so I called on their presence. Through my hands, I could experience light energy travelling along, and going to the woman's energy field. I simply acquiesced with my intention, for the energy to go where it was needed. My body became hot as I could feel Spirit bringing healing energy through my being and outwards from my hands to her womb. I experienced the colors of this healing as a mixture of blue and pink and orange. These colors each had their distinct qualities, but they were mingling and forming a stream of energy that approached and interacted with the dark stagnant blob within the womb area. I could only observe with wonder while the colorful living energy projected through me enlivened this area, and threads of new vibrant energy were able to link with the more healthy energy field surrounding the womb.

Next, I could sense the presence of Berenice as she stood up and came over next to me. She added her energy to the process, and we began to hum together, directing this sound to the entrance of the womb. This sound was helping to steady and relax the energy field of the woman, so she could feel more peaceful and at ease. I felt tremendous harmony with my teacher, and I welcomed her to be with me.

At the conclusion of the healing, I noticed how the darkness in the vicinity of the womb was diminishing, and the threads of energy lines created, becoming more integrated with the woman's overall system.

Soon, I knew that this darkness would disappear completely, and after that, the woman would also recover on the physical level.

Qualities of my teacher, Berenice

I found Berenice to be quite an extraordinary person. She was not like anyone else that I had met. She walked around with an air of grace and calm, but there was an energy and awareness about her, where she was watching and monitoring the activities of all that she met, even those on the very edge of her vision. Inevitably, if there was someone in need or suffering, she would be drawn to them, and maybe give them healing, or instruct me to do the same. Sometimes, she might have a quiet word with them, or direct them to others who could better serve them or heal them. She was a diplomat and problem solver, energetically observing imbalances in people and the environment, and then setting out to make adjustments so that equilibrium could be restored.

Although she had a strong will, and she was not someone to be trifled with, there was a light about her that felt very spiritual. She approached her work with love, and even though there were those that were afraid of her because of her forthrightness, I found her to be very kind. She could be quite challenging to people. This was because she tested them, and urged them towards the highest standards of behavior. Not everyone she encountered was very willing to follow her guidance and advice. But she had a look that could make it very clear to those she addressed that it would be wise for them to do as she suggested.

Most of the time, she did not speak to me very much. In the early years, I either walked by her side, or a couple of paces behind her. Occasionally, she would make some comment about what she perceived to be going on with people in the community, and her insights often moved me and stimulated my thoughts by what she said.

One day, we passed by a boy, one of the older students. He was standing forlornly, with his head resting against a tree. There were tears streaming down his cheeks. For a moment, Berenice hesitated, and we both looked at him. I expected her to go over to him and comfort him in some way, but she did not. Soon, she was striding forward, and I felt torn about what to do. This boy was distressed and needed help! Scrambling, I ran after Berenice, and grabbed her by the arm. Berenice stopped and turned, and looked deep into my eyes. Very gently, she told me that she was not to help him; this was for someone else to do – a soul that needed to help this boy. It was not her path. If this person did not respond to this calling, then the boy was to find answers within his self.

In that instant, I realized how Berenice acted upon guidance that she received from within her Self, and that she tuned into people in a very deep place. It was not always appropriate to intervene. She did not do necessarily what she wanted to do, but more, what she felt she had to do.

In my first years, I felt as though I was treading for much of the time in Berenice's footsteps, and this was what was expected from me to learn her ways. Gradually though, she included me more and more, and when we travelled to distant communities, she encouraged me to engage in the dialogue with community leaders. I came to know her thoughts and outlook, and she was continually testing me to improve my awareness. My respect for her grew and deepened, and it felt, as I became older, when we were working, that our minds blended, so we could work together with the utmost harmony.

We often had to sort out personal disputes that sprang up in communities. When I was puzzled or struggling in a particular situation, I would share with my teacher about this, and often she would draw on her own experience to advise me. Because she was sensitive about my development and maturity, there were some cases in communities where she was the arbiter, and others that she left to me.

The case of two arguing men

Once, we were called to visit one of the southern townships to help with a situation of great strife between two men. These men seemed to even gain sort kind of pleasure from continually arguing with each other, and their actions were causing enormous disruption to the community.

As she usually did, Berenice asked me to 'tune in' before we left, and as I sat under the Yew tree in the Sacred Grove, all I could see was a girl, all huddled up and crying, with her head buried in her hands. When I told Berenice this, she smiled.

Apparently, these two men were contesting the leadership of the community. One claimed the right to be leader through the linage of his ancestors, all of whom had all been leaders of this village in previous generations. The other one had trained with the Order of the Wise and purported to have superior knowledge and qualification to administrate the district. They both had strong followings in the village and claimed authority to make decisions affecting the community. Often, their policies were in conflict with each other, and provoked fighting between differing parties. Their fights were draining the well-being of the village. Many of the population despaired that the men were more interested in exerting power over each other, than in doing what was in the best interests of the community. To me, it felt a difficult case, and in my mind, I did not know what could be done to ease the tensions.

When we came to the outskirts of the village, I felt a restlessness of energy about me. I noticed that my breathing was shallow, and when people came out to greet us, I could sense fear, sadness and aggression. Some of them stiffened visibly when they saw Berenice, but none of them looked happy.

Suddenly, Berenice deviated from the path, and motioned me to follow her. We walked along a small winding track that went out of the town and up an undulating slope. There we saw a dead tree standing starkly in front of us. And underneath the tree was the girl that I had seen in my vision. Her clothes were torn, and there were scratches and patches of blood for the whole length of her body. Her body was twitching and she was whimpering slightly. Because of the way, her body lay, my first instinct was to ask if she could have broken her back. She seemed to have fallen from the tree.

Immediately, Berenice rushed to her to channel healing, and she asked me to assist her by holding the girl's feet. The girl was moaning as the healing proceeded very intensely. All at once, there was an audible crack, and the girl's body went completely limp, and she appeared to lose consciousness. The light continued to stream through Berenice's hands, but it was more gentle now, and I noticed the peace that was spreading through the girl's energy field. Then Berenice came over and sat next to me, and we watched the girl together, and waited.

Finally, the girl opened her eyes, and we gave her a drink. It took a while longer before she was fully revived, and then Berenice wanted to know what had happened. What emerged was that this girl was the daughter of one of the self-appointed leaders. She had just had enough, and although she claimed that she had fallen from the tree by accident, her fall had had a deeper meaning, and had manifested as a symbol to what was taking place in the community. Berenice and I conferred in our minds about this. We did not say anything to the girl but brought her with us.

When we entered the hut to meet the two men, Berenice brought the girl with her, and placed her on her lap when she sat down. She wanted me to sit next to her, and I was only a year or two older than this girl.

Very deliberately, Berenice spoke aloud, and asked the girl to point out which of these two men was her father. The tears were streaming down her face as she pointed at him. His reaction was to be aloof; he could not even look at his daughter, and he endeavored to hide his emotion.

At the back of the room, there was a woman supplying drinks for us all. Her energy was quiet and serene, but she had strength about her. She was very subservient to the men, and they kept ordering her to attend to practical tasks as if she were some form of slave. Both Berenice and I had noticed her, but said nothing of it.

Sitting in front of the men, Berenice asked them both to present their case, in turn. Immediately, they both started talking at once, speaking over each other, and arguing. The girl squirmed in Berenice's lap, and I could feel her love and longing bubbling up from inside her, wanting to express itself through her tears.

The girl's presence appeared to distract the men, and they stumbled and struggled to present themselves coherently, speaking in halting voices, still interrupting each other, and not listening.

In an effort to assert himself, the girl's father raised his voice and tried to impose his view upon the other one, and at this, the girl howled and burst into loud tears, sobbing loudly, and burying her face in Berenice's shoulder.

The men stopped in mid-sentence.

'Tell them what you want,' Berenice told her.

The girl slowly raised her head, and although she was shaking slightly with fear, she could also feel Berenice's encouragement.

'I want you to stop fighting,' she implored them, and for a moment, she looked at her father, directly in the eye.

Berenice nodded to support the girl, and waited for the men to respond. For a while, they looked confused, and did not know what to say. But then, they could not help themselves, and they both spoke up, one blaming the other. Berenice raised her arm, and commanded them to stop. She uttered firmly that she had heard sufficient. If neither of the men were capable of listening to a child, and assimilating what she had to say, then they were neither worthy of being leaders of the community to be entrusted with that position. The men looked down, but had nothing to say.

My teacher asked the men to introduce the woman who served the drinks. What was her place in the society? For some moments, the men were unwilling to talk about her, so Berenice addressed the woman directly. It transpired that this woman was actually more advanced in her training within the Order of the Wise, than either of the men. Berenice had recognized and remembered her from the college. My teacher then looked up at the men and questioned how it was that she was in a lesser position than them when she was much more qualified? They had no answer. She told them that they had acted as bullies, with no thought for anyone except themselves.

Later, in the meeting hall of the village, Berenice spoke before the assembled members of the community. She proposed the woman from the hut to be the Spiritual leader of the village, and explained her reasons for this, and coupled with this, that all powers the men had attested to themselves be withdrawn. On a show of hands, this motion was validated overwhelmingly, and some of the people cheered.

In further private meetings that Berenice facilitated, the girl spoke at length with her father, and he broke down and cried when forced to admit how his actions had affected her. It was the beginning of love being rekindled between them, and the new woman leader agreed that if he could express himself less forcefully, then he could work as her assistant. The other man decided he would leave the community and travel.

I was impressed with the strength of character of this girl, and sensed that one day, that she would be a future leader of the community, herself. She had intelligence and calmness and cared for others.

As we were walking out of the village, the girl came running out after us, and she had something in her hand. She gazed up coyly at my teacher, and asked her to accept her offing with gratitude. When she unfurled her hand, there was an intricate small carving there. This object had been constructed with much care, and had obviously taken her a long time to make.

Berenice stared curiously at the girl, and she told my teacher that the carving was a representation of her inner animal friend. She had been told by him that Berenice would need what she carried. Berenice accepted the gift, and gave the girl a farewell hug. The carving was an exact likeness of a wolf.

The wolf pack

There were many adjustments now in our new hut, living with Mulaid and Kiend and their addition made our home life much more vibrant and interesting. I am not sure that Gracon liked it, because he so much preferred privacy and quietness, but for the rest of us, I believe that we became very close and amiable companions. Mulaid practiced often with his beautiful stringed instruments, and I found the sweet sounds of his music to be quite captivating. Kiend was a friend to the animals, and they loved him. In the evenings, he would offer seeds to the birds and squirrels, and they would eat from his hand. I saw him on many occasions place his hand on some creature and heal them of wounds and injuries that they were carrying. He could speak and listen to them, like my father. In the evenings, he would be gone for hours attending to his favorite creatures in the surrounding area. And in the mornings, when we woke up we were often surprised by the presence of animals sharing Kiend's bed with him. Our hut became rather like an animal shelter. But I welcomed this, and Kiend helped me to gain a much greater appreciation for our animal kingdom.

Our land had many animals, and some of these were dangerous. In our traditions, the animals were honored, and we knew that it was our duty to look after them and give gratitude to them for offering themselves to us as food. We respected creatures and knew that they had consciousness like our Earth, and we chose to live in harmony with them. In each village and township we had people attuned to the animals. Energetically, we created boundaries around our township and along our regular paths, to keep us safe, so the wilder animals would leave us in peace. In return, we respected their right to roam freely.

One day, Berenice called me to come to her. She had received a telepathic call for help from a village that was being terrorized by wolves. A pack of wolves had encircled the village, and at night time, their howls were keeping the children awake. During the daytime, the wolves were roaming along the pathways through the village, generating a lot of fear and panic. Hunters had tried to scare off the wolves and kill one or two of them. But when one of the wolves was injured by a spear, the others became very aggressive and ferocious, and teamed together in their pack, and the hunters had to retreat. In desperation, the governing bodies of the town were pleading that we come and rid them of this threat.

My teacher gave me the carving that she had been given by the girl, and asked me to tune in. I went to the Yew tree, as was customary for me, and closed my eyes. The carving felt warm in my hands, and as I focused my thoughts on the village, it began to vibrate. I saw the people, and I saw the wolves. The people had turned away, and it was the wolves that were staring at me with their determined eyes. What surprised me was that I sensed that it was the wolves needing the help, not the people.

We left early the next morning, and Kiend was coming with us. Berenice was in deep thought, and she told me that she felt that there was far more to this situation than appeared on the surface.

The village was situated a few days walk away, in the southwest of our land, in a fertile area where the local residents had plenty of natural resources to enable their existence to be quite comfortable and secure. The buildings the people had constructed nestled into a small valley surrounded by low-lying hills.

When we entered the township, there was an eerie silence, and hardly anyone to be seen. Doors to the huts were closed, and fires were lit outside the houses to keep animals away. The people were taking refuge inside where they felt more protected.

We were invited to stay in one of the huts closest to the perimeter of the village, and it was clear when we were within this shelter that no-one else had been here for a considerable time. They must have felt too vulnerable to stay here with the wolves so close. For Kiend and my teacher, Berenice, they appeared to hold no such fear, and they were both soon relaxing and having a rest from our walk.

That evening, we were going to go to the wolves. We would wait until night time, so that we could slip out of the village unnoticed. Berenice wanted to learn directly from the creatures themselves, what was going on.

When the time came, we cautiously wound our way through the undergrowth, and up the nearest hill in front of us. The light of the moon helped us to see our way. We went single file. I was in the middle, behind my teacher, and Kiend brought up the rear. At one point, Berenice paused, and put her arms around me, and she tried to reassure me and keep me calm. She could tell that I was a little nervous compared with them.

In the distance, I could hear the sounds of wolves howling in the night. There were many of them. Their sounds punctuated the silence and I felt a nervous sweat dribbling down my body. I found myself praying to my guide, Eurydice, to be close to us, and I felt her peace.

At the top of the hill, we reached a clearing, and there was an old stump from a tree, where we sat down. The howls sounded closer, and I felt very exposed. Even with all my training, I noticed how my body trembled, and I had to stop myself from wanting to run and get away.

Berenice started to hum, and Kiend joined in. He knew this sound; it was quite a high piercing reverberation. For a while they continued to alter it until they were in harmony and at the same pitch as the cries of the wolves. Then there was a pause and the howling of the wolves stopped. They must be listening. Then Kiend and Berenice discontinued their humming. And there was silence. All I could hear was my breathing and the thudding sound of my own heart beat. I did not know what to expect next.

Instinctively, I moved myself closer to Berenice so I could feel the warmth of her body as a protection. Kiend seemed quite relaxed, and he was gazing outwards with great curiosity.

I could not see or hear anything, but I could sense that there were movements in the shadows. The wolves were coming. I knew they were.

Suddenly, there was a tremendous howl right behind us. The power of the wolf nearly lifted me off my seat and was an energy that was terrifying to me. He was so close; I felt that if I reached behind me I might be able to touch him.

Berenice gripped me to try to stop me from panicking, but otherwise, she did not flinch. Kiend turned around to look.

There was another growl, and then, further growls, in accompaniment to the first. They came from all directions. I felt that we were surrounded, and there was nowhere for us to go.

Berenice's hands became warmer, and I felt energy flowing from them into my body. There was a tingling on my forehead, and then in my mind. She was channeling healing to me. I heard Berenice's voice speaking to me through telepathy. Her words had a deep penetrative effect, while she affirmed that I was safe, and I could feel myself becoming calmer as I listened. She told me to slowly turn around with her.

When we did this, it took me a while, but I finally did look up, and then I could see the wolf.

There were other wolves prowling restlessly in the distance, but the head wolf was sitting quite still, in front of us, his eyes gazing intently at us, instinctively watching for signs of fear. I was amazed, as I observed my breathing, that it was now quite normal and calm. The tingling on my forehead was intensifying, and I felt that my consciousness and that of Kiend was linking up with Berenice.

The wolf growled again, but it was a softer growl, and accompanied by answering growls from the wolf pack. I could sense Berenice opening up her energy field, and the head wolf continued to stare at us without wavering. He was sniffing at us, and I could perceive that he was searching our desires and instincts, our identities, and whether he could trust us or not.

There was an unfamiliar deep vibration in my mind, and I knew that this was the energy of the wolf. I was not enough attuned to its frequency to be able to communicate to it, but I discerned that Berenice could do so, and possibly Kiend, too.

For a while, I sat, flanked by my two companions while they engaged in an inner contact with the wolf. With my energy system linked to theirs, I felt some strange inner sensations that were uncomfortable at first, but as the contact progressed, there was an increasingly flow of love, and I felt a growing appreciation and regard for our wolf brothers and sisters, and kinship that we were connected and working together.

The contact was finally completed, and the wolf turned and loped away with his pack. Immediately I was able to relax and feel more 'normal'. We were together again with the silence of the night sky and the light of the moon.

Berenice and Kiend related to me what our wolf friend had communicated. He had affirmed how the kingdom of the animals was very much linked to the Spirit of the Earth, and the well-being of the animals was nourished by energy that the Spirit of what the Earth gave to them. In the township near to where we were standing, there was a powerful portal of energy where the Earth Spirit was able to nurture and activate important forces to help the animals in the area. The wolves were very sensitive to this.

The portal for this energy coincided with the stone circle where the local residents conducted their ceremonies. In recent times, those in charge of rituals in this stone circle had not been honoring the animal kingdom in their rituals. Rather than channeling energy for the well-being of all, and working selflessly to channel the Spirit of the Earth, these people had been attempting to summon the energy only to satisfy their own prosperity for their own gain and comfort. They had been sacrificing animals in a bid to bargain for more power for themselves. While not doing anything deliberately bad, local people had become absorbed in their own needs to the exclusion of the other kingdoms. This was causing disturbances.

The wolves did not intend to hurt the people, but had to try to alert them to the damage that they were doing, and show them that they were on the wrong path, a path where they were becoming increasingly blind to their true Spiritual nature, where, if they did not stop, many animals would be slaughtered for no good reason, and the Spiritual portal in this area would then close.

In the next morning, we went to meet with the town Elders, and Berenice commanded that all the people come outside and gather by the central fireplace in the middle of the village. She told them all to wait there, and she insisted that I wait there with them.

Next, she and Kiend strode out of the village in the direction of the hill where we had been in the night. I noticed the birds that were gathering on the roofs of the houses, and one or two of them ventured close to Kiend as he walked along, and he stroked them.

There were some distant howls from the wolves, and I had to urge the frightened villagers to stay where they had gathered, and for them to trust Berenice.

It took a while, but there came shouts from lookouts placed at the far end of the village. Berenice was returning with Kiend. But when we saw them, they had walking between them the majestic figure of the head wolf.

Some of the people glared at the scene with astonishment, while others recoiled with anxiety and fear. One of the hunters picked up his spear and deliberately aimed it at the body of the wolf. Berenice anticipated this, and she acted quickly, glaring fiercely at the man and then shooting energy out from her hands, as she stopped the hunter in his tracks.

'Leave this wolf alone,' she commanded. 'He wants you to listen to him and value him, and he will not harm you.'

At that moment, the wolf lifted his head, and gave a mighty howl that pierced the air, and the other wolves from the pack answered back. Kiend reached out his hand and patted the wolf, and the animal nestled against him. From the expressions on people's faces, they could hardly believe what was happening.

Berenice motioned the people to sit, so that she could address them. She told them what had transpired with the wolf on the previous evening, and the essential message that he had wanted to impart. Meanwhile the head wolf also sat next to Kiend, who stood impassively, and other wolves slowly came nearer from the outlying areas of the village.

Some of the people gave nervous glances at the wolves, but more and more of them were quiet and thoughtful. There was a change in the mood of the people gathered and the energy became increasingly solemn and serious. The leader of the community, a man who wore quite flamboyant clothes, tried to argue with Berenice, and defend his actions, that they had to look after their own interests. But others did not agree with him, and they jeered as he spoke.

Berenice was quieter while the people argued between themselves. A young woman asked Berenice what the wolves needed so they could co-exist in peace. In response, my teacher asserted again that the wolves just needed cooperation and respect in how they as humans conducted their rituals and their attitudes towards the animal kingdom. With this, the head wolf lifted up his head, as if he knew what was being said.

Now, there was a young man, who was clearly irritated by all the indecision, and selfish fear. Standing up, he brushed past the other people and bustled his way to the hunter who had directed the spear at the wolf. Then, without hesitation, he broke the spear in two on his knee, and before anyone could stop him, he went over to Kiend and stood by the wolf. In response, the wolf dipped his head in the direction of the young man, and then looked up and stared at the other people.

'Who is afraid?' the young man taunted the villagers. For a moment, the atmosphere by the meeting place became tense, but then it gradually relaxed, as people accepted that there was no threat at all.

After some reflection, other members of the town council then stepped forward, and asked Berenice what they must do. She told them they must make a pledge to change their ways. Berenice suggested the words and actions that they must do. She spoke of the need to co-exist with the animal kingdom and honor all the kingdoms of life with reverence. Then she uttered this as an affirmation, and she made all the people repeat it. She wanted them to say this louder, and then again, so that the Earth Spirit and all the life around would be witnesses to their intended commitment. The people proclaimed their intentions again and repeated it, and there was spontaneous cheering amongst them. They were happy to do this, and they knew it was right.

Their former leader slunk away and nobody gave him any attention.

Later that afternoon, Berenice coordinated a Spiritual ceremony with the people that they conducted by the standing stones. The energy felt powerful, and many of the people were moved by it, and felt the presence of forces greater than themselves. This was something that they knew they could continue, something that they had to do. By doing this, they would support the network of life around them, and not isolate themselves and cause more harm. By now, the wolves had retreated, and left the people to carry out their actions. It was a happy day.

That night, the children of the township were able to rest and sleep in peace for the first time in many weeks. While they were doing that, Berenice, Kiend and I went up once more into the hills to give thanks to the wolves.

Progress and learning

My training with Berenice went through many phases, and at times, she needed to work very hard with me, repeating things while I struggled to learn the lessons that she tried to teach me. Sometimes, she overestimated my strength and there were other times when I surprised her.

In one village where we went, the leaders of that community were fighting so much over power issues, that everyone in that village was miserable. It had reached the stage where they were starting to destroy each other's property.

Berenice went with me to the village to try and help resolve their problems. She left me with the main protagonists to seek a solution with them, while she attended to other business. For the whole day, I sat with these leaders, and they argued. I attempted to perceive underlying causes, and point these out, but they would not listen. They were people that were so much absorbed in their own fighting, that they refused to be receptive to anything else. It was like a battlefield.

That night when I returned to the hut where I was staying with Berenice, I cried, and felt an utter failure. I was at a complete loss to know what to do. Berenice listened to my despair and held my hands, and then in a very quiet voice, she told me that the next day, we would return to the meeting room in that village, and speak with those men again. She told me that she had things to say, and that we would not be leaving until we completed what she wished to do.

In the morning, we went together, and sat in the room with the male Elders of the community. Berenice berated them for not showing me more respect on the previous day. She told them that unless they started today to listen to one another and work towards an amicable solution to their problems, rather than seek conflict with each other, then she and I would go to the Order of the Wise, and withdraw support completely from this town and cut off trading ties, so they would need to survive on their own.

At this, they stopped. Some of them were startled; a few still argued, but Berenice was firm, and said she would give them a short interval to decide what they wanted to do.

Before that day was over, we had worked out with them a restructuring of their society so that they could attain greater harmony. As the day went on, Berenice handed back more and more of the responsibility for facilitating this to me, and I was grateful for her support. Two members of the community would come to our college for training to help with the spiritual side of their life. The Elders of the community that had been so vocal would have to take more of a back seat and let others come forward, ones that would be more interested to cooperate together. From there, it was possible to sort things out with this community so they could again live with a measure of harmony and peace.

Berenice was not a person to give up. She had a very determined will, and once she had set herself a task, she followed this forward until she achieved what she believed was needed. She helped me to develop this strong-minded approach to situations too. I was not someone who liked to feel defeated, and that evening where I had cried, was one of the few occasions where I did break down, where a task that I had been set, proved to be too much for me. She and I were well matched in many ways, and as time went on, I found myself able to express more and more of the gifts and skills that she had. This was what the training was all about, and although she rarely said anything, I believed that Berenice was pleased with my progress.

Alongside empathy, one of the skills most fundamental for my training was the practice of telepathy. What Berenice taught me was to place myself inside the mind of the person that I was focusing on. I had to ask permission from that person's Higher Self, and my intensions needed to be pure. My task was to open myself as a channel and let thoughts and feelings come to me. It was important that there was no input that I wanted to add to that person's mind; and nothing in particular that I was prejudiced to receive from the subject. I had to be an open observer, without having preconditions in my thoughts about the person, and having sound motives for my intentions in seeking telepathic information.

Sometimes I found that when I asked the permission from a person's Spirit Self, that it was not possible for me to enter the subject's mind, but most of the time, the permission was given. I had to be careful, because it was a delicate and sensitive process to enter someone's mind, and if my desires were strong in any direction, then this could influence the other person and affect them in ways that went against Spiritual Laws. Berenice spent many sessions with me, teaching me and imploring me to abide by the Spiritual Laws, and one of the most essential of these was to do with respect, not only for human beings, but for all life, and learning how to balance the different needs for respect.

In the early stages of my practicing telepathy, Berenice monitored my efforts and corrected me when what I picked up had more to do with my own thoughts, than what existed in the other person. However, the fact that I could converse with my guide, Eurydice, helped a great deal. With my guide, I needed to be open and let go of my own thoughts, although with her great love for me, this was easier to accomplish than with people on the physical plane. So I had both a human Spiritual teacher and a non-physical Spiritual guide.

Gradually, I began to experience varying layers of the mind. Some people, like our teachers from the Order of the Wise, could have very clear thoughts that were easy to read, but also have areas of privacy within them, where they kept their private thoughts. They could shield their private thoughts and make the more public ones more readily available. I was taught about using my own mind to be able to shield my thoughts when necessary, as well as gaining the ability to read the minds of others.

With people that I met in the villages, their thoughts could be very muddled, with inner conflicts and thoughts going in many directions at once. I had to learn to discern underlying thoughts and to know what was most important in people's hearts. The thoughts coming from focusing on the heart could sometimes be very different from those coming from the head. When I felt fear in a person, this would influence very much the thinking process, and could distort what the person was expressing, so that what they expressed no longer came from a true place. I had to hold to my own inner clarity so I would not be unbalanced by other people's perceptions. My task was to navigate through various thought patterns within the person until I could discern what thoughts originated from the truth that that person felt.

Once I could locate truth within people's minds, I had to encourage that person to find their own way to this truth. When they could express their own truth, this was much more powerful than when I told this to them. When people found a way to express their own deeply held truth, then this was an experience that could be deeply transformative, and would be words and feelings that others would listen to with appreciation.

In a further stage, I had to learn about the collective consciousness of communities, and what may be held as the truth for the whole population of those people. I had to work to gain a perception of what was the underlying common thought of what a particular group of people most needed to express together. This meant that I had to help people discover the inner voice of their overall community in addition to what may be their individual concerns. At times, I needed to articulate those collective truths myself, or better, when I could encourage someone who was within the community, to act as its voice.

When I tried to learn these skills, at first in my mind, I found it all rather confusing, but Berenice urged me to ask for help from my own Spirit Self and guide, and then, when it was needed, to ask for Spiritual support to be connected with the higher collective consciousness of a community. I had to trust and let impressions reveal themselves to me, through thoughts and feelings, reaching for that Spiritual guidance, so I did not rely on my own ego, but those loving forces that were greater than me. I had to open my heart, so that I sought for what would most help people and what would be for their highest good.

At first, I struggled with this, and tried to find solutions with my own mind, and I would invariably encounter obstacles and resistance from outside me when I did this. Sometimes I could sense some truth within a person, but it was not possible for me to find the means to communicate about this truth to the person so they could accept it. If I took some moments to be still and ask for inner help, then very often I would receive the assistance that I needed.

People did not always want to perceive what was true inside them, and often created inner mechanisms to hide from this, especially if they imagined that this truth held pain, and when they were attached to some way of being that was familiar to them or where they felt secure…

It was also interesting for me, how, as we visited people from the north of our land, land, that their minds functioned slightly differently from those nearer to our College. This was also reflected in their speech, which had its own inflexions distinct from our language. Racial qualities were a significant factor affecting my ability to interact with people using telepathy. I remembered back to my early childhood with my half-brother, Skife, and how I sensed his mind to be structured in a distinct manner that was dissimilar from other people in the village. Because the structure of his mind was less familiar to me, I found it to be less easy to enter, and he had resistance to anyone coming close to him in any case.

One thing that I did notice, was how, after our Spiritual ceremonies with the standing stones, or even evenings where we would sing and dance together, or meditate, that people's minds were always much clearer. Being with beautiful majestic trees could produce similar effects. It was fascinating to me how the purity and love of Spiritual influences could bring clarity to people's minds. These times were then the best times for healing and counseling.

From this, it became apparent to me why, when we went to a village to help with a dispute, Berenice would always start a meeting with chanting and meditation. The peace that arose from this set a helpful tone from which resolution work could be done.

As I developed with my skills in telepathy, I could also use this as a means of communication with my teacher, Berenice, and also my friends. It was something that we enjoyed sharing together. There were times, also, when I would attune to members of my family. Their Spirit Selves were very open to me reaching out to them, and this allowed a means for me to check in with them at intervals, especially during those longer periods when I could not physically visit them because of my other commitments. This greatly comforted me, especially with my mother. I felt that we could speak to each other via our minds, and I sense that this assisted her well-being too.

Another avenue of learning for me involved the light of the Earth energy. Berenice taught me about the energy system in our land. As students, we all needed to learn about this. Berenice helped to train me, how, with my inner eyes, I could perceive the various colors and strengths and qualities of this light. Then, I could diagnose the health of a particular area through its Earth light, and also discern places of power where the Earth light was most intense and concentrated.

The top of the sacred hill near to our college, where we did our meditations, was one place where the earth light was powerful. Another noteworthy focus for this energy was at the Sacred Grove, near our encampment, the place where we enacted so many of our ceremonies. Being in these places brought forward feelings of aliveness and sensitivity for people. It is obvious from this how the wolves were instinctively affected by disturbances to the natural flow of the earth light, in their area.

The standing stones had been deliberately placed upon focal points where tracks of this earth energy converged. The stones could be amplifiers of this energy, and when we conducted our festivals and rituals at these sites, I could observe fountains of this energy erupting as we sang our chants and joined together with our meditations. The fountains of earth light energy gave much love and helped our land to be a happier place.

In the early stages of my training, Berenice gave me daily exercises with inner meditations and body movement to help open my inner eyes to the subtleties of the Earth energy light, so I would be able to perceive this more clearly. As I grew to be able to do this more fully, even more than when I was a young child, I could feel the Earth and ground beneath me and the air around me, as being alive and breathing with energy. It felt very important to preserve the strength of these energy tracks so that the Earth Spirit could bring as much love as possible into our lives.

Sometimes Berenice and I encountered areas of our land where the Earth light had become weakened and where the tracks of energy were less clearly defined. Usually, this diminishing of light energy was due to past human activity. Where people had not shown sufficient respect to the earth, and there had been a strong expression of hatred, conflict and fear, or where people had been greedy and selfish, then all these actions could affect the Earth light energy. When people sought to use the resources of the earth for their own gain without thought for the needs of the whole, then this could generate actions that would result in energy blockages, and stop the Earth light energy from flowing as it should.

My initial experience of this had been with Gracon, when we were first travelling to the college. I had sensed then, in the way that she supported Gracon, how Berenice was skilled at healing disturbances in the Earth light energy field. Sometimes, by moving a large stone slightly, or by placing some crystalline small stones in particular places, this would help to activate the energy to a more healthy level. She also, on occasions, planted trees on energy intersection points to enable future generations to enjoy a greater energy flow in times to come. As the tree grew, the living being in the tree would nurture the energy system, as the energy system would nurture the tree, so both could flourish.

What was most important was to educate the people, so that they would understand how vital it was for them all to respect the Spirit of the Earth, and act in harmony with its energy field. By doing this, we could all be happier and living in greater harmony with one another. But this was a process that constantly needed attention and work with all the groups of people that we met. We could not take the Earth Spirit for granted. Nor could we be sure how well our people would continue to respect the Spirit of our Earth, without positive intervention to help everyone along.

In our villages, the position of the houses was important, as was the materials that were used to construct houses. We had advisors from the Order of the Wise that would consult with village Elders whenever significant changes were to be made in the physical structures of the village. Berenice had this knowledge too, and she instructed me, so I could learn and help people that we met.

We travelled very extensively, and there were times when I felt quite weary, and longed for home. For Berenice though, her work with people and communities was her service to the land. Her drive to serve came before any personal wishes that she could have. She instilled in me a passion for looking after our land and its people, and helping to make it the best possible that it could be.

The wild boar

On one of those rare opportunities when I could have a break from my training, I went to visit my family in their village. On my return journey from this visit, I was walking through a stretch of woodland on my own, when I heard a noise.

Although at first, this was like a low, distant rumbling, the volume of the sounds increased and became ever louder and more urgent. My initial reaction was a fear response, and I felt my heart beating very rapidly. I felt that my body was on a high state of alert, and I had to identify what was happening, and what I needed to do about it.

For some moments, I stopped and listened. The direction of the rumbling was from behind me, so I turned and strained my senses in that direction. Placing my ear on the ground, I tried to perceive what this disturbance could be.

At first, I speculated if this might be some tremors coming from within the Earth, itself, but as I listened more closely, I heard what sounded like the thundering of hooves on the ground, not just a few, but hundreds of them. In my imagination, I could see a very large herd of animals rushing madly toward me. Their energy felt like panic.

I had never encountered anything like this before. Animals were part of our life, and we needed to relate with them and find harmony with them as well as we could. But there was something in this noise that was wild with fear, and destructive.

For a few moments, I froze, and did not know what to do, but I had to fight with this part of me. If I was to survive, I needed to act, and without delay.

I had been used to having Berenice as a reference, so that in situations where I was uncertain, I could tune in and feel her support, even if she did not say anything to me. One of the roles that Berenice fulfilled for me was as a protector. I also had my guide, Eurydice, but in a physical situation like this, my guide could do nothing, and I could sense that in any case, my guide had stepped back. This was one situation, where somehow, I had to cope on my own.

The child in me felt helpless and disorientated, so I needed to talk with that child. This was one time when she would need to grow up fast.

I could feel the drops of perspiration forming on my head. What could I do? The path where I was standing was not safe. Underneath my feet, the vibration and rumbling of the sounds of the animals was growing more and more violent. It must be a stampede. I looked around and realized that I had to find somewhere as a shelter from this. In my inner eye, I could imagine the thin trees near to me being flattened, and if I stayed here, I would be flattened too.

Were there any rocks nearby? I glanced around in desperation, but there were none. However, I did notice a clump of bigger trees to my left. Without hesitation, I leapt towards them, and crouched myself behind the base of the trunk of the thickest one. There was a slight hollow under the tree, and I just hoped that it would be enough.

All at once, I looked up and saw them, so many of them, charging through the woods, moving chaotically, in absolute fright and terror. They were wild boar. Their hides were glistening with sweat. They had large and unwieldy bodies, but their sheer mass was both powerful and forbidding to be near. Nothing was going to stop them moving forward, and in their wake, I could see a large swath of destruction everywhere.

There was little time to examine them. They were coming now. So I braced myself, tensed my body, and crouched down with my head in my arms, not knowing what would happen. A few of them smashed against the tree, and it shook, and I prayed that it would not topple over. It went on, and I wondered if the stampede would ever end.

But it did, and the tree held, and I was grateful for its strength. And then there was just an eerie stillness with noise of the stampede receding into the distance.

Now though, with the boar having passed, I could see what was behind them, and it was a group of wild cats. These were large animals, graceful, but deadly. Their teeth were like fangs, and could tear into the boar. What they were doing was to pick off the stragglers, the weak and the injured amongst the boar. Their methods were to jump on the poor animals and then sink their teeth into the boar's neck. The terrified boar would have no chance. The cats appeared to be coordinating their attacks together, and there were numbers of them that extended along the full range of the boar's passage. The impact of this upon the boar was to drive them crazy with fear.

One of the cats was near me, and I saw it attack a young boar that had not been able to keep up with the others. The cat acted as a ruthless killing being, and after inserting its fangs, the boar only lasted a few steps before staggering and collapsing from loss of blood to its wounds. Once down, the boar would not get up again. For a few moments, the cat surveyed its victim, but then it was ready to move. These predators did not stop with their killings, but drove on. They would return for their food later.

I was watching this drama with both fascination and also horror, but then, before I could react, the big cat turned around, and saw me. It must have noticed my scent. There was nowhere to hide. Very slowly the big cat moved towards me. It was staring at me, and I had to meet its gaze, but with the fear I felt, I could not stop my body from shaking. Very soon, I could be dead. These animals did not spare their victims.

In desperation, I cried inwardly for help. I heard a voice from within me, commanding me to become a cat, to meet it as one of them.

Berenice had given me some training with animals. We needed to enter the consciousness of the animal and share that with them, in order to communicate with them. That is what she had done with the wolves. But how could I do that with these cats? They were not like me, but slayers of other creatures; they had no mercy. How could I form a connection?

I could not delay, so I instructed my mind to form the intention. The air around me changed and became charged with all the ingredients of my interaction with the big cat. In my vision, I could see the eyes of the cat coming closer and closer. I moved my attention and allowed my consciousness to enter into those eyes, going deeper and deeper, so my perception was altering, and I began to sense the energy of the cat filling me more and more. I had to give full permission for this process, without resistance, and invoke my own big cat consciousness. Somehow I needed to find that and express it from deep inside me.

My thoughts were focused upon appreciation for the animal and the consciousness that it lived by. There was beauty and grace about this cat. Here was a creature expressing tremendous independence of Spirit, an animal that knew what it wanted, and would meet its needs without hesitation. This animal relished its elegance, and knew no fear. For its survival, it had to kill, and that is what it did.

As I became more attuned, I could feel that I was becoming one of these wild cats in myself. I could sense the sleek body, the majesty and the power. Within my being, I wanted to purr and give my greeting, my communication also for this cat to keep its distance. And so I did this.

All at once, the cat stopped. It was examining me, sensing my being, feeling how it could relate to me. And in my consciousness, I was a cat too, set on my survival. I was not going where the other cats were going, but staying here. This was my place, and they could do what they wanted.

The other cat completed its interaction with me. It had not finished its business of killing and chasing the boar. Slowly, the wild cat turned and continued to lope after its prey. Nearby, the boar that the cat had attacked was still weakly panting and shivering. Soon, its life energy would be extinguished. It was very strange, but with the cat consciousness, I could imagine myself sinking my teeth into the boar's flesh, and feeling the desire to satisfy my hunger with that, until I had eaten enough.

But with my consciousness of Ilsa, I did not want to eat the boar. I had seen enough. Turning my consciousness inward, I asked Spirit to help me detach, and I felt a shiver go through me as my normal consciousness returned. For a long while, I stayed sitting by the tree, but finally, with effort, I rose to my feet and turned to go. I did not wish to be around when the cat returned.

CHAPTER 8
―――――

Transition

The end of an era

During some moments of my training, I wondered if it would ever end. The whole process was so engrossing, that a part of me wished that it would go on forever. However, it was not to be. I had grown from being a young girl to now having the attributes of a fully grown woman. My fellow students had grown similarly. With this growth and change, there was now that crucial question about how we had faired with our initial training, and what we would be doing next.

Our teachers and the other Elders of the Order would decide this, and the resultant award would be conferred upon us at a special ceremony by the Sacred Grove. There were three possible outcomes for all the years of dedication and learning that we had undertaken. The first conclusion for some students would be for them to be able to return to their local communities with an acknowledgement of the training that they had done, but without any status to go with it. The result was regarded as having merit, but would obviously be disappointing for any student who was given this entitlement. The second level of attainment would be for those that could return to their local communities, but in some particular advisory capacity, to reflect the skills that they could offer to help the people. For most of the students, this was what they could expect to be the reward for their achievements. In the generation before mine, my mother had gained this entitlement. However, the feat with greatest honor would be for those who would be invited to go further with their training, with the aim of joining the leadership of the Order of the Wise. Those students would continue to be based at the college until their training was complete. Only a few of the many students from each year would attain this third level of achievement.

None of us knew what our award would be. Our teachers were only going to announce this during the ceremony. In the lead up to this event, we all felt quite nervous and excited, and there was an atmosphere of uncertainty and change in the air.

The ceremony was going to be conducted by our leader, Karka. There was a large stone opposite to the entrance of the Grove, and near to the Yew tree that I loved so much. He would be sitting there. Other members of the senior staff of the order were going to sit adjacent to him. Further around, there was a large circle of stones arranged for us. These were sitting stones, not the larger ritual stones that were used at our festivals.

There was not space for all of us to go through our announcements together, so this was going to take place in stages. For those students who had to share their teacher with other students, and whose education had been more general, they were going to go first. They were likely to receive either the first or second level grades.

The rest of us had received individual tuition as an apprenticeship from one of the recognized senior members of the Order of the Wise. More had been expected of us, for we had been picked out for this from when we were very little. Now we would be assessed and learn if we had expressed the potential of our gifts and capabilities to the satisfaction of our teachers.

I had always felt that, while sharing a house with Gracon and Nianda, and more latterly Kiend and Mulaid, after Greystook died, that I was with young people that possessed exceptional ability. They were

Ilsa

all very dedicated, and I could not imagine any of them not having a successful outcome to this occasion. There was only one other house with students contemporary to us in age where those students were also receiving individual tuition, so I knew that I was among the best in terms of ability.

In the nights leading up to this ceremony, we had many late night talks. Muela was not able to keep us quiet. This would mark the end of the time when we would be sharing a house together, and that precious shared time of youth was soon going to be over.

Over these last nights, we shared our hopes and dreams of the future together, but also our anxieties. We had many happy reminiscences to recount, some sad ones too, such as Greystook's death. We were a group that had been very close, and we had bonded even closer after we had come together as a group of five.

On the night before the ceremony, I suggested that we make a vow together, and promise that for the rest of our lives, we would always be there to support one another. We looked at each other in the eyes, and held hands, and there was a wonderful feeling of love. It was as though Spirit was supporting us. We all agreed to say 'yes' without question. With Gracon and Nianda, there was no need to make such a vow, because that commitment was already understood, but with the others, it felt right and good to make it conscious now. After uttering that vow, we all felt more peaceful, and that night, I believe that we all slept very well.

My time with Berenice in these last weeks before the graduation ceremony was quite tense, but we still had some very intimate interactions. On one day, we were on our own on the high hill overlooking the College. The wind was blowing gently in our faces, and my teacher turned to face me, and she had tears in her eyes. For some moments, she hesitated, and I stayed with her with my gaze, to support her. Then she disclosed to me about an element of her personal life, something which was both unexpected and shocking to me.

I had never realized it, but Berenice had a daughter, who had been born not so long before she had come to fetch me from my home village.

Hardly anyone had known about this. It had been kept very secret. Karka knew, but nobody else in the College.

Berenice told me that she had not intended to become pregnant, but this had come about from a liaison that was not one of her choice. At the time, she was in the midst of her travels, and she had met someone with whom she felt she could trust. But he had forced himself upon her.

When she discovered that she was pregnant, Berenice was startled and confused. Her work was more important to her than anything else, and she did not want anything to compromise that. And yet, she felt this being inside her very much wanted to be with her. She felt that she had let herself down by not protecting herself sufficiently, and she decided that the pregnancy was a sign from Spirit that she needed to keep herself more separate from others so she could do her work to the best possible degree without any other distractions. I felt confused when she said this, but I did not say anything. She went on.

The child was born away from the College, and it was arranged with a family in a village some distance from the College, that they would care for the child in its formative years. Berenice had had only a minimal contact with her daughter through this time. Instead, she had utterly devoted herself to her work, which is what she wanted to do.

I had not sensed anything about this, and Berenice had managed to conceal it within her energy system all these years, but now as she told me, she was crying in a manner that I had never seen with her before. I did feel honored that she trusted me to tell me this, but I also was aware of Berenice's vulnerability, and that was new. For a long time, I held her, and it felt in those moments that our normal roles were reversed.

From the way, Berenice spoke of her child, I could tell that she loved her, and yet, she felt that she could not show her feelings because of her dedication to her work, and she was fearful of being put upon by anyone else and that was why she kept her distance from people and maintained an air that seemed impenetrable to others.

I asked for the name of her daughter, and Berenice told me that it was Shoola.

What Berenice did know about her daughter was that she had Spiritual and psychic ability, so now as she was finishing her commitment to me, she was planning to bring Shoola to the college, and train her in a similar manner to what she had done with me. I could sense that for Berenice, this was how she considered that she could reconcile those different parts of her – the part that had unwavering commitment to her work, and the other part with instinctive maternal qualities, that she could not entirely suppress.

After she revealed this to me, I felt Berenice's attention was divided, and it brought strange feelings through me as I realized that our working time together was coming to an end. In many ways, I could hardly imagine my life without her, because we had been so close, and yet the change was approaching, and I could either flow with it or not.

When I was on my own in these days, I tried to intuit what my next steps would be? I asked Eurydice, and while I felt her peaceful energy, she just conferred for me to trust and be open. At other stages of my life, I had always known which way I was going to move forward, but now it was blank, and it was a big test for me. I felt both excited and afraid.

Awards

Finally, the time of waiting was over, and our group was invited to enter the Circle of Stones by the Sacred Grove. Nianda grabbed my hand seeking for me to reassure her, and I noticed how much she was perspiring. The others also looked nervous, and Gracon was pale. There was nothing I could do or say to help any of them. It was the time of judgment for us all.

In front of us was Karka with his familiar cloak and staff, and next to him sat Berenice. The other teachers stretched around the circle. On the end was Muela, who had been invited as a special guest for the occasion. Seeing her just heightened the sense of emotional finality of what was taking place. The poignancy of this ceremony was that it had the potential to be both very happy, for what we had achieved, and also sad, for the safety, love and security that would no longer be with us. I could feel the debt of gratitude that I owed Muela for all she had given, and could appreciate what a positive influence she had been. As I focused on her, I could sense a lump in my throat, and I had to stop myself from crying.

Karka smiled at us and began to hum. We joined with him, and I closed my eyes. Within the sound of humming, there was silence that brought tranquility with it. When the humming stopped, I looked up and noticed how Karka was surveying each one of us. He smiled a little and then commended us for all our learning and achievements.

Karka spoke of the great need that existed in our land for young people with our skills, and abilities. We were needed to enable our societies to function in peace and harmony, so that the well-being and sense of belonging with all forms of life in our land could be maintained and the connection deepened. He suggested that we all had unique gifts that had been harnessed and developed, and now they needed to be expressed and honed further so they could be placed in service. We were representatives of the next generation of leaders in our land, and it would be a great test for us to shoulder that responsibility, should we choose to accept it.

Our teachers spoke in turn to my friends, and I felt surges of happiness for each of them as one by one they were commended and granted the offer and privilege of being invited to train on and become leading members of the Order of the Wise. They were all praised and each received the honors and opportunities that they had most hoped for in their hearts. I wondered what would be said of me, and how I would be expected to move on from here. It was an endurance to wait till last, but I tried to breathe and stay calm.

The moment arrived when Berenice stood up, and she looked at me in the eyes. As always, I could feel her gaze penetrate deep into my mind. She communicated privately to me by telepathy, that I had done well, and for a moment, her eyes filled up as she silently admitted to me that she would miss me. As I returned a similar thought, the tears rolled down my cheeks. I noticed the others staring at me, and tried to recover my composure.

In her capacity as my personal teacher, Berenice formally noted to the gathering, skills where I had gained competence, and after a short time, she intimated that I had done enough to continue my training. I must have been holding my breath, for I suddenly released an enormous sigh, and part of me wanted to shout and dance on the spot. Looking at my friends, I could tell that they were also happy, for we had all made it to the next stage.

But Berenice was not finished yet. After a telling pause, she declared that for the next stage of my training, my teacher would be Karka.

For a moment, I was stunned, and I gasped inside and there were also gasps from others in the Gathering. I had not known or expected this. Karka glanced at me kindly and smiled, and Berenice sat down next to him. Within the circle there was a murmur that was silenced when Karka raised his staff.

When I sat down, Karka led us in a thanksgiving meditation, and then we were allowed to leave. I needed time to think.

A couple of days later, all of us continuing with our training were called together at the Sacred Grove. Now we needed to make vows of service to the Order of the Wise. There were seven of us, more than there had been for many years. Karka led this ritual around a fire, and we prayed and invoked the presence of the Earth Spirit and our ancestors from our traditions. We each made an undertaking in turn, and our witnesses included our friends in Spirit as well as existing Elders that were present from the Order. Our vows indicated our commitment that even though we were still in training, our service to our land and to the Order, would be of paramount importance in our lives. With this foundation we would dedicate ourselves to fulfill the principles of the Order with the very best of our abilities.

I was happy to make this vow, and felt that it was significant that I did this next to my favorite Yew tree. It pleased me that the Spirit of this tree could also be my witness. As I cast my eyes around our circle, I could see joy in the faces of the others, and we all felt that we were doing what was our destiny and purpose in our lives to do. Our energies at that point felt to join, and I could sense beneath us, the vast love of the Earth

Spirit sharing with us. It was a profound experience of connectedness that would stay with me for the rest of my life.

At the conclusion of the ritual, Berenice took me to one side. I felt very emotional to be with her. In her hand, she had a ring. It was a delicate blue stone ring, and when I held it, it felt very old, as if it had been carved in very ancient times.

Berenice told me that this ring was a ring from her teacher, and from the teacher before that, and right through the generations from our past. It was a ring of truth, and while I acted with integrity and from my heart, this ring would provide protection to me, and would help amplify my intentions and give strength to them. She spoke almost deferentially to inform me that the time for her to pass this on to me was now.

For some moments, she pressed the ring into the palm of my hand, and I could feel the vibration of it flowing through my body. Placing the ring on my finger, I promised to wear it every day, and call on its power to help me with the love in my heart.

During my training, I had noticed Berenice wear this ring, and noticed how at times of crisis, she had sometimes fingered the stone of the ring, and now I knew why. It felt that Berenice was making a sacrifice for me in releasing the ring to my care, but it was also a statement of her own commitment to help and serve and teach and pass on knowledge to others selflessly.

As we looked in each other's eyes, I could feel the love between us, and the tears again rolled down my cheeks. We hugged in acknowledgment of all that had passed, and for the future that was waiting to be born.

Chapter 9

Initiation and responsibility

Living with Karka

I was very sad to complete my apprenticeship with Berenice. I know that, for many people, Berenice was quite a remote figure, and people tended to keep their distance from her, out of respect for her powers, and her sharp nature. Nonetheless, for me, I had sensed her dedication and her compassion, and having worked so closely with her for so many years, I had glimpsed human sides of her that few other people were given the privilege of being shown. She had cared for me, nurtured me and my abilities, through every stage of my growing-up years. As her student, I felt enormously satisfied and grateful for all she had given me.

But now that I had graduated from this first stage of my training, there was a new phase of my learning to begin, and that was about my responsibilities to community, and the nationhood of which we were part. And my teacher in this was to be Karka, the acknowledged leader of the Order of the Wise, the one that was head of the Spiritual government in our land.

Until now, I had had very little to do with Karka. I had seen him at ceremonies, and had watched from the distance when Berenice had conferred with him, but I knew very little about how it would be to relate closely with him. It felt very strange that I had been selected to learn with him, but Berenice had assured me that this was my rightful next step, and my guide, Eurydice, had also been insistent that I go ahead.

It was with a little nervousness that Berenice formally introduced me to my new teacher, and handed me over to his care. But Karka put me at my ease immediately. There was kindness in his eyes, and they twinkled as someone who enjoyed his life. He took me to his hut, and showed me a small enclosure within it. This was to be my new sleeping place. I would be living with him, and accompanying him on all his journeys, and in the performance of his duties. Karka assured me that the best way for me to learn was for me to be close in his vicinity, as he went about his life.

On my first night, I missed Berenice and my friends, and wondered what it would be like to be so intimately bonded to Karka. But from the other side of the hut, I could hear Karka's rhythmic gentle breathing as he slept, and there was something about this that was reassuring. Within me, I started to feel the excitement of a whole new phase of my life beginning.

Soon I realized that Karka had a very different personality to Berenice. Whereas Berenice would keep herself removed from other people, giving herself privacy, and creating an aura where people were almost wary of her, Karka held no such distinctions for himself. He talked and laughed with people as an equal. He would help light the community fires, cook the meals, tend to the sick – there was no task that Karka would refuse to do due to his position. Karka approached his life instinctively, and if he felt that there was a need that he could fulfil, then he would do his best to do it. Because of his attitude, Karka was both very approachable, and very busy. Following his footsteps, there was activity from morning to night, and Karka chose to be attentive to all the many people that came seeking his advice. There was much respect awarded to him, and he approached all his work and tasks with the humility of one who was doing what he felt he had to do, and thus he existed very much in the flow of life.

In the midst of all this activity, there were considerable moments of what appeared to be quiet time, where Karka would retreat to his hut, and in those first days, without him instructing me otherwise, I waited for him outside while he did this. Until, one day, he invited me to join him. He then asked me to attend to his body, as he was about to go on an inner journey. I sat down adjacent to him, and he closed his eyes and meditated. Then I noticed that his Spiritual being was leaving the body. It was like a flash of light wispy smoke, as his Spirit rose up and went. There was a small thread of energy that extended from his body and seemed to trace a line where he had gone. The body that he had left behind was quite inert and breathing very slowly. It felt very trusting of Karka to leave his body in my care, so I attentively watched over him and waited for his return.

The times when I had made most use of leaving my body, had been when I had helped to accompany the Spirit body of people when they died. This was something very important that we did, in support of those souls. I had been privileged to gain a little experience of this when Greystooks died. And there were other occasions on my travels with Berenice, when we had helped people in the process of passing over.

She had taught me how to travel with her, out of my body, and by focusing my energy upon the soul of the departing Spiritual body, I could accompany Berenice and go with these departing souls on the beginning of their journey into the Spiritual realm. Doing this had been a very beautiful process that enabled me to strengthen my faith and inner knowledge about the continuation of life, and that I need fear nothing about death.

Eurydice, she had shown me how I could leave my body to visit my family, and I did this at junctures where I felt that I needed to connect with them, either for their sake or mine.

For Karka, though, I soon realized that these journeys were not just occasional, but a significant part of his everyday life, and something that was almost matter-of-fact, as part of his work routines. Karka informed me that this was his primary method for communicating with people who were long distances away. Not many people could exercise this skill as well as him. For him, it was practical to travel to inwardly visit other people in other parts of the land. When he met these people, they could energetically perceive his presence with them, and they would then do their business together.

The other technique he could employ was telepathy, but he preferred to actually travel in Spirit form, so that he could have his energetic presence directly with the people with whom he was communicating. Now Karka wanted to teach me how I could do these journeys regularly, myself, so I could join him with where he was going.

The first time I did this, I felt rather nervous, but Karka assured me that I just had to follow procedures that I had been taught, and that he would wait for me with his Spirit body until I was there with him.

Within moments of Karka closing his eyes, he was gone, and it was left for me to go through my practice and join him. It felt different from when I had followed departing Spirits. I called on Eurydice, and she coaxed me to relax and surrender to her arms, and trust that my physical body was safe and then I could feel myself gradually floating and lifting upwards. It was easy to do what my guide had suggested, and I could feel her support. There was a slight tremor as I lifted upwards into the light. The feeling was so pleasant that I could let myself be carried by it higher and higher. I would have loved then to continue to be with Eurydice, but I remembered that my aim was to join with Karka.

Within his light body, I could still recognize Karka. His light had a brilliant blue and gold color, but his energy was familiar and when he spoke my name by thought transference, I knew that it was him and that I was with him.

He motioned me to link with him, and suddenly we were travelling very fast. I was vaguely aware of the ground far below me, and we moved rapidly through the air. By conscious thought intention, Karka set a destination for us to reach, and within moments we were there.

There was an Earth mound, and below that, a line of trees, and a solitary figure standing by a Yew tree, very much like the one I loved so much in our Sacred Grove. The man noticed our presence and looked up at us in welcome. He was wearing white robes and was a very humble and peaceful man. Although he was aware of us and communicated to Karka by telepathic thought, we were still in our energy bodies and had no physical form. This man was able to perceive our energy being as naturally as if we were there in our normal bodies.

I had no idea where we had travelled, but when I asked Eurydice, she told me to use my inner senses, and I could feel that we had voyaged a considerable distance north, and not to the east of our land, but to the west. It was not a part of our land with which I was familiar at all.

The name of this man was Rakus, and he was leader of the community in this part of the land. He and Karka were engaged in earnest conversation about problems he had been having with some disruptive elements within the community. There were those who wanted to sacrifice animals to give more power to their Ceremonies, but many, including himself that were opposed to this. Rakus was concerned that there could be conflict and wanted advice about how he could best approach the situation to bring harmony to his people.

In the history of our land, there had been tribes and communities that had engaged in sacrifice as a regular practice. Some had even used human sacrifice. There was the belief that sacrifice would release the powers of those human or animal souls and this could be utilized to help the people in that vicinity. But we felt that this kind of practice was wrong and disrespectful, and would cause immense suffering to those being sacrificed. We experienced that fundamentally, the Earth Spirit wanted peace and harmony, and that our actions needed to facilitate that. From my travels to various parts of the land, I had been surprised how much the tendencies to engage in sacrifice still existed.

Karka listened intently, and then suggested for Rakus to encourage open discussion rather than confrontation upon the issue. By airing views, and creating conditions for genuine listening on all sides, this would allow feelings of cooperation to develop. Karka would send a small delegation of teachers from the College to assist Rakus's community to hopefully help the people to gain insights and understanding to enable them to resolve their difficulties.

While they spoke, I remained silent and listened. Within a short time, they had finished and Rakus waved his farewell.

The journey back to the body was even more rapid, and I must admit, that I struggled to keep up with Karka's pace. My intention was not quite clear, because I was also trying to digest the experience that I had just witnessed. So then, when I landed in my body, I did so with a thud, and for some considerable time afterwards, I had a headache that reminded me that I needed to learn to be more focused.

In time though, I did learn to be gentler, and go at my own pace, and then on return, to ease my way into my physical body with the help of Eurydice, if I needed it. I did not have to go as fast as Karka to be able to complete the travel more gracefully.

Over this next period of time, I went on many inner journeys with Karka. Through my energy body, I travelled with him to many different places in our land, and even beyond. Usually there would be one or more people that we would meet, and it was by this means that Karka could monitor and advise community leaders in the wider reaches of the land.

On occasions, in the course of his everyday life, Karka would suddenly become still and withdraw from whatever activity he was engaged in. What I observed, as I became more sensitive, was that these were instances when Karka was receiving visitors in their energy bodies, and he would be counseling them and supporting them, or in some form, exchanging information. Karka would also visit the sites of ceremonies in his energy body, to be a witness and support what was taking place, without necessarily making contact with any of the members of the Order of the Wise that were there. He just wanted to watch and know what was going on.

With all this, I learnt a lot about Karka and the range of responsibility he carried, and his interest in the Spiritual life of all the communities in our land.

Although it was a great feeling of liberation to be able to leave my body and join Karka on his inner travels, I found that I still preferred the direct Earthly contact that was only possible through being in the physical body. There was feelings of freedom that arose through travelling the inner worlds, but I felt that my purpose was much more about living my Earthly life to the full, and enjoying all my passions and what I needed to express in the physical world. The inner worlds offered an attractive space where souls could retreat, but it was not where I wished to dwell while I still had my work to do on Earth.

For now, anyway, I was acting only as a witness to Karka's energy interaction with others. I did these travels when he bid me to accompany him.

Very often, Karka did need to go to places in person to meet the people, and attend to some task that needed his physical presence. There was that side of his work too. The people in the land needed to be able to talk with him and interact with him, and to see his being as their leader. Only a few could leave their body as he was able to do.

So I went on many physical journeys with him, but these felt very different from what I had experienced with Berenice, and this had a lot to do with Karka's personality and approach.

A meeting of nations

One morning, Karka came striding enthusiastically to where I was sitting by the fire. He was smiling. Today we were going to leave on a long journey, but this would be no ordinary trip. There was a meeting that Karka needed to attend; this was to be a gathering of leaders and Elders from communities of our people, not only those native to our country, but also of people from other lands. It was a rich and important occasion, and one that occurred quite rarely. He looked at me with a twinkle in his eye.

We would be travelling by boat across the sea to attend. As he said this, I gasped in amazement. This was to be my first crossing to another land. I felt both privileged and excited. I wanted to jump up and down but felt I had to restrain myself.

After the first stage of this journey, we gathered in a small encampment by cliffs overlooking the sea. It was a beautiful place, but very windy. Below us, the waves on the sea churned and there was a mix of cloud and rain that seemed unceasing. With us, there were many of the most respected teachers and craftsmen in our land, close associates of Karka. I recognized some of them from inner journeys that I had shared with my teacher. They had come from the far corners of our kingdom for this expedition.

It was quite a joyful reunion for many of them, and around the campfire, there were many stories being told, and singing. We were a people who liked to be happy and to be with each other. Many of the stories were from earlier times and younger days, and I contented myself to listen and felt honored to be part of this assemblage. This was Karka's generation of friends, and it was clear that they had been through a lot together, and this gathering served to rekindle their bond, and remind them of all that they did share.

I wondered about the boats we would use to travel to the big land, whose peninsulas we could see far in the distance. As I looked down to the ocean below, I could see the shape of a boat that had come to our shore from the land beyond, and it appeared so small from our vantage point, so tiny in the midst of the mighty sea, and flimsy as it bobbed through the waves. I experienced trepidation and a shiver of fear, not certain how safe it would be for us to travel in such a vessel. Immediately, I sent out an inner call to my guide, Eurydice, and she reassured me that this boat had completed its journey from the other land, and I felt a sense of quiet gratitude for that. She encouraged me to be open for surprises and new learning and to know that I was protected.

In the morning, we gathered as a big group and said prayers around our journey. We invoked the support of our Earth Mother, the Air Spirits, and the forces of the weather to guide us in secure passage to the big land. In this area, the weather could be quite unpredictable, and storms arrive with little warning. To navigate across these seas on our boats was not an easy task. We had specially trained boat people to take us on our journey. It was in their capable hands that we would place our trust.

The boats were a simple wooden construction, like a raft, with raised edges to try and offer us some protection from the water. In the middle of the boat was a tall mast of wood with a single sail cloth. For each vessel, there were four boat people. Two of these people stood up, one at the front, and the other at the back. The one at the front held a long pole that extended from the water right up to where it was attached to the mast. By working with this pole, the boat person at the front would direct our sail and navigate our way forward. In conjunction with this, the boat person at the back held a thin wedge of wood that could be levered in different directions and dropped into the sea. This wooden structure was the rudder of the boat to give stability and help maintain our direction. The two boat people at front and back needed to work in close cooperation so that our boat could maintain a steady course. Meanwhile the other boat people worked with paddles from the sides of the boat so that the momentum of our journey could continue.

Karka informed me that the boat people had undergone much training, including Spiritual training, so that they could be attuned to the nature elements and work in harmony with them. They worked in teams and practiced inner communication with each other so that in the course of a voyage, they would be in unity with each other.

We had a flotilla of six boats going to the big land, and many articles of trade that we needed to take. The boats were quite laden and lay heavily in the water. At the outset of our journey, there was a gentle breeze, enough for our sail to catch the wind. We had friends to push our boats from the shore, and as we were pushed out into the sea, I found a place on the side of the boat where I could crouch huddled between some blankets.

As we journeyed further, I gazed up at our guides, the boat people. They were very still, and their movements were fluid like the waves. It seemed as if they were in a state of trance, and they appeared to be in deep meditation, totally occupied and focused upon their task. As

I moved my attention from one boat person to the other, it was as if they were in total attunement with each other, and the movement of one corresponded with answering strokes performed by the other ones. It was almost as if they were one being rather than four, and their cooperation with each other was matched by the way they interacted so seamlessly with the energies of the ocean.

During the morning, clouds came into view from the south. By early afternoon, these covered the sky, and brought with them, gusts of wind and rain, so that the waves of the sea were increasingly rough and violent. Although for me, the sound of the waves breaking down disturbed me, and I felt frightened, our boat people remained steadfast and unperturbed.

Inside me, I recognized that in these unfamiliar conditions, my child consciousness wanted protection and comfort. I looked across at Karka, and with his eyes, beneath his hood, he smiled kindly at me. His thoughts beckoned me to keep faith with the boat people.

Karka motioned with his hand for me to look ahead, and as I strained myself, forward to see, I viewed something quite remarkable. Although the waters around us were churning and boisterous in their power and energy, in front of us, there was a small area that was smooth and calm. We were moving into that space and going forward. Our boat was rocking from the currents of the water and the wind and rain, but nowhere near as much as it could have been had we been exposed to the full onslaught of the elements. I could hardly see the other boats, sometimes just gaining a glimpse of one of them between the waves, but I guessed that they were similarly being protected and guided.

It was an amazing feeling when our boat landed on the far shore of the big land, and we were able to stretch our legs and feel the sand and earth of this land beneath our feet. The vibration of this land felt quite different from our own land, but the feeling of it was rich and nurturing, and I welcomed the opportunity of this new experience. There was something vaguely familiar about this land to me, as if from some deep reaches of my soul memory, I knew it somehow. Within me I felt the strong desire and wish to explore.

Ilsa

The gathering of our people from many lands was an immense event and I felt rather nervous being there at first, because there was so much activity. There were different races of people. Some were dark-haired and stocky people, and they came from the south. From the east and north, the people were fair-haired. Each race had its own language. Even the local people, who looked very much like us, spoke in a language that I could not comprehend.

The various groups all appeared to have their own customs and rituals. There were clothes and fabric that I had never seen, and animals, including some large furry ones, that were completely unfamiliar to me.

While I adjusted, I felt quite bewildered by it all, and yet, it was also exciting to witness how all these different people lived, and what we might have in common with them all.

Our meeting had a Spiritual element, and when we came together as a group in the Sacred Grove of our host's community, and we started to hum, there was a quiet unity and love that spread between us. That was when I felt a warm glow in my heart. It did not matter how different we may appear to each other, or what language we spoke, from our inner beings, we were connected. In our humming, music and dancing, we shared one Spirit, and from this base, we could learn together, and assist each other as communities.

Karka was very busy over these days, and he was involved in many meetings. In general, the people that he met greeted him as if they were long-standing friends. He did not expect me to accompany him on all his business, so this left space for me to mingle with others.

I found myself gravitating towards other younger ones like me. One evening, a small group of us made our own fireplace and sat down together. We could not understand each other's speech, but we were able to experiment with our mind communication, using telepathy, where our minds could act as interpreter. We were able to project images of our homelands and friends and what was important to us, into each other's minds. I gradually learnt sounds of their language that corresponded to those images, and they did the same with me. It was quite basic and felt clumsy at times, but we enjoyed each other's company. We enjoyed what we could offer each other, and around the fire, we played games, and laughed and had a lot of fun. We took it in turns to share mind stories from our lands. It was very interesting. I communicated with them about our College and some of the adventures that I had had.

As we tuned in to each other, it came to me, that sometime in the future, these new friends would come to visit me in my home, and that my people would be hosts to a similar gathering to what was happening here. With this thought, I smiled inside me.

At the end of the Gathering, I was very sad to leave my new-found friends. With all the people I had met, my perspective of life had been greatly opened, and my world had been considerably expanded. I knew that I would stay in contact with some of the young ones with whom I had shared most, and we would utilize telepathy and inner travel to do that. I wished that next time, when such a gathering occurred, that I would be able to share this with some of my friends from my home. It had been a precious experience, and there were many warm hugs and tears before we parted on our final day.

The Wise Ones

One day, Karka motioned to me that he wanted me to accompany him to meet somebody. By now, I was used to the spontaneity of Karka's moods, and enjoyed the adventure of what each day would bring with him.

We journeyed up a hill not overlooking, but quite near to our encampment in the College. There was a small hut, about halfway up this hill, nestled into a slight cleft. It was not the first time that I had noticed this hut, and I had been aware of smoke emanating from its vicinity on a few occasions, but otherwise, had taken little notice of its existence.

Although the hut was small and had a very basic design with wood and stick thatching as a base, the interior of it was very tidy, simple and ordered. A man was living here, quite old, and his hair was long and matted, and he wore a straggly beard. I noticed how his appearance contrasted with the tidiness of his home environment.

Karka introduced him as Strilo. He smiled at us, and quickly arranged some rugs where we could sit, and he made a light broth for us to drink from the pot on his fire. For a long time, Karka and Strilo engaged in everyday conversation about the conditions of the land and people they both knew in the College. I was puzzled and wondered what could be the reason for Karka to bring me here?

As I observed Strilo, most of the time, he kept his head down, but periodically, he would gaze upwards sufficiently to remind Karka of his interest. In the corner of the room, there was a pile of stones, and I recognized this as an altar, and could feel from the energy of it, that this man had a very sincere Spiritual practice.

Strilo saw me looking at it, and he asked me about my impressions. When I shared my thoughts, he smiled in acknowledgement, and he offered for me to have one of the stones from his altar as a gift. For a moment, I felt uncertain, because I did not wish to disturb the sacred arrangement of the stones as they were placed. With uneasiness, I glanced towards Karka for reassurance, but my teacher merely nodded, and I smiled towards Strilo in grateful acceptance.

When I handled the stone that had been given to me, I felt it buzzing with energy. I was surprised, and I felt prompted to open my perceptions to Strilo more intently. His aura was very still and white, and I had not seen that before. He said very little, but his eyes were very deep, and I felt that he could see the true me beneath my appearance. For a moment, I felt quite inadequate with all my desires and attachments, and that my own energy was swirling while his was so peaceful. But he just smiled calmly.

Before we left, Strilo gave me a warm embrace and I felt a lot of love from him in his good wishes for my learning. Once we had gone, Karka asked me what I had sensed of Strilo's energy, and I told him of the purity and quietness of it. As we walked down the hill, I felt light and joyful, and began to appreciate what a profound visit this had been.

Karka confirmed about the clarity of Strilo's energy field, and suggested that as a soul, he was more developed than either of us. Strilo had no active role in the government of our community, but his energy was important. He was one of the Wise Ones, and Karka then proposed that there was another one of his kind that he wanted to show me.

When we returned to our College encampment, and sat at the central fireplace, Karka pointed out a woman that was there. Her name was Puela. She spent her days sweeping and tidying, busying herself around the encampment, and helping to keep things in order. She seemed very intent with her tasks and rarely spoke to anyone. If anyone addressed her, she smiled, but hardly interacted with people otherwise. She was an older woman, who dressed very simply, and she was quite bent from all her years of labour. I had seen her about, but again, had hardly noticed her. There were many people in our encampment that drew attention to themselves, but she was not one of them.

Karka asked me to focus gently upon her energy field, and again, I was struck by her purity, and the clarity of her aura. It was not an aura that was brilliant, but in its quietness, there was peace, and, as if awakening from ignorance, I could feel the placidity and peace that she channeled wherever she went.

Karka confirmed that she was another one of the Wise Ones, and then spoke more generally about the place that these people had in our society. Characteristically, these people tended to stay in the background, and it was through their energy that they made a vital contribution to the harmony and well-being of our community. He told me that there were more of them, and that they stayed largely hidden from view. It would be up to me, now, to become aware of them.

He suggested to me that it was best to leave these people in peace. As souls, they knew what they were doing, and the best way that we could learn from them was by observing them and consciously accepting the energy of being that they were expressing.

This was a day when I started to appreciate that there was far more to the functioning of our society than was obvious from surface appearances. It was important that we maintained genuine Spiritual practices so that the underlying support that existed in enabling our society to exist in peace and harmony could be maintained.

Previously, I had been aware of the sacredness of specific places, stones and trees, but it had not been apparent that wise people supported the fabric of our community as well. It was not only in the volume of expression that power could be exercised, and strength witnessed, but much more in quietness and peace.

Gaining responsibility

Over time, I came to respect Karka immensely. He might not have been as still and quiet as the Wise Ones that he had pointed out to me, but I felt him to have his own wisdom and aptitude to life that I admired. He expressed this more in an active and practical fashion. There was not a day that went by, when he was not mindful of the needs of others and how he could serve the needs of our society as a whole. His dedication to his job and life of service was total. Although he was very congenial and friendly towards others, very much acting from a place of solidarity with everyone he met, he had a drive and sense of purpose that marked him apart.

People looked to him for reassurance when they were experiencing doubts or difficulties, and he would be there, often with his laughing manner, helping those who needed it to find confidence in their own decision making and the ability to continue.

I noticed in ceremonies, that there were very few ceremonies that Karka actually led, but he would stand in the background, watching, and being there in case he was needed. If there were ever any important community decisions to be made, Karka would be required to give final approval.

There was a progression in the way that he related and taught me. At first, he did not talk to me much, but shared his life with me. He did show me what he did, and he expected me to accompany him, and blend with his energy as well as I could. As time went on, he talked much more with me, and he explained to me his reasons for acting in the way he did, and asked me how I would have dealt with particular situations that he faced.

Increasingly, our discussions about the day's activities would extend until late in the night, and become more and more detailed. When I offered my own solution to problems he had encountered, ideas that were quite different to his own, he would often roar with laughter, but then he would typically challenge me with further questions so I would learn to consider additional angles to what was being considered. He was a very thorough teacher, and I never felt him to be critical of me; his intention was to help me to grow and to explore my own inner truth and learn from the experience that he could offer me.

We were a people of heart, and our feelings guided us through much of our actions and ways of being together. But with Karka, I learnt to think and plan what was needed, and this helped me to become more knowledgeable of our community and its functioning and how to manage human beings.

Over time, I came to feel very much at home with Karka, and I came to know his approach to life very intimately, and he came to know mine. Gradually, my mentor allowed me more responsibility, so instead of him travelling either inwardly or outwardly to settlements in the land to attend to problems, he would delegate some of these tasks to me. In the evenings, we would again discuss these situations, but now, it was not his actions that we dissected, but mine.

One evening, Karka paused in our examination of the day just passed, and he told me that I was ready for another step in my development. He informed me that it was time for me to assemble a group of workers from the students of the Order of the Wise to accompany me, and for us to work together as a team. We each needed to have our own strengths and abilities, and to be able to blend together as a unit. I would be their leader.

He told me how many years earlier, he had gathered his own team, and they had worked very closely together, and still did. Karka confided that most of the ones who had journeyed with them to the land across the seas for the international meeting of the people, that these were the members of his team.

Many of these Elders were now nearing the end of their working life, and although there were other teams, a new team was needed, and he advised me that I was the one to form this.

For some moments, I felt stunned and unable to speak. Karka suggested that I choose young people, similar in age to myself. I had to assess what skills I needed, what people would work together best, and who had the outstanding abilities that would serve to meet the most challenging circumstances. He suggested that I take time to contemplate upon this, so that I felt peace about what I decided.

Assembling my team

For a time, I felt quite perplexed about who I should include in my team. Karka suggested that I consult with some of the other Elders about who they deemed to be most suitable, and so I did this. Upon their recommendation, my list began to grow rapidly with numerous young students whose abilities and potential marked them out as ideal candidates. There were some who I could exclude because of deficiencies they had, but not enough to enable me to decide.

After a while I felt quite confused; I was sleeping restlessly, and with my mind, I could not work out what to do. In this situation, I did what I had done on previous occasions where I felt uncertain and needed inner help. I went to the Yew Tree by the Sacred Grove, and sought the help and guidance of the Earth Spirit, and my guide, Eurydice.

It took me considerable time to relax, even sitting on the Yew, and this indicated to me that my mind had been too busy. Gradually, I began to quieten inside, and even though my thoughts were continuing to explore the merits of some of the candidates, I could hear the soft soothing tones of my guide telling me to listen to my heart.

As I did this, I became even more still and felt my energy turning inward. I wanted to gaze up and found myself searching to see the hut where I spent my growing years. Most of it was hidden from view, but I was able to discern a corner of it in the distance behind one of the other huts.

I remembered all the experiences that I had had with my friends, and what we had shared and all the support that we had given each other, and what a great camaraderie that had been between us. There were other students living in the hut now that we had all moved on. But the bond that we had built together was unbreakable.

Suddenly, it became very clear to me who I needed to choose, and as it dawned on me, I felt both a deep sense of peace and intense clarity at the same time. I would have to ask them, of course, but at that moment, I knew what their response would be.

In the morning, I sat down with Karka to inform him of my decision. He looked at me with curiosity and merriment in his eyes. He knew by my happiness that I had made the right decision.

I chose Nianda for her healing ability and her loyalty, Gracon for his knowledge of the traditions of our land, and his psychic awareness concerning both the land and its people, Kiend for his sensitivity to the animal kingdom and the balance of our life together, and Mulaid for his artistic sensitivity in relation to both music and ceremony. These were all my companions from the later years we shared in our hut. I needed one other person in the team to complete the skills we needed, and the one I selected was a young man called Wueli.

Wueli did not learn in the same school as us, for his training was for him to become a warrior. However, he did attend many of the same classes as us, and I had felt very drawn to him from a young age. We had been close friends, and I had shared with him a lot about my experiences with my father. I felt a strong love for him, and he felt very right to be in the team.

When I finished speaking and explaining my choices to Karka, my teacher just laughed. He disclosed how when in earlier times, he had had to choose his own group, the ones he had decided upon, were also the ones with whom he had shared his living accommodation. Karka explained how it was natural for me to do that, and was a big part of the reason that we had been placed together in the beginning. He then patted me on the back and congratulated me, and affirmed that he thought that I was doing well.

Later, we all met with Karka in a ceremony together by the Sacred Grove. Our leader led the ritual. As we joined our hands together around the fire, and each voiced our commitment to each other and the land, there was a great feeling of union between us that felt very beautiful and strong. It was not the first time we had felt united, but this was very different. I smiled at Wueli to welcome him to be with us. His tall thin frame stood still but his eyes danced with joy. I believe that this was how we all felt then.

This was the moment when we graduated from being students to full adulthood where we would begin our work as administrators for the land. After considerable time where we had been apart from each other with our individual specialized trainings, it felt good to be together again, and in a new way. We were all ready, and I could sense no weakness from anyone.

Following on from this, Karka gave us group assignments where we would visit settlements in our land that needed assistance. It was like the work that I had done many years earlier with Berenice, but more involved, and we used our telepathic skills to work together so we could draw the best from each other and the people we were trying to help.

With our first mission, we were called to a village where there had been both crop failure and illness, and the leadership of the community had become divided as to how to cope with the problems. There had been blame and antagonism building up between different factions of the village, and in their fear, the people were becoming increasingly desperate.

I needed to use my training to sense beneath the fear and confusion about what these people truly needed, and find the means to communicate this effectively. Wueli was with me to approach the management committees of the community to explore how they structured their society and to suggest how they could do it better.

Soon we discovered how shattered this community had become. Nianda was busying herself immediately and helping numerous people with her healing skills. She had three assistants working with her, and they were all needed to cope with the scale of the suffering before her.

As Wueli and I sat with the administrators of the village and its warring factions, we were soon confronted with the bitterness and anguish that existed, and the people were exhausted from their struggle.

Gradually, we were able to uncover the background details of their conflict. They had had a well-loved Elder called Paigel who had been killed in tragic circumstances a couple of years previously. A few of the young youths within the community had been practicing their spear throwing and competing with each other as to who could throw the furthest. In using such weapons, they should have been doing this in a safe place, away from others, but they had been playing at this within the confines of the settlement. Paigel had been on his way to tell the boys to move their activity when a wayward throw had struck him in the chest.

In the following days, as Paigel lay dying, there was much arguing among the families. The people were used to Paigel's direction and there was no obvious successor to his leadership. This incident poisoned feelings so much between various members of the village that the fabric of the community disintegrated from this time.

From then on, there was no sense of authority in the village. Ceremonies stopped because nobody could agree about who should lead them. Families stopped acting collectively, but each tried to look after its own interests. There was conflict and endless disputes, and nobody could adequately adjudicate about how to solve the problems. Then, following a heavy rainstorm, there had been a flood that had decimated the summer crops, and the people could no longer refrain from asking for help.

That day, I spent a long time with the youth who had thrown the spear to kill Paigel. His remorse was terrible, and in his guilt, he did not know how he could build a worthwhile life for himself after what he had done. His family had been ostracized. There was a lesson for him around impulsiveness, the recklessness of youth, wishing to excel, and go beyond limits. Indeed, he shared many of the characteristics that I had exhibited when younger. What I appreciated in him was his concern, and a genuine despair about how his actions had impacted upon the village.

Within this youth, I could perceive strength of character and the potential to learn and develop his character. I asked him if there was a chance to redeem himself for what he had done, if he would be willing to say 'yes' to that opportunity? With that invitation, his head rose slightly, and I could sense that his energy was brighter. There was hope in our task.

I asked him to search in his heart and tell me what he would most wish to do in the community where he lived. He confided how he wished for peace and reconciliation within the village, and anything he could contribute towards that, he would gladly do. From this base, we talked further and began to form a more detailed vision of a possible way forward. His friends could help him, and I sensed that he had the determination and capacity within him to succeed.

There was a young woman that had received training from the Order of the Wise. Before Paigel's death, she had assisted in the casting of rituals and ceremonies, but had stepped back when the troubles began. Although there was no one to do it with her, she had continued to honor sacred Spiritual practices on her own, even continuing to pray and care for the Sacred Stones of the village, after the local Priestess had walked away and left. When I talked to this woman, I was impressed by her dedication and her deep faith. Her potential place in the community needed to be honored and recognized.

It was necessary to search amongst the inhabitants of the village to find the right ones, the ones that could emerge to lead the reconstruction of the community. I had to trust, with my Spiritual beliefs, that the people needed for this were there, and that the well being of the community could be restored. In the evenings, my companions and I talked together and shared our thoughts and feelings about the task we needed to do.

After many days of exchanges and interviews with most of the people of the village, I felt increasingly drawn to Paigel's elder brother. This man's name was Seigel. He was a much quieter personality than Paigel. At first, I had hardly noticed him, and yet, in his gentleness, there was a feeling of peace about him. His presence reminded me of those Wise Ones that Karka had introduced to me, all that time before.

Seigel had no bitterness for what had happened to his brother. He had gone on working, providing for his family, and Paigel's family, trying to help where he could, being attentive to people's needs, in his own quiet manner. Seigel was not an obvious leader, but I noticed how people would listen to him, and learn. He was a man with positive intent, and he would encourage others to help each other.

Gracon gathered people to tell stories of great communities in our land from the past, and how our culture had been built, and he postulated about what were the important ingredients for communities to be successful and happy. He led them on meditations in their Grove so that they could connect with their own purpose and what they could bring forth to help their community. Through meditation and feeling the Spirit of their land, the villagers began to regain those nurturing feelings of love they had felt for their home previously.

In the evening, people sat around the fire, and Mulaid generated sounds and music to bring everyone together, and I could sense the healing and inner bonds that these souls shared start to grow stronger again in love.

Kiend was able to instruct people about our animal friends, and how they were willing to help and some of them even sacrifice themselves to promote the survival of the village. Kiend sensed that the totem animal of this village was the crow. These were birds that could be ruthless scavengers, but they also had a gift for seeing. During the course of his discussions a crow descended from the skies and landed on Kiend's shoulders, and then stayed there, squawking loudly to announce its presence.

I called on Wueli to give instruction to those with aptitude about organization and arranging systems that would work for them to function socially together. In particular, I directed Wueli to give attention to the young man that had thrown the spear, and help him afterwards so he could learn.

At the end of our stay, I called a meeting of the community and signaled my opinion concerning the three people with whom I had spent most time, and the role that I felt that each could play in the future of the village. After I had spoken, I invited each of them to speak and share their thoughts, and there was an atmosphere of deep and enthusiastic listening. Everyone wanted to give their new leaders a chance.

Next the young woman led a ceremony of thanksgiving to acknowledge our help, but also to call upon the Spirits to help with the collective efforts of the village, to forge links and create vitality and joy for all levels of life in this land. It was a beautiful, but powerful ceremony. I could feel the warm vibration of the Earth Spirit and a clear blue light gathering around everyone to affirm their new faith, and to give it strength. The woman conducting the ceremony was able to hold the energy of it through her faith and sincere dedication.

In this moment, I knew that the future of the village was now safe, and that these people would prosper.

It was our first assignment as a group, but one in which we all felt a great degree of personal satisfaction.

Chapter 10

Karka's fate

Winds of change

With my team, our assignments did not always work out perfectly. People did not necessarily wish to follow our ideas completely, and there were sometimes suffering and divisions in societies, where the people did not seem to us to have a fixable attitude to their problems. In these situations, we would have to accept the limitations of what we could achieve. On occasions, we felt we had to disappoint individuals for the sake of the greater community, and we could not please everyone. There were times when we made efforts to assist specific individuals who had strength, and we hoped that this would help the larger situation in the longer term.

It was not always obvious to us the reason that we were sent to the places where we had to go. In these early stages, we were still under Karka's direction. He gave us our assignments. As a group, there were instances when we would argue, and could not agree about an approach that would work to resolve a difficult situation. Sometimes I felt that I would get much more done if I acted alone, and I had to be patient with respect of the others in the group. Generally, when we meditated, we would find a common thread to lead us to the work that Spirit wanted us to do. We were often surprised, but by doing Spirit's bidding, we could learn and know that we were acting from the highest good.

When I had worked with Berenice, it had felt much simpler and I could rely on her leadership, psychic sensitivity and knowledge to help us through. But now, it felt different, and I was learning to manage our group as well as helping the communities. In previous times, I always had someone in authority with whom I could defer when I was uncertain. But now Karka stepped back and insisted upon me making my own decisions, so I could take on the responsibility of what I was doing fully. At times, I felt that I was floundering, but I found that it was possible to work together with my friends and we did trust each other, so with that emphasis of being a team together, this helped a great deal.

In our discussions, Karka encouraged me to develop a wider vision of how various communities were connected throughout the land, so I could sense that the communities of our land formed the fabric of a coherent whole. With this background, we needed to encourage communities to be in harmony with each other as well as within themselves.

In addition, Karka gave me the task of organizing festivals and ceremonies, and even gatherings while we were on our travels, so people of different communities could get together, learn from each other, and have a sense of working together. I felt nervous about doing this at first, and leant upon the guidance of Spirit to support me and made use of the suggestions of other team members. They were also doing this for the first time, so we could all support each other.

Karka often talked to me of his vision of a peaceful land where people lived and worked in harmony with the Earth Spirit, learning from each other, and joyfully celebrating our existence from a place of mutual respect. He felt that it was the essential work of the Order of the Wise to promote this, and as leader of our Order, Karka felt that he had a responsibility to work tirelessly for this and hold his vision steadfastly.

My desire was to assist Karka to build on his achievements and to work together with him as closely as I could. As time went on, I could appreciate the mammoth task that he had taken on.

He wanted to educate societies that were unfamiliar with our Order, so that they could learn about the Spirit of the Earth and how they could live deeper and more fulfilling lives. His wish was for these people to join us as part of a wider, united family of people living together across the breadth of our land. There were many tribes and groups to the north and east of our land, in particular, that remained independent and adopted different lifestyles to our own. Some of these people, especially in the north, were of a different race and spoke another tongue to us.

Karka was like an evangelist. But he felt driven to bring as many of these people into our fold, as he could. It was a mission that he had set himself. In this respect, he and Berenice were very similar, and carried forward the same zeal of intention.

Increasingly, Karka left to me the duty of delegating and attending to the day by day health and functioning of the society that we controlled in our land through the Order. In this, there were many Elders within the Order that had far more experience and skills than I did, and I would ask them to execute some of the more subtle and delicate work that needed doing. I felt quite in awe of these Elders, and their experience, but found the strength to direct them somehow. I was not afraid. It was with Karka's authority that I acted, and this gave me the power to carry through with my actions. We all had our place and our inner tasks, and Spirit continued to make it clear to me that it was my purpose to lead, and I needed to gain experience with that, as much as I could. There were still some within the Order, including Berenice, who acted independently, and I deferred to them when it was necessary to do so. I had a job to do, that had been given to me, and it needed all my attention to cope with it.

While I continued to gain practice with my new responsibilities, Karka then concentrated his attention upon his outreach to extend the boundaries of our Order and its influence. For long periods of time, I was separated from him while he journeyed, either with his own party of supporters, or on his own. He went through the land to various outposts of civilization. But it seemed to tire him. When I did see him, I noticed a change in him. It was not a change that felt comfortable to see.

Previously, I had regarded Karka as quite invincible. His humor and high Spirits were infectious; his dedication to his tasks unsurpassed. But now, when I was with him, it was different. His demeanor was more serious, and he seemed more remote to me. Increasingly I noticed new lines on his face, and he did not appear to hold himself so upright. He was getting old.

I asked him if he wanted to share the duties that I was doing and have a break from the outreach work, but he insisted on going ahead with it. He would only be willing to rest from it when the job was completed.

For the first time since I had known him, Karka appeared to suffer weakness. A gap existed between what he wanted to achieve, and what he was able to do. This was like a division inside him that brought frustration to him. There was nothing I could do to help him. It was as if, in his mind, he was playing out some destiny that he had decided had been given to him, and he had no choice except to carry on the track he was treading and put all his efforts into achieving what he had set out to do. Perhaps in his inner guidance, he was aware of choices, but whatever other possibilities there were, he had rejected them. Yet, doing what he was doing appeared to be draining his Spirit away.

One evening, Karka was speaking to me about his struggles to communicate with communities where he traveled. People in these places had such different values and beliefs to what we had. He was seeking to find a bridge of common ground, and it was not easy.

Karka sighed, and I could perceive how much strain he was giving to himself. On the one hand, he wanted to convey respect to the various communities and their culture. But he also wanted to inform them of how we lived our lives, and then try to find creative interaction with them to build up a sense of mutual understanding and support. Some societies he met did not want to listen to him, and they could even be aggressive towards him. He could not force himself upon them, but he felt so strongly that there was a need to find unity in our land, and he had to make the effort.

This was like an obsession that was growing in Karka, and I needed to understand the roots of it. So I asked him why he was doing it.

At the end of this evening, Karka shared with me in a low voice that he feared for the future of our land. He dreaded that there could be dark forces of destruction intruding upon our land. If we did not pull together, we would be defeated.

I was shocked, for I could perceive no indication of this, and I pleaded with him to tell me how he knew this. In reply, he told me how he had been having dreams, and they were not ordinary dreams, but dreams of precognition of the future.

No wonder he was looking old – it was not the outreach that was making him age, but his fears. It was the first time that I had observed this, and it saddened me, deep in my heart.

Journey

One day, Karka called me for a meeting. He was planning to head north on a long journey, a lot further than I had ever been. Karka intended to travel right to the very edge of our land, and to the islands that lay beyond that. I questioned him about his purpose for doing this, and he replied, telling me that he had Spiritual Brothers and Sisters there, and he needed to meet and make a link with them, that hopefully could be extended later.

Karka wanted me to accompany him on this journey, just the two of us. As he put this to me, I felt torn because of my dedication to working with my team. But I knew that I could not refuse him. So I nodded to let him know that I agreed.

Karka looked at me very strangely, and in a way that I had not seen in him before. His eyes were vulnerable, and I could feel him pleading with me to look after him and support him with my youthful strength. I did not know what Karka was foreseeing, but I felt a shiver go down my back, and for a brief moment, it felt as if the space between us was shaking. Inside I knew that my teacher was seeking some assurance from me, so I reached out and hugged him, and told him that he could depend on me and that I would stay by his side for the duration of the journey. Karka smiled faintly. After all this time when I had been learning and needing Karka's help and guidance, I perceived truly that the time had arrived when he needed me.

Now it was morning, and we set out together, venturing across unfamiliar lands. The further north that we went, the more I could feel a chill in the air, and wetness. At night, Karka journeyed, and was in contact with a man from the north, one of his Spiritual brothers, who would be our guide for the later stages of our passage. This man was making a supply line for us, with hidden rafts that we would need, to be able to cross the rivers and lochs we would encounter. He had the necessary knowledge about which way we could proceed to reach our destination.

Some days later, we were treading forward to the edge of a large expanse of water. There we saw the outline of a man dressed in a dark robe. He was waiting for us by the river's edge. This was Karka's Spiritual brother. I could recognize him from the inner journeys I had done with Karka.

The two friends greeted each other enthusiastically, and they were focused on each other. I studied our new companion. He was quite a big man, well built and strong. Under his robes, he wore rough skins, and had long straggly dark hair and a beard. His voice was deep, but I could not understand what words he spoke. However, his mind was sharp and clear, and I could receive pictures from his thoughts that made his meaning cogent to me. His name was Arns, and I felt safe with him.

Soon we were organized and traveling much more rapidly through the rather deserted forests of the north. The nights were bitterly cold, and I needed to wrap my skins around me to keep warm. During the hours of darkness, the three of us would huddle close to the fire. At these times, Karka and Arns would laugh and share stories of their lives and work, deep into the night. I remained largely silent as an observer, but was glad to see Karka more relaxed and at ease with himself.

To reach our friend's home, we had to go far onwards through hills and valleys, as the land extended further and further north. Our land was so vast, and I wondered if the expanse of it would ever end. But one day, we reached a bay where the land stopped, and I was aware that we had reached the end of the mainland. I was tired and sore after having walked such a long distance, but I also felt exhilarated by experiencing all these new vistas.

Around the bay, there was a small settlement, but we were not staying there, and so we kept walking. At the far end of the bay, there was a boat ready to take us where we needed to go next.

As we set out, I could see the scattering of islands in the far distance. It was cold and windy, but our boat was sturdy and we made steady progress, taking turns to row. Arns showed us the water channels that we needed to follow to help us along. The further we went from the mainland, the rougher the sea became. In the atmosphere of the air, I could sense serenity and a building of excitement inside me.

When we came near to the first of these islands, we had to stay quite far out from this, so our boat would not be damaged by hidden rock outcrops. There were sheer cliffs welcoming us, with the hooting of a myriad of birds. Rain pelted down, and the wind blew fiercely. It was such a remote place for us to come, but there was also something familiar about these islands, something that drew me like a magnet.

We continued to weave our way around the islands until a larger one came into view that was to be our destination. As we approached the shore, I noticed how wind-swept the trees looked, and substantial vegetation was lacking. It was quite desolate-looking, but the vibration of the land was quivering with energy. Here was a place where the Earth Spirit was strongly felt. The people here must have been doing a lot of Spiritual work.

Stepping off the boat, there were people to meet us. We were greeted not only with courtesy and respect but also as friends, and the dwellers of the islands welcomed us as their guests. Soon I was amongst other young people, and they were showing me around. Although I could not understand their language, their inner skills were developed and I could communicate with them via telepathy. They seemed very pleased to see me, and I enjoyed their company.

Their homes were made of earth and stone and looked very different from ours. Inside them, they were warm and insulated from the weather. They needed to be, for the chill wind outside was unrelenting, and the amount of daylight was much less than I was used to. But these people were positive and joyful, and they had rhythm and ritual about the way they conducted their lives. They honored their food with thanksgiving prayers and showed respect to each other. The Elders taught the young ones practical skills and inner ones. They were a close knit community and treated each other with kindness.

For three nights, we stayed with them, and I hardly saw Karka during this time. But then preparations were made for a ceremony to be held, and this is what Karka had been waiting for.

Although they had their own language, in terms of their spiritual traditions, they were a people similar to us. They had their own very sacred circle of stones, situated in an alcove protected a little from the weather, and this is where the ceremony would be conducted.

All the people of the Community gathered for the ceremony excepting only the sick and youngest children and the ones that cared for them. It was a happy occasion. Karka wore his ceremonial white robe. He had brought with him, seeds, stones and sacred water from our well. These were symbols for the links he wanted to express. Amidst the chanting invocation, Karka and the leader of the island Community made a blood pact together, and allowed their blood to drip into the fire and burn. Healing herbs were added to the flames and smoke billowed high. Wind twirled the smoke around, but at one point, as the ceremony reached its peak, we all gazed into the sky, and the smoke at once made a circle that we could all see. At this point, Karka stamped his staff into the ground, and loudly projected his voice to summon the Spirits and invoke unity for our land. There was a huge answering approval from the island people. The cries of all the voices thundered into the atmosphere, and then were swallowed by the wind. But then, as the people held hands together and hummed, there was love generated between us, and I could feel the Earth Spirit joining us and supporting us.

It was the same Earth Spirit that existed in the Sacred Grove from my home, even though the vibration of energy here was distinct from that. I could feel that the same immeasurable Earth Spirit cradled all life wherever we would walk as physical beings, and this Spirit would love us and nurture our lives as long as we listened and worked in harmony with it. I felt humbled and in awe and peace grew in our circle as we all could realize the kinship that we shared.

Karka had wanted to strengthen the conscious link of loving Spiritual connection along the length of our land, and thereby give it protection. This was the reason that he had come here. I could feel how positive these efforts of Karka had been, but I also felt then, with a strange thought, a doubt whether his efforts would be enough.

Memory flashed into my mind of my mother, when she described to me the terrible raid that resulted in the conception of my brother, Skife. In truth, when human beings chose to disregard the sanctity of our land for their own desires, then no amount of protection would be adequate. I shuddered inside as I considered this, and I had to push that thought to one side.

Tonight, there would be celebrations and happiness. There was dancing, feasting and sharing. It was a hugely energetic occasion with much laughter, singing and stories. Even though I could not understand the words spoken, it did not stop my enjoyment. The whole community joined in. There was a great feeling of comradeship among the people, and I felt completely included. I joined in the dancing and singing, and I was leaping about with the other young ones. It was nearly dawn when it finished. When it was all over, I was exhausted and sank into a long sleep, feeling very contented.

It must have been much later when I opened my eyes, because the sun was already setting in the western sky. Karka was busying himself around me, and I could tell by his aura of well-being and the contentment around him, that he regarded his purpose for coming here had been fulfilled. He announced to me, that when we had rested for one more night, and gathered supplies, we would begin our journey home.

It was hard for me to depart from the island. Part of me wanted to stay and settle here. I could feel kinship with the people, but I knew I needed to adhere to my responsibilities and duties from my home in the South. When I turned to Karka, I could sense his reluctance as well. Yet, with him, there was an uneasy restlessness of Spirit that I did not quite understand.

The next day, we took our sacks of supplies to the boat. When we waved goodbye, I sighed deeply in my chest, and felt gratitude for this opportunity. Our companion, Arns, would accompany us and guide us for the first stage of our journey, and I felt glad of that.

But as we applied our efforts to row the boat towards the mainland, and as the view of these beloved islands receded into the distance, there was a part of me that wanted to cry out and turn back. Suddenly, even in Karka's presence and with Arns directing us, I felt a strange feeling of emptiness and foreboding, and I felt very alone.

Karka's trial

After Arns left us, and we continued our journey, just the two of us, the difficult feelings I carried inside, intensified. I tried to identify if these reactions originated from me or if they were coming from my teacher, Karka. But it was not from me – I became certain of that. The further we went on, the more silent Karka became, and it was an awkward silence, not one that I could easily penetrate. It was as though Karka was removing himself from me, and I couldn't understand why, and he wouldn't talk about it – and this was something that was very uncharacteristic of him. When we sat down at night, he would stare into the flames of the fire, and the only times, he looked at me, his expression wore more of a grimace than anything else.

On the day of the trial, it was a sunny morning. I was glad to meet the new day, but when I glanced at Karka, he seemed even more restless than he had been, and he was looking about him as if in a state of acute alertness and agitation.

I dared to speak and asked him if he needed my help, and if there was anything that I could do, but he fended me off with an abrupt dismissive gesture of his hand, without giving any explanation. As we started to walk, I let him go ahead, but I continued to be drawn to him with my concern. However, the effect of me doing that was to make me feel tired. It was as if he had put up a psychic shield around himself to stop me getting near. I could not support him if he did not want it. So I felt that I had no choice but to focus upon myself, and I tried to take in the warmth from the sun.

As I gradually found my centre, I could turn my attention to Karka without being so affected by his mood. In his energy field, I could sense indications of a struggle going on. Using the training I had received, I opened myself to perceive his energy system. With the jagged flashes of energy I could discern around his head, I knew that there were thoughts he was having that were not in harmony with his inner being. The energy around his body was swirling with many colors, and very unsettled. He was fighting with himself.

I asked Eurydice to help me, and I sensed her perception blend with mine. As I gazed deeper within his energy field, I could sense his core, and the feeling emanating from his core, was serenely calm. I needed to tune into that core energy more fully. Eurydice had to help me.

I felt myself pulled into Karka's being, into that calmness. Somehow I was allowed to do that without intruding on Karka's being. As I opened my senses to it, I could feel a similar calmness growing inside my heart. There was something linking me with him in this, and it was a beautiful, sacred, energy that I was experiencing. Beneath me, I felt this energy in the Earth, too, in the Earth Spirit. There was something special, and wondrous about this.

When I brought my attention even closer, there was a thread of gold that extended from his heart towards mine and also, there were streams of this thread going in other directions, to other souls, and from me as well as from him.

All at once, the realization struck me, that this was the inner thread of commitment that we carried in our hearts, for those of us that were members of the Order of the Wise. These threads were an expression of the vow that we shared. As our leader, the energy light of this vow was gathered in Karka's core in many intricate patterns, and they felt incredibly peaceful.

Suddenly, I could feel the presence of a myriad of Spirit beings that were also present and also weaving this thread through their beings too. As I focused on them, it occurred to me, that these were our ancestors, and members of our Order from the past. So there was continuity. With these beings, the threaded energy flowed freely as pure light, dancing between them like a form of celebration…

This was a demonstration of how we were all connected, and I knew then that the sacred bond of this thread was something that would always be with us. I was amazed at the sensitivity of this vision. The sacred commitment we had made, had an energy component to it, and I could sense the immense magnitude of this, with the greater forces involved, and how the collective of all that we each contributed, was adding to this energy. I could breathe all this in and was in awe of it, but it also puzzled me.

Shifting my attention, I turned once more to Eurydice. Why was this coming into my awareness now? How did this beautiful threaded energy at Karka's core, form part of the conflict occurring within him?

Karka and I continued to walk along, and I was following him and able to continue my study of him. With my energetic eyes, I could sense Eurydice smiling at me but slowly, she moved her gaze slowly in the direction of Karka. As I looked, even though I was physically behind him, it was as if I was standing directly in front of him, and my attention was drawn immediately to his chest. Here, I could sense the greatest concentration of swirling energy.

There was a formation of light here, and it was throbbing in harmony with Karka's heartbeat, but this light was pulling and wanted to lift away from him. Karka did not want to let it go. What was he attempting to keep? Karka was using a lot of his energy to attempt to keep this light formation in place, and I sensed that he knew that his efforts would ultimately be in vain. His Higher self was urging him to let go of the light formation, but he was very reluctant to do so. And the pulling was increasing with its force. I could tell that this formation was part of what he considered to be his identity – that is what it felt like. But it was not his to keep anymore, for it was detaching from him.

I wished that I could gain more information, but it was not forthcoming. All at once, the vision faded, and in my awareness, Karka was returned to his normal form. He had paused for a few moments, sitting on a rock – and it was not like him to need to rest. But soon he was gathering himself again with his staff, for us to be on our way.

Storm

The change in the day occurred imperceptibly at first. There were a few wispy clouds in the east, and from the stillness that had been there before, there grew a breeze that gusted with greater force, as the morning progressed. The cloud cover became increasingly widespread, until by the middle of the day, there was no blue to be seen. And the cloud cover was not static either. There was motion and turbulence in those clouds. The sky looked angry.

As the sky darkened, Karka's step quickened too. It was as though he wanted to outpace the weather and escape from its influence. At intervals, he would gaze anxiously up at the clouds and then hurry along further. I wondered why he did not stop and find shelter, pause in our journey, and seek inner stillness, so we could commune with the Earth Spirit. That is what he would normally do. But today, Karka did not do that. Part of me wanted to intervene, and tell Karka to stop, but the quiet knowing inside me was insistent that I observe and remain passive. My instinct told me that Karka had foreseen what was happening now – he could do that. But for whatever reasons, he continued to resist the events as they unfolded, and he kept me separate from it all. How much longer could he continue like that?

The clouds turned black and the wind became so fierce that I struggled to keep my balance, and then it became a little quieter and began to rain. Even with the drop in the wind, Karka appeared to be faltering, stopping and starting again, as if he was reaching his limits internally. And then, Karka suddenly stopped completely, and became motionless. I could tell that the light around him and inside him was shifting. Then he turned around to me. His face wore a strange demeanor. Something inside him transformed, and I could sense all that swirling energy which had been so troubling, had settled and was still. And with this, Karka gave a small smile.

Finally my teacher had accepted his fate in this situation and he was in harmony with himself. Inside, I felt very uncertain and nervous, for I did not know what would now take place, but I at once felt better, knowing that Karka was now more at peace with himself.

He still did not talk, but from then on, his whole approach changed and he relaxed. After gazing at me with love in his eyes, he then looked up at the sky and put his hands together, as if in prayer. Then he turned to go forward, on the path we had been treading, and stepped ahead with sure steps. I made a move to walk alongside of him, but he made a gesture with his hand for me to stay back. He insisted upon going first.

Now, as I observed his energy, his being had become quite radiant. His inner light was shining as he walked. My intuition told me that I was now witnessing an event in motion that had been predestined because it felt so familiar, somehow. Now, he had let go of control, and was allowing whatever needed to take place, do so, without any interference on his part.

In the distance, I heard the first rolls of thunder above the nearby hills, and the land shuddered with the violence of the sound. We both looked up at the sky, and the clouds were now churning chaotically, with menace. Visibility was poor, and the darkness over the land, was more akin to what it was like just before nightfall. The force of the wind pushed and pulled with the enveloping storm, and I had to reach out for support from rocks and trees to keep going. Karka was striding ahead, as if oblivious to what was going on around him. The temperature had dropped with the gathering storm, and there was a cold chill, that went through the skins I was wearing to my bones.

We were walking across an uneven landscape, and the vegetation became sparser as we climbed slowly upwards. Karka continued to walk ahead with calm and serenity. At one point, as I emerged from the protection of a large rock formation, I felt prompted to pause in my steps so I could observe what would happen.

I noticed the dead tree as Karka approached it. There was hardly any vegetation near it, just stone and rocky ground. This was a tree that stood on its own, and its presence felt lonely. All leaves had been stripped from it, and its branches hung bare. The energy of this tree was like a remnant of something uncomfortable, with memories of times past, which was not very pleasant. I tuned into it and listened. The dead tree had endured suffering and had given its life to protect other life, so other life forms in the area would not endure negative and difficult energies. This had been a tree acting as a conductor to absorb negative energy, and transmute it, but the effort had sapped the tree of its life energy. In appreciation, I noted that this was a great and noble tree, which had given all in self-sacrifice and service to other beings. I felt such sadness as I saw it and felt awe that a tree could do that. The majesty of its power still lingered in the air, and the shell of its stump and dead branches were a reminder of a vital force that was now gone.

Karka was now near the base of the tree and was looking up at it inquisitively. It was strange how Karka too, had given his life in service of the land, and had sacrificed any personal desires he may have had so he could dedicate himself utterly to his task. The two of them were very similar. But the tree was physically dead and I did not want that to happen to Karka. Suddenly I reacted, and wanted to run. But I was too late.

I watched in astonishment as the lightning hit the tree. The sky lit up and the tree was full of flickering flame. It was like a last farewell, and I sensed that the shell of the tree that remained was disintegrating before my eyes. Even the shell of this once great tree had now had its day.

As I stared, I observed Karka, ahead of me, transfixed by the sight of the flaming tree. Moments later, the sound of the rolling thunder shuddered through the air. It was almost in slow motion that the largest branch of the tree became dislodged and began to fall. As it plunged towards the ground, I watched, as if in trance. The wind swirled and carried it at an angle. It did not register with me, the trajectory of its path, until just before it crashed to the ground. And then I noticed Karka. He did not even appear to try and avoid it as the branch crashed into him, and his body collapsed beneath it in a crumpled heap.

My first feeling was overwhelming panic, and I rushed towards my teacher, vainly hoping that I could help him. I could still feel the trembling of the thunder as it echoed across the hills. I feared that Karka had been completely crushed, but on the far side of the branch I could see that the upper part of his body was free, and he was moaning softly. The impact had been so violent, and as I moved, I could revisit the images of the falling branch, over and over in my mind. As I came closer, I could observe that it was his legs that had taken the brunt of the force applied against him. The collision had cut his legs away from beneath him, and one of his legs was still trapped beneath the branch.

I would have to move very quickly, and with great purpose. Karka was groaning, but hardly conscious. I had to first remove that branch, so I called upon my guide and the strength of the Earth Spirit. There was pure intention. I was utterly determined that this branch would come off Karka's body, and I imagined it happening.

I don't know where it came from, but I felt almost superhuman strength rushing through my veins, and it gave me powers I did not know I had. In a few moments, with a surge of effort, the branch was lifted and cast to the side.

Both of Karka's legs were horribly broken, one in several places and there were a couple of pieces of his bone protruding. I did not know what other injuries he had sustained but I sensed he may also have internal injuries. Now I had to put into practice, all my best healing knowledge. Any delay may set damage beyond repair. I wished that I had Nianda with me. She would know much better than I, what I would need to do now.

In desperation, I beseeched my Spirit friends for as much help as they could give me. I called on Eurydice, and the Earth Spirit, and I could feel the presence of a whole host of other Spiritual beings with me too.

I could hear my guide prompting me to work initially on the main part of his body and then upon the leg that had only one break, and to do that first. So I placed my hands on his chest, and felt a huge injection of energy. I heated up but kept my hands there as long as I could, until I sensed Eurydice whispering for me to move on. So I turned my attention to the least mangled of Karka's legs. I shuddered with grief before I started. This did not seem at all easy. I was aware of Karka's moaning, and could only begin to imagine the extent of the terrible suffering that he must be enduring.

This leg needed straightening. The break had occurred just below the knee, and the bottom part of his leg dangled out at the most unnatural of angles. A segment of his bone was visible, and he was bleeding from his wound. How could this ever be healed? I had to have faith. Tears were rolling down my cheeks as I worked, and I felt as though my hands were burning. My whole body was hot and perspiration dripped from my face. I was desperate to help him. Again I felt that there were forces from beyond me that worked with my hands, and I had to let them do that, and not interfere. They were adjusting Karka's leg into a more straightened position, and I had to place my hands where I was prompted to assist this. His leg seemed to just move little by little with the smallest of pressure applied.

I noticed that it had stopped raining, and Karka was lying still, as if in meditation. At once I realized that Karka must have left his body, and with this thought, there he was above me, smiling down and encouraging my efforts in gratitude.

This should have brought some relief to me, but it did not. However much Karka's Spiritual body was at peace, his physical body was a wreck, and he could not stay away forever. With as much concentration as I could muster, I continued to surrender myself to the will of Spirit, pleading for that help, and I felt Spirit working through me to try and repair Karka's body. Finally, I could sense a stream of energy traveling though his leg, flowing in a gentle, steady motion, and as this consolidated itself, I knew that this leg would be OK.

But there was still the other leg, and the injuries to this were much worse. I applied myself to it, and again the heat energy became very intense, and the forces of Spirit were working meticulously to do what they could to help. I wanted it to keep going until all the leg was set right. However, at a certain point, the healing stopped, and I sensed Spirit withdraw. The leg was not fully repaired, it was still crippled. And I urged Spirit to return, to continue the work, but they would not. I heard the voice of my guide, Eurydice, speaking softly to me, telling me that they could do no more: they had healed as much as they could. I looked upwards in astonishment. Surely they could do further healing if I asked for it? But Eurydice gently urged me to accept that they could not. The awareness was given to me that this was an event of fate. I had to recognize that and allow it with humility.

With a jolt, Karka was in his body again, and he started moaning. I had to comfort him. There was no possibility that he would be able to walk. He could not do anything, and I certainly would not be able to carry him by myself. Why did they not help him?

Using telepathy, I contacted Wueli and Nianda, and sent out a general call for help to those that could be listening, summoning urgent assistance for whoever could arrive most swiftly. I felt bewildered, but had to apply myself to making Karka as comfortable as he could be.

Help did arrive finally, and we were able to construct a makeshift stretcher, and after some days, we eventually reached the shelter of our home. Karka had spent most of his time out of his body so he could withstand the pain easier, and we had given him plenty to drink, to assist the healing.

In the College, there were many worried people, some shaking their heads in disbelief. My own instincts told me that he would never recover from this, and it was clear to me with his energetic being what he had not wanted to give up. It was only because he had accepted his fate that his composure was calm now, when all around him was agitated and uncertain.

The Council meeting

After another moon cycle, Karka called for there to be a special Council meeting so that he could put the affairs of the community in order. He was still suffering and experiencing severe pain, but he wanted to quell the uncertainty around his leadership of the Order.

Karka insisted that the young ones who had recently attained membership of our Order be invited as well as the Elders. All needed to be present. For me, as Karka's assistant, I had been able to attend Council meetings before, as an observer, but this was my first time as a full participant, and my friends Gracon, Nianda, Wueli, Kiend and Mulaid were also invited. It was an auspicious meeting that would be held in the Sacred Grove, and there was much nervous excitement in anticipation of what may happen.

When we gathered, Karka was propped up in a central position, with rugs and skins to support him, so he could be as comfortable as possible. Then, next to him, as was customary, Berenice was sitting, with the other high ranking Elders, many of whom had been our teachers and mentors, sitting adjacent. We young ones were placed on the other side of the fire, and I nestled myself in amongst my friends.

Elders burned herbs and made blessings, and we uttered collective prayers, inviting the Earth Spirit to be with us. Then there was a low hum that increased in volume slowly, as we gathered our minds to seek harmony and understanding with each other. At last, this faded into silence, and attention turned to Karka.

There was reverence in the group towards our leader, and Karka gestured quietly to acknowledge the attention he was being given. His look was one of pained acceptance, and it was clear that he did not find it easy that he could no longer stand without assistance. Physically he was a cripple, although it was plain that his inner light still shone brightly.

Karka shared about his process of what had happened for him. For many months, he had been given the information by his guide that his destiny lay in meeting with the dead tree. In this meeting, he would have to surrender what was most precious to him. Karka was courageous enough to admit that he knew what this meant, and for a long time, he had refused to contemplate it. But in the return from the journey to the northern islands, Karka was aware that the timing for this destiny was imminent.

In the night before the storm, Karka related about a terrifying dream that he had had. In this dream, there had been Barbarian invaders, marauding, and pillaging the land. Women were being raped, children murdered, stone circles overturned, and sacred places destroyed. Our precious homeland, as we knew it, was being devastated by forces that did not care. Karka gave graphic details that told of appalling destruction. It was no ordinary dream. Karka grimly told us that the dream was like living reality, and had the feeling of being visionary and prophetic. It was the culmination of many months of foreboding where he had felt that such an invasion could manifest.

On the day of the storm, he had surrendered to his fate, and his legs had been cut down from under him by a tree that had given its life in service to the land. With his Will, Karka had wished for a different outcome, but he could not avert his injuries and the event that did this to him. He felt that when he returned to the Spirit world, his true home, he would understand why this had to happen, but for now, he did not know.

When Karka then asked Spirit to guide him about the vision he had of the invasion, he was told by Spirit that it was fate that these invaders would come, but the outcome of this intrusion to the land was not fixed. If we came together as a nation, to plan and attune to what was needed with the best of our ability, we might be able to prevent the worst of what would otherwise prevail.

The fact that his injuries were caused by the last act of this magnificent tree of service, and his legs were cut down from under him, this told Karka that this was the end of an era and there was not going to be anything that he personally could do about this. His body had been protected from injury so he could be a messenger, but that was all. His own premonition told him, that he was not going to be there when this invasion took place, and in his dream, he was watching it from above. Like the tree, he had done his work now, and it was his position, as head of the Order, that he now had to surrender.

I understood now how Karka must have struggled while we were walking together, knowing spiritually that he had to release all that was most precious to him – his work and position - and he did not want to do that.

Now Karka paused, and there was a stunned silence in the circle. Karka was openly acknowledging his resignation as leader. But this was only one part of our problems. There was much contemplation about our future as a land. Karka was held in the highest of respect, and his visions had always been received with reverence for the truth that they contained. The peace in our circle was disturbed.

Slowly, I moved my eyes around the gathering and surveyed the Elders sitting there. My attention went first to Berenice, and for a long time, I could not move on from her. I was astonished by what I saw. Her expression was so fierce and gaunt. So much emotion was being held inside her, and yet, I saw flickers of something that I had never witnessed in my former mentor before. In her eyes, there was defiance, but there was also fear. I almost gasped aloud when I noticed this, but I had to keep quiet. She would naturally be Karka's successor, for she was the most senior Elder next to him, but something in me told me that she could not do it. Her energy was closed in, and remote. She was too private and removed. Berenice was not connecting with the others, but isolated within herself.

In my heart, it was obvious to me that if we were to be able to modify and lessen the destructive impact of this invasion, we would need to act together, and harness all our gifts and qualities in harmony, to gain the greatest collective force that we could. We would need a leader that could embrace the people. Just now, I realized, to my horror, that this could not be Berenice.

Then I noticed Karka. He was struggling to stand up. Several of the elders were moving to try to help him, but he insisted on doing this himself, supporting himself with his staff, and trying valiantly to gain balance with his better leg. Everyone once more turned to him. He had not finished yet. The others stepped back, and his voice resonated through the Grove.

He shared how, as he lay beneath the tree, his legs broken, pain searing through his body, peace had descended upon him. It was not the moment for him to leave his body just yet. A further vision enfolded him, and he saw multitudes of people, his people, and they were mainly the younger ones, working together, planning, and supporting one another. Coordinating their efforts was their young leader, and Karka had seen the face clearly. He turned and faced towards me.

With all gathered as witnesses, he told me to arise and come over to him. In surprise, I stood up and did what he commanded me to do. Then, as I placed myself before him, he spoke of me to everyone. He communicated that although I was young, and in many ways, inexperienced, that I had heart, determination and ability. I had proven to him that I could work closely with others, but also that I could make tough decisions, when they were needed. In his vision, it had not been his generation, but the following generation that would act to protect the land. It would be the challenge of my generation, not his. It was a time of change, and the only option if our culture was to survive. Karka had seen my face in his vision, and he had to be true to what Spirit had told him. I did not know what to feel!

Now, I perceived that Karka was calling on his guides to help him, and I could sense a golden shimmer close around Karka's energy field. With this in place, he lifted up his staff, and there was an audible gasp from the gathering. Standing for a few moments on his only usable, though still damaged leg, Karka passed his staff to me. I looked in his eyes with wonder and amazement. Then, when I touched the staff, and grasped it, my body was gushing with energy, so much so, that I could hardly stand. But Karka was wavering, and I had to help him. My friend and teacher had such love and compassion in his eyes, but his physical body was still extremely frail.

With the staff in one hand, I gently motioned my other arm to support him, so gracefully, I could assist him to sit again. Now the eyes of the gathering were upon me.

Karka was exhausted, his energy spent. I could feel a change in the atmosphere of the gathering. There were murmurs, and I could feel disquiet. Not all the members of the circle were happy about my nomination. I tried to sense the source of these feelings, and my eyes were drawn to Berenice. She was looking down, and I felt that in her mind, that she regarded herself as being more capable. My training with her told me that she believed that she could take on the mantle of leadership and do better than me. She obviously felt that she should have been chosen.

I tried to compose myself. My friends were there, and I felt their love and support. Then, before I could do anything, Gracon stood up – I could hardly believe that he would do this. But he was also a seer, and his prophecies had usually been very accurate and insightful. I knew that he had great skill. What he had previously lacked was only confidence. But now he stood to appreciate me, and support my nomination.

I was surprised with the power of how Gracon could project his voice. He spoke eloquently and passionately of my leadership qualities, and how much I had helped him through the course of his life. He spoke of my compassion for others, and my strength. And then he confirmed that he sensed that Karka's prophecy was accurate. Members from the gathering gasped again.

Following his example, others rose to support his case, including Wueli and Dosha, Nianda's teacher. I could feel the tears in my eyes, and the emotion. All this was so unexpected. And yet, behind me, I could feel the power and love of Eurydice, giving me energy, making it very clear that this was my moment, and that I was supported by Spirit.

There was a gust of wind, and the smoke from the fire moved over to me, caressing me, and then made a column upwards before disappearing into the sky. I stood still to acknowledge this blessing from the Earth Spirit as well as the messages given in support of me.

They were waiting now for me to speak. I told the gathered group how humble I felt, and what an honor it was to be given this opportunity, and what a burden of responsibility. Our precious land and people needed to be protected and our bonds together needed to be strengthened. I asked everyone to help. It would only be through acting together, with love and determination, that we could withstand and overcome this impending shadow that lay over our land.

I looked around the circle and felt love and support from nearly everyone. Someone began to hum, and others joined in. Soon the energy of this built up more and more until I felt like the sound of it almost wanted to burst. I invited the circle to hold hands and affirm our bond, so we did that, and I could feel a great enthusiasm, especially from my friends. Something in the peace of this evening made it all right. And yet, it was a sad day for Karka and his colleagues, those who knew that their time had now passed, and I needed to feel that too, with all the spirit of renewal.

When I looked at Karka, his energy was now feeble, and he needed to rest. I did not feel that he would live very long any more, and what great service he had given. When I turned to face Berenice, she was nowhere to be seen. She had gone. I sighed and felt unhappy. It was hard for me to take in what transition was taking place with my two most important teachers. I trembled inside to think about it. But then, as I turned my attention to the others, it was apparent that there was something much greater that I needed to consider than the welfare of two individuals, however significant they had been for everyone. I was aware though that I cared about them and loved them very much.

In my hands, I now had the staff of responsibility for all the land and its people. I fingered it to try to get to know it. I had not expected this, and yet, I could perceive how it made sense. What would I need to do?

At the end of the evening, I stayed in the Grove on my own. I explored the textures and feelings of the staff I had been given. I needed some praying time, and some quietness. There was a huge amount for me to take in, and I had to adjust.

Chapter 11

A dark shadow over the Land

Adjusting to leadership

There was no time to adequately reflect – I found that my ascent to leadership had been both sudden and shocking. I accepted my position but felt overwhelmed by it. In many areas, I was unprepared, and I went to Karka several times, seeking advice. But he shared very little to make it easier for me. He told me that he had passed on to me as much as he could, and that his time was over. Karka suggested that I call meetings with the other Elders to discuss problems and needs, and draw on their experience. He told me that although I could seek their opinions and learn how they would act, that I needed to make my own decisions on behalf of the community and not let anyone else do that for me. Karka impressed on me how being leader could be a very lonely position because I could not share it with anyone. Even my closest friends would be more remote from me now, and there were areas of my being where I would not be able to include them.

I had to adjust to this, but he implored me to keep my heart open. If I became detached or unapproachable, I would lose contact with the people. For me to succeed at my task now, my heart would have to be wide open with the light of compassion, and I would need to let the wisdom of Spirit guide me. Karka said that he had to release me to my task, pray for me, and the land, but let me do it how I willed.

At night time, I struggled to sleep. I had to think now, not just about myself, my friends and family, and what duties I might have, but for the community of our land and how to manage it. I don't think that I would have slept at all during these times, had it not been for Eurydice, and her comforting, loving presence.

My friends tried to support me, especially Nianda. Several times, she offered me healing, and I accepted her offers, as it gave me much needed rest. But I did not know what to share with her, and she was baffled by my silence. Thoughts in my mind were turning around, about Karka's prophecy, about all the various communities. I knew so little. What would happen if I made a mistake, if I did not take the needs of some community group into account sufficiently, if I lost my sense of balance through some personal drive that I had? At times, when Nianda was healing me, I would shake, and it was the fear I needed to cleanse from my system, the fear that I would get it wrong, that I would not be worthy of people's trust in me.

I called meetings, as Karka suggested, and used these meetings to discuss policy, to meditate, to become familiar with the situation in various parts of the land, to learn about procedures I needed to adopt, and about personalities that I would have to deal with in my management. It did help me to learn the thoughts and feelings of the Elders. I came to know both their strengths, and also, in some cases, their prejudices and limits of their visions. I had to be respectful to them, and realize that in my present state of ignorance, I too, would have limitations to my thoughts, and I had very much to learn.

Sometimes, I needed for the Elders to repeat themselves, so I could take in fully what they were trying to communicate. I needed time to understand. During this time, I found that my own psychic visions were not as open as normal. I was putting pressure on myself. So many thoughts were buzzing around.

There was one strong instinct that kept coming into my mind. Within myself, I felt that I needed to promote my youthful friends to positions in the Council of Elders. I needed their support and energy, and they needed to gain experience of management too. We had to pool knowledge and work together. The feeling that we needed to work as a collective group persisted. By doing this, there would be far more wisdom and action that would be possible than if I tried to shoulder everything on my own. It would be better with my friends and young Elders with ability, for them to come into the Inner Circle of meetings and decision making from the beginning. Then we could all grow into it together. Hence, I invited Nianda, Gracon, Wueli, Niend, Mulaid and other young graduates from the Order's training, to attend all the main meetings that we had.

Because of my initiative, attendance at the new Council meetings now were quite large, and the process of decision making, cumbersome, and I thanked all who were present for their patience. With the new additions, we had to formulate guidelines for how we could proceed. I made sure to give space to everyone, and I emphasized the need for us to listen closely to Spirit, and to cooperate as a team. In this early stage of my reign as leader, I needed to instill a sense of group responsibility for our decision making. At this stage, there was still a high degree of good will among the delegates to our meetings. And yet, there was also anxiety about what lay ahead of us.

I made a request to Karka if he could attend some of these early meetings and was pleased that he was willing to do this. His mere presence gave blessings and credence to what we were doing. For the most part, he sat silently, and gave little indication of his thoughts. There was one occasion though, when a group of Elders were indicating their disquiet about whether enough was being done to prepare for averting the impact of the invasion that had been prophesized, when Karka stepped in. He simply informed everyone that we had some time, and reminded us that his own physical life would end before the crisis arrived. Although it was quite shocking for Karka to anticipate his own death, I felt grateful for his input, for it reassured everyone and allayed fears. Karka was aware that we needed time to orientate to this, and to prepare, and that we must not rush or be panicked. Besides the limitations of his crippled leg, Karka was in reasonable health, and he smiled at everyone to confirm this.

Gradually, I felt more at ease and the leadership group became familiar to everyone in it. The only notable absentee from our meetings, was Berenice. She seemed to have retreated into her solitary world, although she continued her work, and maintained the respect from others that she had always carried, I felt that she had disconnected from us. I did not know if Berenice accepted me as leader. She had not spoken to me and I tried not to let it worry me.

Support

At first, I did feel very lonely in my position as leader, but I gradually came to realize that the friends and companions I did have could offer me considerable support.

The two that felt most precious to me were Gracon and Nianda. We had grown up together and knew so much about each other, including our vulnerabilities. There was love between us where I knew that I could rely on both of them, and their loyalty to me and my loyalty to them was sacrosanct. Now, both of these companions had now matured into young adults with considerable skills and growing standing within the Order of the Wise.

Nianda, of course, was a fine healer, and her knowledge of healing had become very extensive. Gracon was a 'sensitive'. He had great affinity with the Earth Spirit and was able to work with energy to restore harmony in places within the energy grid where disturbances had occurred. With his psychic gifts, he could see into the future, and I often sought his guidance as to possible outcomes in matters where my own perception could not fully grasp implications within a situation. Gracon continued to confirm the prophecy given by Karka, and with his perception, suggested that the threat was like a fire that needed to be put out. Gracon felt that the aggressors were from a land across the sea, to the north east. They were a barbarian people that did not understand our way, or our Spirituality. They lived by their instincts and their greed. We would need to be cunning and well prepared to be able to repel them.

When I went on travels, Gracon and Nianda would usually accompany me. Gracon preferred a private role for his work and was glad for me to accept the limelight and the responsibility for meeting with people and communities that we visited. While I was meeting with groups and working out policies within communities, Nianda would help individuals and offer Spiritual counseling while Gracon worked with the energetic health of the places we visited and liaised with those responsible for upholding ceremonies and the Spiritual well-being of the people.

I was grateful for all the traveling work that I had done with Berenice, in my youth, and more recently, with Karka. From this, I had gained friends and contacts with various settlements in the land – people that knew me and would support me. But there were still many places where I had not been, and in these less familiar territories, many were skeptical of my leadership.

The purpose of my visits to communities had now changed. Whereas previously, I had been primarily concerned with sorting out problems for the community so it could function better, or administering what Karka had set out for me to do, now I needed to assert my authority, and bring communities together so they would be more prepared for what would be coming.

I was a new leader, I was young, and I had no reputation to go before me. It would be necessary for me to gain respect, not only from the group of Elders, but from the people in our communities as well. I felt I had to prove myself to everyone so the people would be willing to listen to me. Karka may have told us that we had time, but within me, I felt urgency, and wanted to act.

In one village, there were squabbles between members of the leading family, a father and two sons. When I sat down to talk with them, I could sense that they had no interest to listen to me. After all, I was a stranger, and a woman. Why should they take notice of me? I could feel anger build up inside me. How dare they not respect me?

I used my eyes and the power of my intention to attempt to focus their attention, but they still would not listen. When one of the brothers decided that he had had enough, and stood up to leave, I raised the power of my voice and slammed my staff on the ground, and energy bristled from its end. I commanded for him to sit down. They were shocked and astonished, and the brother sat down immediately. Then we were able to start sorting things out.

That was when I realized that I had power that I could use, and the staff helped me, because it was a conductor of energy, and for many generations had accompanied the leader of our land. I had felt the crackling of energy from the staff when I slammed it down. From now on, I would not hesitate to use the staff if I felt someone was disrespecting me. I would not be passive.

Rebellion

For a while, our work as a team was productive, and I felt that I was building up my own network, and gaining respect within the communities. But rumors about the nature of the possible invasion that was coming provoked a growing sense of unease within the land. Rather than forming links between communities, many settlements were building their own fortifications so they could protect themselves more fully against danger. Fear was spreading isolation. Added to this, we had two dry summers where the rains did not come, and the crops failed. Conditions were hard, and people began to feel that perhaps the current leadership was not supported by the Earth Spirit, and that we needed to find another way.

Somehow, I needed help; I needed people to believe in our union, and our capacity to work together to deal with our problems collectively. If we stayed in isolation, our society would be destroyed when the invaders came. I did not know how I could accomplish this transformation.

I sent out Elders to the far corners of the land. We led rituals, tried to reassure people and bring them together, but people had little food, and our words seemed increasingly empty.

I could not stay still either, and I immersed myself in travel, from one place to the next, from community to community, never ceasing. But more and more in my heart, I began to doubt. Maybe Karka had chosen wrongly, and I was not the right person for the job? I prayed each night. But all that came back to me from Eurydice was for me to be patient, and to listen closely to Spirit. This, I agreed to do. But it did not allay my anxieties.

There was news from my family. Conditions were very unsettled with my parents. By now, my younger brother and sister, Luend and Sealbow, both wished to study with the Order of the Wise, but had been held back by the situation in the land. My parents struggled to deal with the vacillations of my elder brother, Skife. And he was causing a lot of difficulties.

For a long time, I had tried to ignore the problems that I could perceive coming from that direction. I did not feel that I could be seen as being distracted by my own domestic difficulties when there was so much of wider importance that needed my attention. However, as I let my own behavior be modified by what I felt that others might think, there was an uneasy feeling in my heart and I felt that I was betraying myself somehow. I could not do this. I had to be true to my heart and its wishes.

Skife was stirring up trouble in the local community where my parents lived. I called a meeting with the other Elders to discuss it. I shared my own reservations about spending energy attending to this, but as the Elders listened and we discussed the issues, we sensed collectively that the challenges coming from this direction were actually quite serious, and needed to be addressed. This was because Skife was starting to involve other people in his reactions to me. The negativity he was propagating was growing beyond the village of my family home. He was trying to stir up as much trouble as he could.

I still held the uncomfortable feelings inside me of the resentment and hostility that Skife had expressed towards me when we were little. His feelings towards me had clearly not changed. I learned that Skife had trained to be a warrior within the village where my parents lived, but had done this without my father's support. Now, he was adamant, with all the talk of invasion, that it should be the warriors to take charge and meet this challenge. With two dry summers and crop failures, his thought was that the Order of the Wise were not up to the job, and these crop failures were indications that the Earth Spirit was not supporting the Order either. Skife criticized my leadership directly, and spoke of me being too young and inexperienced, of being reckless, and of not having a clear focus.

Skife was summoning support for his views, by visiting many settlements in the region. His stance held a resonance for many of those that listened to him. Skife argued that people should put their faith and trust in the warriors, for they were strong and could defend the Land. What could the Order do?

I needed to meet my parents, and traveled to do that. It was a long time since I had physically been with them, although I watched over them regularly with my psychic faculties. To meet them in the flesh confronted me with the reality of their condition and was very emotional for both me and them.

In my first impressions, I was surprised and saddened about how old they had both become – and my mother was ill. They were both very relieved to see me, but there was such a lot of pain within them. Neither of them could condone what Skife was doing. With my mother, I could sense a deep despair, and I felt that she was almost torn in two. On the one side, it was clear that as one of her children, she could not reject her love for Skife, who was her child, however he was conceived. But as a priestess of the Order of the Wise, and with all the feelings of loyalty she had towards me and the fabric of the society in which we lived, she felt utter revulsion towards Skife and his actions and could not reconcile these different parts of her. As I gazed at her energy field, I could perceive a torrent of swirling energy that was weakening her by the day. I asked Nianda to attend to her urgently, and she tried to help, but Nianda told me that she could do little more than ease the pain.

In my father's case, his response was utter rage and contempt. Within his heart, he had struggled throughout Skife's life to accept him and the way his existence had come about. He wanted to confront Skife and fight him, and I could tell that he carried underlying resentment towards my mother for continuing to be loyal to him. Both my parents were experiencing acute torment, and it was hard to be able to help them.

In their relationship together, they appeared to be even more distant from each other than when I had left them. They shared the same house, but for most of the time, barely spoke to each other.

I counseled my father not to intervene. He must be patient, and trust. My father did not want to hear this. And he argued with me. Imploring my father to withhold his anger felt disempowering to him. He felt that he had done this all of Skife's life, but now, surely, the limits of his tolerance for Skife had been breached. My father had to listen to me! I could sense no good coming from a possible fight between Skife and my father, and I also needed to consider the larger picture. It was difficult, but I could not condone my father venting his anger at my brother now. If he did, it would only weaken the position of the Order of the Wise further. My father was very disappointed.

The threats of this rebellion and the possible invasion that Karka had foreseen, could be overcome, but it needed peaceful and intelligent cooperation and not violent confrontation between our people. The fabric of our society was based upon our nurturing the connectedness that we shared. We must not betray that. My conviction was that we needed to act together. Violence would only beget violence, and to begin a cycle of fighting between our own people would only bring ruin to our land. Infighting was not a viable way forward if we were to successfully confront the menace that was approaching us.

After spending time with my parents, I spoke to representatives from the village, and tried to calm them and reassure them, but although they listened to me, I sensed that they were uneasy and questioning. I made little progress, and could not resolve their fears and uncertainties. These people needed hope and some tangible aspirations that they could work towards. I did not know what to offer them.

In despair, I broke off the meeting, and retreated to the family home to be on my own. How could I unite the people and motivate them? In this situation, for the people to be kind towards each other, and to respect our traditions, was not enough. I needed some inspiration, or else, we would be overcome.

Just then, I could sense the energetic presence of Wueli wanting to communicate with me telepathically. As I listened to his thoughts, he told me that there had been a hostile raid in another part of our land. Two villages had been razed and women and children raped and abducted. Many people had been killed and injured. This attack had taken place on the north east coast, in a quite remote community within our land. But it was an area where the people were friendly and loyal to our Order. What was more worrying was that location of the raid was directly in the vicinity of where Gracon had predicted the invasion would originate.

Wueli was concerned that as news of this incursion spread that it would engender panic and fear amongst the people. I asked Wueli about Karka's health and he assured me that Karka was fine, so I instructed Wueli to use that as a means to reassure the people. Even so, I could feel my own pulse racing, and fear was extending through my being.

I called for Nianda and Gracon and shared with them about what Wueli had told me. Gracon tuned in and assured me that he sensed this to be an isolated incident. He did not perceive any further incursions following directly from this. But, as I looked into my friend's eyes, I saw fear, and his skin was pale. With this raid, the threat of invasion had come one big step closer. And, if Gracon felt fear, how would the people in that area, especially, react?

They would be very anxious and need to know that steps were being taken to protect them. The whole situation had suddenly become much more urgent and grave, and I knew that we were not doing enough.

The timing for the forecast invasion was still in the future, but the need to prepare for that and for our people to gather forces together to meet this challenge when it came, was with us now.

Bewilderment

The next weeks were frantic, with meetings, communication across regions of the land, and Elders being rushed to places where there was reported uprising and discontent. There was an echo in various parts of the land about the need for warriors to take a more leading role, and there were many movements proposing that local militia be formed so villages could defend their own settlements. For me, this would only fragment our society, and was the opposite of what we needed to do.

The fact that the past two summers had been so dry, leading to crop failures, had brought into question, in many people's minds, if the new leadership were the best people for looking after the land and its people, and whether we were capable of dealing with the situation at hand. When people were hungry, there were less contented, and more inclined to want to look after their own interests, less willing to pray to the Earth Spirit for support. Sadly though, the doubts that the people had about the leadership was reflected in myself, and increasingly, I held thoughts about whether I should resign as leader.

It was an unceasing struggle, the effort to try and reassure and satisfy the people and to build their confidence and trust in the leadership, while also searching for some course of action that could be effective in meeting the challenges to come.

In conjunction with all this, there were also persistent reports about Skife and the people he had gathered around him, that he was gathering some form of army to take over from the present leadership, and establish a more military government under his command.

My mind was so busy with all this, that it was little wonder that I became exhausted. One day, I could not do it anymore, and I asked Wueli to deal with the administration while I rested.

As I went to my hut, I had little hope that there were any more initiatives that I could make. Desperately, I called on Spirit to help me, and Eurydice, but there was silence, only the urging for me to be still. Whatever this test was all about, they in Spirit were not going to do it for me. I was on my own. With all the anxiety that I felt, it was very difficult for me to be still. At night, I had been struggling to sleep; there were so many thoughts and restless worries. But that evening, after sitting for some considerable time in the darkness, staring into space, I finally gave up my will, and surrendered to sleep, and entered my inner world of unknowing, having put aside my doubts and fears.

Peace and confrontation

In the morning, I awoke with a strange sense of calm. Somehow, I knew that today would be a special day, but I did not know the context; it puzzled me; I would have to trust and open to what Spirit brought forward.

The autumn dew made the ground wet, but it was one of those days where the air was crisp and clear, and the visual details of the local environment with the hills and the forest were as concise as they could be. Such days were rare, and made me rejoice about being alive. For these moments, I could allow myself to enjoy this space. I breathed in and could sense the quiet vibration of the Earth Spirit.

With sensitive deliberation, I walked down that familiar track to the Sacred Grove and my favorite Yew tree. As I reached the tree, I could feel its love, and its great sense of history and belonging to this land. Tenderly, I caressed its branches in appreciation. Then I sat down with my back resting against the trunk of the tree in meditation, soaking up the peace emanating from this beautiful sacred place. I spoke my prayers, wishing peace for the land, and asking for guidance that I could be a worthy vessel to lead and help in the best way possible. As I did that, I could feel myself drifting within, to an inner place of silence that felt very soothing.

It must have been some time later when I was roused, because, as I looked up, I saw that the sun had moved some distance across the sky. Wueli was there beside me, and his manner was nervous and agitated. He had news, and needed support from my authority so he could act.

There were intruders that had been seen approaching our College settlement. They were a large number of warriors led by my brother, Skife, and they had weapons. In Wueli's assessment, they were hostile, and their intent appeared destructive. Wueli wanted my permission for him to post the warriors we had here in the College, so they would be placed around our settlement as an attempt to defend it, and for our other residents to be instructed to retreat to safety.

So, my brother was coming for me. It had been predicted, and all the signs had been there that he would do this. I asked Wueli if he thought we had enough warriors to defend the College from this attack, and after a pause, Wueli shook his head. We were a peaceful people, and we were not equipped for war.

Suddenly, I knew that a great test was upon me. I breathed in the energy of Spirit from around me, and implored Spirit to make me strong. What would these warriors want to do? When I questioned Wueli further about how many warriors were in this party, it seemed that there could be hundreds of them. In numbers, they would vastly outnumber the few warriors that we had to protect our College. If Skife wanted to destroy our College settlement, then we would not be able to stop them with physical force. We would have to find another way.

At that moment, I felt connected to my core, and I could sense my strength with the Earth supporting me. I could visualize myself standing on the edge of our village, alone, and speaking with Skife. I checked with my inner being, and that is what I had to do. I needed to be at the front, for I could put no one before me. These warriors would have to meet me, and they would need to witness me with my brother.

I told Wueli this, and he was shocked. He could not agree to my plan, and insisted instead that he bring his warriors and himself, to stand by my side. Looking in his eyes, I told him clearly that I had to do this myself, and that he and the other warriors from our settlement needed to stand well back to give me that space.

Wueli argued with me, for he knew the hatred that Skife felt for me. He did not want my safety compromised or in danger. But I was certain I had to do this as I had seen it. I was not a girl anymore, but a grown woman and chosen leader. Nobody could be there with me, for this was my time, and I had to act on my own; I had to meet his hostility with my commitment, determination and clarity.

I could sense Wueli's fear and concern, and his love for me. It was his job to protect, and he was doing his job now, and what he thought was best. But there was a knowing in me that my mission in my life depended upon what I did next, and I was determined, with a clear sense of purpose, to fulfill my destiny.

I knew that Wueli did not want to leave me on my own to face Skife; he feared that Skife was unpredictable and he was unsure how well I could communicate with him. Others would also be against me going out to meet him alone, and they would want to keep me safe too. But this was the time when I needed to stand in my power, and trust that power. This was the moment for me to assert my truth as leader of the people, and if the Earth Spirit wanted me to take on this task, and to do what Karka had bequeathed for me to do, then Spirit needed to look after me. I had the love of the land in my heart, and that is what I wanted to express. I counseled Wueli to look after the others, and if anything did happen to me, he must ensure that the others were protected. For a few moments, I gazed appreciatively in the eyes, and then I motioned him to go, and he reluctantly did so, after exchanging the briefest of hugs. I was fortunate enough to have people around me that did genuinely care for me, and I never wanted to take that for granted.

But now I picked up the Staff given to me by Karka, and headed to the rise at the edge of the village, where I would wait for my brother to arrive. Here there was a clearing. My feet felt steady, and as I stood in my white robe, holding the staff in my right hand, I prayed for inner support and strength to see this through.

Ilsa

Once I turned around and I saw a crowd of other members of the Community. They were watching from outside the huts at the boundary of our settlement, and Wueli was keeping them there, preventing them from coming closer – as I had instructed. Amongst them, I could see my closest friends, Nianda and Gracon, and they were watching silently, straining to see every movement and hear every sound. In some of those gathered there, I felt stillness, and that they were praying in support of me. In others I could sense fear and anxiety. I turned back now so I could face towards Skife and his warriors. That was where I had to have my attention.

Finally, I became aware of the warriors approaching. I heard them before I saw them. As they emerged from the woodland, they spread out and made a long line and approached together as a group. Some of them were beating drums. They were war drums, and had a harsh menacing vibration. The sight and sound of all these warriors was most intimidating. It was Skife, striding out in front of the others, and he was riding on some kind of animal that looked like a horse. He looked very comfortable, and almost imperious. Skife wore colorful clothes and protective skins, and carried with him an impressive looking spear. As they came closer, the beating drums became more violent, and the men began to roar; a menacing collective roar intended to engender fear. I could sense members of the Order behind me step back, but I did not flinch.

Skife motioned the others to pause and then he dismounted and stepped towards me. Even though I was alone, he was wary of me somehow. It puzzled me that Skife could have managed to attract such numbers of warriors to walk with him. My knowledge of him had assumed him to be living as an outcast and a loner, not close to anyone. However, as I looked at him now, there was a confidence about him, and I perceived that for him to become part of the warrior group had given him a sense of belonging and identity, a field of endeavor where he could excel. The others behind him looked up to him, and Skife relished this appreciation of his skills.

When they saw me though and saw that I was not frightened, they became quiet and also hung back. It was only my brother that dared to come forward.

But then I could hear scuffles behind me, and I could tell that the number of onlookers from the Order was growing, and they were shuffling closer to me. They must have decided that they could not leave me alone with this. But that was not my wish. I turned towards them, looking sternly at them, and motioned for them to stop. I kept staring at them until they did so. Then I again turned to face Skife.

It was possible for me to feel the coldness of Skife's energy as he tentatively stepped towards me. He was only moving very slowly, and he kept glancing at my staff, as if it might threaten him. Although he tried to look in control, I could tell that he was actually quite anxious. His body twitched and I wondered if he was suspicious of my powers, and what I might do with him. He did not know what Berenice and the other Elders had taught me.

To help with his courage, Skife turned to his warriors and directed them to close in, and form a band of support behind him. They did this hesitantly, but Skife continued to maintain a healthy distance from me. He tried to assert himself by raising himself up and he told his men to be still. Then he started to speak.

I had not heard Skife since he was a boy, and I was interested to hear what he sounded like. He had a low voice, but it was loud and clear, and he projected it well; He must have been practicing for this.

'Ilsa, my sister, you have let down the people of this Land. There is danger at hand, and you do nothing. There has been no rain. The Gods show their displeasure. You are weak; you are not worthy, and our land needs strong leadership. We warriors can defend the land much better than you. We have come to take charge. Move aside – we have come to take your place!'

Skife took a few steps forward and raised his spear, and his men looked on, and raised their spears with him, but I continued to stare at him, and did not move.

Ilsa

Now it was my turn. I slammed the staff into the ground, and a crackle of energy formed a vibration that spread through the ground around me. Upward through my body, I could feel the strength of the Earth Spirit. I felt power. The warriors must have felt it too, for they stepped back and looked at each other in fear and surprise.

'Skife, I would not be here unless I believed that it is my right and destiny to do this task. The Order of the Wise comes from a great tradition of Spiritual leadership with the intention of bringing peace and harmony to our land. The way of the warrior is to fight, and fighting will beget more fighting. And fighting will divide our land, and bring destruction and unhappiness to the people and to our beloved Earth Spirit. We cannot defeat this foreign enemy by fighting alone. They have superior force and will defeat us that way. By fighting, we will play into their hands. We must work together, Skife, in cooperation, and preserve our traditions, and find a way through our unity to repel any intrusion that they can bring. There is an important place for the warriors in this, and I invite representatives from the warriors and from your group to join us as we meet and work out a strategy of unity to decide how we can preserve our land and use our strength and the love we share together to uphold our values.'

For a moment, I paused and then continued, looking straight in his eyes.

'I am happy to meet with you, my brother, and for us to find peace together.'

Inside my mind, I could hear a voice whispering to me, 'Be true to who you are Ilsa. Do not play his game. Be true....'

Suddenly, I knew what I needed to do, and although it was not easy, I placed my Staff down in front of me in a gesture of good will, so I would be completely disarmed.

'I come in peace to you, Skife'.

I stretched out my arms so I would be able to take his hands. But he didn't want that. The warriors and my people were both silent, and watching with intense anticipation.

Skife was clearly uncomfortable with my stance and my words. He did not want cooperation, but a fight. He wanted a reason to defeat me, to humiliate me and impose his might. Skife spat down at my staff and edged backwards. He shouted more loudly, trying to call out to everyone. My gesture had confused him.

'You are weak Ilsa. Your words are empty. You have no power over me.'

In his mind, Skife could not comprehend my actions. It made no sense to him, and he was trembling. In my heart, I attempted to project love to him, but he blocked it.

Skife came forward again slightly, but the other warriors did not join him. The atmosphere around us was becoming very charged, and I could feel the love of the Earth Spirit and my attunement to it. The others were joining in, and from the Order behind me, some of them were starting to hum.

Skife was becoming more desperate. All the feelings of jealousy, and sense of inferiority towards me, that he held, were coming to the fore. The love and peace we projected only served to draw these feelings out more strongly. I could perceive his inner state as a red energy streaming from him. I had to ask Spirit for protection, and a voice inside me ordered me to stand firm. But the more I stood there, the more frantic Skife became.

The Staff in front of me on the ground was giving out this immense energy of calm and peace. I gave inner encouragement for this to continue, and chose to focus on this rather than any vulnerability I would have felt otherwise. The energy from the Earth was radiating outwards, and the volume of the humming was increasing. It seemed to make Skife less secure and unsettled. He was looking around him uneasily.

I shifted my stance so I could be more open towards Skife. At that moment, I could feel both love and pity towards him. I spoke again, with love in my heart, repeating what I had already said: 'I invite you to work together with me for peace, Skife.'

'No'. He shouted defiantly, in rebellion. 'You must die.'

He lifted his spear, and I knew what he would do. There were gasps behind me, and the humming stopped abruptly. In this moment, I had to stand still, even though this meant that I would be a target for Skife. His back arched slightly, and he extended his arm behind him, holding the spear tightly. He could have stopped there, but he didn't. There was a look of seething madness and fierce intent in his eyes. I could not change him. He threw the spear.

In those moments, I stood transfixed. The memory returned to me from early in my life, of the deer in the woods, when I had been with my father and he was sharing his hunting skills, and I was a child in awe of him. But the motivation of Skife and my father was so different. Was I to be a willing sacrifice like that deer?

I also had the memory flooding into my consciousness of all the interactions I had had with Skife in my young days, from the attack in the woods, the boulder he threw down at me when I was going to the College, to all the looks of hostility he had given me. And Spirit had helped me through those interactions, and urged me always, for me to stand up to Skife without fear. Could I do that now? I had to do it.

The spear arced towards me, and in my awareness, I knew that it was directed towards the middle of my chest. Skife was an excellent spear thrower. The target would surely be reached. When the spear penetrated me, I would die. Yet, as all this was happening, I felt strangely calm, as if I could witness it all in wonderful slow motion. And with this happening, a voice inside me was shouting at me, telling me to trust and to be still. Vaguely, I was aware of screams of panic coming from behind in the direction of my friends in the College settlement. I did not want to leave them; it felt too soon, far too soon. The spear was traveling rapidly closer, and I decided to surrender myself to fate, and place myself completely in Spirit's hands for what I needed to experience.

In that instant, there was a change, and a force pushed sharply through me, shifting my body slightly, just enough, so I was jolted to one side. It was only an instant before the spear would impact upon me. The spear was still coming, and I could not avoid it, and my body shuddered in anticipation.

Then it was there, like an explosion, and the thud of the spear into my shoulder was massively painful. I could feel myself collapsing to the ground and soon into unconsciousness. The shock was terrible. My body was writhing in agony as my consciousness drifted away.

Aftermath

Normally, with an injury, I would have left my body to reduce the stress. I had done it many times. But on this occasion, I had stayed too long, right to the moment of impact. And the shock had been too much for me. I had collapsed into unconsciousness, and knew nothing of what happened.

When my consciousness finally started to stir, I was aware of being inside, and lying on the bed. My eyes did not want to open, but I could tell with the smell of the oils that I was in the healing tent. It was warm and I was covered with skins and cloth. Nianda was there; I knew by her energy. However, there were many other people there too; I could hear them and sense their presence.

I must have drifted away again, for as I began to regain consciousness for a second time, I was ready to open my eyes, and I saw all the people there watching over me. Some of them were crying and distressed. It was very emotional. Nianda stopped them from coming too close. She was smiling; she must have been delighted that I had opened my eyes.

I looked down at my body, and the spear was gone, but my body was drenched in blood, and I felt so weak. I could only move the tiniest amount. Nianda tried to give me some liquid to drink. I coughed and spluttered but some of it must have gone down, for I was soon drifting away again.

This happened several times until I was finally more alert and able to listen and speak a little. Nianda was still there, and it was night time. She was with me on her own, and she asked if I was ready to hear the story of what had happened after I was hit? I nodded to her, and she smiled.

Nianda related to me how when the spear was thrown, everyone came forward, including the warriors. They were all concerned, and we were all frantic to save you. Many of the warriors were inconsolable and felt they had done the wrong thing. Some of them tried to capture Skife, but he span away out of reach and got on his horse.

Apparently, Wueli, in particular, was desperate to apprehend Skife, but Skife was too quick, and somehow managed to weave his way free. This did not stop Wueli, and he continued to pursue Skife with every ounce of his energy and he ordered his own warriors to go with him. Even though they were on foot, Wueli was not going to give up.

They had only just returned, and were unsuccessful in their search. At some stage, Wueli realized that my well-being mattered more than finding Skife. He told us how he had felt that he had failed in his job in allowing Skife to throw his spear, and he projected his anger with himself and frustration, by obsessively trying to find Skife. But he had come back to his heart in the midst of the chase, and then abandoned the pursuit. This reminded me so much of what had happened with my father, but I was so glad Wueli had decided to return.

News had traveled rapidly about the confrontation, and many settlements were conducting healing rituals for my recovery. There had been a great outpouring of sympathy and grief for the injury that I had sustained.

Nianda looked at me intently, and with relief in her eyes, to share that I had the people behind me now. There had been a great transformation.

Although this made me happy, it made me want to rouse myself, but my body was far too weak. As soon as I tried to sit up, my body sank back again.

With my inner eyes, I saw Eurydice looking at me. She too, was smiling at me, and I knew then that Spirit had been at work. I was glad to be alive.

Meeting to gather our forces

For a long period after the attack, I had to rest, and I slept for long periods. During this time, I had to delegate the day-by-day running of our government, to the Council, and trust in their judgments. There was impatience in me to be active again, and on several occasions, I tried to raise myself upwards, only to feel so weak, that I needed to collapse again. I would have felt despair about this but for the presence of Spirit reassuring me and giving me peace. Nianda continued to administer healing, while Gracon liaised with me from the Council to inform me about developments in the communities within the land.

While I rested, I had many thoughts entering my mind about what we needed to do as a leading body, and how we could best face the challenges that were facing our people. I felt that we needed to act more as a nation rather than as a conglomerate of disparate groups all acting independently with a loose thread of guidance coming from the College of the Order of the Wise. We needed to coordinate our activities and work out strategies for building our defense. Someone with suitable knowledge needed to take charge of this. If we were to combat this enemy, we also needed to gain a stronger sense of who we were as people together, and a collective vision of what we wanted to achieve.

I shared these thoughts with Gracon and he offered to call a meeting with representatives from various quarters of the Land, and that this meeting could be held as soon as I was fit enough to attend.

Gradually, I did gain strength, and I was very relieved when the day of this meeting arrived, and I was able to be carried in a litter to the meeting area near the Sacred Grove.

Such a large gathering of people were there; I had not expected this. And Gracon was chairing the meeting. He invited me to address the gathering, and I was able to thank them all for their attendance and for all their support during my convalescence.

Gracon's assertiveness surprised me, but he was standing quite calmly, and people were listening. As I surveyed those that were present, I noticed that both Karka and Berenice were present, even though Karka was being propped up by attendants, and looked very frail. Berenice sat a bit apart, silently watching every move, but somehow preoccupied, as if she was in another world. I felt both her love and her detachment, and was grateful when, for a few moments, our eyes met, and she gave a rare smile. Among other people there were Elders that I did not recognize, including members of northern tribes – I could distinguish them by their clothes and demeanor. However, even with the volume of people present, the atmosphere of the meeting had unity and purpose.

Various speakers rose to introduce themselves and speak what issues were most important for them. Many condemned the attack upon me and the raid that had taken place. There was a strong current of thought suggesting that we needed a national force of warriors that would serve and administer the wishes of the Order of the Wise, a group of warriors that would act to defend our land and its entire people, and not act independently to usurp power for their own gain and interests.

When they were all finished, I was supported to stand, and I searched for my power inside to project my voice. Firstly, I acknowledged the strength of feeling about forming a national force of warriors to defend our land from the forecast attacks. I spoke of a need for us to establish a sense of our nationhood, so we could act together to ensure the security and safety for our people. We needed to build purpose into our lives to bring about a transformation in our way of relating together, so this would come, not just from the dictates of the administration of the Order of the Wise, but from everyone. We needed to focus on our Spiritual rituals, but also how we could cooperate together. What was vital was for someone to step forward who could act as a military commander for the operation of repelling the raiders and keeping our land safe – someone with skill but also commitment to serve the people and be respectful of the rule of the Order of the Wise.

There was a pause, and Wueli stood up. He told the gathering that there was a man and his partner, who could do the job we needed. There was a hush in the gathering as Wueli prepared to speak.

He told the story of this man's life. When he was a child, his parents had been killed by raiders, the same race of people that were threatening our shores now. He had been held captive and taken away to a foreign land in their boats. For months, he had endured torture and abuse, being made a slave to obey these people's dictates. His partner had also been held there. But eventually, after much planning, the two of them had made a daring escape, and in one of the boats of the barbarian raiders, they had fled the fortress where they had been held, and completed an almost miraculous journey back to our homeland.

This experience had left its scars, but had also given the two of them lasting impressions of what these people were like, and what we could expect from them. They had formed a group that patrolled the coastline and had repelled many parties of raiders that had subsequently tried to ravage coastal communities. They had studied also with some of the Master Elders of our northern lands, and had a good working knowledge of the interconnectedness of life in our land, and the efforts we needed to make to respect that and work in harmony with it.

I asked Wueli where we could find those two people, and he then gestured and pointed to a couple that were seated next to him, introducing them to us all.

They both rose up, and held each other's hand. The man's name was Verdiff, and he was a well-built man with thinning hair and piercing eyes. The woman sitting with him was smaller and so slight. Her name was Chrisong. They looked very different from each other, but their energy seemed to blend together.

I realized that I had never met these people before, and they were from an older, more experienced generation than mine. But when Verdiff met my gaze, there was a gentle look of kindness and determination in his eyes. Immediately I knew that he was someone that I could trust. As a pair, I sensed that they had traveled through many struggles together.

I invited Verdiff to tell us his ideas, so we could assess them. So he started. He spoke about how he felt it as an inner mission and purpose that he and Chrisong shared that they would be instruments in the defeat of these hostile forces. They had quietly known it as their destiny from the time when they found their way back to our land. With our Order finally preparing for this confrontation, they now could speak and do their work.

As I looked now towards Verdiff, I could perceive a light around his energy field. It was as if Spirit was bringing his soul forward at this time for us to gain knowledge of him and what he could offer to us, as an answer to our prayers.

Verdiff was of the opinion that the barbarian raiders would only want to stay in our land if they considered it to be worthwhile for them, so we needed to ensure that this would not be the case. He proposed that, as a priority, all communities on the east side of our land would need to be evacuated and relocated in another part of the land, at least until the danger passed. If these raiders had no settlements as pickings for their desires and greed, then the purposes for their raids would not be satisfied. They would feel the need to search elsewhere for their plunder, and might leave our land in peace. The prophecy had indicated that this would not be a small scale raid, but a full invasion party, and if we did not deflect them from their aims with complete commitment and coordination on our part, then they could settle and subjugate us to their wills. Verdiff continued and spoke in much more detail about what he felt we would need to do. His plans were well thought out.

Karka nodded in agreement, and there were murmurs in the gathering as we all took in what Verdiff said. Within my heart, his strategy made sense to me and felt right. It backed up the need I had put forward for our communities to work together, so we could all prepare for this.

I turned to Gracon to consult with him about how much time we may still have, and he replied that in his estimate, we may have not much more than one sun cycle to complete before the attempted invasion would come, but that smaller raids would most likely continue in between times until then. The need for organizing our defense forces and those evacuations to commence was urgent.

Verdiff and Chrisong sat down, and the proposals that they made were accepted and plans were put in place to implement them. The resolve amongst all present at the meeting was steadfast and there was a great atmosphere of relief for us to have some form of plan that we could activate. I felt, with all the public representatives that now attended this meeting that the drive for what must be achieved would not only be present in the leadership of the Order of the Wise, but could be nurtured in general public opinion as well.

As the meeting dissipated, I felt relieved and was glad that I had been fit enough to attend. As I waited for aid to be able to return to the hut, I looked across at Karka. He, too, was needing assistance, and I felt disturbed by how weakened he looked. It appeared that in a short space of time, much of his essential life energy had receded. I did not feel that there was very much left.

Karka's death

Over the next weeks, with all the frenetic activity, meetings and planning, I felt an underlying sadness at the edge of my consciousness, which would not shift. In many ways, I did not want to explore what it was telling me because I knew that I would not like it.

Then, one morning, I woke up and heard shouts, and the sound of running. I could stand up now, and had sufficient strength to walk short distances. As I looked out of the entrance to my hut, I could see a small crowd of people gathering around Karka's hut. The awareness of what was happening came to me in a flash. I felt a shudder through my body. Karka had left his body. He had done it silently, and on his own. His time had come, and he knew it. I felt sadness welling up in my heart. He had been my friend and mentor. I owed so much to him. Now he was gone. In the time leading to his passing, he had withdrawn from people, staying in his hut and sending away visitors. His public life had been over for some time, and in his last days, for his own reasons, he preferred to be on his own. I could sense that even in his Spirit being, he had withdrawn a long way. He had not wanted goodbyes, but to go quietly, and let life move on.

I staggered over to his hut, supported by my staff, and others stepped back to let me in. Karka's body lay serenely on his bed. There was a slight smile and peace about him. It was possible to observe that Karka must have felt acceptance for his body to die. I believed that he would have left or his own accord, knowing that he could do that in harmony with the needs of his soul.

His contribution to our Community and the land was immense, and yet, the manner of his death suggested to me that it was not the time to create a big ceremony to honor him. Something quiet and reverent would do. There were other challenges for all of us to face just now. The fact that Karka had now died fulfilled another piece of the prophecy to indicate the approach of the threat to our land and its people that would soon be upon us. The timing of his death seemed perfect to me, although the thought of not having his presence with us brought sadness for me and the community, and there would be many to grieve his loss. I felt fortunate in that he had passed onto me all the knowledge that he could, and even though our association was inevitably drastically affected by the trauma of the lightning strike, I felt that he had completed with me, what he had to do.

I gazed around at those assembled in the room, and there were many crying and bent down, taking in their loss. Within myself, I began to say my own goodbyes to my mentor. I felt a great outpouring of love and gratitude from my soul, and I prayed for his personal evolution of Spirit, knowing that I would meet his soul again.

At last, I rose to go, to leave room for others who would want to be here, when the flap of cloth at the entrance of the hut opened, and Berenice entered. In her eyes, I saw distress, but she also carried with her, an atmosphere of passionate defiance. Her energy was like a whirlwind, as I watched her, and she examined every detail of Karka's body and demeanor. Her expression was intense and other people stood back to give her space. Just as suddenly as she had come, she went again, out of the entrance and walking swiftly away. Beneath her very active exterior, I felt that Berenice was deeply affected by Karka's death. It must have been devastating for her, for they had been so closely linked. In her isolation, I wished somehow, that I could help Berenice. She was someone who seemed to have lost the thread of her link with others in our community, and the place that she had carved out for herself in our Order was one that seemed no longer to operate in reference to others.

As I returned to my own hut, I was grateful to meet Nianda and to receive some healing from her. It was an interesting time, and my intuition told me that there could be more dramas to unfold. But for now, it was a time to reflect on Karka, all that he had contributed to our lives, and give thanks with joy for all that this entailed.

A new addition

Karka's funeral pyre was attended by many, and the ceremony for this was carried out with great solemnity and reverence. It was noted how much energy Karka had put into bringing co-ordination and a sense of shared Spiritual purpose into our nation. It was work that was far from complete. His laughter and ability to relate to all people that he met was remembered with awe. And until his traumatic injury, his efforts at communication with people had been tireless and positive.

When we considered the end of his life and the message that this had for us, it was about how Karka had needed to release his own efforts completely and pass them on to others to fulfill. No doubt, he had had his struggles with this; he would have gained so much personal satisfaction from his work. But he was a person who served the greater good, and the manner in which he had released his own position was an example to us all. The opportunity was there for us to embrace the work that Karka had done, and to carry this forward. With my own process of releasing him, I had done private meditation and prayers to Spirit, but in the public light of Karka's funeral ceremony, it was something where we were able to ask the Spirits to help us to do as a collective.

There were many of us that had inward visions of Karka during the ceremony. We shared these with each other. In all of them, he was smiling and encouraging us. As the fire of his pyre burned down, a great feeling of peace spread through our group.

For me, it was good to be active again, and to feel my physical strength returning. The decisions that had been made at the meeting felt right and had now to be applied by our actions. There was much work to be done. One task was to set up the national group of warriors that would represent all parts of our land, for them to be trained and bonded, and for them to be guided by the leadership of Verdiff and

Chrisong, so they could become a force in harmony with our Order, and successfully defend our land. There was also the matter of evacuating the coastal communities along the east of our land where danger was threatened most. This was no easy matter. Some of the communities there would be amenable to this because they were loyal to our Order, and would trust in the decisions that we made about them. But many of the tribes in these areas, especially in the more northerly stretches, were fiercely independent, and some had no contact or connection with our Order at all. We could not even be certain, if the invaders came, that some of these communities might even form alliances with the invaders and help them so that they could more easily attack us. To persuade these communities to move location, even if only temporarily, would need considerable efforts and diplomacy. This was a daunting undertaking, especially with the limitations of time that we faced. We needed help on all levels to accomplish this. Then, there was also the situation of food shortages brought about by the drought from the past two years. Food and supplies needed to be shared, and support given to those communities that were less fortunate. We needed ceremonies to ask the Earth Spirit for support. There was also unrest in some areas, and we needed to offer counseling and Spiritual help to those people to enable the peace in our land to be preserved. These were just the main areas of concern for our leadership; there was sure to be more.

In all this, I needed to play my part, and to lead. I wanted to be present and active, attuned to Spirit, so that my own contribution would be as helpful as possible.

With all my aspirations, it was good to feel the blood flowing in my body again, so that I could resume my physical activities. I was very much a 'doing' person, and did not feel very comfortable to be confined. It gave me joy to be walking again, and to be able to join in the morning meditations and greet the sun from the top of the sacred mound that overlooked our community. But all was not right with me.

My body felt strangely sensitive, and I was emotionally fragile, in a manner that was not usual for me. Sometimes in the mornings, I was sick, and could not tolerate food. I wondered if I may have acquired a debilitating illness, and it worried me that my health may not allow me to do my duties.

In the days following the meeting before Karka's death, there had been several occasions when I had been intimate with Gracon. I had felt so proud of him, and full of love for his efforts in organizing and co-coordinating the meeting. For us to join had felt right and it was very pleasurable. But now, at the back of my mind, was the thought about what consequences may have stemmed from this action.

One morning when I was meditating, sitting by our Yew tree in the Sacred Grove, I saw a female Spirit standing with my guide, Eurydice. Her being was radiant, and very loving. She told me that she was with me and her body was growing inside me. I felt shocked. So many emotions flooded through me at that moment; I had to compose myself. Finally, I placed my hands on my stomach and prayed.

Perhaps at the time of discovering this, I should have felt joy, but with all my responsibility and was needed to be accomplished in the land, all I felt now was alarm and despair. I needed help; a lot of help. I was pregnant.

CHAPTER 12

A Great Loss

The passion of Berenice

Once Karka died, Berenice became frantic. The pace of her activity increased. She was not prepared to wait while meetings were held and groups organized to accomplish specific tasks. For her, action was needed immediately, and she had no patience for group processes. If people did not support her and go along with her plans, she acted on her own. The shadow that Karka had foreseen spreading over the land was something that Berenice wished to avoid at all costs. She appeared prepared to take on this as a task, single handed.

When she was with us, I watched her, and she seldom laughed anymore. The grace with which she carried herself had been replaced by hurried footsteps. I tried to meet with her, listen to her ideas, and share the load of the responsibility that she felt. But if I managed to find people to work with her, or if I offered to accompany her myself, then she would give herself further assignments, so the pace of her activity never relented. I wondered that she never appeared to tire, but it was as if some hidden force of Will propelled her forward. In her eyes, other people were not doing enough, and she felt that she had to make up for that somehow.

Her dedication to the land and our people was great, but seemed almost like an obsession. She could not bear to allow our kingdom to be compromised or weakened by possible invaders. She had absorbed Karka's vision but wanted to alter it with her Will, so it would not come to pass. And her Will was enormously strong.

I felt doubtful how much the Earth Spirit was supporting Berenice on her missions, despite her energy. There were a couple of occasions as she left our encampment, when I glimpsed her face, and it carried a haunted look. Why was she cutting off from her inner sources of Spiritual connection? With her driving Will, I sensed that underneath that was fear. She was afraid of what would happen if she did not do her utmost for the land, and this compulsion coupled with her anger and self-belief, was an immense force.

Her eyes looked angry, and I wondered how much she felt resentful towards me for taking what she regarded as her rightful position as head of our Order, after Karka's abdication? What could I do?

I felt very anxious about Berenice, more concerned for her in my thoughts, than for our land. But I could not maintain that. When I listened to my own guidance, I was repeatedly told to release her, and that I could not interfere with her decision making. Strategies had to be implemented for the defense of the land, and this is what required my primary attention, because long term planning was needed and substantial community involvement. Vast tracts of the population had to act together in one Spirit to manifest unity of purpose. Involving community groups in the process did slow decision making down. But it had to be done.

Berenice was clearly not satisfied with this. She had picked out tribes and pockets of communities where the allegiance to our Spiritual government was most weak, ignorant or in rebellion, and she set out to convert these people to respect the Order of the Wise by commanding them to do this. She was particularly concerned with those nearest to the north eastern coastal regions where the invaders were predicted to infiltrate first. Many of the people in these regions had the reputation of being quite warlike, and had shown little interest in Spiritual matters for generations. But Berenice believed in her strength that she could change them, and she was determined to succeed.

Over time, even though I was heavily occupied with lots of organizational matters, I tried to keep a watchful eye upon Berenice and what she was doing. I asked Spirit to help me, and provide protection and support for her, even though she had not asked for it. There were two journeys where I insisted on coming with her, and while with her, I listened to her thoughts about averting future peril, and I tried to be sympathetic and urged her to allow us to support her more. She could feel my concern for her, and it irritated her.

In one difficult conversation, she urged me to be true to myself and mindful of the responsibilities that had been entrusted to me with <u>all</u> the people of the land. It was not appropriate for me to fix my attention upon her. Effectively, she was sending me away.

It was as though she had felt rejected, and now she was rejecting me and all the others in our Order, building barriers around her Self, and directing her Will to do what she felt driven to do. She was engaging in her own personal crusade, and did not want me or anyone else to be near her. She found it very difficult to hear me offering her suggestions for she felt pride in her capacities, and she had been my teacher.

Although she made her wishes very clear on that day, I still found it very hard to abide by that. I felt that if she did not change her course, that she could be heading on a route towards self-destruction, for she was isolating herself at a time when we needed to experience togetherness. But she was convinced by her powers of determination as though she was invincible, and she did not need anyone by her side.

As I headed back towards the College on that evening, by myself, I felt a dreadful feeling of foreboding that I might lose someone who had given me so much, and who I loved so dearly. And I could do nothing in my own powers to prevent it.

Several times, I felt helpless at my lack of control over what Berenice was doing, and I wanted to send people after her, and demand for her to co-operate. But I knew instinctively, that I could not impose myself in such a manner. Each day, I tried to force myself to attend to family and the routine concerns of my office, but in my stomach, there was a knot of fear that was growing. I was preoccupied, and stared into the distance. Many times, I attempted to locate her with my telepathic senses, and although I could discern glimpses of her thoughts, there was a deliberate block that she had set up, and her senses were not open to contact. She had goals that she wanted to accomplish, and her focus was exclusively concerned with that.

There were reports of remarkable conversions, of co-operations between tribes that were forged through the tenacity of Berenice's efforts. We all had to appreciate her successes, but I could not dismiss my own niggling feelings that her gains would not last.

Pressures

Of course there were other matters. Communities needed to be relocated, and decisions were needed about where they could go, and the residents had to be convinced to move there. The national force of warriors needed to be assembled, and to be representative of different localities throughout the land. Members of this force had to be vetted to ensure that they would be capable and loyal. Some communities still needed help and support after the ravages of the drought in the past two years. Festivals had to be organized for the people of the land to feel more united. And then there were many fears people had about what would happen when the invasion came to pass, and what dangers existed. It often fell to me to provide as much reassurance as I could.

I could not do everything, and had to delegate more and more of my responsibilities because I was also pregnant and this slowed me down a lot. The further my pregnancy progressed, the more cumbersome my body felt, and I was bitter about this and intolerant of my own condition. Although, it should have been a time of rejoicing, I felt restricted and was very tempted to seek to terminate the pregnancy so I could have my full attention upon my pressing duties in the land, and my concern for what was happening with Berenice.

Nianda counseled me, and I knew that she was right. The soul of this child was calling to be born at this time, with my body, and I needed to respect it and love it. I struggled with myself, and had many sleepless nights worrying, and this did not help my mood.

The pregnancy was much more difficult than I could have imagined. My health was not good, and I had not fully recovered from the wound I had received from Skife before I had to cope with this. There were so many callings on my attention.

As I neared the time of the birth, I was ordered by Nianda to lie down and rest, for my body was bleeding and I felt very weak. Nianda was attending me constantly. Normally, I would have been very robust with my physical constitution, but not now. Nianda was very concerned about my situation. I had fever and little appetite. My body was becoming dangerously thin.

One morning when I was lying down, I felt a strong vibration on my forehead. Closing my eyes, I listened. It was Berenice. She was telling me telepathically that she had decided to go to the Massetti tribe. As I received her message, I felt a shiver go through my body. Every instinct in me wanted to compel Berenice not to go there. These people were fiercely independent and resistant to outside influences. They lived in an enclave by the eastern coast. They were people that had no allegiance to anyone except themselves. I felt that she would need a contingent of our strongest warriors to protect her. But she was typically insisting on going alone. She was adamant that she could cope with them however much I tried to persuade her otherwise.

Why was she telling me? Did she secretly wish for support without being able to admit it?

During that day, I felt incredibly sad, and I did not know why, but every time my thoughts drifted in the direction of Berenice, the feeling of heaviness in my body got worse. I had to shake this off somehow and focus on what needed my immediate attention. I needed to find some resilience, so I sent out a prayer to Spirit for strength, and somehow, from that moment on, I started to rally, and feel calmer. My fever went down. I had to give birth to this baby, and I had to be present for the other Elders and the people, as much as I could. With determination, I was not going to allow despair to overcome my ability to act.

In the last days before the birth, Nianda insisted that I remain in my hut, even though, in my eagerness, I felt I had to be up and about, to engage in the activities within our encampment. It was very frustrating for me being so immobile, and it gave me small comfort to be able to watch others at their work.

One morning, I gazed downwards in the direction of the hut where Berenice stayed when she was around. I expected to see her hut empty, but it was not. There was a small figure sitting at the entrance to the hut, a teenage girl. With recognition, I saw that this was Shoola, Berenice's daughter. It caught me by surprise that Shoola was there, and she looked so forlorn.

I knew Shoola to be an excellent psychic and mind reader, in many ways following in her mother's footsteps. She had been engaged in her apprenticeship with Berenice or some years now. Even though they were mother and daughter, they seemed to work together well, and appeared to be very close. They traveled everywhere together, just as I had done with Berenice, many years earlier. But now, Shoola gave the appearance that she had been abandoned. As a trainee, Shoola had to do what her mother/teacher expected of her, and although she was obedient, Shoola looked absolutely desolate.

For a long time, I watched Shoola, and felt the disturbance in her feelings matched my own. I wanted to help her somehow, but knew not what I could do. At one point, she looked up at me, and our eyes met. As she stared at me, I could feel an immense longing in her eyes, and a sense of loss.

Just then, I felt a sharp pain in my abdomen, and I had to turn away. I was starting to feel the movements and adjustments of my child within me, and I knew that the birth was getting close. But something in me was stirring, and it would not let go.

Ritual

It was a few days later, and I called for the Community to gather for a ceremony at the Sacred Grove. I asked that this be a fire ceremony and entreated my friends and fellow teachers to bring objects of power for us to send light and prayers of protection to Berenice on her mission. The desire in me to offer Berenice help was overwhelming and I could not let it go, without offering some form of inner support for her.

Nianda thought that I was mad. How could I conduct a ceremony in my condition? She doubted very much that I had the stamina, and had counseled me that I needed all my strength for the birth. But I was not prepared to listen. I could feel the strength of Spirit supporting me, and had the inner conviction that this was something that I had to do.

Now I was going to take part in this ritual. Nianda tried to take my arm, but I insisted upon standing on my own feet. Although the sweat was pouring from me, and a large part of me wanted nothing more than to lie down and collapse, I was determined that I would not give in to the weakness of my body.

With faltering footsteps and leaning heavily on my staff, I went first to Shoola. She did not know about it yet, but she would stand with me while I conducted this ceremony. We would do this together.

There was a large gathering of us in the Grove, and it was a still night. So many people had been touched by the compassion and clarity of Berenice's work, that she was recognized as a giant amongst us in terms of psychic and Spiritual work. There was also appreciation for the dangerous task she had taken on. I stared in wonder at all those present while continuing to feel an anxious knot in my stomach. I did not want my friends to know how afraid I felt.

The fire was lit, and the power symbols were deployed, and chants and prayers were uttered. The presence of the Earth Goddess and guides were invoked. There was a powerful positive intent going out from us in support of Berenice and her work. Shoola was standing right next to me, and I squeezed her hand.

My inner eyes were opening, and I could see Berenice's Spiritual form there, and she was looking at us. She knew what we were doing. There was a murmur in the crowd. Others could perceive her too. Unexpectedly, there was a warm smile and gratitude in her eyes, but she only held this for a few moments, and then turned away. I shouted inwardly for her to come back and stay with us. But nothing could persuade her, and it was as if she walked away and faded from all of us. All I could see then was blackness, and it felt so empty.

I did not understand her. Why did she not accept our link more fully? I had to do something. Would she not come back? The more I inwardly pleaded with her to return, the further she seemed to retreat, and I sensed that she was putting up shields to block out our energy and focus on what she was doing.

My intuition then told me something that frightened me. I perceived it as a familiar knowing that I could trust. Although she appeared to have such strength of Will, I felt her energy to be weaker than I had ever known it.

Suddenly, the peace was disturbed. There was a sudden cold gust of wind, and then another. The stillness was no more. There was dampness spreading in the air, as if it was going to rain. But the fire could not go out, not in the middle of our ritual. That would herald disaster, and could portend terrible tragedy for Berenice. We had to keep the rain away. There was a gasp in the crowd and then shouting in my mind. Spirit was speaking. We could not do anything. This was a Spiritual process and we had to just watch and observe.

The wind increased, and the cold made me shiver, and I wrapped my cloak around me more tightly. As I gazed towards the sky, the clear starlight sky was gone, and instead there was a dense cloud cover that even the moon struggled to penetrate. There were drops of rain, and the fire sizzled as the drops fell on it. Surely, this would not herald the end? The wind sprung up again, and fanned the fire briefly, before more droplets quelled the flames further, so with every wave of drops, it seemed more certain that the fire would die. We all watched in utter disbelief. Shoola clutched my hand more tightly. But then there was a further change, and the air became still again, and an eerie silence pervaded the space of the Sacred Grove. The trees and watchers were gathered in silence, and I did not know what their final judgment would be. The flames had died away to almost nothing, and there were only embers that remained.

Nianda wanted me to go so I could rest, and other members of the gathering slowly drifted away with downcast eyes. But I had to stay, and needed to know if there was any hope left, if Berenice could survive this ordeal.

We all knew that in a fire Ritual, Spirit spoke truly and would indicate through the strength of flame, the fate of the person to whom the ritual was directed. I wondered if the outcome could have been different had Berenice inwardly stayed with us rather than turning away.

All night, I stayed there with Shoola by my side. And by the time the sun arose, there were still embers there alight. All was not lost. While the embers and warmth of the fire remained with the sun, there was hope. Even now there was the chance that Berenice might live, but what danger she must be facing.

We completed the ritual there, and Nianda and Shoola helped me back to my hut.

An uneasy birth

Now I needed to bring my attention to the birth and with the effort of bringing my daughter into the world. Suddenly, I felt that I could focus on her, and I felt such a strong pure light associated with this being, I felt that her imminent presence needed to be honored with every fiber of my being.

Nianda, of course, was there with me. And there were many others that came to pay homage. Numerous predictions had been made about this baby from far and wide in our land. Representatives from various communities had come with gifts and blessings for my baby. Many of them had been waiting patiently for days while I had been so preoccupied with the fate of Berenice. I knew that I needed to be more disciplined about where I placed my thought, and surely, my baby deserved for me to be more present with her than I had been. But there was something in this drama with Berenice, something about her being and my love for her, where I could not leave her on her own. At least now, I could rest and follow Nianda's instructions for my care and well-being.

It was not long before I started to feel contractions, and I hoped and prayed that the birth would be over with quickly and easily. But it was not to be. The birth, itself, was long and arduous. I was already considerably weakened and ill with fever and the residues of the wound I had received from Skife. The contractions went on and on, so the efforts of bringing my daughter forth from my body completely exhausted me. There were moments, when I wanted to give up, when I didn't feel that I had the strength. But I had to think for the land and my responsibilities, and I wanted to see things through. I called on Eurydice, the Earth Goddess, and all my Spirit Helpers, to give me the energy to push and help my little girl to find her first breath. And finally, she emerged and uttered a loud cry of welcome to our world!

When I felt her release herself from my body, and heard her voice, I just collapsed with joy and love. It was such a wonderful feeling, such a moment of celebration. The shouts of elation echoed throughout our encampment. I did not fully understand it, but there was something about this baby that felt very precious to me and our community. I wished then that I could have appreciated her presence in my body more fully! Nianda placed her on my tummy, and I could feel her warmth and aliveness. What a miracle! I was glad that it was over.

Nianda gave me an herbal drink, and I just sank back onto my bed. Much as I wanted to remain conscious, I could not do so any longer. I felt myself drifting, and it was such a relief to let go.

I do not know how long I was away, but when I awoke, all I could perceive was stillness, and it was night time. My baby lay by my side, wrapped in cloth, and I could hear her breathing gently. Next to her was Nianda. Her eyes looked tired, but she was still present and attentive to my needs. How fortunate I was to have her with me!

Immediately, I wanted to get up, but when I tried to move my body, I found that I could not. My body was like a heavy weight, and I could not shift it. Nianda gave me another drink, and then I was drifting again, and must have slept. I do not know how many times this happened, but gradually I did feel my strength was returning. It was like a dreamy state of bliss, and I felt so content resting, and being with my baby.

Finally, I found that I could adjust my body and reach out to hold my little one. Another woman from our encampment had been helping to look after my baby, as was our custom.

Now, Nianda gave me a different kind of broth, and the taste was sharper, and I could feel the warmth of this stirring me towards greater energy. My mind became clearer, and I was prompted to begin to think about what was going on around me. What was the news in the community? How were things going? What about Berenice?

Distress call

Suddenly, I wanted to sit up, and I struggled to do this, and Nianda tried to settle me so I would continue to lie down. But I had to ask, and insisted that Nianda tell me all that she knew. From then on, I started to have visitors for short periods, and I attempted to listen and discuss issues so I could contribute to the needs of our government. I had to force myself to do it, but it was important for me not to neglect my duties.

One morning, I decided to tune in to Berenice. Suddenly, I felt a shiver through my body. What was happening to her? As I continued to open my perception to her, it felt very quiet, but in the background, there was an uneasy tremor. I did not like it. Nianda noticed the change in me, and tried to calm me, but now that I had been alerted again to my teacher's plight, I could not release it, for I felt terribly afraid.

It was two nights later when the moment I had been dreading arrived. I had woken in the middle of the night and my body was wet with perspiration. It was not a scream or a shout or a desperate calling, but a whisper that came suddenly like an arrow, and pierced my soul. I sat upright with a jolt. Her voice was in my mind and she was asking me to come.

Berenice was in trouble. She was seeking for my help. The nature of her call indicated that she needed the help now. It was urgent. She had finally realized that she could not do it all on her own. I just hoped and prayed and pleaded with the Spirits that she had not left it too late.

Inwardly, I tuned in with my imagination, to the embers of the fire ritual. They would give me knowledge to help me. And in my mind, they were still glowing, no brighter, and no duller, just as they were. This was enough to motivate me, to renew my hope and belief.

Thoughts were rushing in my head. I had to call our warriors. There had to be forces to protect Berenice from the Massetti. Should we storm their community? It was not safe. We would have to act very carefully. Berenice was calling me. She obviously felt that I could help, and she knew my skills and how we could combine together. But then I cried out in anguish. It would take at least four brisk days of walking to reach her. How could I possibly do that in my condition? I felt defeated. But then, in the turmoil of my mind, I heard Berenice's voice again. It was almost pleading with me, urging me to come. I could not ignore her. It was such a change in her. What suffering must she be enduring for her to have such a change of heart? I had to go. Nothing would stop me. I had to believe that she could hang on, that she could survive until I reached her.

Struggling with myself, I somehow managed to get to my feet. How unsteady I felt, I could hardly stand, and I had to reach for the support of wall of the hut to keep myself upright. Nianda was with me in an instant, and her eyes were full of alarm. But I stared at her and our eyes met, and I communicated with her my intention. She knew that when I decided to do an action that felt important to me, then nothing would sway me from doing that. Nianda glanced despairingly at my body, and then looked up at me again. She swallowed and then nodded in agreement. I could not do the journey without her, and she knew that. Her loyalty to me was not going to waver now.

Nianda gave me a drink and I felt the energy of it stimulate my senses. My body was so lethargic and weak. I called on Eurydice and the Earth Goddess once more, but even with their help, I had no notion how I could manage this journey. But then I thought of Berenice, and the preciousness of her life. She would not refuse me if I needed help. I could not refuse her.

Looking around the hut, I saw my baby sleeping, and she looked so peaceful. I felt a lump in my chest. I would have to leave her, but there were others who could look after her. There was only one choice for me, and that was to stay standing and move.

It took a while to get organized, and I could only watch while Nianda gathered supplies and medicines that we would need. Meanwhile, I leaned heavily on my staff and waited. We then went over to the entrance of the hut. Even those few steps were agony, but I managed it, and it was a start. As I looked outwards, someone else was waiting. A set of eyes met mine at the doorway, and there was just as much determination in those eyes as I felt myself. It was Shoola of course. Berenice must have called her too. She was not going to be left behind.

I placed my arm around Shoola's shoulder to welcome her. The three of us smiled together in acknowledgement and we were ready to begin our travel.

Desperate journey

The others raced off ahead, but for me, every step was pain. I tried not to show them. How could I do this? Even with my staff crackling the Earth energy to surge through my body, I could only stagger along at a very slow pace. Shoola, in particular, was so much longing to make progress. But it was not long before I felt breathless, and I had to call out to Nianda to lean on her for support. How was I possibly going to get there? I looked up at my friend, Nianda, in despair. Even with all her healing, my body was absolutely exhausted and desperately needing rest. I was trying to force it to do something that was completely alien to its needs. In my heart, I was committed, and I had to go on. I could not abandon this quest for others to take my place.

But then, after a few more steps, my body gave way, and I slouched down on the ground. The warriors might be able to help, but Berenice had called on me. Maybe it was her pride and lack of trust that enabled her to call me and Shoola and no one else? Even for her to admit her vulnerability to the two of us was a considerable achievement.

As I sat, I concentrated my inner attention on Wueli. I needed to call the warriors to be ready and go there. If I could not reach her, others must. I could not let my own pride obstruct this. I could sense Wueli's energy and our thoughts exchanged the nature of the situation. He was naturally concerned for my health, but I insisted that I was traveling and would be there if there was any way for me to manage. He understood, and knew better than to argue with me. The warriors would wait at the entrance of the Massetti enclave unless I gave orders otherwise. It was agreed.

For some time, I sat in Nianda's arms and prayed to Spirit, and slowly I felt the beginnings of energy pulsing into my body. As I then tried to raise myself, I heard a voice within me telling me to find a rhythm. The words were being chanted to help me locate that rhythm. I leaned on my staff and listened more closely, and tapped the rhythm with my hand against my thigh. Next I began to make little steps with the rhythm, one foot at a time. It was working. There was something comfortable about this steady rhythm, something that was almost relaxing, so as I concentrated on the rhythm, I could forget my body, and let the rhythm propel me forward.

Slowly, I lengthened my stride with my long legs, keeping each leg moving at that same rate, so I could sustain it, and the others were staring at me in astonishment. Soon I was the one setting the pace, but it did not take long before Shoola was once more moving ahead of me.

The vibration of the chant was a mantra and meditation for me, and while I listened to that and adhered to that, I could keep going, and the others joined me with my rhythm and it helped them too. With my body, I concentrated upon my breath so it was in tune with the rhythm of my walking, and I focused on that so completely that I heard no other sounds, and just went one step at a time and felt joy in my heart that we were making progress.

The day passed and the force of commitment in me was unwavering. We climbed terrain where we had never been before, but with my inner sight and knowing, there was a clear line of direction where we had to keep walking. On occasions, I listened inwardly for communication from Berenice, but there was silence. This comforted me, for I trusted that she would only communicate if or when her trials became acute.

Every now and again, Shoola looked back at me with a pained expression in her eyes. She was so desperate to reach her mother alive, and if she had been traveling alone, she would have gone faster, I am certain of it. In typical style, Nianda was attentive to me, and most of the time when the track was wide enough, she would stride alongside of me, and check that my energy levels were sustaining themselves. I was happy to be able to smile at her, and keep walking, and it was only when the cold air of the night closed in on us that we agreed to pause and rest.

When I did stop, I felt suddenly that all the energy had gone out of me, and I collapsed down onto my skins. Every bone and muscle in my body ached, and I was desperate for something to drink. Nianda had to work quickly on me for I started to hemorrhage, and it was only the strength of heat from the healing rays that poured into my body through her hands that steadied me and prevented my condition from deteriorating. I must have slept again, for when I awoke, the full moon was lighting up the sky and there was a burning fire in front of me. My companions were staring at me and grateful that I was conscious again.

We all needed to sleep, and I needed to sleep much more. If our expedition had had any other purpose, I would have felt pleased with the progress of our journey that we had made after that first day. But there was uneasiness in my stomach, and I still had a gnawing doubt and fear that our progress was not enough.

I woke up several times during that night, and my body was drenched in perspiration. I must have been having disturbing dreams for

I felt very unsettled. Then I opened my eyes and the others were awake too. The sky was only just beginning to lighten from its velvet night and we were all alert with a feeling of urgency that we had to move.

For me, the hardest part was to physically get up, and to make a few steps so I could inwardly tune in to that rhythm again. For some moments, I did not think that I would find it, because the pain in my bones was so terrible. But I was determined to do it, and I asked my guides and Eurydice in particular, to help me. Just making a few small slow steps, I took some deep breaths and began to be in motion. Nianda wanted to assist me, but I insisted on maneuvering my body by myself. I had my staff to lean on, and that was enough. The others had to be patient with me, but gradually, after a few stutters, I found my rhythm and began to increase my pace as I had done the previous day.

So our journey continued, over three, long exhausting days, until at the end of that last day, the foothills of the enclave of the Massetti tribe came into view. What relief I felt then.

An alien land

The following morning, we surveyed what was in front of us. Normally, when we wandered through our land, we would feel the vibration of the Earth Spirit through our feet. It was like a friend, and we could feel the lightness of our Earth Spirit lifting us up, and when we were in tune, we would want to leap with elation because of the love in the connection that we felt. That is what had sustained me in our journey until now.

Somehow though, as we gazed ahead at the woodland before us, the vibration was markedly different. My psychic sight could still see glimpses of light fluttering across the ground, but it was not the steady supportive presence that was familiar to us. Here, there were dark swirls of dancing energy, twisting and contorting the space that was there.

The Massetti had a fearsome reputation. It was said that they practiced blood sacrifice regularly, not just animal, but with human blood. They made rituals of sacrifice with the intention of enhancing their powers. And they had no respect for the Earth or anyone but themselves. They seldom ventured far from their enclave except to find victims for their rituals. Our people tended to leave them well alone and keep distance from them. With this reputation, I did not understand what had possessed Berenice to consider that she could enter their land and presume to change their ways, without any support, purely as a solitary individual. Inside, I felt that I wanted to cry out with frustration that she would do this.

Our warriors were close, but not quite with us. Wueli had instructed them to hold back until I arrived, and a big part of me felt like waiting for them, for I did not want to enter this place rashly. But then, suddenly, I felt a violent shiver ascending up my back, followed by a scream. It was an inner scream, for there was no sound in the air, but the violence and shock of it was so great that I staggered and would have fallen had it not been for my staff. The horror of this made me wince, and I saw the instant dismay in the expressions of my companions. They had heard it as well.

'Ilsa, help me.' It was Berenice. She had opened up her psychic channel. I could feel her struggle and her desperate efforts. Inside, I was frantic.

The three of us looked at each other. In a moment, we were running, faster than I had ever run before. There was no thought of pacing myself, no time to adjust to a steady rhythm; I just had to go. We all did. I tried to communicate to her that we were coming, but I do not know if she heard me. Her energy sensed to be totally taken up in her battle.

As fast as I was going, Shoola was going even faster. I had never seen anyone so desperate to reach her destination. We could use the channel Berenice had opened up to guide us. She was close. We had to go up the hill. It was only a small path, and the foliage grew quite dense. This slowed us down, and we hacked relentlessly at branches so we could keep going. The plight of Berenice was intensifying. Her energy was becoming erratic. She needed us urgently.

Outcome

The space in front of us was clear now, and there was a path that wound around the contour of the hill. We were close, so very close now, but not there. I was determined to keep up with Shoola.

Each step brought an explosion of memories through my mind. Berenice had played such a vital role in my life. She had attended me since I was very little, and taught me both skills and leadership. It was the child in me that was scared. Berenice had been like a mother to me, not in an ordinary sense, but I trusted her utterly, and she had nurtured so well, my inner life. Berenice and Karka had acted as my Spiritual parents. I had lost Karka, but I couldn't bear to lose Berenice too. As I gazed ahead at Shoola, I could only shudder to imagine what she would be feeling.

I strained my ears to hear sounds, and from the very edges of my awareness, I could hear footsteps receding faintly in the background. Why would they be going away? The energy from Berenice had gone very quiet. I did not like it. It was too quiet. Where could she be? I sensed that they were afraid of her, and that she had used her powers to keep them at bay. That is why they had run. She must have done something to ward them away. I still did not like it, but I dared to hope. Could she have found a place of safety? I so much wished for that.

Memories continued to flood into my consciousness. I remembered the fear in Berenice's eyes when Karka had shared his vision, and the obsession that had followed. I could not blame Berenice for that. She only wanted to protect our land, and preserve it. Fear and pride had stopped her from reaching out for support. It was such a revelation that Berenice was capable of possessing fear, but I suppose that it taught me how we all have vulnerability, even those that appeared most strong. I rather wished that Berenice had dared to share her human sides more fully with others, and that she could have dared to do that. She could have been helped. It had not needed to come to this.

Just then, I felt that my thoughts were no longer private, but that Berenice was listening to me, as though she was nodding in agreement and comforting me. I heard her voice in my mind. 'It is all right Ilsa; it is all right. Be peaceful.'

The quality of Berenice's voice had a quality of love and a lilt to it that was very different from what she had been expressing, but it was her being without a doubt. I sensed that reaching her was imminent. My heart leapt with delight that I might find her alive. But then, as we came around the next bend, Shoola motioned ahead and screamed. I felt chaos in the air and violence.

There was rustling in the trees. The energy of the land was terribly disturbed. Pools of blood were scattered along the track, and off to the side, Shoola was crouching down. She was holding someone, rocking them, grasping at them. She wouldn't let go. It was Berenice, and she seemed in a horrific state. I cried for Nianda, and tried to pull Shoola away so she could get through. Nianda worked crazily, but as I examined the body and noticed the extent of the blood loss and the lifeless stare in Berenice's eyes, I knew that very little could be done.

Her body was still warm. We had been so close. Nianda kept working, but Berenice's body was empty of blood. Gradually, she eased off. I looked back at Shoola and made a space for her to come in again, so she could be close to her mother's body. She was howling with grief.

Berenice's staff was half raised to indicate that she had battled to the last. As I studied the scene, along the path were pools and trails of blood, suggesting that her death struggles had been extended and bitterly painful. Within me, I knew that her connection with physical life was over.

Confrontation

I felt drawn to look up into the tree, and just beyond that, there was a light. My inner perception went there as though pulled by a magnet, and I recognized immediately the being that emanated this light. It was the Spirit of Berenice. The love I felt from her now was enormous and I wanted to embrace her and hold her and take comfort from her. She smiled and let me come close, and I was almost lulled into a feeling that what had happened was acceptable. But it was not to be condoned. It was awful; a horror beyond words, and a force of emotion was stirring from within me. I felt rage rise up in me, and I felt anger with Berenice. She had brought this on herself. But how dare the Massetti do this to her. Did they not realize who she was? She would have not wished any hurt upon them, and yet, what had they done to her? I had to go to them. I needed to seek justice for this. This could not go unanswered.

I motioned to Nianda that I was going on. She was torn. Her natural instinct was to accompany me, but Shoola needed her just now. So I left them and proceeded forward.

I do not know from where I found the strength, but I strode forth and marched right into their encampment. I was not afraid; I was summoning the Earth energies as I had never done before.

'Who did this?' I bellowed. My voice thundered through the clearing, and I am sure that everyone heard me. If they did not understand the words, it did not matter, for my intent was unmistakable.

A few tribesmen sheepishly looked around from the corners of buildings. But some were more defiant, and proceeded out to challenge me. I was not going to excuse anybody. With the intensity of my emotions, I could perceive their minds. They were not going to get away with this. One of them was bolder than the others. They appeared to look to him. I surmised straight away that he must have been the instigator, without allowing reason to balance my conclusions. He was moving towards me with a group of his followers. They had spears and were poised to use them to stop me. They must have believed that they would have strength in numbers.

That must have been what they did with her – attacked her en-mass. How dare they do that! How dare they destroy such a wonderful life! The rage in me was ready to kill. I lifted up my staff and directed it threateningly towards this man's body, and I could feel the emotional impulses in me urging me to kill him. The energy and rage I felt could have gone right into his heart. He would die. But voices in me shouted 'no' and I hesitated. Something woke up in me, just enough, just enough to alter the course of my rage.

The energy shot out of my staff with tremendous power; there was too much force behind it for me to halt it. But just in time, I lowered my hand, and the energy plummeted into the ground in front of this man. He stopped in his tracks, and the others looked on in bewilderment. I stamped my staff into the ground again and a huge burst of flame exploded out of its ends and drew out between the onlookers.

They were frightened, and I knew with certainty, that if any of those tribesmen would try to defy me, that I would use the staff again. I gestured to the crowd, and commanded them to bring the leading man to me. The tribesmen shouted and gesticulated and slowly the man stumbled forward towards me. He was trembling now, and in his terror, I made him lie down in front of me, on his stomach, so he could not see me and he was most vulnerable.

When he finally lay still and the others had drawn back, I placed the staff on the middle of his back, and directed energy into him. But it was not anger anymore that I held within me, but healing intent, and as I asked Spirit to channel this for me, this leader of the Massetti was made to feel the energy I was channeling, and he sobbed. He sobbed softly at first, and then more and more emotion poured out of him. The tribesmen looked on in astonishment. I could sense light around him, and the tears came from his loving soul. From above the nearby huts, I could sense the presence of Berenice, and she was smiling.

One by one, I motioned the tribesmen of the Massetti to come forward, and the Spirit of Berenice drew closer to work with me. I did a similar process for each person, and Berenice helped me to channel the energy from Spirit so each of these people could connect with their souls. It was an amazing process, and somehow, it was making it possible for Berenice to complete the work she had come here to do. If only she had not tried to do it all on her own, she might now still be alive. It was a terrible thought.

The atmosphere in the tribal village was changing now. Gradually, the tribesmen were becoming willing to do my bidding, and some of them were even moving forward without me motioning them to do so.

They all lay down in turn, and Spirit continued to help them transform so they could all be connected to their souls.

When it was over, I called them to come together. We needed to talk. Even though our language was different, I could reach their thoughts through their minds, and they were ready to listen to me. They had to change now. The times of rebellion were over. It was time for them to join us, for us to work together, and I was going to start the process.

I kept working with the Massetti, using my staff, talking with them, learning about them, and addressing their ways and customs, and insisting about how these needed to change into new ways of being. They had heard it all from Berenice, but with her, they had countered all her efforts with a thick wall of resistance. Berenice had started to break down that wall, and I could now go further. It was like a mass conversion to a new form of consciousness, and somehow inside, it must have been what they really wanted, or they would never have cooperated. Something in their dealings with Berenice must have started to change them. I sensed how hard Berenice must have worked, but she had never faced people that were so violent and self-absorbed before. I hoped that they had not hurt her too much. She did not deserve it.

Only when I was convinced that my work with the Massetti was done did I return to Shoola and Nianda. In the last steps I made as I came around the corner to them, I staggered. My energy was completely spent. I could feel myself falling, collapsing, but somehow Nianda must have caught me.

Ceremony of farewell and appreciation

Later on, our warriors came. Nianda worked tirelessly to offer me healing and replenishment. I could only rest while the others prepared Berenice's body. She was dressed and made up as well as could be. Shoola would not leave her mother's side, and was still extremely distraught. In a very welcome gesture, members of the Massetti helped our warriors to build a litter to carry Berenice's body, and one also for me so I would not become even more depleted.

We would have to bring the body of Berenice home. She had to be honored. The grief in our land would be overwhelming because she had been such a powerful figure and a force for good in her unending dedication to the well-being of our land and its people. So many communities had been touched by her clarity and Spiritual attunement.

And we did manage to bring her body home, and the funeral ceremony for Berenice was immense. People came from all over our kingdom, and beyond. Our encampment had never been so populated. All the Elders of our College were present, and they lined up with me for the ceremony. Tributes had poured in from all corners of our land; such was the reputation of Berenice. Many had brought gifts that were placed as offerings with the body.

At the time appointed, I gave the keynote speech; I spoke of the lifelong dedication that Berenice had given to the land and its people. I gave emphasis to her concern about possible invaders and how much passion she had to wish to keep our land safe. In her work for the communities of the land, she had acted from a commitment she held to truth and from a wish to support people and their highest good.

There were members of the Massetti tribe present. I had invited them. In the middle of the ceremony, I gave them a large quartz crystal stone as a gift from us and as a symbol of our willingness to incorporate them into our society. I spoke about how the very presence of the Massetti was a testimony to the power and passion of Berenice's work and how much was possible if we all applied ourselves. The people shouted their approval and I could sense a great feeling of unity and purpose in the gathering.

It was Shoola who lit the funeral pyre. I could sense the sadness in her eyes, but she stood tall and did not waver from her duty. She stood by me throughout the ceremony, and when it came her moment to light the fire, she performed this task with power and dignity. I felt in that moment that the mantle of Berenice's role in our community was being passed to her daughter...

She would need further training, and she would stay with me. I would look after her and make sure that she learned all she needed to learn. We both had had the same teacher. Shoola accepted that, and even welcomed it. I knew that in future years, there would be times when we would work very closely together, but just now, she needed to heal and be nurtured.

In the moments after Shoola lit the fire, she stepped back, and the flames roared. Shoola held my hand tightly. We both turned our gaze skyward, and I was sure that I could see the Spirit of Berenice watching in the night sky. As the flames diminished, the vision faded and I knew that we were ready to begin a new phase of our lives together as a community. Slowly, when people drifted away from the sacred Grove, there was a palpable feeling of peace, and strength, that we would surely need in the times to come.

CHAPTER 13

The time of trial for the land

Preparations

I looked up at them as Verdiff and Chrisong stood at the top of the rounded hill overlooking the North Sea. It was cold and windy, and the sun had set, leaving those two figures as darkening silhouettes against the twilight sky.

Verdiff was not a tall man, more stocky, but very determined, and with intense eyes. Even though the wind was fierce, he stood there with his skin coat wrapped tightly around him, just swaying ever so slightly, but with balance and focus about the tasks he had set himself. He was doing what he had been doing each evening since we had made our camp; he was surveying every stretch of sea that he could view, straining his eyes to notice any slight sign of movement. In his mind Verdiff knew that the barbarians were coming. His mind was on high alert, but his body was calm.

Beside him was his faithful companion and friend, Chrisong. Her frail looking thin small body did not do justice to a woman whose strength of will and strategic mind complemented Verdiff perfectly. They were close enough to blend their thoughts through telepathy, so at times when we heard them talking, it was as if they were one person.

And their commitment to the effort of repelling the invaders was total. Together, they looked like two trees rooted to their environment, at one with the elements where they stood.

The moment expanded as I watched them and they remained together. Their intention was to make absolutely sure that we were safe, and they would stay there observing, until the last speck of remaining light had gone. Once it was dark, it was only by sound that we could hear them returning. Even then, their footsteps moved so silently that I could hardly notice them.

The time was almost upon us. I could feel the anticipation and nervous tension within me, and within everyone in the camp. As I reflected, I recalled how amazing it had been, that after the Massetti had converted to our ways, then other tribes and groups had also listened to our pleas, and had acted with haste to join us and move their communities to safety. Suddenly, the vision of what we needed to do to build our defensive plan was put into action and manifested, with cohesive endeavors towards this from all sections of our society. And it was Verdiff and Chrisong that emerged at the forefront of all our efforts, guiding and directing, advising from their expertise. We trusted them, and I was happy to acknowledge that in this, their leadership would be vital for the survival of our people and our way of life.

Not everyone was in harmony with us though. The two villages on either end of the bay beneath this hill had been amongst the last to evacuate. They had been so stubborn, insisting that they were safe. And while we continued to argue with them, the barbarians had struck, not once, but twice in quick succession, first to one village, and then to the other, raping and plundering, burning huts and taking captives. The only survivors were so traumatized; we needed several healers to help them. After this, of course, the remaining inhabitants did agree to go, and we constructed shelters for them much further inland.

Verdiff surmised that the barbarians could well return here a third time, and base their attack and invasion from this bay with the much larger force that we knew was coming. They knew this area now, and the local residents had been so easily overcome, that the prospects of more pickings from this area would probably attract them. It had been decided to keep a small fire burning in the two villages on either side of the bay, as a spur to attract the barbarians to this spot.

We did not know exactly how they would arrange their invasion fleet or where they would position their attack, so we had to guard long stretches of our coast line with warriors and lookouts. This is where we needed the experience of Verdiff and Chrisong. We needed to know how the barbarians were likely think so we could anticipate them and concentrate our forces in particular places. Verdiff and Chrisong were familiar with their consciousness from having been captive for so many years in their presence. We depended on them.

Verdiff had assembled a large segment of our forces here by this bay in readiness. Gracon, with his inner vision, concurred that this was a likely target for the invaders. So with warrior groups concentrated in selected positions along the coastline, members of the Order were present in every battalion of warriors, so that telepathic communication could be maintained, and we could be as well organized as possible.

Nianda, Gracon and Wueli were with me. Wueli had been assigned to be my personal guard with the task of protecting me and as a coordinator between the warriors and the Order. When I looked at Wueli, I was surprised at how edgy he appeared, but it was not an easy time for any of us.

The night times were occupied with strategy meetings, working out details of our contingency plans, with Verdiff checking through our members with all the warrior forces along the coast, monitoring everyone of them for signs of danger or hostile presence that would demand an immediate response. My impression was that Verdiff and Chrisong hardly slept, and I believe that they relied on Spirit energy to keep them going.

I could not stay up with them, and I let myself surrender to sleep each night to ensure my physical fitness would be as sturdy as it could be. With all that I had been through, I knew that I was still recovering, and needed to look after myself. I shared a makeshift shelter with the others of my group, and we huddled together in the night for warmth.

It was Verdiff's opinion that we could not hope to defeat this enemy in direct battle. They were bigger and more physically strong than us. Even if we did manage to overcome some of them through our tactics and numbers, they would not respect this. They were a race that desired to crush and conquer any opponents. And if they lost one battle, this would only make them more determined to return with more brutality, to gain revenge and triumph. They were not a people that could easily be deterred.

So what could we do? Verdiff had thought of an ingenious plan, and what it involved was for us to deprive our enemy of plunder, and attack their supply lines. We had to lure them into a trap so they would deploy tremendous effort, but their thirst for blood and conquest would not be satisfied, and their will would be weakened to such an extent that they would regard any further effort as futile. It was a bold vision, which at first glance seemed virtually impossible to fulfill. But after considering many options, it seemed to be our best chance, and we all agreed that we had to commit to it.

From my perspective as leader of the Order, I had to reconcile the fact that we faced a potentially very violent incursion into our land that we had to counteract for our survival, and yet, underpinning of our society were the principles of peace and upholding the sacredness of all life. I knew that if we were entirely passive, it would be a catastrophe for our land and its people. We had to act to defend ourselves. But if we fought and killed in great numbers, this would betray all the ideals we stood for. There was appeal for us in the Order in what Verdiff proposed, for it was based around the need for self-preservation and defense, rather than offensive action. It was a compromise, but given our situation, there was little else we could do.

The Incursion begins

It was a still morning. Even the sea birds were quiet. But I was awake early, and I felt an urgency to arise to meet the day. Within minutes, there was commotion and warriors rushing past me. I could see Verdiff

Ilsa

and Chrisong issuing instructions, directing our people to action. The first sightings had been made.

Our own lookouts had seen not just one but several large boats on the horizon, and the sightings had come from more than our area. From all along the coast, communications had been arriving thick and fast suggesting a huge numbers of boats approaching our shores. This was no ordinary raid. It was clear that the predicted invasion of our land was about to begin. As I tuned in with Verdiff, it appeared that there were four distinct parties of barbarians approaching our coastline in different areas along the coast. Fortunately, we had each of them covered with our warriors, but the numbers of invaders was huge, and Verdiff was furiously organizing people as preparation, and so we could put into place the measures that we had planned.

As I came up to the top of the rise, I could see for myself, and I noticed the distant sails and shapes of at least seven large boats. Inside, I was trembling and my Staff was quivering in my hand. Part of me wanted to fight these people. I could not leave this to others. Inside, I felt a rage growing in me, questioning about how these people dare to disturb the peace of our land. It was our land, not theirs. They had no right to be here.

I thought about the women who had been raped, children whose parents had been slaughtered and held captive, and men who had been tortured. These invaders were ruthless. They did not care about human life. All they wished to do was to assert their dominance, and express their lust for blood. They could not be allowed to demean the respect we held for the land and our people. We had to stop them. I wanted to do my part now, and not just be a spectator. At that moment, I could have easily charged down the hill to the beach and taken these Barbarians on by myself. But I could not do that, so I took a deep breath. Just then, I felt a comforting hand on my shoulder so I looked around and saw the supportive figure of my friend and companion, Wueli. How grateful I was for his company.

Soon we gathered on the far side of the hill, the side facing away from the beach. It was my job to lead the prayers, and I did that, praying for the support of the Earth Spirit for our defense of the land. I could not help it; I slammed my staff into the ground, and there was a fierce crackle of energy, and a vibration that spread through the ground around us. I wanted to give strength to our forces, and if it wasn't for our need to be completely quiet, I would have shouted out my cry of defiance to send these invaders away.

Inside, I was struggling, for I could feel the warrior impulses of my father pulsating in my blood, and I had to suppress this for the sake of discipline in our ranks.

With my inner awareness, I linked with other members of the Order along the coastline, and I could sense my friends joining me. I said a prayer for the leadership of our commander, Verdiff and his partner, Chrisong, offering ourselves in service to their wisdom and direction, and inwardly pleading that we all act together with vigilance to carry out Verdiff's orders. It was a tense situation, and I stepped back to give space for Verdiff to make his own announcements.

I could feel Wueli's presence next to me. He could sense the dilemma that I was having. His thoughts wanted to enter my mind, and I chose to let him. He told me that the warriors needed my Spiritual leadership. I must not become involved. The physical fighting and execution of Verdiff's plans were for the warriors and not me. They had been trained for this. Now was their moment. I had already put my physical self at risk far too much already in recent times. If anything happened to me, it would weaken the morale of our forces tremendously. This was one time where I had to look after myself. What I could offer was inner encouragement via telepathy. I could link to the Spirit of the land, and do the inner work for which I had been trained within the Order of the Wise. Whatever was to transpire, I was a witness, and the story of this day needed to be preserved for our future.

Before he could say much, Verdiff was called up the hill by one of our lookouts, and soon, he and Chrisong were standing together, talking earnestly, and pointing back and forth along the coastline. The boat party in front of us was not travelling quite where Verdiff and Chrisong had anticipated, but was headed towards land a little further down the coast. They called a meeting with us and all the warriors. The forces with us needed to become two groups. We needed to assemble our army of warriors on either side of where the invaders would land. This way, we would be better prepared for whichever way they decided to move. Chrisong would take one group, and she needed to move under cover with her group, immediately and swiftly, so that they could be situated on the south side, while Verdiff would stay with the remainder of the forces here on the north side. Both groups would be far enough away to be hidden, but in a position to be able to counter and follow whatever the enemy would decide to do.

Wueli motioned to me and pointed out a hill adjacent to the one where we stood. He motioned to Nianda and Gracon nearby. This hill was closer to where the enemy would land. It would provide us with a vantage point away from Verdiff's warriors, from where we could view developments as they unfolded. I wanted to go there immediately, and we soon set off.

Landing party

The boats did not come directly to the shore, but fanned out as they approached. I speculated that they were seeking signs of settlement where they could wreak their havoc. For some horrible moments, I thought that they may change course and land in some altogether different place from where Verdiff had supposed. But they didn't, and it was a long stretch of beach where they secured their boats, right in front of us.

From where I was, the men in the boats looked quite tiny, but they were busy, with much activity, unpacking their boats, collecting wood for a fire, and then groups of them spreading out into the surrounding area. I wondered if they may come to the hill where we were stationed, but they chose another one next to ours, from where they could gain a view of the nearby landscape. We hid while they did this. They were obviously conducting a reconnaissance mission to ensure the safety of their base, while also determining options for where their operation could go next. Groups of them went to either end of the beach to the remnants of the villages that they had raided previously, and they must have been disappointed to find these deserted, but it did not seem to deter them.

By early evening, the raiding party had all gathered again on the beach. From my communications, I felt relief that none of our forces had been discovered. This was the stage of patient waiting. We did not know for how long they would stay here. Verdiff and Chrisong supposed that they would make camp overnight by the beach and make their moves in the morning. This anticipation proved to be correct.

They were a noisy crowd, and there were shouts and the sounds of revelry that filled the air. Their fire crackled and flickered in the darkening sky. The noise from their gathering did not quieten until very late in the night. It was only then that I felt that I could rest. Finally, I did get some sleep, only to be woken by Wueli nudging me urgently after what felt to me to be the briefest of intervals.

It was a grey morning. The enemy was on the move. A large group of them were heading inland, and they were going by a southern route. As I watched them, I observed that their route would take them very close to where Chrisong and her forces were concealed. I felt anxiety in my stomach, and hoped that Chrisong and her group could remain hidden. Our warriors had acquired skills to hide traces of their movements. Verdiff and Chrisong had trained them in that. I had to trust. The barbarians must not discern our presence, at least, not yet. The plan would be for Chrisong and her group to follow behind the barbarians on the move, and monitor them.

I waited anxiously while the group of barbarians proceeded. After a while, they moved out of my range of vision, so I remained crouched down in my position, wondering what Verdiff would do.

There was a problem for our commander, because too many of the invaders remained behind. They were a huge group, much more than I had imagined, and the majority of them were still lingering around the campsite. I could tell with Verdiff's energy, as I tuned into him, that he was anxious and uneasy.

If only a few had remained, our plan had been to hole and break up their boats, but we could not do that with so many still there. It would mean direct conflict and much loss of life.

Verdiff was hoping that because there was no signs of living settlement left in the vicinity, that this would encourage the invaders to go further inland, but then they would need to carry supplies, supplies that would be heavy and burden them. Therefore they would create a supply line, and hopefully leave these only lightly guarded, especially if they surmised that the area where they were exploring was unpopulated. These would be what we would attack, for if we could dismantle and destroy their supply lines, then this would weaken them and make them vulnerable and frustrated.

But Verdiff's plans were not working out as he wished. He did not like to be separated from Chrisong, and he could not understand what the remaining barbarians on the beach front were doing there. Why had so many of them stayed behind?

Chrisong and her group were now in pursuit of the warriors that had gone inland. I took my mind awareness to the beach where the rest of the invaders were gathered. I felt them to be slow moving, gathering their energies and supplies in a very steady manner. But then, I had a sudden realization. These barbarians were obviously tired from their night of celebrations, but they were not going to be idle. They wanted their plunder, and I could see signs of increasing activity. I could hear sounds of shouting from their ranks, and all at once, a large majority of those that had stayed there were on their feet, and on the move. In horror, I realized what would happen. They were headed south like the others. It was clear that they were planning to go and join up with the other barbarians that had gone inland.

Verdiff appeared to have the same thought as me in the same moment. We were tuned in with our minds, and I could see him in the encampment below me, indicating frantically to our warriors that they needed to get ready. The barbarians were moving; they were going fast, in the footsteps of their companions. Only a small group was remaining. Chrisong's group would be sandwiched between the two groups of raiders. If this following group stayed together, she may be able to avoid them, but they weren't; they were spreading out. Chrisong had to be alerted to the danger.

I felt Verdiff's agitation. He wanted to go after them, and was clearly desperately worried about his mate. Chrisong and her forces would need a lot of support. Verdiff wanted to move in a hurry. Only a small handful of his warriors would remain. Verdiff spoke to me in my mind and requested if Wueli could take charge of the beach operation. He needed to go immediately.

It was with some shock and exhilaration that I realized that we might yet be involved in some significant part of the mission. We had to remain in our new encampment with the residual warriors that stayed behind, and assess the situation that lay before us.

There were now only a small number of barbarians left to guard their boats. They must have felt safe. I realized that for us to fulfill our objectives with their boats, then these guards would either need to be killed or incapacitated, so we could achieve our ends. I wondered what Wueli would consider as the best action for us to do. My intuition told me that although it was ruthless, that these guards would need to be killed.

I spent some time in silence. Gracon and Nianda joined me, and we prayed. These men invading our land still had souls. They needed compassion, and we asked the Earth Spirit to grant them passage that would best support them on their own personal journeys. Meanwhile we waited. The time for us to strike would be in the dark.

Sacrifice

It was a very long day, and I found it hard to keep still as the sun slowly crept across the sky. I did not want to impinge upon Verdiff while he was involved in active command, especially with regards the delicate nature of the circumstances of the operation. But I had to open myself to what was happening on the ground and how our plans proceeded. On the edges of my mind, I felt increasing agitation within me. Wueli was on his feet and walking around uneasily, shaking his head. He was also tuning in, like me.

Our attention was with Chrisong. She had received telepathic communication from Verdiff about the situation with the second group of barbarians, and Verdiff's main concern was for them to make themselves safe. The second assemblage of barbarians continued to spread themselves outwards, and this made matters much more challenging. They were noisy, and their forces covered a wide arc. Increasingly Chrisong and her warriors were being hemmed in.

Chrisong and Verdiff were not happy that they had failed to anticipate this. The barbarians were not a people that stayed very easily together. They were loud and needed space from one another. It could have been that they were also searching for evidence of the local population, and for tracks that would lead them to small communities hidden in the undergrowth. They would not find any. But Chrisong needed to be very careful for her warriors not to leave and indications of their presence.

What she would have preferred to have done was to move over to the edge of this second group of barbarians, and then, as they moved forward, to come in behind them. But the size of her group of warriors was too large, and they would soon be detected. She would have to act quickly, for the second group of barbarians was closing in and making much swifter progress than the ones ahead.

The numbers of barbarians in both groups were far greater than the forces that Chrisong had at her disposal. She did not want to risk direct conflict. This would play directly into the invader's hands. Far better for the invaders not to even realize that they were there. That was the plan that she had formulated with Verdiff. So how could they do that now? The strategy that they decided upon was to break into small groups, and for each group to try to find the means of winding back through the enemy on an individual basis, and then regroup from there. If any single member of their group was discovered then, they might be killed, but the overall integrity of the mission would be preserved. It was only if there was the danger of many of them being discovered that the operation could face serious problems.

Chrisong started to split off her warriors to accomplish this aim. She urged them to keep to the Earth energy paths and ask Spirit to protect them. Ahead of her, she could hear distant shouts and noises from the masses of barbarians that were there. They were not that far in front.

When they came to a rise, Chrisong could view the large hill in front of them. This is where they were headed. The summit of that hill would give them a vantage point from which they could survey a long distance into the surrounding countryside.

Chrisong gazed in dismay as she saw that in the landscape below the hill, there were no trees. It was heath land. When they reached the heath land, they would be totally exposed, there would be no cover. Chrisong had to move her warriors urgently.

Listening to the shouts and drum beats of the barbarians behind her was very unsettling. Even though, from her mind communication, Chrisong knew that Verdiff was closing in and approaching with his own warriors, this provided no comfort. Her beloved companion could do nothing to help her. Chrisong just had to pray that all her forces could find a way through. And of course, she had to leave her own small group till last.

Chrisong organized the groups with as much clarity as she could. She gave directions and encouragement. All were willing and determined. There were only a few groups left and only a small expanse of undergrowth remained for cover. She prayed that they would all make it. But then, what Chrisong had dreaded most suddenly came into manifestation. Some barbarians from nearby behind her started shouting and alerting the others. Someone had been seen.

Chrisong swung into action. She had to do this. With all the turmoil in her mind, she needed to act. If one was seen, the others would be in grave danger too. Everything they had hoped to gain through being hidden could be lost. Without hesitation, she quickly maneuvered herself to the base of the biggest tree she could find in the area. She was a very skilled and agile climber. With the remaining

Ilsa

groups, she instructed them to go forward and then to fan out just before the heath land began and then to double back as the others had done. She kept only three warriors with her, and in her heart, she felt the pain of knowing that she was condemning these three loyal friends to certain death. She hugged them, and they knew what she was asking of them. Not one of them wanted to leave.

As soon as she was high enough in the tree, Chrisong yelled at the top of her voice. Being female, her voice was distinctive and aimed to lure the barbarians towards her with alacrity. So it turned out to be. As they came to her, the others could get away. It was the only way to save them and safeguard the mission.

When Verdiff sensed what she was doing, he pledged to come and save her. She told him to stay away. Verdiff argued with her. She had to let him help her. She refused. He argued with her, over and over, again and again. But she was adamant. The success of the mission was more important than her life. He had to let her do this.

What passed between them, via their thoughts, was immensely painful, as they both realized the finality of what was unfolding. For Verdiff to be in this position where he could not help the one that he loved was the worst possible torment that he had ever endured. He struggled with it. But every time he wavered, she fiercely countered his impulse, reassured him of her love for him, and insisted that he must be strong.

Chrisong waited in the tree, her warriors close by around the base of the trunk. The wild Barbarians were soon upon them. It would not take long. They had spears and knives. Chrisong instructed her friends to let death come to them. Better to die quickly than to be tortured and violated and suffer a lingering death. These attackers had a lust for enjoying suffering and brutality. They would probably prefer to keep at least one of their victims alive if they could.

The barbarians came on to the warriors like wild animals. To prey on the local population was what they had been hungry to do. In a short space of time, her friends were all dead. Chrisong scrambled higher up the tree, right to the top most branches, to give herself some respite. She communicated with Verdiff and tried to encourage him. He was desperate for her to find some way out. Surely, she could slide into the undergrowth and escape. But Chrisong knew that she needed to stay, for if she got away, those barbarians would continue to search for her, and they would not give up, and the whole mission would be imperiled.

Chrisong was now swaying in the wind on those high branches and she felt a strange sense of peace as she watched the scene below her. The barbarians were clambering over each other to try to climb the tree after her, but they were clumsy climbers, and could not get near her. Their spears were falling short and they were growing increasingly frustrated.

Chrisong continued to speak with Verdiff, and recalled precious moments of love that they had shared. She insisted that he must complete the mission, and that she would never leave him in Spirit, but this did not satisfy him. The barbarians were starting to chop at the tree with their axes. Once again, he pleaded with her, but she was steadfast. She could not linger much more.

Chrisong sent a powerful bolt of energy to her lover in farewell, and came down the tree to a lower level. The barbarians looked up at her with lust in their eyes. A few of them threw spears that fell short, but then one came that reached her level, and Chrisong was grateful to the blessing that this presented to her. By leaning to her left, Chrisong was able to move into the path of the spear. She let it strike her in the chest. As her body collapsed and fell, she felt disappointment and acute sadness that her life had to end like this, but then she also felt relief as her Spirit rose up and left. It felt good for that to be over. For Verdiff though, he felt the spear as if it was striking him. He let out a gasp that would have been a gaping scream, but was prevented from doing this only because the barbarians were so close.

From a military perspective, Chrisong's actions had been appropriate; she had been prepared to sacrifice her own life for the sake of being true to her mission. From a personal perspective, her actions had torn a great bleeding wound into the heart of all that Verdiff and Chrisong had wished together.

Verdiff's grief

Verdiff was devastated. I could feel his utter despair, and I had to hold on to my friends, to Nianda, Wueli and Gracon, so I would not collapse and feel crushed by the weight of what Verdiff was feeling.

We could see him now in our minds. He had broken down and was sobbing. No one could console him. He wanted to withdraw from the mission. His energy was very volatile. He also felt a huge anger and wanted to lash out. I could sense all this as I tuned in to him. I had to try to reach him and speak directly into his mind. It was not easy. He was tightly closed.

I tried many times, until finally with a burst of determination, I did get through. Verdiff pleaded with my mind to bring Wueli over so he would be able to take over the leadership of the mission. He did not want the responsibility anymore and refused to do it. I could not allow that. Within me, I felt that I had to see him in person. Nothing I said to his mind would make any difference. His soul was quite broken, and needed both healing and space to grieve. But we also needed him, not only for the sake of our group, but for all the other groups too - and the land. Without his presence, the morale of our warriors would plummet.

I stopped speaking into Verdiff's mind and grabbed Nianda. We needed to go. Wueli wanted to come too, but I told him that he was needed to monitor the invader's party that remained on the beach. It was not the time for him to be with Verdiff. Together we ran. Verdiff was immobile. We had to go to him. Somehow, on this occasion as with others, I could trust my instinct and intuition to lead me where we needed to travel. Nianda stayed with me, and we both knew the urgency of the situation before us.

It was late afternoon when we reached him. The warriors were resting, and as we arrived, many of them looked up, acute anxiety written on their faces. There were several dozen of them, but not one of them knew how to deal with Verdiff's grief. Fortunately, a few scouts had gone ahead to continue to monitor the progress of the barbarians. We needed to know where they would be.

Verdiff was sitting apart, head in hands, completely disconsolate. His energy was grey and unyielding and his skin color looked drained and divorced from his vitality. It was hard to see someone who was normally so strong and capable in such a resigned state. And yet, as I examined his energy state further, I noticed above his head, that there was a light. As I focused on this light, it became brighter and brighter, and I recognized it, of course, as Chrisong. How typical that she would be there so close to him. And he was oblivious of anything except his own sorrow.

If only he would notice her. I reached out gently and offered to place my arm around him. He was even resistant to that, but I could tell how desperately he needed love. Inwardly I prayed repeatedly that he would open up to receive help. I kept my arm there and eventually he responded and moved his head around to my shoulder and cried huge sobs while I held him. The more he cried, and accepted contact, the less stiff his body felt. Nianda went behind him to channel love and healing into his heart. We could feel the presence of Chrisong helping. We had to revive him, somehow.

It took a considerable time before Verdiff's sobbing subsided, and he finally looked up, and spoke to me.

Verdiff could not understand why Chrisong did not allow him to bring the warriors in to rescue her. It had been a terrible choice that he had been forced to make, and it was not something that he could endure. He had done what she had insisted upon, but in his heart, he felt something fundamental had broken.

His life had been hard, and she had been his only love, and what made all his ideals and purpose meaningful. How could he carry on without her? He broke down again. They had pledged that they would do this together, that the love they shared would be enough for them to lead this mission and preserve the land from these savage intruders. Now she was gone, and their defense of the land had hardly begun. All their planning had been in vain. Verdiff felt that he had no strength, no will to continue. We would have to find someone else to lead the mission.

Ilsa

I heard all that Verdiff said, and I could sense his resignation, but some force in me told me that Verdiff could do it, and that he had to do it, that this was his test and the moment when he could shine.

I told him to look up, and he would not budge. Then I told him again, and he still would not stir. So I shook him and I spoke to him as loudly as I dared, for him to look up. And I shook him again. He was so irritatingly stubborn! Verdiff questioned me, and asked me why, and I kept insisting, until he finally did raise his head, and I told him to raise it higher, until he finally saw her, and perceived her light. And he smiled.

'Is it really you?' He repeated this over and over again. And all the time that he looked at her, her light shone more brightly, and seemed to merge with his. They shared thoughts and feelings together, and I felt Verdiff's strength returning. She was trying to reassure him, comfort him by her presence and reaffirm the commitment that they both had made to further the mission that they had started, and lead it through to its completion.

Verdiff felt that she was with him, and that she would be with him, and while she was there, he could do it. And she urged him to affirm that and give the mission all his strength for it to succeed, and to be a shining light himself, where others could follow, and do what was required to carry out the strategy of defense that they had put in motion. She had to repeat herself many times for it to sink in and for him to agree, but she stayed with him until he got it.

Finally Verdiff stood up. He called the warriors over, and he spoke to them. He affirmed how precious our land was, and our way of life, and that this was a time when we needed to stand up and ensure that no one would destroy the good that was here. Our civilization was the guardian of a way of life. The values that we lived were to respect our land and all its creatures, something which these people coming in their boats did not recognize. Their brutality had to be countered, and they had to be persuaded to go elsewhere. He was going to lead, and he wanted our warriors to work with him, and for the Order of the Wise to add its support, for us to succeed in this together. Verdiff then looked up at all of us in front of him, staring in our eyes, and as he did this, he affirmed to us all that he would continue his efforts as commander until all the objectives of the mission were complete, and every last barbarian had left our land for good.

There was a great energy of love and determination, and the light of Chrisong and many other Spiritual beings joined us in encouragement and acknowledgment of what we needed to achieve. We would go on, and I knew that our warriors were in safe hands.

I had had communication from Wueli that there had been messages from our other groups. Wueli had been taking these and dealing with them. There was great concern about Verdiff and his state of mind, but Wueli had urged all the groups to keep going – that in this situation, there would be setbacks, but we needed to continue the effort until we won through.

We had to get back to Wueli now, for he would soon have his own trial and challenge, and a task to perform, and I knew how much this would test him to his utter limits. I could not leave him on his own for this.

A time to kill

It was evening now, and Wueli and I were laying on our stomachs, observing through tufts of grass, the beach below us, where the remaining invaders were gathered around their camp fire.

From where we lay, we could see about twenty of them, mainly men, but a few women and children too. They had lit their fire was near to their boats, and were huddled around the fire to keep warm. Every now and again, there would be shouts and garbled noises coming from their group. They were not a people to enjoy silence. Close to the fire, they had erected simple shelters with sticks and skins where they would sleep.

We knew now, from our other warriors that the two larger groups of barbarians had now merged into one group, and were now at the vantage point on the high ground where we had anticipated that they would be. They had made camp there, and now Verdiff and his group had found shelter nearby, and were continuing to monitor what they were doing.

Our warriors were basically peaceful people. They were trained as guardians and protectors of our village life. Often, they were the hunters and providers of food for our communities. If there was a natural disaster, or an attack by wild animals, our warriors would be there with their strength and spears to help the people. They were people we could rely on, and their function was to serve the local community in whatever capacity they were needed. In the case of a dispute, the warriors would be there to support the Order of the Wise, to help maintain stability and well-being in our land.

It was very rare that our warriors would ever be called upon to hurt or kill another human being, and when this happened, it would only be with extreme reluctance, and usually this would occur defensively, in response to some violent attack. Our warriors were there to protect, not to kill. We were a society that respected life, and not destroyed it.

But now, that had changed. The village warriors had been summoned as a group to help form a national force of warriors, trained to resist and defend our land from invasion. There were new rules in place to deal with this threat.

Many discussions had taken place to determine strategy for how we would cope with the barbarians. Verdiff and Chrisong had been given command of this mission, and their thoughts contributed greatly to the policy that we adopted.

We would have to kill. To hole and destroy their boats, we needed to be prepared that the best course of action may be to kill those guarding them. To remove their sources of food and drink from their supply lines, we may need to kill there too. Verdiff argued that the only means to deter these people from incursions to our shores would be by killing some of their number. Brutal as it were, they were still people that tried to look after each other, to some extent, and they would not want to live in an environment that they did not consider safe.

But to kill these people, we would need to do it as painlessly as possible, with prayers for these people's souls. We did not in any form want to instill or encourage a lust of bloodshed in our warriors. We had to do what was necessary to achieve our objectives, and not more. In adopting this policy, we would also seek to avoid any form of direct conflict, so that loss of life would be kept to an absolute minimum.

With these aims, Verdiff had supervised the training of a number of warriors in the art of killing painlessly, using knives, and pressure on certain parts of the body. During his life, Verdiff had travelled extensively, to various societies, and during these excursions, he had gained skills in the art of killing. We had to approach this very sensitively, but it was something that felt right to do.

Wueli's trial

Wueli was one of those warriors trained for the purpose of killing barbarians. He only did the training because he felt responsible for doing as much as he could to defend the land. As the warrior in charge of security at our College of the Order of the Wise, he felt it as a duty that he would need to take an active part in this combat operation. But the thought of killing revolted him.

Wueli was one of my closest friends, and I knew him very well. He was a kind and compassionate man, someone that I could count on, a friend and colleague that never wavered in his devotion. And here he was, volunteering to act against other human beings, in a manner that went completely contrary to his heart. He tried not to show it to me, but I sensed that Wueli struggled with this dilemma very much. I had seen him with his head down, even crying on one or two occasions, but he would not speak of it, or openly ask for support. During the build up to the invasion, it was as though he carried a wall around him to keep his emotions held inside him.

Now, though, the night had descended and Wueli would need to take his group of warriors to attend to the barbarian's boats and those that guarded them. Gently, I reached over and squeezed Wueli's hand as we watched them from the hill. He did not resist and welcomed my touch. I moved a little closer to him. As they sat by their fire, we could see their shadows moving sometimes against the flickering flames. Their raucous laughter and shouting betrayed their presence. They did not expect that anyone would approach them, and they were quite unaware of us.

A little while later, I led our group with prayers for the barbarian's souls, and invited various beings of Spirit to be with us and support us in our efforts. We asked for the souls of the barbarians to be released in peace, and that our warriors could perform their task with respect, but also purpose for the sake of our land.

We would have to wait until all was quiet, so I sat with Wueli, and I could tell that his energy was suffering with both fear and sadness. Reaching out my hand to him again, I touched him, and he welcomed me with a squeeze and a quiver. This was very difficult for him, and he needed to know that he was loved. I had tried to reassure all our warriors, but with Wueli, I had a special bond.

We had sympathy for the barbarians, for they were souls like us, but we had to protect our land, and the barbarians were simply ignorant, and did not respect life in its sacredness, as we did. We could not let ourselves be destroyed, and we had to stand up for our way of life. These killings were a necessary act.

In our earlier discussions, I had offered to participate in these killings, myself, as an act of solidarity, but with us being a peaceful nation, it did not feel appropriate. My role was first and foremost as the leader of the Order of the Wise, not a war queen. What I did would be an important symbol for our people. I could be a witness, but not a participant in this. So it was to be done by Wueli and his fellow warriors.

Deep into the night, we waited until the barbarian encampment finally settled, and with our patient waiting over, Wueli knew that the time had come to strike. Most of them, at least, would be sleeping now. Wueli gave one pained look towards me with his dark eyes, and then, with a gesture to the others, and a flick of his body, they were gone.

There were only a small group of us that remained. Gracon, Nianda and I stretched out at the top of the rise, and tried to see what would happen. Wueli had requested to me not to intrude upon his mind while he did this. He wanted privacy, and to draw from his own inner resources while he undertook this task. It was not easy for me to restrain myself. I cared about Wueli, and I knew how vulnerable he felt just now. Part of me wished that I could be there with him, or even to kill those people for him, so that he wouldn't have to endure the anguish of it. But I could not, and I also had my duty and my position to consider.

The fire of the barbarian's encampment had burned very low. We were aware, that because of the fermented liquids that they drank, that they would sleep heavily and be little able to defend themselves. It was the ideal time to do this.

There was a soft breeze, and we could also hear the hypnotic crashing of the waves in the distance, but, other than that, there was nothing to give away any indication of the sequence of events that was unfolding.

Gracon's body was twitching and his face contorting. He had left his body, and although his physical self was next to us, his Spirit Self was on the beach. Gracon had also vowed to stay clear of Wueli through this, but he wanted to support the other warriors and witness what took place. Nianda reached over and held my hand. This was not easy for her either. At one stage, we did hear a short muffled sound, like a scream, but it died quickly away, and then there was nothing further. Nianda and I shuddered and held each other tighter.

We watched and waited for what felt like a long time. Then suddenly, Gracon moved and opened his eyes, gazing over at us.

'It is done,' he reported blankly.

We waited in silence, and eventually Wueli and his troop of warriors appeared over the rise. Wueli was very controlled, and he communicated the success of the operation. All the barbarians had been killed without incident. None of our warriors had been injured. Solemnly, we came together to send further prayers, and then everyone retired to their shelters.

I followed Wueli. He tried to motion me away but I would not go. Wueli was shivering. Before he reached his shelter, he vomited and staggered. He could hardly stand. I sat down with him, and lightly held

Ilsa

him for a while, and waited. He needed to talk, and finally he was able to do so. I had never seen Wueli so vulnerable.

He had not wanted to kill people. Everything inside him screamed that it was wrong, that human life was sacred, but he also knew his duty and commitment to our land.

As I listened, gradually the story of what happened to him seeped out. When he had gone down to their encampment, there had been one barbarian sleeping under skins. He was only young, maybe sixteen summers. When Wueli had approached, he had opened his eyes. For a brief instant, Wueli had seen terror and incomprehension in his eyes. Wueli could not bear it, and had stuck his knife into this boy's chest before he could think. It was the most terrible act. How could he ever forgive himself? Wueli was inconsolable. I would stay with Wueli on this night. He needed me. He needed love. It was certain that he would not be the only one wrestling with haunting and disturbing thoughts. In the new day, Nianda would be very busy, and she would also have her own distress about this.

In the morning, we gathered the bodies and made a large funeral pyre for them. We had to do this immediately, rather than to give them the usual three days that we would give for full Spiritual release. We also attended to the boats, and worked hard to break them up, and used their wood for the fire. We deliberately left one boat untouched and a further one that we holed severely, but left by the water's edge, as a tactic that had been decided upon.

By the time we burnt the bodies, it was late afternoon. I conducted the ceremony, and Gracon helped with herbs and invocations. We all held each other, and there was much weeping and sadness. I was glad of that; we needed to feel our solidarity, emotions and love. It was a hard time, and not something that could be put right easily.

My thoughts turned to Verdiff now, and how his work with the mission was proceeding. His mind had been open to mine during the day, so I knew that a lot had been happening.

Paul Williamson

Supply lines and animals

Our land must have appeared to the barbarians as a country offering great opportunity. They were a travelling people, explorers, but they also had strong instincts to dominate others, and overpower them. Their wooden boats were quite elaborate and large, constructed with care to withstand choppy seas. They were basically rowing boats with simple sails, but they must have been capable navigators, with physical strength to direct their boats where they willed. For their journeys, they packed their boats, not only with their own warriors, but also with supplies, so they could maintain their strength.

One thing they had in abundant quantities was jars of the fermented liquid. They seemed hardly to be able to exist without it, but we noticed how much this weakened them, in addition to making them loud and vulgar. But they had also brought with them sacks of root vegetables and grains for making soups and broths. With salt from evaporated water, they were able to preserve meat for considerable periods, and had many bags of meat with them.

All the food that they had was there with the aim that they would be as self-sufficient as possible, so they did not need to hunt or scavenge for food in the country where they journeyed.

In previous raids to our land, the barbarians had gained rich pickings from their incursions. They would not have had such a lot of supplies then. The barbarians appeared to extract enormous pleasure from destroying villages, creating havoc and terror, killing, torturing and raping the local people. But they also took to satisfy their wants. So people were captured as slaves for sexual pleasure and labour. Skins and articles were collected and taken. Food stuffs were also commandeered. They were a people whose primary purpose appeared to be to satisfy their own wants and desires, with no regard for anyone except themselves.

On this expedition, they were a much larger party than we had ever encountered, and the ones we had seen were only one of several groups along the coastline. They wanted to raid, but also find bases from which some of them could stay and settle. Even with all the supplies they had brought, we anticipated that they would have brought hunters and hope to find game from which they could sustain themselves for a longer time. We had to ensure that this would not happen.

As much as we could, we needed to make conditions so difficult for them that they would be deterred from ever returning here again. It was a challenge because their previous visits had been so satisfying for them. This is what they expected on this occasion too. But they would not find it so.

By their boats, the barbarians had left a large measure of their supplies. They would want these provisions to be kept in reserve for when their warriors returned from their explorations. On the day when we destroyed their boats, we emptied their fermented liquid into the sea, and sacrificed their vegetables and grain to be burnt on the funeral pyre of the bodies of the barbarians that we had killed, alongside all their meat as well. When the mass of warriors returned, they would have nothing to feed upon, or drink.

This was just the beginning. We anticipated that the invaders would also create storage areas at points and stages along their journey, so they would have ready provisions when they needed them. Our intention was to ensure that these would be disposed of as well. The barbarians would not be able to attain satisfaction of their wants and desires while they were hungry and thirsty. It might drive them crazy, but we needed to know that all those that could leave, would do so, and not return.

There was one more preparation that we made to help our cause, and this involved the animals. My friend, Kiend, had a special kinship with the animals, and there were others like him. For this time of the invasion, we had brought all those people together, and assigned them with a task. It was not easily possible to communicate with all the animals of our land, and for them to be amenable to our instructions, but with some, this could be done. Kiend, for instance, had a special affinity with the wolves. What he and his friends had to do, as much as they could, was to persuade the animals to stay away, and to withdraw from the area where the barbarians would land, so that none of them would be killed. Then the barbarians would not be able to find any game to satisfy their hunger. We wanted them to regard our land as being desolate, dangerous and inhospitable.

Our group of animal lovers approached their task with passion and enthusiasm. Kiend was the leader of the group connected with our forces, and during the night when Wueli and his warriors went to do their task, I listened out to the hills behind us. In the distance, I could hear the faint howling of wolves. I knew that this was Kiend. He was with his friends. His strategy was to use the wolves as guards to shepherd the other animals away.

Stalking the enemy

The barbarians acted in a manner exactly as Verdiff and Chrisong had foreseen. They had made a small supply base on their way to the hill summit where they made their encampment overnight, and then they had left a much larger supply base on the hill when they went on in the morning.

We had cleared all trace of village life in the areas closest to the sea, and in the adjacent land further inland, we had evacuated the people and hoped that most of those settlements would be spared from attack by the invaders.

Verdiff was concerned about what the barbarians would do. From their vantage point overnight, they would have been able to gain sight of the empty villages that were further inland, and they might seek to ravage some of these. There would be nothing in these villages that they could want. Animals and stores had all been removed. It would be frustrating for them to discover this, and Verdiff hoped that they would then turn back. However, if they decided to persist and travel further to the next larger hill in the distance, they may then be able to view settlements that were still populated, and this represented a real danger.

Verdiff's scouts were able to inform him that the barbarians had split into two groups to attack the various distant settlements that they had seen from their overnight encampment. So now, Verdiff prepared to go with a group of his best warriors up towards the vantage point where they had left their supplies. This was a very delicate operation. They could not approach this from the near slopes because it was open heath land, and they would have to advance from the other side of the hill that was visible to the barbarians in the valley beyond. At least, here there was good tree cover. As they edged upwards, the warriors slowly spread out so they could encircle their enemy. There was only a small group of the barbarians that remained, and most of them seemed to be sleeping after their raucous night activities. But Verdiff made our warriors wait until the right moment. It would only take one barbarian to alert the others in the valley for all their efforts to be lost. Upon his signal, they raced forwards in a coordinated effort, and although there was one large barbarian that put up a struggle all the others were killed almost instantaneously.

Despite his success, Verdiff could not relax. He had also sent other warriors to destroy the intermediate base the barbarians had made the previous day, and while his warriors started to dispose of the supplies, Verdiff himself gazed anxiously over the vantage point at the valley below him in an effort to see what the two main bodies of barbarians were doing. He had scouts following them, and they were able to inform him telepathically what they knew. Verdiff did not like what he saw.

The leading group of barbarians had gone beyond the villages from the valley, towards the more distant vantage point, and had lit fires to inform their comrades to follow them. They were not turning back. Verdiff felt disturbed by the speed of their movements. It was as if these barbarians were determined to gain some rewards for their endeavors. They must be feeling very frustrated. There were villages under threat beyond the distant hill. He had to try and inform them. These people would need to leave immediately.

There was a network of contacts available to support this. The Order of the Wise had members of its circles in all these villages, ready to administrate and assist in this situation. But this was an emergency, and the people would need to leave without taking more than the most essential of their belongings. They must not be delayed. These barbarians could move fast, especially if they had the scent of prey to catch. The villagers would have to move at night, for the barbarians would surely make another encampment first.

Fortunately, for Verdiff and his warriors, there was plenty of woodland in the valleys between these hills. They could follow in the footsteps of the barbarians quite silently. There were energy pathways where they could tread and replenish themselves, and make greater progress. This was our land, and here our warriors knew how to look after themselves. For us to obtain food and water to replenish ourselves was not a problem, for we could listen to the Spirit of the Earth, and all its creatures, trees and plant life to help us.

We were a people that felt our world to be alive. At this moment, and with this mission, we felt the loving support of all the life that we encountered, for we knew that the Spirit of the Earth was on our side. It was a great source of comfort, and in exchange, we knew that the balance of this support was for us to continue to offer the respect that we needed to give to our fellow life forms. We needed to demonstrate commitment to honor and cooperate with all that lived with us, and for us to dedicate ourselves in service to that.

Even in the short space of time that the barbarians had been with us, they had left their trail of desecration. In following their footsteps, there were trees that had been uprooted, plants that had been trodden on. We felt pain when we saw this; we felt the pain of the plants and the trees. These were a careless people, the barbarians. They did not even realize the extent of damage that they were generating. But there was also no care or wish on their part to learn either. They wanted to conquer and claim this land as their own, but without concern and awareness. It would be tragic to have to let it go.

By now, the barbarians had climbed to their new vantage point and made their camp. Their groups had come together, and shouts and revelry could be heard as they drank and settled down for the evening. Verdiff and our warriors made camp in a hidden valley close by, concealed by the structure of the neighboring hills, and woodland. Scouts kept a close eye on the movements of the barbarians to ensure safety for our people.

During this day, I had travelled with Wueli and our group, to the first vantage point where the barbarians had camped on the previous night. We offered prayers for the slain barbarians and energetically tried to clear the space of the disturbances of the previous day. As we had done on the beach, we lit a funeral pyre and placed the dead barbarians upon this. It was another somber occasion, but one that we endeavored to treat with respect.

Throughout the day, I had been in communication with various groups along the coast about the progress of our mission. It was a busy and tense process as the raids continued. The villages beyond the new vantage point, where the barbarians had gathered to camp, were now being cleared. I gave gratitude for the network of cooperation that was helping us to coordinate our moves during this time.

As we looked into the valleys before us, there were remnants of several fires, where the barbarians had razed the ground of all the buildings within the villages that they had encountered. I wondered what thoughts they would have regarding finding so little active civilization in our land. It would be so different from what they would have expected. Perhaps this is why they pressed on. Instinctively, they must have known that the settlements would exist somewhere. But would they reach a point where they gave up looking?

The barbarians were on the move from first light the next morning. The ardency of their advance suggested to Verdiff instinctively that this was their last thrust. They were desperate to gain returns for their efforts. It would be sad for some of these villages to be destroyed. We all prayed that after this, they would turn back.

Verdiff and his scouts monitored the invaders anxiously. They continued to go forward and they ravaged and burned all the empty villages that they passed. Verdiff continued to hold the faith that they would turn.

In the meantime, our warriors were able to destroy the supply base that had been left on the second vantage point, and there were only a few men that had stayed behind this time, so it was possible to kill them without creating additional disturbance. Our warriors acted quickly to clear the space, and Verdiff was encouraged that so few had remained.

How would the barbarians react when they returned to their bases and found their supplies gone and their warriors slain? Verdiff knew that he had to be very careful. He needed for our warriors to be far enough away that they would not be found, but close enough so that they could stay connected with the barbarian's moves. We had the warriors that knew the local terrain. There were hills with rock clefts that provided excellent cover for our assembly of warriors. It had been impressed upon us numerous times how important at this stage it would be for us to be out of sight and reach of our enemy. It was not a time to settle. Verdiff had instructed Wueli to return with our party to the beach encampment and to wait there. What happened next had the potential to be the most dangerous and potentially liberating phase of the mission.

Retreat

It was the middle of the afternoon when their groups came together, and for a while they appeared to argue among themselves. I had travelled out of my body so I could watch them. For some, it was clear that they felt that they had travelled far enough, while others were not prepared to give up without being able to mete out their savagery. One of them pointed back towards the beach and their earlier supply line, and shouted earnestly. The others looked, and paused in their discussions. A group of them began to trail back, anyway, and let their feet do the talking, and soon the others followed.

Among those of us in the Order that had been following the events, there was a huge sigh of relief. From there, things moved quickly. Once they reached the nearest supply point, they cursed and shouted and screamed out to alert the others. The barbarians must have been enraged, and in vain, they sent search parties to find and apprehend whoever had done this. But they were not doing this in an organized manner, and it was noticeable how their discipline was breaking down.

They were afraid. It was perhaps a new feeling for them. Finding only traces of their comrades burned in a funeral pyre, and all their food and drink gone, must have been the most awful of surprises for them. Verdiff and his warriors were safely hidden, and some distance away, and he commanded them all to be as still as they could be.

One or two of them were throwing articles around to offload their rage. There was something compulsive and maddening in their behavior. They were not going to stay where they were. Even though the night was encroaching, they were turning and charging like a mass of animals down the hill. There was no fire from the vantage point where they had been on their first night. They had to get there. The barbarians were rushing with a mixture of fury and fear, determined to reach that vantage point, and they must have been anxious at what they would find.

The barbarians would exhaust themselves, but they were driving themselves on with pure adrenaline. Our warriors had to stand clear of this. If any of our people were found, we were sure that they would be hacked to death without mercy. The barbarians continued to run, and while they ran they roared. They were going too rapidly, even for their drums. Knowing a little what they were like, they must have been craving for their drink, and fearing for their comrades. Our warriors could not keep up with them.

It is hard to imagine what they must have thought when they found their initial vantage point base also destroyed. We wondered if they might stay there for the night, but they didn't. They were frantic. Even though it was a dark night, they were not going to wait until day break. They lit a fire briefly, to try to get some more light. From our inner perceptions, we could tell that their anger was starting to turn in on itself, and they were beginning to blame each other. Their raid was becoming a disaster for them.

While they paused to light the fire, it gave Verdiff and his warriors the opportunity to come a little closer, but he wanted to continue to keep as much distance as possible between our forces and theirs, while still monitoring them. The main concern that he had was if they decided to stay on our land and think, and look for revenge, rather than panic. It was still a very delicate process, and Verdiff was very thoughtful in his planning. His judgment was that the barbarians were an instinctive race, with little thought capacity, and therefore, without their drink and food, he anticipated that they would not be able to function, and their madness would only increase.

The night turned to day. Some of them were straggling behind, but the bulk of them kept going. There was some desperate urge in them to reach the sea. It was probably here that they felt most at home, safe and familiar. More and more, we could detect that they were starting to fight and compete with each other. No one wanted to be left behind. There was a herd instinct driving them, but also a survival instinct that was even stronger.

Verdiff and his warriors went as fast as they could. He sent communication to us, and was insistent to Wueli that we must be concealed, so they would have no vent for their fury besides themselves. We were watching from our hill, and I did a simple ritual, and asked the Earth Spirit for a special protection for all of us during this time. But even though there was no physical sign of them yet, we were all lying so still, we hardly dared even to breathe.

In the distance, we could hear shouts and commotions from the southern end of the beach. It was the leading members of the barbarians, now approaching the beach. They would suffer a massive shock to find their supplies from here also gone, and their guards and boats burnt on the funeral pyre. What would they think when they saw their boats? Only the two boats remained, and one of these was severely holed, deliberately. There were far too many barbarians to fit upon this one boat. How would they deal with this? We had to wait and watch.

There was utter chaos. The barbarians were rushing around. They could not control themselves. The madness and fear in them appeared to reach fever pitch. Some of them made a move towards the boats. They wanted to get away and save themselves. But they were beaten back. Now they were fighting each other with knives and spears, lashing out at each other, and the water was turning red with their blood. They had turned their anger on each other, and we could hear their screams from the wounds they inflicted upon each other. I felt compassion for them.

They were all so desperate to get on a boat and not to be stranded on this land. When they discovered the state of the second boat, this made things only worse. At one point, there was a group of them that appeared to almost break free, but the other barbarians made a surging effort to draw them back, and more bloodshed resulted. No one seemed to be able to bring sanity to the proceedings, and so, the killings and mayhem went on.

There was one woman. She was not very tall, but strong. She shouted at them and tried to pull them off each other. Soon, she was knocked down, and sank into the water, but she must have recovered, and she struggled to the shore. Climbing up the beach, she tried to encourage others to withdraw and wait, but very few would listen to her. She shouted at them until she was exhausted, and then sank to her knees. This woman had more sense than the rest of them. I could tell. In a moment, she began to look around, and stare at the surrounding landscape. She was searching for us with her eyes.

As I kept gazing at her, her eyes wandered to the hill where we were watching, and for a while, she seemed to be staring right at us. My perception told me that she was a woman that knew. She was a woman that could lead these people with heart and awareness, and was important to them. From my heart, I sent her my appreciation and asked Spirit to give her strength.

This woman then stood to the side and watched what was happening in the water, and I did the same. The fighting barbarians seemed to be utterly exhausted, and there were only a small number of them now standing. The few of them that had been sensible enough to withdraw while the fighting continued were now able to dare to step forward. These were the ones that had the best chance to leave on the last boat. They were still quite volatile, but the woman I had seen was now issuing instructions and trying to organize them. They were listening to her just enough so they could work together and board the boat.

Not all the barbarians were dead, but the ones left were so injured that with all their groans and moaning, they were not able to do anything to interfere. It would be up to us how we would deal with these injured ones. I felt that it might be kind to help them heal and repair their other boat so they would be able to use that to leave. In my instinct, I felt that we would not lose to do this for them.

Some stragglers were still also arriving on the beach and joining in the panic that was there.

From the hill, we had gazed in astonishment at the frenzy that had unfolded before us. Verdiff had still not reached us, but we could sense him coming. Slowly the one barbarian boat edged out from the shore. They had no food, and little liquid, and so, we were not certain if they would have the strength to make it back to their native land. But they seemed more resolute now to go. Some of them were looking back, taking in the memory of what had happened. I hoped and prayed that at least some of them would survive to reach their native terrain. With that woman on the boat with them, I felt hopeful. She was a survivor, and she had the determination to ensure that her people survived too. In our hearts, we knew that it would be a long time before they would attempt to come to our land again. And with that, we were glad, and felt huge relief.

When Verdiff did join us on our hill, and observed what had taken place, he danced around and shouted like a little boy. We were all very happy just then.

Over the coming days, we heard news of the other groups and trials that had been proceeding along our coast. Generally, the success of our mission had been repeated elsewhere. In one area, there had been fighting, and a number of our warriors had been killed, but the overall strategy that we had tried was successful. There was one cluster of barbarians that had sought not to leave our land when they found that their boats were destroyed. A decision was taken then to kill these invaders, even though it meant loss of life, for it was felt necessary so none of these people would be able to gain a foothold in our land. The people of our villages had been saved, and we felt that we had been protected and guided to achieve a great victory to preserve the traditions and way of life of our people.

There were prayers and services to honor the dead. On the beaches, and places of battle, our healers cleansed these areas as well as we could, to help the energy of our land return to its former peaceful state. Warriors who had been hurt or involved in the trauma of battle received counseling and healing too. We tried to care for those who had actively supported our efforts.

Later, we held memorial services, in gratitude for what we had achieved, and also to honor those that had sacrificed their lives for our common cause. In the large central stone circle in the south of our land, we held a public ceremony that attracted thousands of people from all over the land. It was a great coming together, with a mixture of solemnity and rejoicing that we could all share.

I waited with my own celebration, until we conducted our more private ritual in the Sacred Grove at our College encampment. We lit a fire. This was a service for the Order of the Wise. Verdiff was regarded as a hero in the land for his leadership in our trial, but here, in this environment, he could allow himself to be more vulnerable, and to acknowledge his feelings of loss for his precious partner, Chrisong. He broke down and cried, and we held him gently to allow his tears.

There were others we had to acknowledge too. For me, I remembered Karka and Berenice. They had both given so much. We had to go deeper, and give gratitude to the Earth Spirit, for our friends in the animal and plant kingdom, and the mineral world. As the flames died down, many of us could see an inner light that shone brightly over our Grove. It was as though those Spirits of our ancestors and loved ones that had passed on, our guides too, were with us at this moment, marking a momentous occasion, which meant a great deal to all of us. Looking around, there were several there with tears streaming down their faces, and I felt it too, great joy in my heart.

Gracon spoke from his own inner awareness. He felt that our efforts to repel the barbarians had been a success, and that the invaders would not return, not as an invading force, in our generation.

We all felt peace then, and we stayed together in silence for a long time, until all that remained of the fire were a few glowing embers on the ground. And then we celebrated. We were a people that loved to delight in our attainments. That night, we danced and sang; we played music, hugged and embraced each other. The happiness was immense, and it was only at daybreak that I finally went to my hut and to sleep. It had been a good night, and a new dawn for our people and our land.

CHAPTER 14

Family Tragedy

Nightmares

The celebrations for our victory over the barbarians were a great relief to all of us. Now we could turn our attention to the aftermath, and how we could move our society forward to embrace more secure conditions. I would have liked to have felt free to dedicate myself fully to this task. However, it was not yet a time when conditions would be easier for me, and there were other matters of a very personal nature that were flooding into my consciousness and emotionally testing me to my limits.

In those times immediately after all the celebrations were over, I started to have recurring nightmares concerning my father. Suddenly, as I slept, he would be there in front of me and he would be screaming in agony and despair. And then his face would turn towards mine and his eyes would be looking into mine and pleading with me. At this point, I would wake up with a start, and with perspiration dripping down me.

At first, I tried to ignore these dream visions, for although I knew that my father needed help, I had all these other national issues that had to take priority and needed my leadership. But every night, the vision would repeat itself and my father's expression became more compelling and urgent. It was as though my father's Spirit was trying to connect with me. His earthly body would not approach me, but his Spirit wanted to reach me through these visions. As much as I hoped that other members of my family, or his community could reach out to him just now, his gaze towards me was very deliberate, and I could not turn away from him.

The build up

This prompted me to reflect back over my father's life. He had had a lot of problems. It was not just about the dramas that had taken place around my half brother, Skife, for my father was haunted and wounded in his soul. On one of my visits to our family village, my mother had told me how, when she was a child, my father had witnessed the death of his father, cut down and slain by raiders, before his eyes, just meters away from where he had been placed under some bushes so he would be safe from attack. My father had been devoted to his father, and had felt part of his life ebbing away from him as he witnessed the last movements of his dying parent. It was a miserable start to his life, and gave a base for how much he hated any raiders to our land and the destruction that they brought. I suppose with the trials that we had with the barbarians, this would have only acted to trigger memories and feelings associated with his own past.

My father was a proud man. He had loved my mother very much, and the well-being of our family was completely central to his concerns. It must have been doubly devastating to him when my mother was also raped and hurt by raiders and made pregnant by them. We all knew how much at pains my father felt even to accept my brother Skife's very existence, and the division that had then resulted between my mother and father. It must have felt to them both, like they were being torn apart. And added to that for my father, was the sense of responsibility that he must have felt for what happened, not only to my mother, but to their whole community, that through his attention being elsewhere on a hunt, at the time of the raid, he had not been there to uphold his position. He must have felt a huge sense of inadequacy. It is little wonder that he became withdrawn afterwards, and when I left, this tendency became more and more etched into his way of being.

My father, increasingly, could not cope with Skife, and although he tried to act as if he was tolerant and accepting, inside his heart, he did not feel it. For the sake of our family, and his relationship with my mother, he tried to support her at every turn. However, the way in which my father orientated himself, with the anger and resentment he felt towards Skife, and indeed also, less directly, with my mother, especially following occasions when Skife expressed cruelty to others, was for him to retreat, and take long periods of time in the woods, on his own. The inner division that wrecked my mother's and father's relationship became more and more exacerbated, until they could hardly communicate together. Internally, my father held a smoldering resentment around the whole situation that he could not easily suppress.

After I left, Skife's hatred directed itself towards my brother, Luend, and my sister, Sealbrow. Skife had an unrelenting craving to feel a sense of belonging. He wanted to be in a position of acceptance in the family and community. When he saw Luend, Sealbrow and I and how much our lives flowed and blended into the community around us, Skife felt almost insanely jealous. He did not have any of that, and this perception of lack encouraged his beliefs and tendencies to act as though he was an outsider. But Skife went further than that, and he positioned himself as an outcast and rebel. Within his heart, there was a seed that germinated that contained the desire to destroy what he did not have. As he grew older, this seed extended its roots until it was ready to express itself outwardly.

I only learnt later about incidents that occurred concerning my brother and sister with Skife. Sealbrow had a great love for animals. One day, Sealbrow was sitting quietly, playing with a squirrel, when Skife came from behind her and bashed her with a rock over the head. She recovered, but never felt at ease after that, whenever her brother might be around. Sealbrow could not trust him. On another occasion, Skife taunted Luend with a spear, and wanted my brother to fight with him. My brother refused, and this provoked huge anger in Skife. This built up and found its expression in an appalling incident when Skife stabbed Luend in the arm with his spear. My parents were horrified, and my father broke his spear and burnt it in the fire, and kept Skife confined in our hut for days until he apologized and promised not to do it again.

But it was not long after that, when Skife left the family home and started searching for kindred spirits with whom he could share his ways. He was not reformed, and he would not change under pressure from anyone else. Skife then did the only thing where he felt comfortable, and he chose to live the life of a warrior, but not one serving our community, but one committed to undermine that. He was determined to make his own decisions now, without influence from either of my parents or the society where he felt he had been forced to live while he was growing up.

When I came on visits, my brother and sister pleaded with me that they could come and live with me. They did not feel safe around the village anymore. My mother also wanted to join me. Although she could not reject Skife in her heart, entirely, she no longer wanted to live near him, nor have members of her family threatened by him. But father would not leave. With his pride, he would not let himself be bent by Skife's will. The village was his home, and he was determined that this was where he would spend the rest of his days. This caused a further split within the family, for my father still relied so much upon us all for his well-being. How could we leave him on his own? But for now, they would all stay. It was not a time, with the crisis in our land, when my brother and sister could come to the College to do their training and be accommodated there. The Elders of our College community were too busy. They would have to wait.

This visit occurred during the time of famine, when for two summers, there was very little rain.

After the attack when Skife tried to kill me, my mother was extremely distressed. This was when she became ill, and my father snapped too. At last he went into action, and vowed that if Skife or any of his followers came near to their village, he would kill them rather than let them destroy our community or affect our allegiance to the Order of the Wise. My father tried to summon support from others in the community; he wanted to lead an expedition to locate Skife and capture him, so that he would not be able to do further harm. The community leaders would not agree to this. We had our principles. If we were aggressive towards him, then what we would be presenting would be no better than what he did. A basic creed of the Order was that we needed to be models of peace through all that we did. After the way that I had met Skife with love and peace when he attacked me, the community leaders affirmed that we needed to remain true to this approach, and not seek revenge. My father was desolate, but would not back down.

Despite her illness, my mother tried to beseech my father to be calmer. She needed him to give his love, and my brother and sister did too, but my father could not stay with my mother anymore. He felt driven to go out in the woods and look for Skife.

After he threw his spear, Skife felt humiliated by how everyone reacted to him, but before they could turn on him, he managed to escape, and his guile and determination propelled him out of reach of his pursuers. My father zealously tried to trace and track him, but Skife had made rapid movement travelling far to the west. Going on what other people had reported, my father eventually found his trail and continued to follow it until stopped by the sea. On the stony beach, there were markings to indicate that there had been a boat waiting there for him to leave our shores. In my mind, I sensed that it was very unlikely that we would ever see Skife again. For the rest of my family, this did not bring peace though.

For my mother, Sealbrow and Luend, they were insistent now, and all wanted to come and live with me. My mother was weak with a coughing illness and needed much healing and rest. Sealbrow and Luend both had sensitivities that could be developed within the Order of the Wise. For them to come to the College would not be inappropriate, even though Luend was almost fully grown and older than many of the other students. But my father was a shadow of the man that had taken me hunting with him as a child. He wanted to teach Luend the skills of hunting so that his son could follow in his own footsteps and become the village's leading hunter and warrior. My father was desperate to have someone from his family with him.

It was a struggle, and this tested Luend and his loyalties to the extreme. To be a hunter and warrior was not Luend's inclination. He was a story teller, and he had sensitive gifts that could be developed. But Luend also had a great love for his father. Although I could see the pained look in his eyes, I supported my brother's decision to stay with my father – at least I would support that decision for now. Sealbrow and my mother would come with me.

My mother and father had not been able to relate intimately for many years. The division between them would not heal. Without intending to cause harm in their relationship, my father could not reconcile his own rejection of Skife with my mother's love for him. They argued occasionally, but mainly they had kept a continuing uncomfortable silence between them. Together with my brother and sister, we all felt the pain of a family that was severely wounded.

Mother's passing

The health of my mother deteriorated. She carried a lot of guilt, shame, and an acute sense of failure. And she now felt utterly defeated. As much as I tried to reassure her, even with the help of healers such as my beloved friend, Nianda, nothing really made any difference.

One evening, she confessed to me her regret that she had not made efforts to have an abortion when Skife was conceived. It had been her sense of the sacredness of life and her growing love for her unborn child that had driven her to allow the pregnancy to follow its course. However, nothing that she had been able to give had been enough for Skife. Because of the love and attention that she had given him, others had suffered, and she also felt for Skife, and what he must be feeling now, as a result of his actions and the exile and permanent isolation that he had ultimately imposed upon himself. Nothing she could do now would make things right, and she felt resigned with no purpose left with which to live further. Those of us that tended her could feel that her life Spirit was withdrawing more and more. There was nothing we could do to restore it.

On the night that my mother died, Nianda and I were attending her, and Sealbrow was also with us. Nianda had hold of my mother's feet to offer support and Earth energy, but we could all sense that she would soon be going. There was a growing peace in the room, and we felt a wonderful presence of Spirit light with us. I knelt close to Sealbrow, and told her to tune in to me and for her inwardly to stay me during the process of what would unfold. Then, when my mother's Spirit left her body, Nianda and I travelled with her and Sealbrow came with us. We all rose up with her into the light, until we could go no further, and we could sense other Spiritual beings reaching out to welcome her. We could perceive my mother looking back in gratitude, and we joyfully bade our farewells. All that time, I was holding Sealbrow's Spirit hand with my own, and I could feel her trembling with the majesty of what she had experienced. In a moment, we were back in our physical bodies. For some time, we just sat in silence, and then Sealbrow cried, and sank her young head into my shoulder.

We respected mother's wishes and celebrated her life and cremated her ashes in a funeral pyre at the college of the Order of the Wise rather than in her home village. She did not feel anymore that she could have any association with the village where we had been born and where she had lived the main part of her life. Although I sensed that this amounted to a rejection of her life, and would have liked for her to decide differently, we needed to do what she wanted, for she did not wish her body to be buried in a place where she had experienced so much pain.

Protecting Luend

My father did not attend the funeral, but Luend did, and with both my brother and sister with me, I promised them shelter, and that they could stay with me and build a life for themselves.

When my brother had arrived for the funeral, he had been very tense and unhappy, but the longer he stayed with us, the more he relaxed and even started to laugh and enjoy himself. But there were issues to resolve. Luend was in conflict with himself. Although in his heart, he felt much more at home to be at the College and to be with Sealbrow and me, he could not feel completely at peace with this. To honor himself, he needed to develop his gifts, and be where he could be happy. But what would become of his father if he was not with him?

I put to Luend that he needed to go and talk with our father, but I offered to him for me to accompany him and stand with him while he did that. It was an important situation where Luend required both support for emotional solidarity, and to have a witness to be there with him to help him find balanced perspective afterwards. My father would not want Luend to go, but it was a situation which necessitated him to also consider the needs of his son.

My father was not at home when we reached the village, but I could sense that he was not far away, and we found him in the woodland at one of his favorite places of retreat.

I stood by while Luend haltingly tried to explain how he felt to his father. There was not much that my father said in reply. In his blank expression, he appeared to have put up inner barriers so he could remove himself from us emotionally. I stepped in and confirmed about Luend's gifts and that the life of being a hunter and warrior did not suit him, and that being at the College and training there was where he could be happy.

My father looked up at Luend with sorrow, and checked with him that this is what he wanted to do. For a moment, Luend hesitated. For much of his life, he had been the one to try and please others. He had not enjoyed my parent's arguments and had tried to act at times to pacify them, rather than asserting himself. This was a major test for his character and he was not very strong with it. Slowly, Luend took half a step away from my father and towards me. In a weak and wavering voice, he then confirmed my thoughts and affirmed his decision to come with me.

I again made the offer for our father to come with us. He could work as a hunter around our college and help with our food supply. There was a place for him, if he wanted to be with us. We both pleaded with him, over and over. But he would not budge, would not even consider it.

This was one of those very hard days, because I did not know what would become of my father, how he would manage for himself. Even with the offer we were making, he would feel that his family had totally abandoned him. It was not true, but in his mind set, this would be his reality. The only place where he was willing to be was in these woods and the land where he had his roots. He would not feel at home anywhere else. But I doubted that he would feel at home here either.

I promised to visit him as regularly as I could, and Luend joined with that undertaking, but it was not a short distance from here to the College community, and we both knew that those moments in between visits would be very long and lonely for him. We did not know how he would cope.

There was sadness when we left him, but also relief. I knew that for Luend, the decision was right. For Luend to have been any longer with his father, would have had a difficult negative impact upon him. He would have been dragged into his father's suffering, and my brother did not need this. He needed to be with the living rather than with someone who had all but given up his life. Yes, at the same time, my father needed support, if he would allow it. I could only ask Spirit to help bring this to him, but I did not know, with all my responsibilities, how I could be there for him to any significant degree, myself.

The end of the rope

Time had elapsed. Now the attempted invasion by the barbarians was over, and I was having nightmares about my father. They were haunting me, and in my heart I knew that I could not ignore them. One particular night, I dreamt of my father in chains, and cut off from everyone. No one, including myself, could reach him. Looking at the expression on his face, there was complete despair and resignation. His eyes were vacant, and the life was going out of them. I woke shaking in a cold sweat, and desperately needed someone to comfort me. Gentle Nianda was there, and she held me. But there was something in this dream that was very real. I needed to go to him without delay.

In the morning, I discovered that Luend had been dreaming of my father too. We both felt that compulsive urge to travel to him immediately, and Nianda insisted upon coming as well. Sealbrow saw us as we made our preparations, and she implored us to let her join us, and it felt appropriate, so we all went together.

While we travelled, there was a strange atmosphere of silence and uneasiness between us. We were each preoccupied with our own thoughts. I tried to consult with my Spirit friends for guidance, but all I could sense was a mist, a cloud of unknowing. Whatever was happening was something that we could not be forewarned about. It was an experience for our humanness to encounter, and a test for us, how we would respond.

When my mother died, I felt acceptance. Even though she had been deeply hurt by events concerning Skife, I had sensed with her death that this was the time when she had to die, and her passing marked a graceful transition that felt very peaceful when we celebrated her funeral. With my father, I felt differently, and my stomach felt tightly wound in a big knot like I held a fear that I could not quite understand. Why was I feeling this association with death?

I did not like my father's isolation; it did not feel natural or right for him. His mind had been tormented, but without company, his thoughts would become obsessive. I did not perceive any peace about him, and this disturbed me greatly. As a child, I had received inspiration from my father, and I had admired him. This was my real father. What was there now felt like it was only a shell. And that made me feel sad, because I sensed that it could have been different, and that he could have been happier. I just wished that we could help him.

When we came to the village, we asked people about my father, but no one had seen him for many days. He was not at our house. My brother and sister looked worried. The fear and foreboding in our group was growing and gnawing at us. As I checked with my instinct, I felt that we needed to go into the woods. By an old beech tree in the middle of the woods, there was a small clearing where my father and I had had many talks when I was young. I knew it as being his special place, like a refuge where he could relax and feel comfortable. Whenever I had thought of this place in the past, it had brought forth warm memories of times when the two of us had shared together. For Luend, this place was also familiar, but I could tell by his face, that with the more recent associations that he had held regarding this place, and that these were not as positive as mine. We agreed to go there.

The closer that we came to this clearing, the tenser I became. I reached over and held Sealbrow's hand, and tried to draw Luend closer too, but he was resistant somehow. Nianda drew a little closer to my brother, to offer as much comfort as she could. I felt a shiver as we came to the last logs we needed to cross over before the clearing, and we stopped for some moments before we dared to look. We could hear birds, and the gentle sounds of the breeze blowing through the branches of the trees, but nothing more.

At last we stepped forward. The beech tree was standing there in full leaf, a magnificent tree, standing alone, with other smaller trees around. We had always regarded this beech as a guardian for the land in this part of the woodland, a messenger of abundance and peace for all the creatures in its vicinity. But that was not the message that it was giving now.

Near the base of this tree, but above head height, there was a low branch that extended thick and almost horizontal for several meters. Around this branch, there was tied a rope, and on the other end of the rope, there was a noose. Within this noose was my father's body. His eyes were strained and tortured. He did not look peaceful. By the smell, and decay around his body, he had been dead there for some time.

I cannot begin to describe my horror. I wished that I could have spoken to him, and tried to dissuade him. I had been given no indications until the dream. And by then it had been too late. We had not been allowed to intervene.

Swiftly, I rushed forward to his body, and detached it from the rope. Nianda helped me to let it down. My sister was howling, but it was Luend, that we needed to help most and he was clearly in shock. For a long while, we just stood there in our despair. The tears flowed from all of us. Even Nianda was overcome by it, for it reminded her of her own family tragedy. We could not speak yet, just let out our grief. I came over to Luend, and reached out to hold him. This must have been the support that he needed, for his grief then poured out of him, and his body was shuddering with the release of so much pent up pain that he had been carrying. I encouraged him to express his feelings. The loss for us all was tremendous. We all felt for my father. He had been a good loving man. The most important thing that he had wanted was a happy family, and a good working community life. He could not accept what had happened. His dream had been eroded, undermined and broken, and he had not been flexible enough to adjust, or to seek help and solidarity with others. His will had been too strong, and his guilt had made him isolated. I wished that he had loved himself more. His life was worth more than this. We had all loved him. It would have been possible for him to join us at the college. He would have found some happiness with us. I was sure of it.

This was one of the saddest days of my life. I was so grateful that we had each other.

For some time, I allowed my own grief to express itself as the others were doing, but the responsible part of me knew that I needed to support my brother and sister. This loss would etch itself more deeply into them, especially my brother. We needed to make arrangements too, with the local villagers.

Release

The funeral had to be held in the clearing where we had found his body. This was his place, and the most appropriate setting in which to leave his ashes. There was a large gathering of people from the village that joined us. Many were touched and mourned my father's death.

Any misgivings were put to one side, as we appreciated all that he had contributed to the life of the village. The safety and security of people was always a priority for him, and he had been generous in his time, giving help to people that needed it. His hunting had provided food for the people, and during times of scarcity, he was someone that could be relied upon to ensure that the people did not go hungry. He had a very reverent connection with the animals and the land. As we prepared his funeral pyre, we could feel the blessing of that magnificent beech tree that had carried his body when he died. Even from the land there was sadness and regret. We could feel it.

The funeral ceremony, itself, was very quiet. There was somber and deep reflection from all present. We watched patiently during the burning until all the embers had stopped glowing. Only then did we go. Throughout the rite, I could sense the presence of my father in Spirit, overlooking proceedings. I perceived his quiet dignity observing and giving thanks. Inwardly, I spoke with him and offered to accompany him to go higher to his guardians in his home in the Spiritual world. He gratefully accepted my offer, and I lay down and went with him, and we travelled upwards, but I almost had to pull him up. Part of him did not want to go. He was not able to go as high as my mother's soul went. His energy became lighter as we rose together, and there were others to comfort him and support him as I reached the place where I had to leave. It was a sad goodbye, but this was as far on his soul journey as my father's Spirit was prepared to go, for now.

Once the villagers had gone, I stayed behind with my family and Nianda. We did a cleansing ritual to clear the space around the beech tree of the residues of my father's actions. Later, we returned to the family home. We needed to conduct rituals there too, including one for Skife. It was not Skife's fault for what my father had done. There was no blame towards him for this, but we needed to re-evaluate our relationship with him in the light of what had happened. My brother and sister and I felt as one on this, and so we proceeded. We felt that we wanted to release Skife from our family. If it was his wish to join us later, then we would consider this, but it was obvious from his actions that he had rejected us, and there was no need for us to torture ourselves by trying to maintain his link with us. It would feel better if we could create a clear space for both him and us, to get on with our lives in peace. At the same time, we did not wish to carry bitterness towards Skife – we sincerely wished that he could find fulfillment in his own life, and we wanted to send him love.

We did a beautiful meditation in which we concentrated our hearts to bring a collective ball of love to send to him, both to wish him well on his way, but also to release him from us. At the end of the meditation, we all felt much lighter, and it felt like a burden had been lifted from us. If only we could have done this earlier, while our mother was alive, I wondered whether circumstances could have worked out differently.

As we completed the meditation, Luend, Sealbrow and I, had a joint vision. Our minds united. We saw with our inner eyes, that our mother and father were standing with each other in Spirit. They were smiling at us and saying 'Thank you'. It was as though we were completing a Spiritual task with them and for our family, together. There was a strong energy of love.

We had further work to do. In the family hut, there was much there to remind us of our childhoods, articles that had been given to us, a fireplace laden with memories, our beds and personal objects, but there was also that feeling of isolation and inner conflict that permeated the space, and which we had to release. We talked about our relationship with the family home, and I encouraged my brother and sister to express all their feelings, and I did this too. We spent a long time, going over memories, both, pleasant and unpleasant, to acknowledge all the main associations that this hut had for us. We had to honor and give gratitude for all that had been for us in this home. But at the end of the day, we stepped outside, and put fire to the hut so that it would be no more.

We did this in consultation with the elders of the village. This hut could not be a memorial for my mother and father, after all that had happened, and it would not be appropriate for anyone else to live there. This hut, as a family home, had died too, and it needed to return to ashes. We watched in silence, holding each other, while flames devoured this precious artifact from our past. For our people, it was important to mark an ending completely before we could fully open to the new.

At the end of that day, the four of us left the village, and we all had a sense of putting the past behind us, and we were going to move forward into a fresh phase of our lives. It felt good that Nianda travelled with us, for she needed a sense of family, and we were all happy to include her. Luend and Sealbrow would live at the college of the Order of the Wise, with me now. We would have our own independent lives; Luend and Sealbrow both needed to study and learn. But we would be close enough to nourish each other when we needed it. The love of our family could not be broken. If anything could honor the Spirit of our dead father, it would be this.

Cleansing

Later on, at the College, I often looked out for my brother and sister. Even though they were both engaged with their inner training, they would also need time to recover from the trauma with my father. My attention was particularly drawn to my brother, Luend, and I noticed how he was becoming very withdrawn from others. Something in him was not at peace.

One evening, I spoke with him, and asked him what troubled him. I reached out my arms to him, and he broke down sobbing. I could sense an inner conflict in him, but did not wish to enter his mind unless he consented to this. But Luend needed to talk.

Even though he was studying with our community's story teller, Uandi, and learning to express his inner creativity in service to others, Luend felt guilt that he was not being true to his father's wishes for him, and that his study was a betrayal to his father's memory.

For many hours, I talked with Luend, and encouraged him to tell me what was true to his heart. He tearfully confided to me that he loved his study and could never feel comfortable in his being a warrior, but he struggled to know whether he had let his father down.

I suggested a fire ritual, and invited Uandi and Sealbrow to be present. From a stump of wood, I proposed for Luend to carve into this wood, representation of all the guilt that he had felt about his feelings connected with his father and his chosen career. For several days, Luend worked on this very intently, until he felt that he had finished. Then we gathered together around a fire in the sacred Grove, and we invited the Spirit of our father to join us. The smoke from the fire waved about and then became very still. We hummed and threw herbs of purification upon the fire. Luend then felt the presence of our father; we all did, and Luend heard the thoughts of his father in his mind. He was asking Luend for his forgiveness, and giving Luend a blessing for him to be true to his heart. It was a beautiful moment, and we all cried. I asked Luend about what path he wished to follow. He then threw the carving into the fire, and as it burned, he joyfully announced that he chose to follow the path of his heart.

We all hugged each other, and sang and told stories until the fire had died down. Only then did we feel the Spirit of our father leave us. And Luend smiled.

Chapter 15

Children

Our ways with children

During the course of my life, I had five children. They were all quite different from each other, and all precious in their own ways. There were also four different fathers to my children, and in every case, my children were conceived with love.

In our society, and especially within the Order of the Wise, we were mindful of how character and abilities within a child could be affected by the linage and genetic combination of the parents concerned. Sometimes, we would plan pregnancies to give the best chance of bringing into our world a child with outstanding gifts, if that was something that we needed at that time. We did not place any restrictions upon who we could be with, but it was usual for members of the Order of the Wise, to conceive children with each other, as a means to preserve and nurture the existence of individuals with psychic sensitivity and dedication to Spirit, so that our Order would continue to function well.

We did not have marriages as such, in our society. However, we did have men and women that chose to be together for a lifetime, and we honored that choice with ceremonies if it was what those people wanted. When members of our Order had a child, the babies would usually be looked after by one of our team of child carers, so that, as members of the Order, we could continue to do our work and attend to our duties. But, as soon as we were not required for those tasks, both mother and father could have a full role in the responsibility of looking after the child. Then, later, when children were old enough to attend training classes, they could do this and live with other children of their own age, rather than the parents. But contact and the love bond with parents would be maintained. Children grew up with a sense more of belonging to a community than exclusively to one set of parents. This arrangement seemed to work well for us.

Breien

In my own case, my first conceived child was my daughter, Breien. As I have described earlier, the birth process for me with her, was quite difficult. During the pregnancy, I felt a lot of anxiety about the state of our land, and the possibility of the invasion, carried a heavy sense of responsibility for all that. Then, in the later stages of pregnancy, there came the problems with Berenice. Several times, I had had the thought of not wanting my daughter and feeling that it would have been much easier without her. I struggled. Gracon was in wonder that I was pregnant but also became quite fearful with my struggles. I knew that he would be a devoted father, but he was not confident when it came to relating closely with other people. He was uncertain how skilful and relaxed he could be around our child.

Breien was quite a sickly child. Perhaps the thoughts of not being wanted made her unsure about whether she should really be alive or not. She needed a lot of care, but in the early stages of her young life, with my occupation around preparation to withstand the invasion, and all the tension and travel involved with that, I was not very much available for Breien, and neither was Gracon. She did receive love and attention from our carers, but the absence of both Gracon and myself in these early times, must have affected her.

When conditions settled, I devoted myself to give much more support to Breien, and I took a close personal interest in all that she did. As she grew older, she did grow stronger, and she played with other children and her heart did sing. But she was always the child that took an interest in others that suffered, and struggled to feel at ease with their selves. There must have been some component of unsettlement that remained in her soul, and then wanted to express this through helping others. As she grew older, Breien gained a reputation as one who was very sensitive and able to help the suffering in our settlements. She learnt healing, but her most impressive gift was how she could help with the healing of the mind, those that had been traumatized or felt uneasy with their thoughts.

Lunto

My second child was with Wueli. After the invasion had been repelled, I wanted so much to give Wueli love. He had been so brave and courageous to kill those barbarians, and I did not want him to feel haunted by his actions. I wanted him to feel accepted and supported. Wueli responded to my love and we conceived a child. This child was my son, Lunto. We wondered if he might express some powerful warrior blood in his nature, and this did prove to be so.

Lunto was a very physically active child, and he seemed to gain great pleasure in helping to resolve and manage conflicts. I sometimes felt a vague apprehension that he may seek conflicts a little too much, for in his young life, there were occasions where he would instigate and generate disturbances between people so he could test his skills. If all was in harmony around him, Lunto could easily feel bored. He craved excitement, and the tension of pitting his wits against someone else.

Lunto trained with the old master, Verdiff, and was tutored as his potential heir. Over time, Lunto appeared to tone down his recklessness under Verdiff's influence. As they worked together, the two of them became very close. Verdiff took Lunto on some long travels and taught him about other cultures. They would laugh, talk, and tell storied for long hours around the fire.

Wueli and I sometimes wondered if Lunto may eventually become the next leader of our Order because of his leadership and management qualities, and we hoped that our son could be a force for good in our community.

Theo

My third child was a quiet sensitive child named Theo. Another girl, Theo was conceived with my musician friend, Mulaid. The pregnancy occurred during one of the happiest periods of my life, a time when all the struggles of invasion and family issues were resolved, a time of relaxation and joy in our community. Mulaid and I had always been close, and when I listened to his music, it took me onto amazing inner journeys. There came a time when we felt that the spirits around us were beckoning for us to join in physical love. The pregnancy that followed occurred very gracefully, and as much as I could in my everyday life, I exposed this child in my womb, to waves of Mulaid's music.

The child that was born was a delicate child with pale skin and dreamy eyes. Theo loved the woods and the trees, and would laugh with the nature spirits and enjoy their company. It felt like she lived a lot of her life in the other more Spiritual worlds, rather than the physical world. But she brought the joy of those other worlds into her play, and it felt a great blessing to have her around. Then, as she grew older, she developed great gifts of music playing and storytelling. Even though he was much older, my brother, Luend, and Theo, formed a close bond. The stories that they channeled together were quite magical. Luend played with Theo, and the two of them went off into the woods. The creativity between them just flowed.

Theo was a girl that we had to protect from the hardships of the world, and we could only introduce these elements to her very gradually, as she grew older. She preferred home life rather than travelling, and passionately cared for the environment where she lived.

Huntle

Occasionally, there were conventions where we would meet and exchange with our people from other lands. It felt important for us to cooperate and learn together. In the trip that I made with Karka while I was still training, I had connected with a group of others of my own age, and we had maintained contact as we all grew to positions of responsibility.

Much later, we had one of these conventions in our own land, and this was held near to the large stone circles to the east of our College. My hopes had been that this meeting would help to strengthen our bonds of nationhood together, and unite us in common purpose. However, the meeting turned out to be quite fractious, and delegates appeared to be more interested to promote their own vested interests rather than helping and supporting each other. The approach of some of the delegates angered me, and there were a number of arguments in which I became involved. Many of the delegates were only regarding the convention as a form of business meeting to expand their trade and influence, and this was not what I felt needed to be our priority.

During the meetings, there was a leader from the Gaullist people, who expressed similar thoughts to me. He was like a shining light in the midst of all the squabbling and haggling that was around us. I remembered him, for he had been one of those that I had met in that very first convention that I had attended with Karka. Although I had not been close to him then, I had noticed him, and he had been in our group. But now, my respect grew for him enormously. His name was Vieta.

Before the convention closed, we formed an alliance, and conducted a ceremony by the stones, with the intention of bringing peace to our people. Mulaid played music, we hummed and prayed, and the presence of Spirit was felt very close. Many of the delegates attended, and the atmosphere of proceedings completely changed afterwards. It was as if this ceremony helped people to wake up and realize the true purpose of what we were here to do together.

When the convention was over, I invited Vieta to our College, and shared with him the Sacred Grove. We sat together upon the branches of the old Yew tree that I loved so much, and we felt the whispers of Spirit and Mother Earth urging us to create a union together.

That afternoon, I allowed myself to have physical intimacy with Vieta, and we conceived a child. As well as being a leader, Vieta was also a healer, and our daughter, when she was born, brought with her the gift of healing, which flowered more and more as she grew older.

When Vieta became aware of my pregnancy, he was happy to release the child to my care. The child's name was Huntle, and even though she saw her father only rarely, at least in her early years, I encouraged the bond between them, and she had the awareness to be able to establish telepathic contact with him, and she often told me of the conversations that they shared together. Huntle was fully accepted as a member of our family group, and was an inspiration to many. She was a symbol that the love we felt as people, did not need to be confined exclusively to the people of our land, but could be extended far and wide.

Varnu

My body was quite tired and worn from carrying children by the time I conceived my youngest child. This was again with Gracon, and we had the impulses from Spirit that a soul wanted to join us for some time before we relented and made the opportunity for this child to manifest physically. The psychic energy around this child was very strong as I carried it, and I felt many strange thoughts about our ancestors come into my mind while pregnant. When this baby was born, I knew that I had had enough with conceiving children. It was a boy that we had, and his name was Varnu. He had a quiet and intense nature.

As he grew, we became aware how Varnu had knowledge beyond his years. From psychic sources, he knew about threads of our civilization, how we had evolved, and the highs and lows of our nationhood. Varnu was someone who rarely spoke, but when he did, it was worth listening to. He was quite a remarkable child, and quite solitary. Even so, he was very close to Gracon, and I could foresee at least one element in his destiny; he would be a record keeper for our people, someone with inner information that we needed to acknowledge, in order to bring our civilization forward.

Siel

The only other child, it feels important to mention is the one conceived by Nianda. I had doubted if Nianda would have any children, because the subject of children for her on a personal front appeared to be a vulnerable issue for her, and brought with it, feelings connected with her own childhood. However, throughout our adult lives, she devoted herself to the care and well-being of my children. When I came to give birth to each of my children, Nianda was the one present to welcome the souls into our world; she would speak to them, administer herbs, and spiritually ask for protection and for the awareness and conscious recognition of the soul's guides to be known and acknowledged.

Nianda had a close connection with Kiend. They were both very sensitive, and Nianda also developed a deep love of the animal kingdom that she could share with Kiend. They lived in a hut together for sleeping, and yet, for a long time, they were no more than friends. But, after my fourth child, Huntle, had been welcomed into the world by Nianda, in the ceremony that we had by the Sacred Grove, I looked into Nianda's eyes, and saw a glow about them as she lovingly held my baby. Something in her had changed.

Soon afterwards, she gave me the happy news that she was pregnant. We were all so excited. When her baby boy, Siel, was born, I had the privilege to perform the duties of welcoming her child into the world, in a similar fashion to what she had done with mine. I felt great joy for my friend, and knew that it was a moment of tremendous fulfillment for her. Nianda and Kiend became devoted parents, and Siel blended in with my children so we became together a very happy extended family.

Paul Williamson

Our family

It was as though with Gracon, Nianda, Mulaid, Kiend, and even Wueli, that we had been like family to each other from when we were young, and now we continued that through the children that we shared, and there was great love and support between us. In addition, there was Berenice's daughter, Shoola, my brother, Luend, and sister, Sealbrow that also belonged with us, and we were all closely bonded.

Our family energy encouraged other similar groupings throughout the College. This was a change in the structure of our College from how our community had been in Karka's time, and it was not without its challenges. We had to be mindful of our work so that we did not become too inward looking upon our families, but maintained an outer focus too. From our training, we had all made vows to commit ourselves to service, not only to our extended family, but to the wider community. If we could keep the balance right, the inspiration we gained from our family life, could help others learn how they could bring more love into their lives too.

Not everyone was happy. Those who did not have family, and felt more isolated, could become jealous of the comradeship we had, and want to undermine it. One woman, in particular, challenged me, and publicly accused me of creating a family culture at the expense of the individual Spiritual training purpose that had been so central to the activities of the College previously. I could not deny the attachments that I felt to my dearest friends and family, but I had never forgotten my own duties in the position I held.

When I listened more deeply to this woman, I could sense her loneliness, and feeling of lack, and so I asked her what she wanted and needed. Tears came to her eyes, and after more questioning, she broke down and admitted how much she wanted children of her own, but she had not been able to conceive. I offered for her to train to be a midwife, so that she could have a much more active role with the children of the community. Once she considered this, she felt joy, and ultimately equipped herself well, in this new role. I was happy that she was able to support me in the delivery of my two youngest children.

We were fortunate that after the dramas of the attempted invasion of our shores, that there was a long period of peace in our land now. It was possible for us to enjoy our family life and the nurturing love that this could provide for us all.

Chapter 16

Later Stages

Renewal

In the repercussions from the incursions by the barbarian invaders, there were ripples of unsettlement that continued to disturb our society for a considerable period. Much psychological repair work needed to be done. The celebrations that extended throughout the land were tinged with unease. For a long time, there were those that were wary and afraid, in case the barbarians would return. Gracon was convinced that they would not, but many people, particularly those in the east, found it difficult to trust.

Wondrous stories spread through our communities of the feats of our warriors, but these stories brought with them, their own anxieties. The fact that our warriors had been so brave alerted people to how difficult and potentially dangerous the situation had been. It placed into question the safety and security of our homeland. Because it appeared to have been primarily the warriors that had been responsible for defeating the barbarian attack, and the Order of the Wise had acted in a secondary, supportive role only, this placed into question the authority and power of the Order, and there were those that wanted the warriors to have a more prominent position in our society. But in my mind, if the warriors claimed the power in our land, then this would encourage the aggressive instincts of our people to play out, and we knew from our history that the Spiritual well-being of our communities would suffer as a result.

It was only gradually that communities began to rebuild themselves on the north east coast. Numerous ceremonies and rituals were performed around the areas of the incursions, in an effort to heal the land there, and it was a big relief when people did feel able to re-establish their homes there once more, although many of them chose new positions for their communities rather than return to where they had lived previously.

It was a time for regeneration. In our seasonal festivals, we gave thanks to the Mother Earth for preserving our land, and giving us the chance to continue to be guardians and custodians of it. There was a humbleness and joy that accompanied that prayer and its acknowledgment of gratitude. Within the Order, it felt important to nurture and encourage gatherings that would build our community Spirit and express appreciation, not to be occupied with creating stronger defense structures to protect us from possible future attack, but to affirm our intention to live in peace and harmony. The longer the seas remained clear, the more people could feel at ease, and start to enjoy what we had.

Some of the warriors and others that had been involved in the fighting carried within them psychological scars. They needed care and support. Wueli was one of these. Sometimes, in the night, he would awaken, and his body would be soaked in perspiration, and he would have nightmares about killing those barbarians. I tried to work with him, and took him on inner journeys so he could talk with the Spirits of those barbarians that he had killed. Even though he could do this, and feel that in Spirit, these souls had no anger towards him and accepted what had happened, this did not totally alleviate the problem for him. It needed time, but because of the feeling of wrongness that he carried about killing another human being, Wueli could never quite find peace about what he had done. He just had to accept that it had happened, and try to move forward.

Conceiving a child with him did help, because it gave him an outlet for his compassion and love, and this nurtured more positive feelings within him. When our son, Lunto, was born, Wueli was full of joy. Now, Wueli wanted to dedicate himself to a life where he could help and support others, and he had a great abhorrence for any form of conflict. He hoped so much, that our son would take on another path than to be a warrior, but sadly, Lunto, as he grew, had other ideas.

The outcome from this conflict with the barbarians could have been so much worse, and it was a miracle that our plans had worked according to the shared vision we generated together, and that the barbarians had been repelled with so little bloodshed. We were fortunate that we could continue the way of life that had served us so well, and with all the efforts that we had made, we deserved this too. The horror of the battles and loss of life and suffering was not a life that we wanted. For us, there was much more happiness for us to experience through living together in cooperation.

I worked tirelessly to put these ideas across to people. At many gatherings in various settlements throughout the land, I spoke to the people, and tried to encourage them, and rouse them into feeling good about themselves. I travelled far and wide. Others from the Order did the same, and there was a force of good will that spread like waves of peace through our communities, and the time came when our people could share a great deal of happiness in living simple lives together.

Problems still arose as they always would do, and for us within the Order of the Wise, we had to be vigilant, and attend to disturbances that existed, both on a human level, energetic level, and also in terms of organization and general management of resources. But gradually, the ripples of unease settled and became more and more still. Tensions eased, and people smiled. It was a time of joy for our land.

Family happiness

As the consciousness of our people shifted to that more relaxed way of being, I could spend more of my time within the homely environment of the College, and attend to the needs of my extended family, and students who were training in the College. My life continued to be busy and full, but more satisfying and less fraught.

With Shoola and my brother Luend, I spent a lot of time, so they could feel loved and heal from their losses. They needed encouragement to find meaning and build new foundations in their lives. Only then would they be able to open themselves to a positive future and express the love in their hearts.

Another member of the family held my attention even more. I wanted to dedicate myself to nurture my relationship with my eldest daughter, Breien. In some ways, I felt ashamed of my neglect and at times, rejection, of her, during the pregnancy and the early stages of her young life. Nianda and I worked with her, giving her regular healing. Many times, I took her with me, and sat with her by the Yew tree in the Sacred Grove. There, I spoke to her mind and tried to reassure her, and explain to her my actions and my preoccupations at the time, so she could understand that she was loved. I gave similar attention to my other children when they were growing, but the need with Breien was critical because of the influence of what I had brought to bear within her.

Our extended family lived in a circle of huts within the College, and we had our own fireplace where in the evenings we often gathered and spent time together. Initially, not all of us were completely familiar with each other. For example, my brother, Luend and sister, Sealbrow, had not previously known Kiend and Mulaid. And Shoola was new to many of us as well. But there was an openness and willingness to embrace each other, and over time, bonds between us developed and deepened, so we did feel like a family and we could trust and look to each other for emotional nourishment.

Our circle was open, and we did not insulate ourselves from others in the College, and we would sometimes join with other circles so that interactions between us and the larger community were maintained.

I suppose we broke with tradition with our children, because, as they grew and trained, they still spent a great deal of time with us, even though they were supposed to be with the other young ones with whom they were learning and sharing together. Our family bond was such that they would not have wished for anything different.

I did miss Berenice and my father and mother. Within my heart, I wondered if I could have helped my father, but I had to remind myself, that he had been the parent; I was his child. As a soul, he had faced his own set of challenges, and I could not take that away from him.

Now, I my own life, I became at ease with my responsibilities, and I was pleased that within the Order, that there was harmony between us, and the dedication among members of the Order was high. Although my work continued to involve journeying to places, many of my duties involved being present at celebrations, and supporting group activities where people were happy and could share together the joy of being alive. However, the times I valued most were being with my extended family, talking, singing, playing, eating and generally finding pleasure in our simple life.

Changes

For a long time, I hardly noticed myself becoming older, and I relaxed very much into feeling that my happy life would extend on indefinitely. Indeed, there were many moments of contentment when I marveled at the miracle of life. Watching the children grow and play together was very satisfying. It gave me great pleasure when Shoola graduated to become a full member of the Order of the Wise, and then, one by one, my children attained their positions as well. Outside the family, I had many friends and contacts throughout the length and breadth of the land. All was well, and our lives together were good.

But slowly, the wheel was turning, and the movement of the seasons brought closer, endings and fresh trials that I did not particularly want.

One morning, I was by the central fireplace in our College listening to some beautiful music that my daughter, Theo, was creating. Suddenly she stopped, and I felt a tearing pain in my chest. As I tuned into it, I wondered at first if it was an attack upon my own health, but it was not. As I tuned inwards, the face of Mulaid came to me. Theo came running to me. She was a young woman by now. Before I knew it, she had flung herself into my arms and buried her head into my shoulder in tears. The pain stopped, but I had a strong sense that something terrible had happened. And Theo had the same thought.

That day we waited anxiously, and Theo could not stop shaking. We both knew, and Theo would not leave my side. Later, in the day, when one of our warriors ran into our encampment to tell us the news, the foreboding we had felt became real. Mulaid had been killed in an animal attack – a group of wild cats. I felt stunned. From my own senses, I felt that his physical death had occurred quickly. But that was a small relief. We had to go to his body.

When we reached him, we could both see Mulaid's Spirit standing by a tree nearby. There was extreme sadness in his eyes. Mulaid had not wanted to die, and I had not wanted him to die either. Theo ran towards him to try and embrace him, but she could not. She had been extremely close to her father, and would be lost without him. We sat down by his body and sobbed. The grief I felt for Mulaid's death was enormous, and for Theo, it was devastating. For both of us, it would take a long time to recover. The others would miss him very much too. He had brought the Spirit of music and creativity to our worlds, and although his gift had passed on to Theo, all that Mulaid had expressed was unique and could never be replaced. There had been many occasions where he had lifted my Spirits with his gentleness and his inspiration, and there were many who had been similarly touched. His place on our Earth had made our lives happier, richer and more fulfilled.

Later, it was precious to be able to accompany him with Theo and Nianda on his journey into Spirit, but the love and light of Spirit, even with the Celestial music that we heard, could not dissolve my own sadness and feelings of despair. For in my heart, I felt that this marked the beginning of the end of a beautiful dream. It was the first fracturing in the unity of our family.

But with all the grief of this loss, there was another one approaching that would tear apart the structures of my life even more.

Lunto's mission

Of all my children, the one who was most obviously outstanding with his charisma and presence was my son, Lunto. We all held high hopes for Lunto. He was tall, lithe, and a compelling leader with long flowing hair that would blow in the wind. When he spoke, he commanded attention, and people would look up to him. Because he had trained with Verdiff, he was held in great esteem by all the people of our land. He was my eldest son, and the natural heir apparent to take over from me when the time came.

After he had completed his studies with Verdiff, his teacher then retired and Lunto took over the responsibilities for tending to the security of our land. Lunto had gained a lot of knowledge and experience from Verdiff, and also insights about how warriors were trained and fought in other lands. He wanted to train our warriors further in the art of combat, so that when raiders came to our land, we could more actively defend ourselves, and this would enhance the level of protection that we would have.

Verdiff had tried to teach Lunto patience, and about the value of life and seeking peaceful solutions to conflict, but he had not been entirely successful. For Lunto enjoyed to show his prowess, and even seek situations of conflict so he could express his abilities. He impressed many with his skill, and Lunto enjoyed the adoration that he received. In many ways, he reminded me of how I related to the world as a youth, but although I learnt lessons about that, I am not sure that he did.

I felt uneasy about his proposals concerning the warriors, because I felt that it contradicted that values of peace that were so central to our society. Lunto argued with me, suggesting that a powerful ability to defend our land would help people feel secure and create peace. I was not convinced, and although I loved my son dearly, I felt that he may be a little on the impetuous side, but I could not change him.

Over time, Lunto organized our warriors and they successfully withstood and reduced the incidence of raids that took place on the west coast. However, in the north, there was beginning to be incursions from the barbarians of the east again. Gracon counseled that he felt that provided our people if, that these raids would be spasmodic and do little damage, because of the memory that the barbarians still held, of what had happened before.

But the thought of these barbarians and their savagery produced terror among the local inhabitants of that region. They wanted a protector, and Lunto was happy to fill that role. Gracon furthered counseled that if the barbarians were provoked by our aggression towards them, that this would feed those responses in them, and could escalate the raids on our shores. Lunto would not listen to this, and resolved to meet the threat of these barbarians directly.

In one spectacular triumph, Lunto managed to organize our warriors so that a large party of raiders, were (with only a few exceptions), all killed, and their boats disabled, with only minimal casualties on our side. Lunto was hailed as a hero, and people felt that his military abilities were remarkable. The more that people adored him, the more that Lunto's confidence appeared to swell. There were rumors of a further possible raid by the barbarians, and Lunto wanted Wueli and me to accompany him, so that we could witness his fine strategic arts first hand.

For many years, Wueli had stopped having any involvement with our warriors, and instead, he had acted as an advisor in the peaceful governing of the regions of our land. He was a very skilled administrator. Many times, he had tried to persuade Lunto to broaden his interests and develop other facets of his character, but Lunto was headstrong and wanted to make his own decisions. Wueli confided in me that he did not like what his son had become. He felt much foreboding about this trip.

Lunto could be very insistent, and although I also felt uneasy about it, I felt that I needed to honor him, so Wueli and I agreed to come, with Nianda in attendance as well. Afterwards, I wished that we had stayed.

My son felt so convinced of his judgment and abilities that he felt that it would be unnecessary to evacuate the town where it had been foreseen that the raid would take place. If the people remained, it would entice the barbarians to come forward and meet his trap.

Ilsa

The warriors were positioned and given instructions, fully expecting a daytime raid that would be quite imminent. We were not in a position to interfere, even though everything in me screamed that he was mistaken in his strategy.

As it turned out, the raid occurred at night when nearly everyone was sleeping. Our forces were unprepared. I woke with a start to the sounds of screams and burning. We had been placed in a position overlooking the town, so that there would be no danger to our safety. My body was shivering. I could see in Wueli's expression that it was agony for him to stay behind with us, when so much destruction was taking place in the community nearby. He looked at me imploringly, and I could see desperation in his eyes. I told him that we would stay safe, and that he must do what he felt was right. Wueli was consoled by that, and his expression softened. In a few moments, he turned and picked up his spear and was gone. I prayed that he might be able to help our son.

Throughout the night, the fighting continued. Nianda and I watched from our vantage point in dismay to see so many of the village huts burned to the ground. I could not relax and my fingers gripped into Nianda's hand. With every scream, I wondered if that would be my son's death throes. Towards morning, I could see evidence of the barbarian boats burning and signs of frantic activity as they tried to escape. Inside, I could feel a little more hopeful. After that, it became quieter. Nobody came to us. In my stomach, I felt a knot of fear.

A little later, Nianda and I ventured out and slowly approached the village. There were bodies and blood wherever we looked, with just a few injured survivors. In the distance, I could see someone familiar, organizing the collection of the dead. A few warriors were with him. I always knew that Wueli would survive this; I did not worry about him. But with my son, Lunto, I was afraid, and my fears turned out to be well founded.

When he saw me, Wueli stopped what he was doing and came over to me. There were tears in his eyes, and I knew then that my fears had manifested. We embraced and wept together. Nianda joined us. It was a devastating tragedy that seemed completely unnecessary to me – not only for the death of our son, but for all this community.

Wueli told me that he had discovered Lunto with a spear in his back. He must have been surprised and attacked from behind, and in all probability, was one of the first to die. Wueli had covered his body with skins and left it by the side of the ruins of the main house, and had then taken charge of the defense of the community.

Now, Wueli took me over to show me the body of our son. It was a pitiful sight. Wueli bent down and placed his spear next to Lunto. He never lifted a spear again.

For the rest of that day, Nianda busied herself helping people and offering healing and help to the people of the village. I should have helped as well, but all I could do was to stay with Wueli and grieve.

When it came to the cremation of Lunto's body, there was much sadness. I visited Lunto's Spirit body, and could sense the disappointment. It was a situation where the wishes on Lunto's part to impress others, completely obscured his better judgment.

There was emptiness inside me regarding Lunto, but I felt, somewhere, that Lunto, as a soul, had fulfilled the most likely scenario for his life. For him to have found some humility and patience were the keys to his survival and gaining learning, but ultimately, the impetuous side of his nature had been too dominant. I had to release him, and pray for his soul, that he would not judge himself too harshly, so hopefully he would do better next time.

Father and son

Wueli had ensured that there were no survivors from the barbarians that raided the village. That way, he managed to prevent further large-scale raids and incursions. It was typical that he would consider the needs of our communities before his own feelings. As a result of this, our life was able to return to a form or normality.

However, Wueli had lost part of his self and purpose in life through Lunto's death and he never regained his full vitality again. I noticed weariness in myself, too, and my other companions were all suffering increasing limitations through their age. There was a sad knowing that stretched between us. Gracon, in particular appeared increasingly frail. He had been involved in an accident some years earlier, and hurt his leg, so now he walked with a limp and the help of his own staff. Sometimes, I saw him looking to the sky, and he struggled to attend to his duties.

One day, Gracon met with our daughter, Breien, and for many hours, they were engaged in intensive private discussions. At the end of them, Breien was holding Gracon and sobbing, and they stayed together like that for a long time.

The next morning, Gracon came to me and informed me that he wished to walk with me and our son Varnu on a journey to his homeland, where he had been born. Looking in his eyes, I could tell that this would be the last journey that he would make. There was a grim determination in his expression that would not take 'no' for an answer. I wanted to cry and to hold him, for I felt highly emotional, but now did not feel to be the time to express those emotions, and so, I held my feelings inside, and contained them.

Varnu, by now, was a young man, and had been accepted into the circle of the Order of the Wise. He and Gracon had always shared a very close relationship, and it was Gracon who had been Varnu's main teacher.

The journey we made was largely in silence. I thought we would need to assist Gracon, physically, because of his weak leg, but in his will, his intention was clearly to complete this passage unaided, and that is what he did. In the evenings, we did reminisce; there was much for us to reflect upon, that we had shared together. But the words we spoke had finality about them, and as we spoke, my throat often felt clogged up as if I was carrying a lump of sadness there.

Finally, when we did reach Gracon's home village, he directed us to the burial mound where the ashes of both his parents lay. I still did not know the full story of Gracon's childhood; he had never revealed it, but it was his private wish for this to remain inside him and not be revealed.

Gracon climbed up onto the burial mound and told us simply that this is where he would die. He had a necklace with sacred stones and bones, a necklace that had stayed with him throughout his adult life. He took this off and gave it to Varnu. He was passing the mantle of responsibility and knowledge to his son now, and Varnu accepted this gratefully.

Gracon kept a low profile on the mound and closed his eyes. For a while, we both stood next to him and prayed. But then we both found places so that we could lie down too. My companion was ready to leave his body. He wanted a conscious death; for he knew that it was his time. Varnu came with me in his Spirit form when Gracon undertook his transition. On an energy level, as we left our bodies, we felt as though Gracon was embracing us with thanks. I could sense the happiness emanating from Gracon's soul. He was rising upwards rapidly. It would be a joyful homecoming for him. There were other beings, including his guide, that were waiting for him.

I could feel the intensity of Varnu's light besides me, and was able to sense that he had a very developed soul light. We had to let Gracon go now, and I only did this reluctantly, and then it was over.

In a moment, Varnu and I were stretching our bodies on the mound, while Gracon's body rested completely still. We would need to wait and prepare the body for its cremation. I could feel that Varnu accepted his father's death – he knew that the time had been right, and he honored that with love. There was an atmosphere of quietness about him. I was more upset, and felt resistant to the change that Gracon's passing brought into my life.

Later that evening, Varnu looked over at me with imploring eyes. I steadied myself so that I could focus. Going into his mind, I could tell what Varnu wanted now; he needed to learn from me about the skills of leadership. Just then, I felt the presence of Eurydice, close by me, and offering encouragement. There was a strong affirmation coming from her for Varnu's request. I had to do this; it was important to help Varnu live out his destiny. And suddenly, I could see ahead to a time when Varnu would be standing in front of crowds of people, doing the work that I had been doing all these years.

It was like a light going on inside me, and I realized that my purpose in my life extended to ensuring a continuation of the leadership of the Order, and passing this on to my son. All my adult life, I had enjoyed what I had acquired and had celebrated that. Now I had to release my position, just as Karka had to do all those years earlier. In my case, it was easier because in my life, I had achieved all that I wanted to do. But I would apply myself to share my knowledge and teach my son all that I could, to the very best of my ability. I turned to my son to acknowledge my agreement, and Varnu smiled.

Passing the mantle

There must have been a stirring within me when Varnu asked for my assistance, for suddenly, I roused myself with renewed energy and purpose, and I sought to apply myself in my position of responsibility with improved passion and determination. There was a time approaching soon when I would no longer be leader of this land, and in the interval before that happened, I wanted to pass on all the knowledge that I could, and immerse myself in the administration of my duties, so that when my time came, I would know that I had done my very best, and left a strong foundation for those that followed me.

With Varnu, I spent time with him, tested him and gave him challenges and ever greater responsibility. I endeavored to train him with as much thoroughness as Karka and Berenice had trained me. He was a responsive student, and rapidly learnt the art of executing decisions and leadership. With Gracon, he had developed his inner knowledge and capacity for psychic perception. But Gracon had always been more withdrawn and retiring from the world. With me, my son needed to open himself to deal directly with people, and learn management and skills at communication. This needed time, but over time, Varnu became a powerful speaker, and I tried to encourage him to express his compassion through his words. He had much depth for a young man, and he needed to be able to channel that in a way that reached people.

Besides Varnu, I wanted to spend time with my other children, and my grandchildren. With each of them, I wanted to listen to them and nurture and support them as well as I was able. My daughter, Breien was following in Nianda's footsteps and becoming regarded as the foremost healer of her generation, and Nianda was glad to help her. All my surviving children had their gifts, and I was pleased, also, how my sister, Sealbow and brother, Luend, had found happiness and families of their own within the environment of the college. Shoola had stayed a little aloof like her mother, but found it easier to ask for help than her mother had ever done.

I felt pleased with how love had helped shape contentment and fulfillment within the members of my extended family. And among the Elders, there was also now a mutual understanding that had been molded over a long period of familiarity with each other.

I travelled with Varnu to the far corners of our land, so he would know all the communities of our people and they would know him. With my energy, I pushed myself, until one day I knew that I had done enough. On that morning, I awoke with a clear knowing that the time had arrived for me to pass on my staff and withdraw from my office.

I called for an extended Council meeting, and announced my resignation from leadership. The members there were aware of my feelings and so what I had decided came as no surprise. They were ready to endorse my choice of Varnu as the one favored to take my place. I believed that he now had sufficient character to take on what could be a difficult job.

We had been blessed to have had a long period of peace in our land, but now, I could feel restlessness in the Spirit of the land, and although I could not define it exactly, I sensed times of unsettlement ahead. Each new period of our history had brought with it change and opportunity, and sometimes difficulties. I knew that the Earth Spirit supported Varnu to take the position that I had held now. There was a light about him today, and it gladdened my heart to be able to pass on

Ilsa

my staff to him, when he was willing and ready to take the position. In my mind, I felt much more confident with Varnu taking on the mantle of leadership than I would have with Lunto.

In the ceremony that followed, I opened my heart to wish Varnu well, and gave him the staff that I had inherited from Karka. My son's training was over. He accepted the staff now gratefully, and he held it up for all to see and then stamped it on the ground. As he did that, there was a crackling of energy. This was the sign that we all wanted to see; the acceptance that he now not only held the instrument, but the power within the staff, and that the Earth Spirit was with him too.

For me, it felt a relief to let it go, and I felt lighter inside. My wish now was to enjoy a few more years, being able to appreciate the fruits of my life, without needing to carry the burdens anymore of responsibility.

That afternoon when I returned to my home hut, I felt stillness and wonder at how life moved on. I could never control it, and on this day, I gracefully accepted it.

CHAPTER 17

My transition to Spirit

The place where I most liked to be when I was older was by the central campfire we had in the middle of our college settlement. By now, my own family had expanded and moved on to the next generation, and they were no longer such a close knit group. I was still enjoying my life though, and I liked to feel involvement with all the community around me. From this fireplace, I could watch the various activities going on, the children playing, and the purposeful strides of the students and members of the Order as they attended classes and meetings and went from one place to another. If people needed my help or advice, I was there, but I felt quite peaceful sitting back, having earned my right to be a retired Elder. Some of my grandchildren would come and sit on my knee and I would tell stories to them. These were happy times.

Each day, I would partake of my meditation practice, and I would spend time with my guide by the Yew Tree in the Sacred Grove. Walking longer distances was not so easy for me anymore, and my legs had stiffened, so I needed to go gently when I walked. But as long as I accepted these limitations, my inner life was as alive as ever.

I could appreciate the work of my son, Varnu, and the specialized skills of my other children. Varnu had a very different temperament to me, and I sometimes felt him to be somewhat emotionally withheld. Usually, he kept a strong sense of his own boundaries, and he tended to be very focused with an intensity of purpose about what he needed to do. He had a clear deep mind, and people respected him for that.

Two of my other children, Breien and Theo were also now in the Council of Elders, as was Nianda's son, Siel, and Shoola. My other daughter, Huntle, served more as a roving ambassador and travelled a lot between our land and other communities beyond our land where our people inhabited. She helped to bring about many connections between people and groups, and sharing of resources.

I did feel that the land was in safe hands, both with Varnu and other members of the leadership. Whatever unsettled times may lay ahead, for now it was peaceful, and I enjoyed that.

My most faithful companion was still Nianda. Although she still did some healing work, she now mainly acted in an advisory capacity. Often we would sit together for many hours by the fireplace, keeping ourselves warm, and observing the life of our settlement, while feeling contentment inside.

In my mind, I often reflected upon my life and all its contours. I would think about my companions that had now passed on, and I wondered what it would be like when my time came. I asked Eurydice about this, and she allowed me to explore some of the inner realms of Spirit and accompany her to experience some of the inspiring realities that we could meet there. I was not afraid of death, but there was a reluctance to release all that I had acquired in this physical life. It was satisfying how much I could appreciate of the community life that I had shared with so many wonderful souls, and I also felt some pride in myself for what I had contributed.

When my time came, it came quickly. I was not allowed to linger forever. One day I was bitten by an insect and the wound became infected. After a couple more days, I started to have a fever and I needed to lie down. As I lay in my bed, my body was hot, and I could feel myself growing weaker. Nianda attended me as she always did, but her expression was concerned. She could tell with our shared thoughts we had, that my time was near. I sensed that it would not be long before she followed me and that we would be reunited again.

News must have spread about my illness. I was surprised how many people came to visit me. It was not just family, but many people from the Order, and even leaders from communities that existed further distances away. I did not realize that my presence carried such significance to people any more. But I welcomed this appreciation of my being, and I tried to reassure all of them of their future without me.

Just before my passing, I felt a strong awareness of my Spirit body, ready to draw me upwards. I sent love out into the surroundings, and there was a deep feeling of peace that pervaded the physical space by my bed. Then I knew that I had to go.

The movement of my Spirit leaving my body for the last time was exhilarating. Nianda was with me, and we travelled upwards into a sphere of intense light and love. There was the urge in me that I had to keep going, and Nianda needed to turn back. She did not want to go. In the slight pause when she stopped and retreated, I felt immense gratitude for all that she had given me, and all that we had shared.

Eurydice was now with me, and we continued to ascend. I felt that where I was going was new ground, experience that my soul had not known before, and we finally stopped in a plateau of light, that was stunning in its beauty and intensity. From this vista, I could observe an overview of my life and other lives that were calling me. Eurydice congratulated me and told me that in my life as Ilsa, I had acquitted myself well, and now I could reflect for a while and allow the Spiritual truth to permeate of what I had achieved. As I gazed at my surroundings, I had a sense of other lives and challenges that I still needed to meet. It was not all done. And I was able to perceive how in some lives, I had faltered, but in this one, I had stayed largely true to myself, and learned the lessons that were necessary for me. At times, in my life as Ilsa, I could have been more patient, especially in my younger years, and I could have given more for others to do rather than trying to do so much myself.

But then, in my eagerness, I was in another place in Spirit, a realm where I could meet with some of those many souls whom I loved and loved me. It was like a blissful reunion where we could all give thanks and laugh about what had just taken place on the Earth plane. As I observed the various souls, some of them were glowing and very happy, obviously pleased with their growth, while others had a more pensive air, where perhaps they had not fulfilled all their goals as souls. This gathering felt familiar, like an event that would follow all incarnations, with a flow of souls arriving and others moving on.

There were some souls in particular that drew me, old friends whose presence felt much more complete and magnificent in Spirit. By seeing these souls, I could appreciate much more fully, my relationship with them, and qualities about them that I could only dimly perceive while in my physical form. Although we had social time all together, there was also the opportunity to meet with my soul friends individually in private. This was a process that was very intense.

The souls I met did not reveal themselves in any particular order, just appearing as I was ready to greet them. Gracon was the first one with whom I met. For both of us, it was a relief how well we had managed to relate to each other in that life. We were long standing soul friends, and had been together many, many times. Like me, the experience of that incarnation for him, had been very positive, and he had been well rewarded. It was gratifying to be together again.

Following on from him, other souls stepped forward. In turn, I could perceive the souls of Berenice, Mulaid, Wueli, my mother and father from then, my son, Lunto, Karka, and many others. There was so much in each of them where we could relate, learn and share love with the presence of each other, and we did that. Each meeting affected me emotionally, and I felt enormous gratitude for what we could offer each other as souls.

Each relationship held mysteries and had to be sensed as fully as possible to be acknowledged. What we had all shared in that lifetime just past added to each of those relationships and gave them all greater soul love. There was much to digest.

Eurydice informed me that at the right moment, I would need to travel to the realm where I could meet with the soul of my brother, Skife, for he still felt very ashamed of his actions, and needed to communicate with me and to accept my forgiveness so he could feel able to move forward.

For now, I needed a space so I could begin to integrate all the experiences I had had, so I could bring this with me for where I needed to go next.

CHAPTER 18

Reflections

According to my instinct and inner vision, the setting for this story of Ilsa's life took place as follows:

Ilsa was born in the area that we now know as southern Wales. The raiders that came and raped her mother, I sensed, came from Ireland. The civilization in Ireland at that time was more primitive than the Celtic society, although they did have rafts that were sufficiently robust to be able to cross the Irish Sea.

The college of the Order of the Wise, was situated in the area where the town of Glastonbury exists today. It is possible that the hill where the members did their meditation was the Tor, or some other hill in the vicinity.

The meeting that convened with the various Celtic nations, took place in southern France, and included representatives of Celtic people from across western and central Europe, but not from northern Europe.

When Karka went on his journey north, he travelled along the eastern part of Britain and went all the way to the Orkney Islands. The people in the Orkneys then were an independent advanced civilization that had many links and similar practices to the Order of the Wise.

They were like a sister civilization. Karka made the journey in a quest for unity with them.

When he returned, the tragedy with the storm and being struck by the dead tree, this occurred in the border region of southern Scotland.

The main battle with the barbarians occurred in the north east of England and could have been near to what is now Scarborough. The Massetti tribe lived further south than this, possibly around the area of Skegness.

What I called the 'barbarian' race came from various locations in the north of Europe, and these people could have been ancestors of what became later, the Viking people.

According to Eurydice, the Celtic civilization extended for many thousands of years across Europe and Britain. Within Britain, what I have termed, as the Order of the Wise, was an element that continued in various forms, throughout the history of the race. Sometimes the influence of the order was stronger than at other times, when the society was more fragmented and existing in isolated pockets. There were also periods where the Order existed in quite a dark capacity, and the stones then were used for blood sacrifices, and even human ones. Usually, during the times when there was an expansion of the use of the stones, then this corresponded to lighter epochs, when people were more spiritually aware, and adhering to sacred principles in their everyday lives. The time of Ilsa was in the middle of one of the more positive eras where the Order of the Wise held a very constructive influence upon the society of the time.

Eurydice communicated that the Celtic people were influenced by the civilization of Atlantis, when this land perished, and survivors came to European shores. Skills that these people brought with them, fed the Celtic race with ideas and practices that helped them. However, it was from a civilization to the East where the Celtic people originated.

Ilsa lived at about 1200BC. She was in her late fifties when she died.